CALEDONIA SWITCH

STEVEN LANE SMITH

outskirtspress
DENVER, COLORADO

Outskirts Press, Inc.
http://www.outskirtspress.com

ISBN: 978-1-4787-0082-1

Library of Congress Control Number: 2013915386

Outskirts Press and the "OP" logo are trademarks belonging to Outskirts Press, Inc.

PRINTED IN THE UNITED STATES OF AMERICA

For Aileen, Austin, and Travis

Chapter 1

JOHN WESLEY HARDIN

"PUT DOWN YOUR arrows and swords," Miss Annette Laval commanded her Brighton School third graders as they milled around the classroom restlessly like a mob that could turn ugly at any moment. "Knives, too. No one should be holding anything sharper than a tennis ball." A timid nine-year-old in the front row dropped a Cerulean crayon like it was a red-hot poker.

Miss Laval scanned the classroom for non-compliance as she motioned with her arms for her students to return to their seats. "Put everything back in the props locker. If anyone is maimed or killed," she exaggerated for maximum effect, "we'll have to cancel this year's Historical Figures Program." Her dire warning restored order but did nothing to stimulate voluntecrism.

Competition for a leading role in Hollywood can be brutal, but the only thing brutal in Miss Laval's classroom was the silence that met her request for a volunteer to be "first out of the chute". She used the rodeo slang in hopes of inciting someone to action. Jargon borrowed from astronauts, race car drivers, and baseball players had worked in the past. When that approach failed, she appealed to each student's sense of duty by calling the lead-off position a great honor.

Sinking a little lower in their chairs, the reluctant thespians tried to appear unworthy of such an honor. Even Raymond Delacroix, a notorious risk-taker, exuded terminal indifference. The lone exception was John Wesley Hardin, who blissfully gazed out through a classroom window at the brilliant yellow leaves that crowned the school yard maples. He was a master practitioner of the art of daydreaming, and he was ripe for picking when Miss Laval finessed him using an orthodox teacher technique — *entrapment.*

"Now, who wants to go first?" Miss Laval asked in her most disarming voice. "Would you like to go first, John? John?" Miss Laval repeated to interrupt his reverie.

"Yes?" John replied as his head swiveled toward the front of the room.

"Very good, John," Miss Laval beamed. "Class, we have our lead-off batter."

Known for her leaky bladder and flimsy intellect, Rita Fontaine, who routinely applauded at the slightest provocation, clapped tentatively. That started a spontaneous mini-ovation among John's nineteen balky classmates.

John didn't fight the tide. Over the next fortnight, he embraced his role, designed a world-class costume, and memorized his lines obsessively. It was his way.

Five minutes before John's stage acting debut, a flutter of butterflies bivouacked in his nine-year-old stomach. Peeking through a break in the curtains, John inspected the crowd.

In a small New England village like Caledonia, it wasn't un-usual that a third-grader would know a few of the names of villagers gathered anywhere in the town, but John could attach a name to every single person in the audience, includ-ing the late-comers standing in the rear of the hall. John had a mighty memory. The many hours he had spent practicing his scripted lines were complete overkill, because he was the least likely boy in New Hampshire to forget *anything*. John spotted his father, Dan Hardin, seated beside his maternal grandmother, Marie Laval.

Fidgeting in the fourth row, Dan suffered the forebod-ing that had distressed him on John's first day of school. Dan remembered leaving John on the Brighton School steps like a lamb, a sacrifice to Life. Dan was prepared to face any challenges in his own life, but, when John was involved, Dan felt vulnerable. He harbored insecurities about his ability to shield John from unnamed threats. Dan's wife hadn't been on the steps for John on his first day of school and she wasn't in the hall for John's inaugural stage performance.

The face of Marie Laval, John's grandmother, was an aloof, stoic mask among the crowd of faces that faded into ob-scurity as the house lights began to dim. Marie was shackled to a secret like a prisoner to a ball-and-chain. Privately, she felt responsible for the desertion of John's mother. In hushed moments like this, Marie feared that her secret might be un-veiled someday, allowing village gossips to discover that she was to blame.

The hum of the audience trailed away when the lights extinguished. The only sources of light in the room were a filtered line of backlighting at the bottom of the curtains and red letters over a door that said "TIXƎ". For two weeks, Annette had pleaded with the custodian to reverse the sign, but the custodian claimed to be a busy man. In an effort to draw attention away from his sloth, the custodian had pointed out that the sign read correctly when viewed in a mirror.

John left his covert observation post to prepare for his entrance. Simultaneously, the curtains swished open, the stage lights flared fully as bright as a welder's torch, and John strode to the center of the stage. John's appearance might have been even more stunning had the custodian remembered to start the Vivaldi *Four Seasons* tape on the amplified sound system. In Annette's mind, the oversight was proof that the janitor was lazy and forgetful. Annette tried to pantomime the motion of a violinist drawing a bow across violin strings. The janitor was also unimaginative. The amplifier speakers remained silent.

As John stood in the center of the stage illuminated by thousands of watts of incandescent light, a pleasing sensation unlike anything he had ever experienced spread through his body. Adrenalin. He paused dramatically like a model on a runway waiting for Vivaldi's genius to fill the room. This pause gave the audience ample time to admire his dark blue military jacket with its classic double rows of gold buttons and its gold-fringed shoulder boards. His black *bicorne* sat smartly on his head, and his blond hair curled at his temples. His right hand remained inserted in his waistcoat. Offstage, Annette motioned wildly for John to deliver his speech. His white-gloved left hand caressed the ornate handle of his sword before sweeping toward a fictional horizon as he delivered his lines flawlessly.

"Exiled by my nation, I retired to Elba." His innocent blue eyes scanned the audience as he asked, "Who am I?"

A slide projected on a side wall presented three choices: Andrew Jackson, Napoleon Bonaparte, and John Paul Jones.

"The Nutcracker!" The gruff voice of Thomas Bruguiere bellowed from the rear of the room. His interjection netted a few involuntary laughs from people in the audience who knew all too well that Bruguiere, the only one-eyed janitor in town, suffered from Tourette's Syndrome. More accurately, Caledonia suffered from Bruguiere's symptoms of Tourette's Syndrome, because of his almost ritualistic outbursts at Town Hall Meetings and summer concerts at the Town Gazebo down by the town docks. Caledonians tolerated Bruguiere the way one might tolerate a plantar wart when the remedy seems more of a vexation than the malady.

In accordance with program instructions and three years of tradition, members of the audience voted for Jackson, Bonaparte, or Jones using Interactive Response Units (IRUs) built into each of the sixty chairs in the assembly room. Most of the adult members of the audience had previously approved a warrant article to spend tax money to pay for the Brighton School expansion and for the IRU system housed by the expansion. Proponents had promised that the expenditure would produce some of the brightest children in New England. Even if that promise had gone unproved or even unfulfilled, the tax payers in the audience were eager to get their money's worth out of the IRU system.

"*Au revoir*," John declared grandly as he turned to exit the stage. His indiscreet improvisation seemed to rule out Jackson and Jones, but John was so wedded to his role that the words just popped out. IRUs clicked all across the room as the respondents registered their votes before the buzzer sounded. The auto-tabulator recorded the IRU clicks, and Napoleon won in a landslide total of 55 votes to one stray vote for Andrew Jackson. Some in the audience supposed that Thomas Bruguiere had cast the erroneous vote in ignorance or even protest. The slide projected on the side wall read, "Napoleon Bonaparte was exiled to the Island of Elba by the French government in 1814. He escaped in 1815 to lead French forces to their defeat at Waterloo. Napoleon Bonaparte was played by John Hardin."

John took the enthusiastic applause as validation of his Napoleon costume design work and his eloquent delivery. One look at the tears in Teacher Annette Laval's eyes told him he had hit a home run. As he exited the stage, his sword dragging on the wooden stage behind him, Napoleon, a.k.a. John Wesley Hardin, knew he not only had knocked the cover off the ball, he had smacked it out of the park.

John brushed past the next featured historical figure played by Paul Bruguiere as his classmate shuffled onto the stage with a look of dread in his eyes. Paul, nephew of Thomas Bruguiere, was dressed completely in black from his borrowed lace shoes to his top hat, a crudely-made affair that even the most casual observer could recognize as the unskilled union of glue and black construction paper. Paul's liberally self-applied mascara, intended to represent the facial wrinkles of a worried man, had a creepier, more sinister effect, and, as Paul turned to face the audience, several people gasped. Paul's menacing appearance wasn't the only bump in the road of his presentation. Paul refused to recite, "Four score and seven years."

"Not even my Uncle Thomas knows that 'score' means 'twenty'."

Miss Laval, willing to attest to the paucity of Thomas Bruguiere's vocabulary, assured Paul that virtually everyone recognized the famous words. Paul wasn't swayed, however, so Miss Laval relented, allowing Paul to write his own script, which he proceeded to mangle in a loud, trembling voice.

"Eighty-six years after the founding of my country, I proclamated an emancement," Paul said robotically, his hands gripping his lapels in a nod to oratorical convention. "Who am I?"

The choices projected onto the wall were Thomas Paine, Daniel Webster, and Abraham Lincoln. Although Paul had completely slaughtered his lines to the amusement of some, his question was not an insoluble puzzle for the audience.

"Jack-the-Ripper," Paul's uncle called from the back of the room. His call-out garnered a couple of chuckles.

John Hardin could remember asking his father why people encouraged Thomas Bruguiere by laughing at his blather. Like most fathers, John's father sensed that "I don't know" was an acceptable response only in matters like nuclear fission, origin of the species, and so on. In most every other area, he knew he had to swing the stick and hope to hit the *piñata*.

"Stockholm Syndrome."

John was no dunce at geography. He knew the capital of every country on the globe, including Africa where the names of cities and nations seemed to change with the seasons. John knew about Stockholm, but it was the first he had heard about a syndrome.

"What's Stockholm Syndrome?"

"Hostages bonding with their captors," Dan had said, displaying the brevity ascribed to natives of New England.

"Someone should muzzle him," John had said.

"Be patient. Most people are doing the best they can."

Watching through a seam in the curtains, John questioned whether this was the best Thomas Bruguiere could do.

The IRUs clicked almost in unison. The mellow buzzer sounded, and the votes revealed that Abraham Lincoln had won handily with 53 votes to none for the other choices. The seven votes unaccounted for could be credited to indecision or incompetence. A much-relieved Lincoln exited to perfunctory applause as his accomplishments were projected onto the side wall.

As it turned out, Bonaparte and Lincoln were the only runaway choices of the evening. Votes were much more evenly distributed among the notables who followed. When Eddie Rickenbacker took the stage, Bruguiere called out "Rocky-the-Flying-Squirrel". Chief Sitting Bull elicited "Tonto" from Bruguiere; Moses, "Jesus H. Christ"; Betsy Ross, "What's-her-name"; and Richard Nixon, "Tricky Dick".

Even Zorro – the most historically problematic of the presentations – won only a plurality of electronic ballots cast because of active voting for Batman and the Count of Monte Cristo. Zorro's intense stage fright, resultant mumbled lines, and clumsy sword play (his foil was a citizens' band radio antenna) rendered clues meaningless and resulted in the electoral horse race. Even Thomas Bruguiere was baffled into silence.

The real sensation of the evening was the appearance of Robin Hood. Controversy had surrounded Corky Gleason's casting as Master Robin from the moment Corky had announced his intention to play the part.

"Porky Corky ain't no Robin Hood," Raymond Delacroix had rasped. Raymond was the closest thing to a bully in Annette Laval's class. "Porky steals from the poor to give to the rich." It was a convenient harpoon to throw at Corky, because his father was president of Tremont Savings, one of Caledonia's three banks.

Corky's birth weight had been over eleven pounds, a figure that had been revised upwards in Caledonian mythology over the years to something of a record among almost three hundred years of recorded births in the village. Starting out at an eye-popping eleven-plus-pounds, Corky had never looked back, and he was the tallest, heaviest, and roundest child in Miss Laval's class by a wide margin.

"Please," Annette had quieted her animated students, "no name calling. Do you want to approve Corky to play Robin Hood, or do you want to skip recess and stay indoors to talk about it?"

"Cor-ky! Cor-ky!" Raymond Delacroix had chanted, showing how quickly public sentiment can reverse in the hands of a skilled arbiter. The jackals had backed off. Elated, Corky had thrust his pudgy arms into the air victoriously.

Annette's opinion was fine theoretically, but, as a practical matter, it didn't take a soothsayer to predict the outcome of pouring Corky's obese *corpus* – better suited for the part of Friar Tuck – into the attire of Robin Hood. The awed audience inhaled in unison as Corky waddled onstage like a verdant Pillsbury doughboy whose bright green leotards (complete with a baseball crotch cup) and green silk ski under shirt were stretched to the point of semi-transparency.

An inspired Thomas Bruguiere called out, "Peter Pan!"

No one with a trace of common sense could imagine this green apparition defying gravity, at least not with the current state of technology. So, no matter how unkind Bruguiere's interjection was, even an adult could be forgiven a snigger or a snort. Corky's father coughed loudly and shifted in his chair in the front row. This settled the audience. Corky was no stranger to ridicule, and tears welled in his eyes as he recited his lines.

"I take from the rich to give to the poor. Who am I?"

The choices were Robin Hood, the Jolly Green Giant, and Sir Lancelot. When the voters had expressed their collective will by way of the IRUs, the Jolly Green Giant edged Robin Hood by 30 to 24 votes, a completely absurd outcome in light of the hand-made bow and arrows gripped tightly in Corky's knobby hands. Some kind of elaborate voter fraud had just occurred, John thought.

"Ho, ho, ho," Thomas Bruguiere intoned from the rear of the room.

When Corky exited the stage with his chin tucked into his chest as he stifled a sob, it was a compassionate John Hardin who put his arm on the shoulder of Robin Hood and told him, "Nice job, Corky." It was a grand gesture befitting Napoleon.

Bruguiere's insensitive callouts eventually earned him

universal condemnation. An exasperated audience cheered for Andrew Gleason when the portly banker insisted that Bruguiere leave the proceedings. Bruguiere mumbled a face-saving rebuttal as he retreated from the room for a two-block walk to the nearest pub. Humor, he thought, is a dehydrating business. The third graders on the other side of the heavy curtains watched the distraction through breaks in the draperies. John felt sorry for the rabble-rouser's nephew, Paul "Lincoln" Bruguiere, whose worry lines had deepened in proportion to the appalling conduct of his uncle.

Order reverted to the mean, however, and, at the end of the program, all twenty presenters formed a line on the stage and bowed in a sequence resembling a wave. The audience cheered wildly for the troupe and for Annette, the highly-regarded third grade teacher who had put the whole thing together. As the house lights brightened, Annette could see her mother – Marie Laval – leaning toward John's father – Dan — to comment as they clapped along with the other spectators. Annette felt welded to her mother by a secret that they shared, yet she felt her affection for her mother compromised by the same secret.

Annette bowed in unison with the children, and she motioned toward her students proudly. Her left hand lightly ruffled the blond hair of John Wesley Hardin, who attached deep symbolic meaning to the gesture. A star was born. The curtains closed.

Backstage, Miss Laval was promptly cornered by Corky's father, Andrew Gleason, a corpulent man in a corpulent man's business suit. Annette knew that her twin sister Trinette had snubbed Andrew Gleason ten years earlier on the day of Trinette's wedding to Dan Hardin. Andrew's sour disposition was well-known around Caledonia, and his decade-long animosity toward the Laval family had become public knowledge. His face was crimson, and his jowls jiggled as he spoke.

"You made a fool of my son in front of half the town tonight, Miss Laval."

The accusation startled Annette. She stammered in an attempt to reply, but Gleason interrupted her and continued his verbal assault.

"It was obscene. Corky has a thyroid condition...and... obscene. Remember, I sit on the School Board, and your continued employment is very much in my hands."

Annette already knew that Gleason was on the Board, because her own father, Phillip Laval, also was a Board Member, and he, too, was president of a bank – the Bank of Caledonia. She tried to assure Gleason that she had the best interests of her students in mind, but he crowded toward her even closer and stage whispered his final threat as his pasty index finger invaded the space around her face.

"I warn you, Miss Laval, you're on thin ice. Don't give me a reason to take action!" He stormed away leaving Annette shaken.

Gleason's sentiments were completely at odds with the attitudes of the other members of the audience. As they filed out of Brighton School into the crisp October evening, many of them commented on Miss Laval's endless creativity.

"Always thinking outside the box", said one mother, whose choice of metaphor was *not* outside the box.

In truth, Annette had invented the Historical Figures

Program as an antidote to Halloween. She was no fan of Halloween, citing its satanic overtones, its demonic subtext. She disapproved of the commercial exploitation of parents and children alike. She looked on with distaste as costumed imps and goblins spread like a horde of scavengers throughout Caledonia on the prowl for Candy Corn, Tootsie Rolls, and miniature Snickers bars.

Using the power vested in her as Brighton School's Third Grade Teacher, Annette had devised the Historical Figures Program to take the devil out of Halloween. Children still wore costumes, but they wore them for an uplifting reason. As a bonus unforeseen by Annette, costumed children delivering lines they reliably botched never failed to amuse audiences, and the popularity of the Historic Figures Program grew each year. Except for the distressing encounter with Andrew Gleason, the results of her innovative thinking had exceeded her expectations.

One unintended consequence of this year's program, however, was that John Hardin, whom everyone knew to be Annette Laval's nephew, became so enamored of the *persona* of Napoleon that he wore the military jacket around his home for many days after the program as he repeated aloud the lines that had, in his estimation, shaken the Caledonia theatrical world.

His fixation became clear to Annette the very next day when he showed up early for class attired in his Napoleon jacket. It gave him the appearance of a Caucasian Michael Jackson making a belated curtain call. John's obsession knew *some* boundaries; his *bicorne*, leotards, and knee-high boots remained at home neatly arranged on his bed. Wearing the jacket didn't bring back the adrenalin thrill, but it reminded John of his stage success – the anticipatory silence of the audience broken by his immortal words, the applause, and ultimately the approval of his teacher.

Annette kneeled down beside John's desk as he doodled away the moments before the arrival of other children in her classroom in Brighton School.

"John, your Napoleon jacket is wonderful," she said. "But think about the other kids. They might think you're bragging."

"I *was* the best." John's words displayed vestiges of infantile omnipotence that marked much of his behavior.

"Everyone knows it," Annette said, "so you don't need to say it…or wear the jacket."

John pondered her words. "I'll leave it at home," he promised.

That afternoon was the last time John's classmates saw him in the stunning dark blue military jacket. It was the last time Raymond Delacroix could shout out "Ya fairy!" based on John's attire.

John walked the sidewalks from Brighton School toward his home on Lake Tremont in his customary manner: He stepped carefully so his sneakers not only did not step on cracks but did not step on an imaginary line drawn on a forty-five-degree angle from each of the four corners of each concrete slab. He visualized the forty-five-degree lines as clearly as if they had been troweled into the concrete. They were John's reality, just as he really had been, for however short a time, Napoleon Bonaparte.

Chapter 2

THE LAVALS

TEACHER ANNETTE LAVAL'S complicated journey to her Brighton School classroom began when she and her identical twin sister Trinette were born in Caledonia Hospital in 1966. Her parents, Phillip and Marie Laval, had immigrated to the United States from Canada six years earlier in search of employment for Phillip. Within two weeks of their arrival, Phillip interviewed for a job as a teller at the Bank of Caledonia.

The bank president who interviewed Phillip didn't abide oafishness or sloppy personal habits among his employees. Phillip's timidity passed for dignity. His impeccable grooming, the result of thirty-minute sessions behind the locked door of his bathroom each morning, made an immediate positive impression. Phillip had his share of faults, but he was neither oafish nor sloppy, so he shone where it mattered most.

When the president asked Phillip to name a special skill he possessed, a skill not apparent on his resume, Phillip said, "I'm very good with numbers." The president, having heard a range of responses from "needle point" to "imitating loon calls", found Phillip's answer refreshing. Phillip's claim happened to be true. He was an auditor's dream. Furthermore, Phillip was polite yet firm when firmness was required. He asserted himself on behalf of his employer to resolve levels of conflict that drove him to full retreat in his own home. To top it off, he was a willing listener in a town populated by lots of willing talkers.

Phillip had a charming way of describing his grandfather's motivation for leaving France for Canada as "wanderlust". *Wander?* That his forebears had wandered was evident *ipso facto* by his presence in the New World. But *lust?* No one could think of Phillip and lust in the same context. It was comical to think that Phillip had descended from a line of lusters of any description. One former bank colleague, who had been fired for misappropriating funds, remarked in parting that Phillip was such a prude that he had impregnated his wife telepathically. The preposterous slander outraged Phillip's coworkers, and they rallied to support him against all charges by the disgraced embezzler. Phillip's position in the bank was secure.

Phillip never once asked for a raise, but raises came with regularity as he ascended through the ranks of the bank. At the age of thirty, he was named Branch Manager. Eight years later, he was chosen to serve as President of the Bank of Caledonia, when his predecessor keeled over dead while cross-country skiing only moments after commenting on how "alive" the crisp air and exercise made him feel.

Phillip subsequently accepted an invitation to serve on the Board of Directors of Thornton Academy, Caledonia's prep school perched on the banks of Lake Tremont. Phillip was the youngest member on the board. He had risen to social prominence in the village in only seventeen years since his arrival in Caledonia.

Phillip's wife Marie was not a wall flower. She was good-looking and she knew it, but she had the good sense to refrain from showing that she knew it. She had grown up in a French-speaking home, so her French accent was a distinctive trademark in Caledonia.

Soon after arriving in Caledonia, Marie became active in the Caledonia Garden Club, in the King's Yacht Club, and as a volunteer at the St. Paul's Catholic Church food pantry. She dressed more formally than most villagers, and passers-by commonly assumed that she was one of the wealthy seasonal visitors who kept homes on the shores of Lake Tremont. Her female detractors claimed that Marie was too headstrong and her airs too grand to fit in with Caledonia society. Her detractors' husbands thought Marie fit in perfectly well.

In search of a rare laugh, Phillip sometimes called his wife "Chairhuman". By the time Marie was forced to take time off for the delivery of her twins, she was simultaneously serving as Village Beautification Chair of the Garden Club, Membership Chair of the King's Yacht Club, and Food Pantry Logistics Chair at St. Paul's. She returned to serve in those positions within three months of giving birth to twins, Annette and Trinette.

Marie's daughters were the center of her universe. In the manner of her own mother, who had returned to live in France, Marie reared her daughters to be ladies. At home,

Marie conversed with the girls in French. She took them to lessons in tennis, sailing, equestrian, and piano. She imposed iron-clad schedules for practice, and she encouraged them to participate in tournaments and races. The twins, like their father, wisely complied with Marie's wishes.

Annette and Trinette were born only six minutes apart, but, judging from their contrasting personalities, a realignment of stars must have occurred between the two births. Annette was studious, forgiving, and a good listener. Trinette was restless, grudging, and too self-centered to take advice or instruction from anyone.

Annette was courteous on the tennis court. She accepted umpires' rulings without complaint, and she was gracious in victory and in defeat. Trinette, on the other hand, could be a tempest on the court. She distracted her opponents by pouting, frowning, and sighing theatrically. She exulted when an opponent double-faulted. She could instantly morph into a screaming banshee if a linesman made an adverse call on an important point.

Trinette won the girls' tennis club championship when she was fifteen and again the next year. At the latter awards ceremony, she insisted that the *Caledonia Reporter* photographer take another photograph, because she thought she had blinked when he snapped the picture. He did. Then he asked her out for a date, and Trinette said, "You've got to be kidding." The reporter had the last word as the newspaper published the picture of Trinette with her eyes closed.

Despite their different personalities, Annette and Trinette had a deep affection for one another...within certain boundaries. They shared some of their secrets and gave advice to one another that they seldom followed. For example, Trinette encouraged her sister to speak up for herself during tennis matches.

"Don't let the judges walk all over you!" Trinette lectured her sister. "Take charge! Push back!"

"You want to win more than I do," Annette told her. All Annette wanted was peace.

"One day," Trinette warned her sister, "you'll pay a heavy price for not standing up for yourself."

In Sunfish races at the King's Yacht Club, Trinette's antics were less of a competitive advantage. She lodged protests over the slightest perceived infractions and she even rammed a competitor once for spite, costing her three positions at the finish. Annette, on the other hand, sailed by the rules and made no excuses for a faulty read of wind or water. Her competitors copied Annette; they tacked when she tacked and they steered parallel courses to hers in the hopes of finding favorable wind. Annette won her class three summers in a row when she was aged fourteen through sixteen. At the last ceremony, Trinette stomped away grumbling, "Nobody gives a flip about sailing." In the privacy of their home, however, Trinette hugged Annette and congratulated her.

"Why do you blow up? Why do you say the awful things you say?" Annette asked.

"Because it gets me what I want. You won't get what you want unless you fight for it."

During the summer when the girls were thirteen years old, Marie took Annette and Trinette to France for a two-month holiday at the simple country home of Marie's widowed mother. The twins adored their Grand'mere, who returned their affection by letting them sleep late, setting no structure for their days, and letting them swim unsupervised in the little stream that separated her garden from a neighbor's vineyard. The twins could play on the neighbor's clay tennis court any time they desired. When the girls played tennis without an audience, they didn't keep score. Challenges and ill temper never interfered with the long rallies they enjoyed.

Grand'Mere served tea in her garden at about four o'clock in the afternoon. She told her granddaughters stories about their grandfather. Marie already knew these familial tales, but she took pleasure in the recounting and seeing her daughters' curiosity. Grand'Mere told them how she and her husband had moved to London in 1938 "just in time" and then on to Montreal in 1940. Their grandfather had volunteered to serve in the Canadian Armed Forces in World War II. An infantryman in the Glengarry Highlanders, he had been killed in Holland three months before the end of the war. She told the twins about returning to France after their mother had married Phillip. Grand'Mere's brother was ill at the time, and Grand'Mere lived with him in her present house until he was taken by cancer.

One afternoon, two sons of the neighbor's groundskeeper rode on horseback to a spot across the stream from the garden while Grand'Mere was serving tea to Marie and the twins. The boys invited Annette and Trinette to ride with them, but the twins demurred.

"Go with the boys now," Grand'Mere told them. "You'll have time for tea later."

Each bareback horse carried a boy and a girl as they

cantered away on the path between the stream and the vineyard. Grand'Mere and Marie watched the dust clouds linger in the afternoon sun after the horses' passing.

"You've raised two beautiful young girls, Marie," Grand'mere said.

"You showed me how." Marie's compliment had a self-congratulatory scent to it, but not so strong as to require retraction.

Seeing how happy her daughters were in this tranquil place, Marie wondered if she pushed them too hard back home. She wondered whether status and achievement were too important a part of her life. The uncomplicated love shown by her mother fulfilled Marie in a way that made club chairmanships and her busy social life in Caledonia seem petty.

On the other hand, Marie had seen disastrous outcomes in the lives of children whose parents set no goals and no standards for behavior and achievement. Marie resented the lack of excitement and opportunity in her own childhood, and she was committed to teaching her daughters how to excel in a variety of interests and in education. The two-month stay was a blissful interlude in a place of unadorned tranquility. Marie returned to Caledonia before the start of school with her girls who were sun-tanned, happy, and comfortable speaking French.

The twins enrolled at Thornton Academy when they were fourteen. Their ninth grade peers and teachers couldn't distinguish between the two girls in photographs. In the flesh, however, even the dim-witted recognized the chasm that separated the twins' tastes and personalities.

Even after turning seventeen, Annette seldom dated.

When she did, she came home before her mother's eleven o'clock curfew. Trinette treated the curfew as a suggestion, like the donation recommendations on a United Way solicitation card. She felt that way about rules in general. Speed limits applied to other people. Age restrictions on drinking alcohol also applied to other people. Criminalizing marijuana use was stupid. Her serial dating led to countless trespasses on the eleven o'clock curfew.

Annette lay in her bed immobilized by foreboding as she listened to one typical midnight intervention precipitated by Trinette's tardy return from an evening of frivolity. Downstairs, every light on the first floor of the Laval house was illuminated, giving the darker demons of Trinette's nature no place to hide.

"You are grounded!" Marie chided her.

Trinette scowled impudently. She disdained the term "grounded". She wasn't in the Air Force.

"Are you jealous, Mummy?" Trinette taunted Marie. "I'm out having fun while you're stuck at home with Daddy?"

That was Phillip's cue to speak. "Breaking curfew is disrespectful and selfish."

His counsel wasn't necessarily wrong, but he didn't know his audience very well. He longed to be almost anywhere on the planet besides his own living room at this moment. He knew the outcome of this brouhaha: Three days of the silent treatment by Trinette and a week of Marie's lectures about shirking his duties as head-of-household.

"Be firm with her, Phillip," Marie chastised him.

Trinette snorted and averted her gaze from Phillip dismissively.

"I'm a woman!" the sixteen-year-old revolutionary shouted. "Your rules are for little girls!"

Annette could hear Trinette's defiant footsteps on the stairs. As usual, Trinette had to have the last word: "I've had all the crap I can stand for one night, so I'm going to bed. I'd be asleep by now if you didn't have these friggin' rules!"

Upstairs, Annette prayed for peace in the Laval household and, while she was at it, in Northern Ireland and in Palestine. These kinds of confrontations made Annette nervous and filled her with gloom. If only people could get along. Phillip had once confided in Annette that he had considered entering the priesthood. Annette felt certain that her father wished at this very moment he had acted on his religious impulses.

"You've got to be the disciplinarian, Phillip!" Marie rebuked her husband. "You're not supporting me!"

"I'm the man you married, Marie, not the man you want to mold me to be."

Annette hoped her sister hadn't heard the last exchange, because Trinette was always emboldened to know that she was causing friction between her parents. Trinette, who had already flopped on her bed, heard everything. With the lights extinguished and the Lavals retired to their respective beds, no one in the Laval Family believed for even a second that Trinette had broken curfew with impunity for the last time.

During their prep school years, Marie often served a glass of wine to the girls at dinner in their home. Outside their home, however, Annette shunned alcoholic beverages in compliance with the state drinking laws that Trinette routinely flouted. Trinette's diary revealed that, by the age of seventeen, she had personally tested a score of different beer varieties and twelve different labels of vodka. The evidence of her prowess was an album of labels she had soaked off bottles and then pressed and mounted.

Annette was north to Trinette's south. Annette was positively charged, and Trinette was negatively charged. Recognition of their polarity reinforced their behavior. This disparity in behavior by the identical twins gave them the confidence of having a twin and the satisfaction of being a distinctly unique person.

The consensus among boys at Caledonia High School and Thornton Prep was that Annette was great to look at, but Trinette was the twin you wanted to date. Identities were bound to become tangled in the minds of some. Rambo Johnson, who viewed himself as the pick of Caledonia High School's stable of studs, had a riotously good time with Trinette late one evening courtesy of a stolen bottle of vodka and the cabin of the town Fire Boat tied up to the town docks.

Just as conquering one river was not enough for Lewis & Clark, so it was – by analogy — with Rambo. Intending to make a clean sweep of the Laval offspring, Rambo invited Annette to go out a week after his evening with Trinette. Annette had no knowledge of her sister's prior escapade with Rambo when she accepted the invitation. Taking a bit much for granted, Rambo attempted to pick up with Annette where he had left off with Trinette. Rambo's tag team dream was not to be. Early in Rambo's campaign, Annette slapped him with enough force to permanently thwart Rambo's intentions. Rambo took Annette home promptly. Then he started a rumor that Annette was schizoid.

On another occasion after the twins had played in a field hockey game in Maine, the girls paired up with a couple of Camden High School boys. Trinette convinced Annette to switch field hockey jerseys and dates half-way through the evening for the fun of it. Trinette's real motive was to be able to make out with both boys in the same evening. She achieved her goal. Both boys were hopelessly confused, however, because they thought they were with a moody set of twins – willing one moment and decorous the next – when they were actually sharing time with one willing twin and one decorous twin.

From the rabble of boys seeking Trinette's attention, Daniel Lee Hardin emerged as the leader by not seeking her attention at all. Dan had stumbled upon the formula that winning a girl's affections lay in not trying too hard. He was six feet, two inches tall, sandy haired, and reasonably handsome, especially to Trinette who had a preference for cleft chins. This son of the owner of Caledonia's only hardware store possessed a nonpareil cleft chin. Dan lettered in three sports at Thornton Prep – football, hockey, and track. His muscular build and reluctance to speak too quickly or too often established him as a star among his peer group of smart-mouthed slackers. Trinette called him a "breeder". She wanted him for her boyfriend, and she got him. She and Dan dated steadily during their last year in prep school. They often double dated with Annette and Scott Harrington, Dan's best friend.

When the two boys bought the *War Wagon*, an aged, spacious sedan, the four youngsters had the freedom to roam

the roads around Lake Tremont. They skied together in winter and went to dances in the summer. Dan and Trinette
had squatters' rights on the *War Wagon's* back seat where the
two wanna-be lovers panted through acrobatic maneuvers so
energetic that the *War Wagon* rocked on its ancient suspension. Annette's defenses were more formidable, so after a little kissing and a little groping, Scott usually suggested that
they walk down by the lake for a while. Annette preferred
Scott over every other boy she dated, but she was perceptive
enough to know that Scott wasn't a one-girl kind of guy. She
kept her infatuation with Scott a secret for many years.

Trinette continued to date Dan even after he and Scott
headed southward to college at Princeton, the only Ivy
College that accepted both Dan and Scott. The twins head-
ed northward to enroll at McGill University in Montreal.
During the summers of their college years, Trinette and
Dan picked up where they had left off the previous autumn.
Because the train schedule between Philadelphia or New
York and Montreal was inconvenient and slow and because
flights to Dorval were expensive, Dan visited Trinette in
Montreal only once during each school year. Trinette kept
Dan in a special place in her heart, but she was a big-hearted
girl, so she dated a lot of other men in Montreal.

Laurens, a student from Brussels, became the leader of a
pack of boyfriends who filled Trinette's social calendar to the
detriment of her academic pursuits. Laurens had qualities
that appealed to Trinette: He wasn't possessive; he had plenty of money; he didn't complain when she drank too much or
smoked pot; and he didn't panic and head for the hills when
Trinette became pregnant in January of her junior year. He

paid for Trinette's abortion.

Trinette shared a little white lie with Annette, who sensed that something was wrong. Trinette knew that Annette would be horrified to know that she had resorted to abortion, so Trinette told Annette that she had suffered a miscarriage. Annette believed her. Abortion was too abhorrent for her to contemplate. Trinette even convinced herself to believe the lie. The twins kept the fictional secret secure.

Annette's only serious brush with romance at McGill occurred during the same semester that Trinette had her secret "miscarriage". Josh Walker was an agreeable match for Annette. He was a serious, almost scholarly, undergraduate student in the Faculty of Dentistry at McGill. Annette met Josh while conducting a survey of students at the McGill Pain Center for a non-profit opinion research company.

Josh entered the interview room as the third interviewee of the day. Unlike most other interviewees who brashly sat down and sprawled out like they were at home on their own couches, Josh sat down only when she invited him to do so. Sensing that his gaze was solely on her, she wrote down Josh's data quickly, but his bemused manner made her nervous, and she had to erase some entries and reenter them correctly.

"You have dazzling eyes," Josh said. It didn't matter that he was a student of dentistry, not optometry, because his compliment wasn't intended to be a medical opinion.

"I hope you're not too dazzled to answer this questionnaire," Annette replied. She was a lot more flattered than she let on. "Okay, you're Josh Walker, aged twenty, from Plano, Texas."

"And I'm free on Friday night. How about dinner?"

Annette smiled and nodded her head slightly. "If I say 'yes', will you let me finish the survey?" she said.

Josh said "yes", and so did Annette. They had dinner on Friday night.

Unlike most of the other dates Annette had at McGill, Josh didn't try to impress her with his intellect, his wallet, or his virility. He seemed genuinely interested in her, and he didn't press her to do what he wanted, which, Annette presumed was what most men wanted. He was patient and considerate. He reminded Annette of Scott in many ways. She didn't like the fact that she compared every date she ever had with Scott, but such comparisons were second nature. Josh was as tall as Scott, but he didn't have Scott's wide shoulders and muscular build. Josh's manner of speaking was more sincere. Scott's conversations were peppered with exaggerated images, borrowed jargon, and phrases of his own invention. If Josh described someone as "homely", Scott would have purloined a phrase to say the person "had a face only a mother could love". Both men could get to the same destination, but Josh's route was more direct, if less scenic.

Annette dated Josh for almost a year. She even invited him to visit her family in Caledonia during the summer, but Josh didn't have time to make the trip. Annette was very fond of Josh, but, in the back of her mind, Scott was always there damping whatever chance she had of falling in love with Josh.

Josh left her life with the same randomness he had entered it. He was good-natured in his parting. He told her how special she was and how much she had brightened his life. At one point, he said, "Our paths will cross again." Trinette's method of boyfriend retention was a half-nelson head-lock followed by seduction. Unable to summon Trinette's will power, Annette simply watched Josh walk away. Graduation was the last time Annette was to see Josh for many years.

Trinette's parting with Laurens in April had a completely different flavor. She spent a weekend with Laurens in a hotel on Rue Sherbrooke. He was going back to Belgium and she was returning to Caledonia. Trinette complained that Laurens didn't care about her enough, but, if he made any statement to suggest that he did, she turned to ice. She wanted not just Laurens, but the whole world, to adore her. She was in love with the notion of love, and no one person could sate her appetite for affection. They said their goodbyes in the lobby of the hotel. He walked west on Rue Guy and she walked northeast on Rue Sherbrooke.

On the rare occasions when Trinette took time for introspection, she recognized that she had always intended to marry Dan Hardin as though she had made a reservation. Everything and everyone between her freshman year and the date of her wedding was purely ego satisfaction and entertainment.

Dan had an open door policy on dating girls at New Jersey College, Bryn Mawr, Swarthmore, and Rutgers's consistent with a very different view of marriage. Technically, he didn't have a view on marriage, because the idea had never crossed his mind. He had known all along that the Hardin family plan was for him to earn a degree and return to Caledonia to replace his father as owner of Hardin's Hardware. Like puberty, marriage was simply a condition that happened when the time was right.

The right time, according to Trinette, was June of 1987, right after Dan had graduated without honors from Princeton and Trinette had barely managed to graduate from McGill. Moments after receiving Trinette's call from Montreal, Marie walked into her husband's den to give him the news.

"Trinette says she's going to marry Dan Hardin," Marie announced. "She just told me on the phone. She never asked my advice. She never even hinted that she was getting married. And *he* never asked your permission!"

Phillip stared at his wife blankly. "Trinette probably proposed to Dan," Phillip mumbled as he rubbed his eyes.

"He's not French and he's not Canadian."

"He's an American," Phillip said. "And so are you. Think about what you're saying." He reached out for Marie's hand. "It's Trinette who's marrying him, not you."

"He's going to be working in a hardware store."

"And I was a bank teller when you married me, Marie. It's going to be all right."

Marie recovered from the shocking news in time to assume command of wedding planning. Marie and Trinette argued about wedding details on the telephone daily. When Annette and Trinette graduated and returned home from Montreal, Trinette and her mother no longer needed telephones; they were free to fight like cats in person. Annette, always the amicable peace-maker, acted as referee and smoother of ruffled feathers, and helped escort her mother and sister through wedding planning battles without the loss of limbs. The cost to Annette was chronic anxiety and the loss of peace of mind.

On a sunny mid-June day, Dan Hardin and Trinette

Laval were married. Lavish by Caledonia standards, the ceremony was conducted at St. Paul's Catholic Church at the insistence of Marie Laval. Although Dan was a Protestant, he agreed to the terms laid out by his ardent future mother-in-law, and the wedding came off without a hitch. The reception did not. In fact, hitches abounded at the reception aboard the *M/S Franklin Pierce*, the largest vessel on Lake Tremont, with a passenger capacity of 300.

Trinette felt liberated in her new role as bride. No more curfews. No more secret beer parties behind her parents' backs. She was a married woman. She could do anything she desired. As the *Pierce* plied the waters of Lake Tremont, Trinette issued her declaration of independence by imbibing a prodigious amount of booze. Four years of partying with her McGill friends in the bars of Montreal had made her a hardened amateur alcoholic. She downed enough champagne and gin to embalm a hippo. That hitch set the stage for several other hitches.

That Andrew Gleason was President of Tremont Savings, a competitor of Phillip Laval's Bank of Caledonia, was the only reason Andrew had been invited to the wedding by Marie Laval. Andrew, however, acted as though he had official status in the celebration. He glad-handed others in attendance, passed out business cards, and sated his large appetite by pillaging food trays and chugging glasses of champagne. Trinette agreed to dance with Andrew when he asked. His massive stomach, his bad breath, and his ineptness at this thing called dance disgusted her, and Trinette disentangled from him as soon as the band hit the last note of the song.

Within thirty minutes, Andrew returned to ask for another dance with the bride. Trinette declined his etiquette-trampling request by claiming to be exhausted. Within seconds, Trinette and a double-jointed groomsman were contorting themselves wildly across the dance floor. Andrew interpreted this sequence of events correctly as a social rebuff, and he headed for the second deck bar to drown the insult. He had no sooner wetted his whistle with his third Martini of the day when, off to his right, he observed another hitch in progress.

One of Trinette's McGill classmates, an immensely likeable girl from Boston, was performing a gymnastic move on the top bar of the second deck railing when her balance deserted her and she tumbled twenty-five feet into Lake Tremont. Even in formal wedding attire, the girl was a strong swimmer, and she easily stayed afloat until the crack crew of the *Pierce* could maneuver to rescue her. Most of the wedding party crowded the starboard rails to witness the voluptuous young lady emerge from the crystal clear waters of Lake Tremont assisted by a cadre of eager rescuers. Physically fulfilling every man's dream of a mermaid (minus the tail), she shouted out as salty as any sailor, "It's a dry old ship; how about a drink?"

Another hitch occurred when Best Man Scott Harrington rose to toast the groom. In accordance with the rule-of-thumb that Best Men think they are about three times funnier than they really are, Scott launched into recollections of a childhood misspent with his best buddy Daniel Lee Hardin. Mercifully, Scott neared a conclusion.

"And, finally," Scott said, as he moved down the head

table to stand behind Annette, "we turn our attention to Trinette's twin sister and Maid-of-Honor. We are celebrating marrying off one of Marie Laval's two lovelies," he said as he leaned over to kiss Annette on the cheek, "but, now, let's lift our drinks to the last free Laval Gal, Annette!"

Annette, embarrassed by the attention and the insinuation, gamely smiled and nodded to the guests who clapped uncertainly. Marie Laval was not amused, but she sipped her champagne like a good soldier. Phillip Laval, not one to find insult in the air, toasted along with the rest of the wedding party before accepting the microphone from Scott to deliver brief Father-of-the-Bride comments without a hitch.

When the *Pierce* docked back in Caledonia, a few revelers among the well-fed, well-lubricated wedding party showered grains of rice on Mr. and Mrs. Dan Hardin as they disembarked from the vessel. Best Man Scott Harrington led the newly-weds to their waiting limousine. The limousine whisked Dan and Trinette away toward Boston amid cheers and blasts from the horn of the *Pierce*. After a night in Boston, the newly-weds were booked to fly to Paris on the following evening for a week-long honeymoon.

Members of the wedding party were leaving the *Pierce* to return to their cars parked throughout the village. Almost an hour of sunlight remained as Scott located Annette Laval on the docks in a group of bridesmaids and groomsmen.

"Who's up for a sunset cruise?" Scott asked in a voiced powered by too many whiskeys and too few *canapés*. In an agreeable state of mind, the celebrants unanimously volunteered. Scott pointed across Caledonia Bay to a white wooden boat house a mile away.

"Do you see the sailboat with the navy blue hull next to the white boat house?" he asked.

"Yeah!" they all cheered.

"Be there in twenty minutes for cast off!"

"Yeah!" they all cheered again. Group whooping and hollering came easy for the inebriated throng.

Scott grasped Annette's hand and led her to the *War Wagon* parked on the main street of town. She teased him by saying she shouldn't go with him in light of his embarrassing toast. Scott apologized and admitted that adlibbing with a microphone in hand wasn't one of his core competencies. Not surprisingly, Annette forgave him as a reward for his self-deprecation. Scott drove to his parents' house and parked in the circular driveway in the south lawn, the front of the house.

The Harrington house was a white Greek revival structure built in 1841. Three sides of the three-story dwelling were graced by extensive porches with sturdy columns. The three acres of grass lawns that surrounded the house were dotted with maple trees. Two docks and a boat house were situated at the end of the north lawn on the southern shore of Caledonia Bay.

Annette removed her high-heeled shoes. Scott led her by the hand as they walked across the western side lawn and down the sloping back lawn to the sailboat. Annette boarded the twenty-seven-foot vessel with Scott, who threw off his shoes and prepared the boat for departure. Twenty minutes went by and no one had arrived at the dock. Scott started the small motor to let it warm up. Ten more minutes passed, and not a single bridesmaid or groomsman had shown up at the dock. Blame it on disorientation, too much bubbly, indifference, or poor navigation, no one showed.

"We're casting off," Scott told Annette and she nodded assent.

Thirty minutes of daylight remained as Scott moved the vessel under power away from the Harringtons' docks. On flat waters and in calm winds, Annette and Scott watched sunset's last rays turn Lake Tremont to gold as they motored four miles away from Caledonia Bay to an anchorage among several islands on the east side of the lake.

Without speaking a word, they removed their wedding clothes and let them fall to the deck. They dove from the transom through the red reflection of sunset on the surface of the lake. They surfaced and swam toward one another until they held one another gently. Each could feel heat radiating from the body of the other in the coolness of the early summer lake water. The silence of night engulfed them and a canopy of stars twinkled ever brighter in the darkening sky.

Chapter 3

THE HARDINS

SEASONALITY WAS A key impediment to entrepreneurial success in Caledonia. The population of the town quadrupled during the summer months, so most businesses enjoyed a feast in the summer and suffered a famine the rest of the year. Restaurants opened and closed like morning glory petals. Dan Hardin's father, Benjamin, who rarely thought of an original idea if he could borrow a hackneyed one from the past, often plagiarized the *Twelve Days of Christmas* to say that Caledonia was served by twelve doctors, eleven policemen, ten antique shops, nine B&Bs, eight bars, seven restaurants, six real estate companies, five lawyers, four dentists, three banks, two grocery stores, and one hardware store.

"That hardware store, of course," he said, after reciting the list from memory, "is my store – Hardin's Hardware." Hardin's Hardware enjoyed monopoly status for many years, but even monopoly status couldn't guarantee success in the hardware business, because of competition from mega-hardware stores in towns less than an hour's drive away. Benjamin

Hardin's monopoly was unexpectedly challenged when a rival appeared in the person of Simon Bruguiere, the father of Paul Bruguiere and the older brother of Thomas Bruguiere, one-eyed handyman of Tourette's Syndrome fame.

Shortly after winning $87,000 in a multi-state lottery, Simon had a vision of starting a business. He described his alleged epiphany over pints of Guinness at local taverns. Pub regulars helped Simon burn through the first $1,000 of his windfall by encouraging him to retell the story of his vision as a means of getting Simon to pay for a round of cheer to guarantee an audience. Simon had an appetite for the spotlight. One evening as Simon finished a wearisome description of the store he was going to open, two wealthy summer residents bellied up to the bar, ordered two drafts, and asked who owned the green Fiat 600 out front.

"That's my baby," Simon said proudly.

"What year?"

"It's a 1957," Simon replied. "It's got 633 cubic centimeters and twenty-two horses."

The wealthy summer residents were as impressed by Simon's facts as they were *un*impressed by Simon himself.

"I can lift two wheels of that little beauty off the ground by myself," Simon bragged.

"No way," one of the rich guys said after a generous swill of beer that left foam clinging to his mustache like runaway shaving cream.

In a flash, Simon recognized a chance to generate a little cash on a wager. Nothing pleased Simon more than the thought of unburdening the pockets of rich guys.

"A hundred bucks says I can." Simon was sure of himself,

because he had, in fact, tied a loading strap onto the front bumper, routed the strap across his back, and leg pressed the front wheels of the Fiat 600 off the ground. That kind of foreknowledge was one of the benefits of having a lot of time on one's hands.

"Make it a thousand," the rich guy prodded Simon.

"Make it *two* thousand!" Simon pressed, knowing he had a sure thing.

"Okay. I'll bet you four thousand bucks you can't lift the *rear* wheels off the ground."

Simon was tipsy, but not completely daft. He knew the engine was in the rear of the car, but he also knew that engineers try to distribute weight as evenly as possible over the axles of their cars. He had lifted the *front* wheels off the ground without requiring a hernioplasty, so he was pretty sure he could lift the *rear* wheels off the ground, too. Technically, this was no longer a sure thing, but, in Simon's estimation, it was very close to a sure thing.

"If I lift the rear wheels clear of the ground, you give me four thousand dollars?"

"That's the bet."

"Done," Simon said. "This is too easy," he whispered in Thomas' ear, which was enough to make Thomas grin stupidly and wonder how much he stood to benefit by his brother's win.

Simon cunningly had trapped the rich guy just as he occasionally had made a buck or two betting on a winning horse after the conclusion of a race that the loser thought was still to be run.

"All you have to do is find a schmuck who doesn't know

you're betting on a sure thing," Simon repeated as though Thomas' visual impairment also affected his ability to comprehend complicated concepts such as cheating.

Simon walked out of the bar followed not only by the rich guys, but by every customer in the joint. Simon retrieved his loading strap from the back seat of the Fiat. He attached the strap to the rear bumper, routed the strap across his back, and prepared to leg press the rear wheels of the Fiat off the ground.

Witnesses made side bets and positioned themselves to verify the pending feat of strength. Simon recalled that the curb weight of the Fiat was 1,300 pounds, so he needed to leg press about 650 pounds. Plus or minus whatever, he thought. This was the easiest money he had ever made with the exception of the recent lottery windfall itself.

Simon made a great show of inhaling and exhaling as he had seen weight-lifters do on television. He squatted deeply once to stretch his leg and back muscles. He raised himself from the squat enough to take slack out of the loading strap. He winked confidently at his brother Thomas, who refrained from winking in return, because, when a man wearing an eye patch winks, he is out of the vision business, and Thomas didn't want to miss knowing the outcome of his twenty-dollar side bet.

Simon put all his effort into the leg press. He was able to extend the Fiat's shock absorbers to the full length of their travel, but his first thrust didn't get the rear wheels clear of the ground. Veins the size of licorice sticks protruded from his neck and forehead. Early in the thrust of his second attempt, something internal popped like the sound of a cork separating from a champagne bottle. Simon deflated like a ruptured balloon, the Fiat struts compressed, and the weight of the car fell back onto the suspension springs. Simon whimpered as he fell limp onto the rear of the car. In silhouette, Simon appeared to be fornicating with the Fiat.

"I think I broke my back," he announced in a dispirited voice.

"That didn't sound good," Thomas said somberly as he helped his brother recline onto the sidewalk. "What made that popping sound?"

"I don't know," Simon whispered. "I could be sterilized from the waist down."

"How do I get my money?" the rich guy asked, his fiscal concerns clearly outweighing his compassion.

"Here, tomorrow at six o'clock," Simon wheezed.

"I don't know you."

"He's good for it," Thomas said. "He'll be here tomorrow to give you your money."

Simon wasn't cheerful about relying on Thomas to wheel him down to the pub in a rented wheel chair the following evening so Simon could grudgingly hand over a check for four thousand dollars to the rich guy.

"Another example of the rich getting richer," Simon grumbled.

It was a brief ceremony marred by ill will when the rich guy recommended Simon not shoot off his mouth so fast next time. The payout reduced the balance of Simon's winnings to less than $82,000. Simon spent the next week in bed, so he had lots of time to think about his next step, if, indeed, he was to be a stepper in the future. He decided to fulfill his vision and open a business soon before he blew through the rest of his winnings.

Simon regained the use of his legs. His favorite part of rehabilitation was the Oxycodone prescribed by a local physician. Deep in the fog of self-administered double-doses of OxyContin, Simon sold his Fiat 600 at a loss because it conjured up too many sad and painful memories. Once he was back on his feet, he leased a small space on Main Street to open a shop he called *Nuts & Bolts*.

His enterprise was plagued by missteps from the very beginning. He bought an expensive wooden sign with rich gold lettering to be hung in front of his shop. He very much wanted a "Colonial look". He placed a bulletin in every postal box in every town around Lake Tremont. The bulletin layout was as confusing as the creepiest works of Hieronymus Bosch.

On June 15, Simon hosted a grand opening at which he served Spam on crackers and plastic glasses of New York State champagne. Including Simon, Thomas, Paul, and a photographer from the *Caledonia Reporter*, eight people attended the gala affair. Simon proudly claimed that not a single bottle of champagne remained unopened, which qualified the grand opening to be called a raging success. The citizens of Caledonia knew that the Brothers Bruguiere considered *any* drinking binge a success, so Simon's wildly optimistic opinion piece published in the *Reporter* was met with general skepticism.

"My vision is to provide the consumers of the Lakes Region with every nut and bolt they will ever need," was his exact quote in the *Reporter*.

Simon imposed a strict "no return" policy. In other words, he proposed to sell exactly the same collection of nuts and bolts stocked by Hardin's Hardware, and, if a customer bought the wrong sized bolt, the unfortunate consumer was stuck with it for the life of the bolt, because Simon didn't give refunds. To the surprise of few, *Nuts & Bolts* folded before the first snow fell.

In the words of one town wit, "The owner of *Nuts & Bolts* was nuts and he bolted."

Simon bolted so unexpectedly, in fact, that not even brother Thomas knew his whereabouts. All Thomas knew was that he was left holding the bag. He had to return inventories and he ended up paying the landlord to cancel the store lease. Thomas was also left with the responsibility for raising Paul.

Benjamin Hardin, the owner of Hardin's Hardware, felt pity for Thomas, so he bought the *Nuts & Bolts* sign from him and hung it in Hardin's Hardware in the appropriate aisle. Thus the incident became memorialized in local folklore. Summer visitors and local gossips alike perpetuated the tale at the Bruguiere Family's expense. Caledonia was back to being a one-hardware store town.

Compared to *Nuts & Bolts'* harsh return policies, Hardin's Hardware had a lenient policy on refunds. Hardin's staff was proud to have offered quality goods at a fair price for over sixty years. Richard Hardin, John Wesley Hardin's Great Grandfather, bought the store in 1937 from the estate of a previous owner financially ruined by the Great Depression. The bankrupt owner was driven by grief and shame to jump to his death from the village clock tower. It wasn't an overly tall clock tower, but it was tall enough to do the job. To the present day, anyone brave enough to climb the aged clock tower staircase could see the sign "DO NOT JUMP" posted as a safety precaution at the top step in the aftermath of the merchant's untimely death. Richard Hardin passed the store down to his son Benjamin in 1963. Richard stayed on to work in the store, and Benjamin strived to show that he deserved his father's trust by improving the store in any way he prudently could.

Two years prior to his ascension to the throne at Hardin's Hardware, Benjamin had graduated from Bates College in Maine and married Helen, daughter of Dutch-American parents from Fishkill, New York. Many people perceived Dutch girls to be really good-looking and sturdy. Helen lived up to that perception partially; she *was* really good-looking, but she wasn't sturdy. She died within twenty-four hours of giving birth to Daniel Lee Hardin in 1966.

Benjamin never remarried. Benjamin was a self-deprecating man who stoically stored the sadness of his wife's death in a private locker in his heart. He was a generous contributor to charities and he was ethical beyond reproach. He adored his son Dan, and he guided him with a tender touch, never raising his voice or his hand in anger.

Benjamin's counsel to Dan was often tentative as though he feared being sued by his son for defective advice. For example, he once said, "Dan, I could be wrong, but I think you'll be a better hockey player if you don't drink alcohol until after college." Needless to say, that particular piece of Benjamin's advice didn't stick to the wall very well.

When Dan announced his intention to marry Trinette, most fathers in the town, despite their secret fantasies of dallying with Trinette themselves, would have said something like, "You're marrying the wrong twin! Trinette's nothing but trouble." Benjamin, however, told his son, "Trinette Laval is a lucky girl to have you as her husband." Benjamin's glass was, if he wasn't wrong, always half full.

Dan was less sensitive and more economical with words than Benjamin. Dan wasn't an abrasive person, but neither did he mimic the wishy-washy conditional statements of his father. Dan was "New England blunt". Some observers believed that Dan needed to be something more than blunt with his new wife Trinette.

No sooner had she and Dan returned from their honeymoon in Paris than Trinette, emboldened by a series of *Mai Tais*, announced brazenly at a local restaurant that she "wasn't working in any two-bit hardware store". Dan wasn't threatened by her bombast, because he knew her so well from dating her all through high school and off-and-on in college. Diners in the restaurant, however, were shocked by what they heard, and they reported Trinette's outburst to friends not fortunate enough to have witnessed the scene first-hand.

Dan had always assumed that Trinette would work in the family store, but, now that she had declared her independence, he told her, "In that case, let's start a family." From the point of view of the sperm and ovaries involved, that initiative had already been launched on their wedding night in Boston, followed by more of the same during their honeymoon in Paris.

Dan detected a first hint of his pending fatherhood in

late July when he offered to make a Martini for Trinette to take down to the beach to watch sunset. She refused on her mother's counsel. That was a powerful hint. He made a gin-and-tonic for himself and poured a glass of water for Trinette. They walked down to the lake shore and settled into their favorite chairs.

"I have something to tell you," Trinette said. This second hint electrified Dan. He was keyed up for a surprise like a tightly wound coil spring. "I went for my doctor's appointment in Manchester today, and," she paused playfully, "we're going to have a baby."

Dan launched from his chair in the direction of Trinette, and he pulled her up to him for a long embrace.

"That's great," Dan said. His first thought was an immature one: He had married the best-looking girl in Caledonia, and now he was going to have the best-looking kid in town.

Trinette nodded and rested her head on his chest.

"Let's call everyone right now," Dan said excitedly.

"Call *your* family," Trinette said. "I've already called Grand'Mere because I knew it's too late for her in France when you get home from work. And then I called my mother and Annette to beat Grand'Mere to the draw."

"So you told your sister before you told me?" Dan teased her. "Who helped you make the baby, Annette or me?"

Caledonia's metabolism began to slow with the arrival of September. Summer visitors left their lake homes to migrate back to their primary residences. Marie Laval received word that Grand'Mere had suffered two minor strokes, so Marie immediately booked a flight to France to look after her mother. Annette postponed her plans for a year of traveling in Europe to accompany her mother. In a move that surprised Dan, Trinette decided to go with them, too. Dan knew that Trinette had a deep affection for Grand'Mere, but he thought it was an unnecessary risk for her to travel in her condition.

"You're three months pregnant," Dan tried to reason with her.

"I can fly up until the seventh month."

"Your mom and Annette can give Grand'Mere all the help she needs."

"You don't have a grandmother, Dan. You don't understand the tight bond we have."

"Why don't you wait until after the baby is born?"

"She needs our help now. I'll be back soon enough."

Without fanfare, the three Laval women left for France at the end of September. On his fifth night as a newly-wed-turned-bachelor, Dan telephoned his long-time companion Scott. He knew Scott was bursting with plenty of his own news, because, after receiving his commission through Air Force ROTC at Princeton, Scott had begun a year of Air Force Pilot Training at Laughlin Air Force Base near Del Rio, Texas.

During previous calls from Del Rio, Scott had been full of the joys of life, and Dan expected more of the same. Dan let Scott tell his news first. Scott was well into jets, now, and according to Scott's account, he was possibly the best formation and acrobatic pilot who had ever lived. Then it was Dan's turn. He told Scott about Trinette going with her mother and sister to France to spend a month minding Grand'Mere.

"Do you think I should have let Trinette go?" Dan asked. "Do you think it's safe?"

"I'm not a physician," Scott replied. "Correction: I'm not a *licensed* physician." He paused to allow his razor-sharp humor to sink in. "Of course, it's okay. Women are all checked out on that reproductive stuff. Besides, do you think you could stop her? Get real."

"I suppose."

"When it comes to women, don't think too much. Just roll with the tide."

Dan couldn't just roll with the tide, however. He called Trinette the following day to try to convince her to return to Caledonia as soon as possible. His persuasion gained no traction during that conversation or during successive weekly calls. As Thanksgiving approached, Dan realized that he had only a week or two to convince Trinette to return to Caledonia, because of the doctor's prohibition against flying after the sixth month of pregnancy. Dan knew how unlikely it was that anyone on earth could pressure Trinette to do anything, but he had to give it a shot. He turned up the intensity of his appeals.

"Come back to deliver the baby in New England," he pleaded. "You need to come back now while you can still fly."

"Grand'Mere's had another stroke. She needs us here."

"She doesn't need three nurses!"

"You have no idea how much she depends on us."

"Having a baby in France is like having a baby in the Third World," Dan said.

"Don't be absurd! Infant mortality in the U.S. is almost double the rate in France!"

"It's like the Dark Ages over there. Socialism and guillotines."

Dan wasn't making a lot of sense and he knew it. He just wanted his wife to return home as soon as possible.

"No one's had their head sliced off since 1977. And the French banned capital punishment in 1981!" She appeared to be well-informed about death in France.

"I don't want the kid to be a French citizen," Dan groused. He felt pushed to the point of saying anything.

"Our baby will be an American citizen, too. Did you learn *anything* at Princeton?"

"I miss you, Trinette. I just want you here."

"Baby, I want to be with you, too, but now's not the time to be thinking of ourselves. Annette's canceled her entire year of traveling around Europe to help Grand'Mere. I've got to do my part, too. Besides, morning sickness has me on my knees. I had no idea it could be this debilitating."

Dan surrendered. "Ah, well," he sighed before registering his unhappiness with one last stereotype, "maybe the kid will play a wicked good accordion."

The plan to deliver the baby in France was in concrete by early November. As Trinette's bouts of morning sickness worsened, Dan made a reservation to fly to France right away. He called Trinette to inform her that reinforcements were on the way.

"Absolutely, not!" she said. "No man on earth should be exposed to the hormones raging in this house!"

"I'm coming," Dan insisted. "I'll stay in a hotel."

"You're not listening to me, Dan. Do *not* come to France!"

Of course, Trinette got her way, and Dan backed off.

"She's probably right, Stud," Scott told Dan during a subsequent mental health telephone call. "Imagine Trinette with morning sickness; it could scar you for life. How are Mrs. Laval and Annette holding up?"

"Trinette said her mom's a rock and Annette's a saint," he said, noting that Trinette wasn't a habitual exaggerator when it came to praising the virtues of others.

"Best to lie low and concentrate on minding the store, Champ," Scott said.

Dan had noticed Scott's frequent use of names like "Champ", "Cowboy", "Hoss", and "Stud" since he had begun flying. Was it the jets or was it West Texas?

"Yeah," Dan agreed. "Trinette says to wait to fly over the week before the baby's due. Buying a ticket at the last minute like that'll probably cost a fortune, but I'll do it."

"Buy a ticket now and pay a penalty to change the travel date," Scott advised him. "That'll save you some *dinero*." Scott could come up with brilliant ideas like this, because his mind wasn't loaded down with worries about a wife and a child. He was a free agent.

The two friends conferred weekly during the next several months. All the news was good. Trinette called at least once a week to update Dan so he could keep Benjamin and Scott informed. Trinette's father, who got his information straight from Marie, seldom called Dan, but when he did telephone two days before Christmas, Dan spontaneously invited him to join the Hardins for drinks at the Caledonia Inn. They met at half past six to toast the pending arrival of the newest Hardin with pints of Tuckerman's Ale.

"Well," Phillip sighed after a dainty sip of his ale, "here

we are — the Three Musketeers."

"Three Stooges," Dan said after a long swallow of ale.

"Kingston Trio," Benjamin added thematically as he sniffed the head of his beer.

"Peter, Paul, and Mary," Phillip said. Another sip.

"Three Amigos," Dan said. Another chug.

"Three Blind Mice," Benjamin said. He sniffed at his beer again.

"Three Magi," Phillip said after swallowing a manly portion of his beer.

"Three Wise Men," Benjamin said. Sniff. Sniff.

"Same thing," Dan said to his father. "Dad, that's not cologne; please stop sniffing and start drinking." Benjamin took a drink of his Tuckerman's.

"The Father, the Son, and the Holy Ghost," Benjamin pronounced liturgically.

The three men exchanged glances. Game over. If this was any indication of the quality of the pending conversation, this meeting could be over before their beer glasses were empty.

"You're probably wondering why I called you here this evening," Dan said, using a line so old and so tired that Phillip didn't even fake a smile.

"Yep, yep," Benjamin sighed. "So, Phillip, I guess we're to be grandfathers soon?"

"Mid-March," Phillip affirmed what they all knew.

"Yep, yep."

"Your life'll never be the same," Phillip told Dan.

A man in the on-deck circle of fatherhood could take such a statement a lot of ways, but his father-in-law's tone was cordial, so Dan took the prediction amicably.

"Having a child will be the high point of your life."

"Some may disagree," Benjamin added, "but I believe being a father is the highest calling of man on earth." That lofty declaration, however qualified, pretty much capped off that subject.

Their conversation continued, but it moved awkwardly like a horse with an injured leg. Marie Laval had whisked Phillip's daughters away to France to mind Grand'Mere without consulting Phillip. This left him on his own at home for an extended period for the first time in his twenty-eight years of marriage. Phillip knew that Benjamin's wife had died birthing Dan, so he avoided saying anything to resurrect sad memories.

Benjamin privately was skeptical of Marie Laval's decision to take both daughters to France to care for Marie's mother. He also had doubts about Trinette's decision to stay in France for her pregnancy instead of returning to New England to be with Dan, but he believed that expressing those doubts served no good cause.

Dan felt out-of-step, too. The last thing he wanted to do was cause his father pain by unlocking memories of Helen's death. The second-to-last thing he wanted to do was to insinuate that he placed his own needs ahead of the needs of Trinette and her family.

In short, the king was wearing no clothes, but none of the three men saw any reward in saying so. It was a lot easier to talk about football and the New England Patriots. Dan picked up the tab for their ales, and the three men paused in the lobby for a parting handshake and a Christmas greeting.

For the first time in his life, including at Dan and Trinette's wedding, Phillip hugged Dan. Benjamin, who hadn't hugged Dan since he was whippersnapper, did the same thing to maintain familial symmetry. Snow had fallen all day, leaving a downy blanket that muffled sound and made the spheres of their individual thoughts seem small and intimate and lonely. They went home to their three empty houses.

Dan joined his father Benjamin at noon on Christmas Day for the traditional turkey dinner Benjamin had prepared every year for twenty-one years. Dressing, cranberries, sweet potatoes, and the turkey were prepared exactly the same way Benjamin always prepared them. The wine and rich food put the two men in a languid mood. They gazed contentedly across Caledonia Bay where ice fishing bob houses lay beneath two feet of virgin snow. Oak logs crackled in the fire. The radiant heat made them feel impervious to the cold outside.

"Before I take my Christmas nap," Benjamin said, as he placed his arm on his son's shoulders, "I want you to know that I'm very proud of you, Dan, and I love you very much."

Dan had never before heard these words from his father. Tears moistened his eyes and tightness gripped his throat. He hugged his father without speaking. It was the best he could do.

"Do you ever feel lonely, Dan?"

"Sometimes," Dan admitted. A second later, he felt selfish for complaining after only a three-month absence by his wife compared to over twenty years of solitude for his father since his mother had died. "Marriage isn't turning out the way I expected."

"It seldom does," Benjamin said.

He shuffled off to his bedroom and Dan settled into a chair by the fireplace. This was New England: A lot of deeply-held sentiments went unspoken in this land of little-worded men. Dan assumed he'd not hear the words "I love you" spoken by his father until he — or his father – lay dying. Dan wondered if he had become so pathetic that his father pitied him.

At four in the afternoon Eastern Standard Time, night time in France, Dan called Grand'Mere's telephone to chat with Marie, Annette, and Trinette in turns. Trinette sounded a little foggy and he asked how she was feeling. "I feel goofy. It's these French morning sickness pills," she explained. Dan signed off feeling no less lonely than when he had made the call.

Throughout Christmas Day, Hardin's Hardware employees had called to thank Benjamin and Dan for their Christmas bonuses as they did every year. It was a revered tradition started by Benjamin's father and continued for fifty years. As nice as it was to hear their happy voices, however, darkness had descended on Lake Tremont, and it was a time for reflection. Dan turned off the telephone ringer, added new logs to the fire, and resumed reading Winston Churchill's *The Gathering Storm* in the vain hope of cheering himself up.

Dan's plan to be in France for the birth of his child never materialized. A momentarily misplaced ski tip while Dan clattered down an icy black diamond slope early one February morning sent him cartwheeling down the steep slope, arms and legs flailing, head whiplashing until he came to rest near the bottom of the run separated from his skis by fifty feet. At first, he couldn't move. Moments later, after he *had* moved a little, he wished he hadn't. The Ski Patrol cautiously lifted him into an ambulance for transportation to a hospital.

Two days later, Dan was confined to bed and in traction in his father's house. The doctor told him he should remain there for six weeks. Benjamin took over Dan's duties at Hardin's Hardware, and he tended to Dan's needs in the evenings after work. Dan tried to be a good patient to reward his father for being such a considerate care-giver.

Then, on the Ides of March, the call came. Marie told Dan that Trinette couldn't talk at the moment, but the baby boy was fine. The mother was fine. Everyone was fine. Dan was ecstatic. Trinette had already named the child John Wesley Hardin. Dan wasn't quite as ecstatic about that, because he and Trinette had previously chosen Benjamin Lee for a boy's name. He asked his mother-in-law to confirm the name.

"John Wesley Hardin," Marie repeated sweetly.

"Wasn't he an outlaw?"

"He was the son of a Methodist minister," Marie assured him, displaying considerable ecumenicalism for such a devout Catholic.

"Who was an outlaw," Dan added.

"I believe so," she said. "The papers are all done."

"It's all done, huh?" Dan repeated. He knew how single-minded Trinette could be. Her addictive personality sent her off on tangents all the time. She could have been reading a story about John Wesley Hardin the very morning of his son's birth and, *voila*, that's the baby's name. He told himself he was fortunate she wasn't reading a boxing magazine, because she just as easily could have chosen Mohammed Ali Hardin or Sugar Ray Hardin. Trinette's unpredictability was enough to make him shudder.

"Tell Trinette I love her and I'll talk to her tomorrow."

Events flowed predictably after the initial shock of John Wesley Hardin's arrival and unexpected nomenclature. Dan left his traction bed and was in his earliest days of rehabilitation when the three Laval ladies and young John flew into Boston Logan Airport. Phillip drove a rented van with Dan down to Boston Logan to pick up their women and the new arrival. To see the women and child emerge from Immigration and Customs was a magic moment stored in Dan's memory. Almost a month old, John was an angel with pleasing features and strangely unfocused eyes that seemed too big for his head.

"He's so handsome," Dan exclaimed. Trinette looked wonderful, too. She gently handed the bundle that was John to Annette so she could embrace her husband. The women cooed and Phillip clucked as he fiddled with John's tiny hand.

"I almost forgot what a rock you are," Trinette whispered in Dan's ear. Six months of separation and consternation were forgotten.

For the most part, it was a quiet two-hour drive. Marie sat in the front passenger seat beside her husband who did the driving. Annette sat in the second row of seats with John, who slept almost all the way home in his portable cradle. Trinette fell asleep with her head on Dan's thigh in the third row of seats.

Phillip left Dan, Trinette, John, and Annette at the Dan Hardin house. Annette planned to stay with Trinette for a few days, so she settled into the guest room, her bed a few feet from John's cot, to allow Trinette to sleep uninterrupted and to adjust to being home with Dan. Dan and Trinette needed time to get accustomed to being together again and to get started on their new life with John Wesley Hardin.

The Hardins had their family.

Chapter 4

THE HARRINGTONS

ON SUMMER DAYS when Dan Hardin and Scott Harrington weren't working at Hardin's Hardware, they were most likely fishing together on Lake Tremont, unless their little fishing boat was driven off the lake by whitecaps churned up by squalls blowing inland off the coast of Maine. In the early afternoon when the sun was high overhead, pastrami grinders, ice-cold lemonade, and frequent dips in the clear lake water compensated for the lack of fish willing to clamp their lips on a hook. Scott's father Joe T. saw them off from the Harringtons' dock on a particularly warm August day before the start of the boys' senior year at Thornton.

"There's no use fishing now," Joe T. opined, reflecting a mistaken belief shared by many that fishing was primarily about catching fish. "Any fish worth his salt has gone deep in this heat." Joe T. was a clever mathematician, but he could scramble a metaphor in his sleep.

"We're going after the ignorant ones who don't know they're supposed to be deep," Scott responded as he steered the little boat away from the dock.

Joe T. was on his way to a reception for parents of pro-spective Thornton students that afternoon, but he stayed to watch the boys make way toward the mouth of Caledonia Bay. He felt a nostalgic tug on his heart as he remembered his boyhood days in Odessa, Texas when he and his best buddy terrorized the bass in Red Bluff Reservoir. He could remember his own father's send-off: : "If y'awl catch a fish in this heat before eight o'clock tonight, you'll know you just caught the dumbest fish in West Texas."

With the boat at anchor, Scott found that, indeed, not all the fish had gone deep. He had been snorkeling for half an hour and was returning to the boat when he discovered a bass loitering in the shade beneath the hull of the boat. That lone bass, he thought, could turn an otherwise dull affair into a money-making opportunity. He climbed into the boat to join Dan, whose solid hour of casting had been unrewarded.

"Any bites?" Scott asked.

"Nope."

"I bet I can land a bass in this boat inside of three minutes."

"You haven't landed any kind of fish in this boat in the last three *hours*."

"I can do it."

"No way," Dan insisted. "It's hot. They've gone deep."

"Five bucks?"

Dan nodded. Scott removed the red-and-white spoon from his line and quickly rigged a plain Number Six hook with half a worm and a single steel weight and dropped the line over the side. Within five seconds, the bass under the boat struck the worm and Scott set the hook. He brought the bass in, removed the hook from the fish's mouth, and placed the fish back into the water.

"Five bucks Sucker," Scott said.

"That's not fishing."

"I landed a fish and you owe me five bucks," Scott said. "It doesn't matter whether I harpooned it or shot it with a bazooka."

"Put it on my tab." It was too hot for Dan to argue with his designing, manipulative, alleged fishing buddy.

Dan was not known for paying his debts punctually, so Scott penciled an IOU on a piece of cardboard and passed it to Dan to initial.

"I'll pay you your stinkin' five dollars!"

"You certainly will. Now, initial the IOU."

Dan scrawled a "D" on the IOU and returned the promissory cardboard back to the hustler. Dan cast his lure into shallow water near a granite ledge. Scott removed the hook from his line, replaced it with a fluorescent yellow, floppy bait and also cast toward the shore, inadvertently crossing his line over Dan's.

"Scott, you've got an entire lake you can cast into, but you toss your stinkin' Chinese bait across my line."

Apart from complaints about injustices such as crossed fishing lines, Dan generally abdicated the duty of talking to Scott. As on dozens of afternoons in the past, the two anglers drank lemonade and swam and fished while Scott yapped about hockey and football. Dan was the quarterback of the Thornton Prep football team. Scott was his favorite wide receiver, because Scott, unlike the other fumble-prone receivers, had a reasonable chance of not only receiving the ball but holding on to it as opponents pummeled his body to the ground.

The two best friends could communicate with a wink, a twitch of an eyebrow, or a simple hand gesture. In the game against Oxbridge Prep, Dan touched the ear hole of his helmet with his index finger to change Scott's route to an "out", thereby amending both the play he had called in the huddle and his subsequent audible at the line of scrimmage. The play netted seventeen yards and became a fundamental proof that the two friends were "on the same wave length".

With the help of photo albums, Scott could trace the chain of causation enabling his friendship with Dan Hardin back to the day his parents – Joe T. and Joyce — met at West Texas State University in Canyon, Texas during a period Joe T. called the Mesozoic Era.

Joseph T. Harrington graduated from Odessa Permian High School in Texas in the spring of 1958 at the same time Joyce Kruger graduated from Fredericksburg High School in the Hill Country of Texas. Joe T. took the bold step of sitting beside Joyce in a freshman philosophy class. The two had a lot in common. They were unspoiled by parental favors too freely given and they were uncontaminated by selfishness. Joe T. liked Joyce's short hair, amicable smile, and freckled nose. Joe T. remembered the first time he kissed Joyce. He told her she smelled like a terrycloth towel hung out in the sun all afternoon – clean and comforting. She took this as a compliment, just the way Joe T. intended it.

Joyce liked Joe T.'s open face and his big, wide shoulders.

She could recognize his unhurried walk and his six-foot, three-inch frame from two hundred yards across campus. Joyce did her homework on Joe T. by reading his philosophy papers. His very first essay was titled *My Personal Philosophy*, but, she thought impishly, a more appropriate handle might have been *Ode to Tautology*.

"The average person is pretty average and can use a little slack. I figure my job on earth is to give it to them," Joe T. had written.

This Joe T. was no Kant or Nietzsche, but how could Joyce not love a guy who thought his mission on earth was to be considerate of other people? He was patient with others, and he was quick to help them feel better about themselves. Joe T. was a popular guy, and Joyce was at the front of the line of his admirers.

Joe T. and Joyce graduated from West Texas State in 1962, and they were married in Fredericksburg a month later. On their wedding night in a luxurious hotel room overlooking the San Antonio River, Joe T. lay in bed curled up like a jumbo shrimp shivering involuntarily. Fearing that he was suffering from a serious ailment, Joyce lay close to her new husband and wrapped her arms around him to comfort him.

"Darling," Joyce said as empathetically as she knew how, "do you want me to call a doctor?"

"No," he said. "Just hold me for a while." Although he had never experienced these symptoms before, he knew that the shivering was simply a nervous reaction to the most exciting moment he had ever experienced. He told Joyce, "This is the most important day of my life, and my nervous system has shorted out."

No matter how she interpreted the incident, Joyce took it as the most personal, sincere compliment she could have received. When the fit of shivering passed, Joe T. and Joyce sealed their marriage in gentle, sometimes urgent, acts of lovemaking that set the pattern for their marriage.

Joe T. went back to West Texas State to complete his work toward a master's degree in education. He served as an adjunct in the math department for a year and then was hired first as a teaching assistant and then as a mathematics teacher at Hardin-Simmons University in Abilene, Texas. Scott was born to Joe T. and Joyce in Abilene two years later in 1966, the same year Dan Hardin was born in Caledonia, New Hampshire.

Joe T. was a well-regarded educator and administrator. His outdoorsman's appearance and his cordial personality appealed to people. He was honest, plain-spoken, and motivated. He spent more time and energy on his students than other instructors. Joyce was well-suited for Joe T.'s disposition and interests. She was the most optimistic person Joe T. had ever met. Nothing seemed to shake her confidence in people. When someone was ungracious toward her, she refused to be offended, rationalizing that the person was having a bad day. Joyce didn't resent the long hours Joe T. worked, and she welcomed into their simple home the students Joe brought home for pecan pie and milk at late night tutoring sessions during their six years at Hardin-Simmons. Joyce's loyalty was instrumental in the growth of Joe T.'s meritorious reputation.

The Harringtons were a great team. In 1970, they moved to San Angelo, Texas, where Joe T. was named chair of the mathematics department at Angelo State University. He served in this capacity for almost ten years, the last four of which he served concurrently as Assistant Dean of Students. His ability to work well with people, elicit their inputs, and mold sometimes competing interests into an actionable plan made him a respected problem solver.

Joyce, who had chosen to stay at home for the upbringing of Scott, volunteered as a teacher's aide at Scott's schools in San Angelo. Largely because of Joyce's good sense and innate optimism, Scott grew up to be curious without being mischievous, self-confident without being arrogant, and committed to being the best student and athlete he could be. Joe T. gave Joyce full credit for encouraging Scott's stellar academic grades and success in football and track, and she deserved it.

Bad news was a stranger in their home until 1979 when Joyce was diagnosed with early onset of muscular sclerosis. Her physician told Joyce that her tolerance to warm weather was bound to decrease over time, and he recommended that they move to a cooler climate.

Joe T. immediately focused his job search on schools in Washington State, Michigan, and New England. The job offer that appealed to him most was an opening as Headmaster at Thornton Academy in Caledonia, New Hampshire. The Thornton Board of Directors, which included Phillip Laval, unanimously ranked him head-and-shoulders above the other candidates they interviewed. Joe T. eventually served as Headmaster or President of Thornton for twenty-one years.

Joe T. was not an avaricious man, and he didn't lust for power or prestige. His ability to connect with sometimes troubled young people and to turn their lives around was the fuel that powered his life engine, and he rapidly made himself indispensable at Thornton. Joe T.'s son Scott first attended Thornton at the age of fourteen. Seated beside Scott in his first class on his first day at Thornton was none other than Dan Hardin. Historical events had occurred in the proper sequence to allow their friendship to begin.

Because Dan's mother had died giving birth to him, he was more conscious of Joyce Harrington's many acts of kindness than her own son, Scott. Joyce treated Dan as if he *were* her own son. Both boys benefitted from Joyce's sunny disposition and her baking. Dan spent a lot of his free time in the Harrington home.

The two boys enjoyed the same music and sports, and they were even similar in appearance. Scott was a couple of inches shorter than Dan. Scott's hair was so blond it was almost white, while Dan's hair was the color of wheat. Their facial structure and body builds were similar enough that strangers often mistook them for brothers. Their relationship was more harmonious than most of the actual sets of brothers in their school.

In addition to playing alongside one another in football and hockey, the boys competed against one another in the four-hundred-meter run, placing first and second in the New England Prep School finals in their junior year. Scott won in 49.22 seconds, and Dan took second with a 49.33. Their times didn't match up with times by athletes in California or Texas, but they were respectable for rural New Hampshire.

During the summer months, Benjamin Hardin hired Scott to work full-time beside Dan at Hardin's Hardware.

The boys pooled their earnings, and, about a millisecond after Dan turned sixteen years old, they used the money to buy a ten-year old Chevrolet they dubbed *War Wagon*. When Scott turned sixteen, the first post-pubescent cracks in their partnership began to show. They squabbled about paying for gasoline, and they lodged complaints when one of them needed the car and it was being used by the other.

They were believers in the rule of law, so they settled their disputes with a coin toss. This worked for a while, but Scott began filing appeals in the form of whining "best-out-of-three" or "best-out-of five". Dan got tired of this wheedling for do-overs, so he suggested a "rock, paper, scissors" method of conflict resolution.

Eventually, this procedure also led to disputed verdicts, so the boys turned to a neutral party – usually Annette or Trinette. Each boy wrote his name on a piece of scratch paper and dropped it into Dan's Red Sox hat. The neutral party averted her eyes and pulled one of the pieces of scratch paper out of the hat to determine a winner. Scott insisted they abandon that method when he caught Trinette conspicuously *not* averting her eyes to ensure Dan's win.

To escape the morass of charges and counter-charges, Dan and Scott reverted to the dollar bill game method of resolving disagreements. They pulled a dollar from each of their pockets and compared the last two digits in the serial numbers to determine the winner. Not surprisingly, Dan noticed that Scott was collecting dollar bills with "97", "98", and "99" appearing as the last two digits, so he called foul and refused to accept a verdict. On occasion, the boys determined a winner after exhausting appeals and do-overs only to discover that they no longer remembered the basis for their quarrel.

Why don't you two grow up?" Annette said once. "For God's sake, flip a coin."

Trinette was even less charitable. "You two are so stupid! I'll never understand how you get straight *A*s!"

The potentially worst squabble of all was set up when Dan botched a parallel parking attempt on the Thornton campus in the autumn of their senior year. Dan reshaped the left rear fender of the *War Wagon* by scraping it against the hundred-year-old bark of an improvidently situated maple tree, a very stout maple tree growing too close to the curb. Dan leaped out of the driver's seat to survey what he had wrought. It looked bad, and it looked even worse when he moved the *War Wagon* forward away from the tree for a clear look at the damage. Everyone knows that one's good deeds are seldom noted, but witnesses crawl out of the woodwork when one messes up. Sure enough, Scott came upon the scene.

"Who's the ignoramus who smashed the car?" Scott asked.

"I did it," Dan whispered as though secrecy might minimize the damage.

"What?"

"It's my fault," Dan said a little louder.

"I'm glad it wasn't *moi*."

"I'll make it right," Dan mumbled reluctantly.

Later, when Dan found out that the lower of two repair estimates was $900, he lost some of his ardor for fixing the car on his own. The insurance policy had a $1,000 deductible for collision coverage, so he began shopping around for an alternative remedy. Riding to his rescue was a most improbable white knight, a peer at that, a senior in the vocational crafts department at Caledonia High School. The savior was a poorly dressed seventeen-year-old trouble-maker with a reputation for saying the wrong things at the wrong times. The young man, who many townspeople considered a ruffian, had shot his right eye out spectacularly with a bottle rocket on the most recent Independence Day, and he wore his eye patch like a badge of honor. Thomas Bruguiere claimed he could make the *War Wagon* whole for $300.

"Done," Dan said.

"I'm in for half," Scott offered nobly, now that the cost of "half" had decreased by $300. "It's the least I can do to help out."

Notwithstanding the handicap of working with a solitary eye, Bruguiere beat out the fender and showed considerable skill at filling, sanding, priming, and painting to produce a repair that the boys agreed was top notch. Dan and Scott gladly paid Bruguiere the promised $300, and they heralded Bruguiere's skill far and wide.

When Benjamin Hardin's janitor at the hardware store went to jail for selling marijuana within 500 feet of a public school, Bruguiere's recent fame made him a shoe-in for the vacancy. Unfortunately, Thomas's fortunes soon took a turn for the worse when he mortally insulted the wife of the President of Tremont Savings. Mrs. Gleason sourly instructed Bruguiere to pick up a rack of canoe paddles she had knocked over while squeezing her abundant buttocks through one of the store's narrower aisles. Her commands were imperious and condescending. Amongst the clattering of paddles in the rough hands of Bruguiere, witnesses affirmed that they had heard Bruguiere say, "Sure, I'll pick up the paddles, you overfed sow."

Hardin's Hardware didn't have a formal customer service training program, but it was widely understood by Hardin's employees that calling customers names like "overfed sow" wasn't condoned. Mrs. Gleason squealed her outrage. Benjamin Hardin raced to the scene of the atrocity and got an earful from Mrs. Gleason. Bruguiere lurked around the rack of canoe paddles, malice radiating from his operative eye ball.

Benjamin fired Bruguiere on the spot, but Benjamin's generosity kicked in when the heat of battle had subsided, and he closed the Hardin's Hardware chapter of Bruguiere's *curriculum vitae* with a payment of four weeks' wages and a recommendation for employment as a janitor at Caledonia's only boat showroom where the janitor's work was confined to a night schedule when no customers were on the premises. As a result of this chain of events, Thomas Bruguiere harbored a reluctant appreciation for the Hardin family and a profound grudge against the Gleasons.

A month later, Joe T. invited Benjamin to join the Board of Directors of Thornton Academy. Phillip Laval backed Benjamin solidly on the basis of Joe T.'s recommendation. Benjamin didn't pretend to be an intellectual; he brought a practicality and level-headedness to deliberations before the board. Benjamin and Phillip became friends, having no idea that, five years hence, the marriage of Dan Hardin and Trinette Laval was destined to make them in-laws. As their friendship developed, they included Joe T. and Joyce in their invitations with a frequency that led to group vacations together in Banff, Prince Edward Island, Iceland, and the West of Ireland. During the months when snow piled up around the white wooden houses of Caledonia, Joe T., Joyce, Phillip, and Benjamin often played pinochle in the Laval living room while Marie knitted or read in a chair beside the fireplace.

Eight months after the *War Wagon* battered the maple tree and two months after both Dan and Scott had been accepted to enroll at Princeton University in the autumn, the boys graduated from Thornton. The worst grades on Dan's transcript were a handful of *B*s. Scott's record was even better; he had received straight *A*s except for a *B* in chemistry. He earned a *B* in chemistry because he had used a Bunsen burner to superheat a quarter which he tossed onto the floor behind the stool of a notoriously cheap international student from France.

"Someone lose a quarter?" Scott asked innocently.

The moment the French boy saw the quarter on the floor, he said, "It's mine."

Almost a full second passed from the time the boy picked up the quarter to the time he first yowled at the top of his lungs and tossed the hot quarter away. In the ensuing investigation, Scott was identified as the culprit. He received counseling on the perils of superheating alloys and a *B* in the class.

Dan and Scott worked together all summer in Hardin's Hardware. When they weren't working, they took road trips in the *War Wagon* with the Laval Gals or went fishing on Lake Tremont. Dan and Trinette were considered an item, but Scott was a free agent much in demand in Caledonia and other villages around the lake, so Scott sometimes substituted a newly-discovered lass in the place of Annette. With the arrival of summer residents in the resort towns situated on the banks of Lake Tremont, there was no shortage of attractive lassies.

Annette refused to take offense when she was replaced in the starting lineup. Jealousy was beneath her standards of behavior. Even though her crush on Scott never waned, she had inherited a healthy dose of her mother's intuition, and she knew better than to overplay her hand.

Scott's intuition, on the other hand, was almost non-existent, which is to say he was a typical American male in his late teens. A little golf here, a little tennis there, and a cute sun-tanned girl beside him in the *War Wagon* pretty much satisfied his survival needs. Annette went on dates with Scott whenever he asked her out, but she kept the depth of her infatuation with him a secret even from her twin sister.

At Princeton, Scott joined the Air Force Reserve Officer Training Corps. Ever since Scott had first laid eyes on a fighter pilot standing beside an F-4 *Phantom* at an air show at Hanscom Field in Massachusetts, he had dreamed of becoming a fighter pilot. At the time, he didn't fully grasp the job description of a fighter pilot, but the gaggle of groupies who surrounded the officer standing by his air machine suggested there were perks to the job. Scott concentrated on mathematics and science and he selected physics as his major.

Dan chose a different path. He viewed his pending ownership of Hardin's Hardware as inevitable based on historical precedence. He had even questioned the wisdom of spending so much money to go to Princeton when it was widely known he was the heir apparent. But his father Benjamin encouraged him to attend the best college he could get in regardless of the cost. Dan studied economics. The two friends often plotted their futures over pitchers of beer at a bar on Nassau Street, one of the streets bordering the Princeton campus.

Unlike most freshmen who rarely finish on the same path they started out on in their freshman years, Dan and Scott followed through with their plans. Dan earned his Bachelor of Arts degree in Business from Princeton in 1987. On the same day, Scott earned his Bachelor of Science degree in Physics.

"Can you believe we actually pulled this off?" Scott asked Dan at *Clyde's*, a place where the boys frequently held vespers. There was no Clyde, but the alcoholic Portuguese bartender was good about keeping the pitchers of Yuengling beers coming.

"Miracles happen," Dan replied.

"Sometimes I wish I had tried a little harder."

"You don't want to use up all your ammo on the first wave," Dan said, vaguely invoking lessons learned at the Battle of Bunker Hill and Corregidor Island. "Always keep a little effort in reserve."

"Four more days," Scott said, "and I'll be a lieutenant. I get sworn in, and they pin on my butter bars."

"The Air Force will never be the same."

It was Scott who was never the same. The path to his commissioning had been strewn with obstacles. Close calls with low grades in chemistry and physics had scared him into unprecedented, frantic studying for weeks to maintain his

ROTC eligibility. An excitable doctor's detection of calcium deposits on Scott's lungs while reading his chest x-rays had threatened an end to Scott's quest until a more experienced doctor interceded and saved Scott's future by explaining that the scarring had been caused by childhood histoplasmosis. Scott attributed the disease to his steady diet of bat guano and kitty litter during his rustic youth in San Angelo.

A couple of weeks after reciting the oath at his commissioning ceremony and receiving his Second Lieutenant's bars, Scott served as Best Man at Dan's wedding. Three weeks after the wedding, Scott began Air Force Pilot Training near Del Rio, Texas. After a year of pilot training, he finished second in his class, high enough to claim one of four fighter assignments. His dream of flying fighters was coming true.

Chapter 5
BOOMERANGING

THE ENGLISH LANGUAGE was insufficiently stocked with words to meet Scott's needs, so, according to Scott himself, a rogue gang of underemployed neurons in the left cerebral hemisphere of his brain fired off synapses via axons to invent words spontaneously. Random word generation had become a habit for Scott. He could coin a term for just about anything. For example, he called his trips back to Caledonia "boomeranging". The world throws you out like a boomerang, and you come back to where you started was Scott's loose definition of "boomeranging".

Dan's theory on Scott's alternative word habit was that Scott saw concepts visually, not textually. Scott's world was inhabited by metaphors and analogies, according to the theory. Dan acknowledged that the colorful words and phrases that peppered Scott's speech imposed a translation tax on his listeners. The habit could have been an annoyance but for Scott's amiability.

"The deficatorium" was "the bathroom".

"The fornicatorium" was "the bedroom".

"Beamed" meant "went", as in "we beamed across the lake".

"He screwed himself into the ceiling" meant "he was irate".

"He left like a scalded-ass ape" meant "he left in a hurry".

"He was screaming down on me like a wounded wombat and I shot him in the lips with a laser" meant "a high speed bandit attacked from above and I destroyed him head-on with a radar-guided missile".

"Boomeranged" meant "went home".

The Air Force gave Scott two weeks of leave and travel time for him to "boomerang" before he had to attend survival school as a prerequisite for F-15 *Eagle* training. Scott flew from San Antonio to Boston where he rented a car for his triumphant return to Caledonia. He felt on top of the world as he drove along the narrow Colonial roads of New England and eventually down Main Street toward his parents' house on Lake Tremont.

On his first full day back in town, Scott called Dan to set up "vespers" that night at the Caledonia Inn. Next, Scott called Annette Laval, and she agreed to have lunch with him in the early afternoon before his reunion with Dan at seven.

Scott hadn't seen Annette since Dan and Trinette's wedding night the year before. Neither of them made reference to the night they had spent together on the Harringtons' sailboat. Scott, a self-taught expert at judging feminine beauty, still graded Annette a "knock-out". Her thick, chestnut hair fell to her shoulders, framing her cherubic face. Her lignite eyes sparkled, and her gaze was earnest and engaged.

Scott thought she may have gained a couple of pounds since graduating from McGill, but, if so, it enhanced her attractiveness in his opinion.

Annette controlled her desire to fix her gaze on Scott. Gaping at handsome men was a practice specifically forbidden by Annette's social behavior mentor – Marie Laval. Scott's military posture and well-muscled frame broadcast confidence. His trimmed blond hair and sun-tanned face and forearms were marks of an outdoorsman, an athlete. He was a man accustomed to the approving long glances of women and the camaraderie of men. Scott had fascinated Annette when she was fourteen years old, and he fascinated her now. As in the past, Annette cautioned herself against responding to him too eagerly.

Scott asked her about her post-graduation travels in Europe, but she didn't warm to the subject. He asked her about her time with her Grand'Mere in France, but she didn't show interest in that subject, either. Finally, he found fertile soil to till, and he got her talking about the pending start of her first teaching job in Boston. She had a soft spot in her heart for children, so that subject got them through the meal. Over dessert, Scott asked her how Trinette had settled into her new role as mother and home maker. When Annette ran out of superlatives to describe young John, their conversation stalled, and the two former classmates, the former Best Man and former Maid-of-Honor parted awkwardly.

That night Scott and Dan met at the Caledonia Inn bar to "prime the Guinness pump". Having confirmed that their elbows still worked, they walked to a pub down by the town docks to quaff pints, a talent they had fine-tuned at Princeton. Scott steered clear of talking about his new life as a jet pilot, because he thought the contrast between his glamorous career and Dan's box-canyon existence in Caledonia was sure to be uncomfortable for both of them. Scott imagined two people trying to converse in two different languages. "Going up" for Scott meant roaring straight up in his jet with afterburners blazing. "Going up" for Dan meant climbing a twelve foot ladder to reach a toilet plunger. Instead, they talked about subjects where they had common ground.

It was safe for the two recent graduates to retell college anecdotes. It was safe to rehash their misadventures while playing football and hockey at Thornton. Their memories matched up pretty well, because not enough time had elapsed for "memory drift" to occur. "Memory Drift" is what Scott called the mental process whereby a two-hundred-yard passing game becomes a *three*-hundred-yard passing game or whereby a 49.5-second four-hundred-meter time becomes 48.5 seconds. When Scott got his old friend talking about his new son, Dan got really animated.

"John's got big hands," Dan said, "so I think he's going to be a quarterback. I'll start him out with light footballs so he doesn't throw his arm out."

"How old is John now?"

"Four months."

"He's four months old and you've already decided the weight of his footballs?"

"Sure," Dan said. "As you are aware, I know rather a lot about throwing footballs."

"Rather," Scott conceded. "I thought kids were pretty

much chimps until they turned three."

"My son ain't no chimp, Texas Boy."

"I mean he's not really interactive, yet, is he?"

"Well, okay, he sleeps a lot," Dan said. "And there are lots of diapers to change."

"Not for me. I suffer from *vromikospanaphobia*."

"And that," Dan asked, "is…?"

"Fear of dirty diapers."

Dan dismissed the comment. In years past, he had listened to Scott recite real and imagined Greek phobias while fishing until Dan had begged him to stop.

"Go by the house tomorrow and see him for yourself. Trinette can introduce you."

The next morning, after his breakfast beside the lake front, Scott drove to Dan and Trinette's house situated on the southern shore of Caledonia Bay down the street from the Harrington house. The Dan Hardin house, built in 1903, was a three-story New Englander – an eclectic style of home that blended a Colonial Revival core with a Victorian wrap-around porch. Scott knocked on the front door. Trinette answered the door with a huge smile on her face. She jumped into Scott's arms and gave him a dramatic kiss.

"Wow, you look terrific!" Scott exclaimed. He meant it. Trinette was wearing a cotton gauze loose-fitting top and khaki shorts and boat shoes. She was tan and trim and Scott couldn't remember a time when she looked any healthier.

"So do you, Jet Jockey," Trinette purred. "Get in here and tell me everything." She pulled him into the house by one hand. "First, come see the most handsome baby in

New England. He's sleeping, so keep the noise down."They stepped inaudibly down the corridor to John's room. He lay in his cot on his stomach with his head to one side. His breathing was so shallow Scott couldn't even see his body move. This was no chimp.

"He's beautiful," Scott whispered sincerely. "I didn't know a baby could look that good." Trinette beamed, took Scott by the hand, and led him out of the bedroom and down the hallway to the sun porch that looked out on Caledonia Bay.

"How about a gin-and-tonic?" Trinette offered.

"Sure," Scott said. "What time is it, eleven o'clock in the morning?"

"It's summer. Time doesn't matter in the summer." She iced two tall glasses and added Bombay gin, tonic, and a slice of lemon.

"I can only drink one at a time," Scott said.

"One's for me, Silly."

"Doesn't that mess with Big John's cortex?" he asked.

"I'm not breast-feeding. Big John's on the bottle."

"Wow. Mr. Independent. Has he started dating, yet?"

"He needs a little more time to catch up with a lady-killer like you."

Trinette handed Scott his drink. She still was a tease, Scott thought. She had a flirtatious tone of voice and her movements and facial expressions were seductive.

They sat on the back deck off the sun porch watching sailboats on the lake just as if Scott had never left Caledonia. Trinette — the twin with the heavy responsibility of child-rearing – seemed lighter-hearted than Annette had been the day before. Scott told Trinette he was leaving town the next morning. He asked whether she minded Dan joining him that night to shoot some pool.

"What's with you guys?" Trinette responded with a trace of agitation in her voice. "Dan's taken me out exactly one time in the past three weeks. Now, you come to town and he's ready to play pool with you all night."

"Is that an 'okay'?"

"Go for it. You're his best friend. I'm not going to stand in the way. But it's no fun being left out."

Scott started to invite her, too, but the baby stirred. It was best if he left.

"I'll see you next time I'm in town," Scott said as he moved for the front door.

"No you won't," Trinette said softly. Her eyes had tears in them. "You'll go off to do all that aviator stuff and you'll be world famous and you won't think about me once."

Scott stepped toward her and took her in his arms.

"I'll think about you."

"No, you won't," she said as she hugged him desperately.

When Scott and Dan met up at a pub to play pool that night, Scott dispensed priceless tips on child-rearing harvested from a lifetime spent nowhere near a child.

"Get him swimming early," Scott said. "Get him comfortable underwater."

"I already have, Dr. Spock."

"Get him on the ice as soon as the lake freezes."

"I will."

"And don't make a big deal out of every time he gets a scrape or a cut. You don't want him to be a whiner."

One of the great benefits of Scott's nearly non-existent experience with children was a scarcity of facts to interfere with his opinions.

"You've gotten used to giving orders, Lieutenant," Dan said. He missed his shot on the seven ball and leaned on his pool cue. "You know, Scott, it's okay for you to talk about your new life. You've avoided bringing it up all night."

Scott held up on his shot and waited for Dan to finish speaking.

"It's like you're afraid to say anything that might make me feel like a hayseed living a dull life in a little burg while you're scooting around to all these exciting places. It's worse when you say nothing."

"I'm not holding back."

"You certainly are. And it's insulting to the hayseed."

Scott sank the eight ball in the side pocket, and Dan gave him the two dollars lying on the rail.

"Time to go," Dan told his friend. "I'm done for the night. We hayseeds have to work in the morning."

They walked out into the gentle July night to find their cars.

"Hey, Dan…."

"Let's don't do any of this 'goodbye stuff', Scott. I can't stand it."

"I'm not talking about goodbye. I'm just saying don't sell our friendship short. We spent eight years together at Thornton and Princeton. So don't throw it away. I don't care if you're a goat herder and I'm an astronaut, we're friends."

They shared a man hug, and they went their separate ways both aware that their relationship had changed.

Scott completed his survival school courses and reported to Luke Air Force Base, Arizona, for six months of F-15 *Eagle* training. After graduating from F-15 school, he drove his new Porsche to Langley AFB, Virginia to be checked-out in his first operational fighter squadron. During the year since Scott's last Caledonia "boomerang", Scott and Dan conversed by telephone monthly. They seldom talked for very long, but it was enough to nurture their friendship. On the positive side, Dan's baby boy was growing up fast. On the negative side, Trinette was spiraling downward fast. At first, Dan only vaguely hinted at her growing estrangement from him, but the longer the problem persisted, the more details Dan revealed.

In the autumn after Scott's last visit to Caledonia, Annette had moved away to Boston to start teaching elementary school as planned. The leaves fell in November and the snow came in December on schedule, but this year the coming of winter and the absence of her sister seemed to depress Trinette. She started to drink more as the daylight hours shortened. She began to ignore house-keeping, and she seemed bored with the constant demands of an infant. She provided for John's primary needs, but she hired baby sitters with increasing frequency and she did so without advance notice to Dan. The first he knew about his wife's evenings out was when he read a note on the refrigerator door when he got home from work at about seven o'clock. Sharing a hot meal with his wife was pretty much a thing of the past by the time March rolled around. When Dan tried to talk with Trinette about it, she pouted and told him not to be so stodgy.

"I'm only twenty-three years old, Dan; I want to have some fun."

Trinette planned a weekend in Boston with two of her McGill girlfriends, and she countered Dan's misgivings by claiming to have hired the best child care provider in town. Trinette claimed that the forty-year-old woman was so competent that she must be called "nanny", never "babysitter". Dan was not a suspicious man or a jealous man, either, but this wasn't the way he had pictured marriage. He reluctantly agreed to her weekend in Boston and to a similar four-day junket to New York City in April, knowing that she was going regardless of whether he approved.

Trinette returned from her "girlie weekends" as restless as she had left, and she seemed to be slipping away from him like a dinghy with a severed line drifting away from its mooring buoy. Dan ran out of patience when Trinette was cited for driving under the influence in April, a month after John's first birthday. Trinette's mother partially insulated her daughter from Dan's new assertiveness and from scandal in the town by placing Trinette in a rehabilitation clinic in Canada. Dan set up a bedroom for the "nanny", because she practically lived in their house in Trinette's absence.

Dan was embarrassed, depressed, and angry, and he told Scott frankly how he felt during their telephone conversations. For once, Scott had no advice, so he just listened. It was no fun for Scott to hear about the loss of joy and love in the Hardin household. He came to dread the phone calls with Dan, but he made them anyway.

Things improved for a while in the summer when Trinette returned from rehabilitation and Annette came back to Caledonia for the summer. Annette slept in her parents' house, but she spent most of her days with Trinette and John. Trinette was affectionate with Dan again, and she rarely drank alcohol, so they seemed to be restoring the relationship they had shared for so many years.

Dan, Trinette, and Annette often played Scrabble late into the night at the end of long summer days and well after John had retired for the night. Laughter returned to their house as they each tried to record monster scores with equally monstrous non-existent words. On the mornings after the Scrabble marathons, John, who was teething and had never met an object he didn't want to stick in his mouth, always made a grab for the letter tiles. The letter "Q" once got as far as his lips, but Annette snatched it away from him at the last second.

Unfortunately, summers in New England come to an end. Annette moved back to Boston for her second year of teaching. Dan and Trinette took John for long walks in his stroller during the glorious month of September. As if ordered by the calendar, as the leaves turned to yellow and red in late October and as the November winds blew them to the ground and as the days grew shorter, Trinette began drinking again.

Dan hardly noticed at first, but by November it was impossible not to detect her slightly slurred speech as she got up from the couch to greet him when he got home from work. Dan reverted to washing clothes and cleaning house as he had the first time Trinette had gone into decline. Notes on the refrigerator door became more frequent. The "nanny" came more often. Trinette refused to talk with Dan about what she was feeling. The rejection hurt him and he could actually feel his heart ache.

Dan spent all his non-working time with John. He took him everywhere he went except to work at the hardware store. In January, while Trinette was in Boston for three days with girlfriends, Dan cleaned house. He wasn't only cleaning house, he was looking for clues. What he found stashed in an antique jewelry box in Trinette's underwear drawer was more than a clue; it was evidence — white powder in a small plastic bag. At first he felt sick. Then he lost control of his nerves and his hands began to shake. And, then, he got angry. He felt betrayed, and he wasn't going to let Trinette get by with it.

Trinette didn't return from Boston until Tuesday night. Dan, who had no idea of when to expect her, had put John to bed and had settled in his favorite chair to read book pages without retaining their content. All he could think of was what he was going to say. His anger and disappointment had put him in a frame of mind where he didn't care what the consequences were any more. Trinette stumbled through the front doorway at just past nine o'clock.

"Honey, I'm home," Trinette said too loudly. Dan shushed her and reminded her that the baby was asleep.

"Well, *I'm* not asleep," she slurred. "Let's party." Her eyes were puffy and she seemed off-balance.

"Did you drive in this condition?"

"Of course I drove, you nit-wit. You think I have a limo driver?"

"Sit down, Trinette."

"Oh, Tough Guy," she mocked him. "I don't want to sit

down." She stared at him defiantly.

Dan tossed the bag of powder at her.

"You raided my stash."

"No more of this, Trinette. No more drugs. No more booze. You're going to go straight and you're going to act like an adult."

"I'm going to do what *I* want, you knucklehead!" Her words were mush, and she fought to string them together. "You don't order me around, Princeton Boy! You're so smug! You know nothing! Nothing!" She motioned with her hand as if pushing Dan away as she turned her back on him. She put the powder in her purse. "You're so stupid!" She turned to face him. She pointed her finger at him and lurched to keep her balance. "You don't even know I had a miscarriage in college."

This shocked Dan, and he started to speak, but Trinette shushed him.

"You're too stupid to know I was with a guy last winter in Boston, and he was hot! And all you can do is pack me off to rehab." She walked away from Dan toward her suitcase by the front door. "You're so boring, Hardware Boy. And you're so stupid. Stupid. You know nothing." She picked up her suit case and opened the front door. Dan was afraid to touch her, because he didn't know the limits of his anger. "I'm outta here!" Trinette shouted as she slammed the door behind her.

Dan stood in her wake, his heart pounding and his mouth dry. Why did she hate him so much? She couldn't drive in her impaired condition. What if she injured another driver or herself? He was partially responsible. On the other hand, if he called the police, her arrest would be in the public record just as it was the year before. Trinette's mother might freak out if she found out that Dan had informed the police. Marie had scolded Dan the first time Trinette was cited for DUI when he had no part in her arrest. He could hear his mother-in-law: "Why didn't you do something?" Dan angrily turned the question back on Marie in his mind, "Why didn't you do something? She was yours for twenty-one years!"

Dan called the police. A New Hampshire State Trooper stopped Trinette twelve miles south of Caledonia. She blew the lid off the breathalyzer. They got her for DUI, speeding, resisting arrest, and possession of narcotics. Trinette's mother went ballistic when she learned all the details of Trinette's arrest, including how the police were notified. Phillip hired a talented Concord attorney who kept Trinette out of jail. Phillip also paid her fines.

Marie took Trinette back into their home while the scandal ricocheted around Caledonia. Marie and Trinette spent hours together with John during the day. Dan hired the "nanny" full time. Marie's oversight of her daughter ensured that Trinette shunned drugs and booze. Trinette's license had been revoked, so she depended on Marie for transportation.

The episode was excruciating for Dan, and it seemed to drag on forever. Embarrassing incidents occurred frequently, because his acquaintances were curious, and not always prudent. Scott was Dan's main link to normalcy, because he felt he could tell him anything. Telephone calls to Scott were Dan's lifeline. Dan said he felt broken beyond repair.

In May, Trinette's father called Dan at home.

"Dan," Phillip said, "Trinette's run away."

"Where to?"

"Europe."

"When?" Dan asked. He felt so estranged by Trinette that he wondered if her moving to Europe even mattered. Was 3,000 miles of separation any worse than six blocks of separation?

"She left two days ago. It's taken us this long to find out that she emptied her bank account and got a ride to Boston. We also know she caught a flight to Brussels."

"Did she leave a letter?" It crossed Dan's mind that Trinette may have written a manifesto detailing all of his faults. She hadn't been shy about slamming him the night he had confronted her with the bag of cocaine.

"She did," Phillip answered. "I won't show it to you because it's too hurtful to Marie, but it says she's going to live in Belgium with some guy she knew in college." This was difficult going for Phillip. "As hard as this is for us, I know it has to be harder for you, Dan. I'm very, *very* sorry for all you've had to go through."

"How is Marie taking it?" Dan cringed to think of how Marie must be responding to her embarrassment and loss of face.

"She's crushed right now, but she'll recover. She's mad at you at the moment, but I told her that you couldn't have stopped Trinette the night she was arrested. I know you *had* to call the police for safety's sake. You're a fine person, Dan. And a great father to our grandson. Time'll heal all of us, and we'll find our ways through this. Stay strong."

Dan thanked him and hung up the phone. Dan's life had been disrupted in a way he never could have predicted on his wedding day. He had made the journey from happy-go-lucky bridegroom to despondent, lonely failure in less than two years. He reminded himself over-and-over all through the sleepless night that he had to be strong for John.

Scott joined his operational fighter squadron at Langley AFB in the spring. He was subject to deployment to Saudi Arabia after finishing his check-out. Scott "boomeranged" to Caledonia on leave two months after Trinette's departure for Belgium. Joe T. and Joyce welcomed their son home and settled him in the comfort of his old bedroom. Scott's parents were in good humor and evidently proud of him, but they didn't hide their concern about him flying combat sorties over Iraq in the near future. His parents had provided for his security for most of his life, and that wasn't an easy switch to turn off.

One evening Scott walked down to his parents' docks on Caledonia Bay and saw his mother and father intertwined in a hammock beside the boat house. For the first time, Scott saw them as three-dimensional vibrant figures, not stereotypical cardboard cutouts. Knowing how much pain the Lavals had been dealing with made him grateful that his parents were steadfast and predictable.

His appreciation for his parents made it easier to talk with them than ever before, and it wasn't because he was afflicted with "tomorrow-we-may-die" syndrome. He didn't even think about dying. An old saying went like this: "If you don't know who the greatest fighter pilot in the world is, it ain't you." Scott subscribed to the theory. He was, at least, *among* the best in the world and he felt truly bullet-proof.

When his parents brought up combat flying, he reassured them. He avoided the subject altogether when talking to Dan Hardin.

Dan was even more centered on John and protective of him than before. Except during working hours, father and son were inseparable. Mother was absent. Dan bore single parenthood like a heavy cross. On the other hand, John, a cute bundle of coos and dribble, didn't have a care in the world. The two-year-old seemed attracted to Scott, perhaps because Scott didn't goo-goo and make a big deal over him. Dan had told Scott the blow-by-blow of his troubles with Trinette by telephone, so he avoided rehashing the sordid story with Scott in person. At one point, Scott asked Dan where Trinette got the money to live on. Dan guessed that Marie was sending money to Trinette, with or without Phillip's knowledge.

"Is Marie still pissed at you?" Scott asked

"It's better now. I think she knows I did the best I could. It's just that she's run interference for Trinette ever since she was born."

"How about Annette?"

"She's an angel. Now that she's back in town for the summer, she comes by all the time to spend time with John. She takes him for ice cream down by the docks and she swims with him almost every day. John's crazy about her."

Scott took Annette to lunch the following day. She was even less forthcoming than at their lunch together the year before.

"Are you mad at me?" Scott asked.

"Of course not. Why should I be mad at you?"

Scott tried to think of all the reasons why she might be angry with him. Neither Scott nor Annette even hinted at the night they had spent together. They kept their conversation firmly on the level of the superficial. Annette told Scott she was not returning to Boston in the autumn to deal with the little Southie thugs who had made her two years of teaching a misery. She had landed a teaching job for the coming year at an elementary school in Portland, Maine.

"Are kids in Portland less thug-like than kids in South Boston?"

"Kids in juvenile prison are less thug-like than kids in South Boston," she said.

Annette talked like a diplomat, who, in the effort to avoid offense, ends up saying nothing at all. She reluctantly admitted that she had wasted two years of her life trying to manage her class full of South Boston hooligans. Scott also was careful. He stayed away from the subject of his life as a fighter pilot. They spoke as though they had signed a treaty to prevent a clash of two incompatible worlds. The time Scott spent with Annette and Dan left him feeling that Father Time had picked his pockets.

Scott took his parents to dinner at a harbor restaurant in Ogunquit, Maine. He called it the Last Supper in jest. Their conversation was flavored with nostalgia. Joe T. had once told his son to find something he could do really well and replicate it over-and-over again short of the point of boredom. Scott had found his "something" in flying fighters. His parents listened with interest to his aviation stories.

Scott examined his parents singly and as a couple. He was proud of his strapping, sun-tanned father and his pretty, freckled mother. What a contrast their tranquil, loving marriage was to the hurricane union of Dan and Trinette. He was proud of his parents and the happiness they brought to so many people.

The next morning, Scott hugged his father farewell and kissed his mother goodbye. He flew unscathed through his combat tour based at King Abdul Aziz Air Base in Saudi Arabia. He and his squadron mates flew Operation Southern Watch missions south of the 32nd parallel over Iraq for eight months without losing a single pilot. His mother and father visited him in Virginia when he returned from Saudi Arabia and later in England while he was stationed at Lakenheath Air Base for three years.

During the same intervening years, Annette taught in Portland for four years before moving back to Caledonia to begin teaching third graders in the Brighton School. After her return to Caledonia, she spent a lot more time with Dan and John. She was the closest thing to a mother John knew.

Dan Hardin continued to write occasional letters to Scott even as their telephone calls ceased. At least once a year, Dan sent Scott a picture of John, who was growing up to be a very good-looking, healthy toddler. Over the years, Dan received nothing from Trinette except a couple of postcards postmarked in Belgium. As far as he knew, she was still on a self-induced high in a manic search for happiness and thrills.

Back in Caledonia, Joe T. and Joyce Harrington continued to travel with Phillip and Marie Laval and Benjamin Hardin at least once a year. They continued their evenings of pinochle, and the men continued to play on the same golf team at charity events. The old friends continued their practice of telling brief vignettes of the lives of their children.

The Harringtons told their closest friends before anyone else when Scott was promoted to Captain. The friends were the first to know about Scott's upcoming change of duty station from Lakenheath to Holloman Air Force Base in New Mexico.

Benjamin Hardin gave glowing accounts of John's prowess in elementary school with understated grandfatherly comments like, "The kid's a genius."

The Lavals retold amusing incidents that occurred in Annette's classroom at Brighton School, but they said nothing about Trinette. Judging by their conversations, even with their oldest friends, Trinette didn't exist.

Chapter 6
DAVY CROCKETT

JOHN WESLEY HARDIN'S obsession with Davy Crockett began a few months after John had exhausted himself and his father Dan with all things Napoleon. For weeks, John had peppered his conversation with French phrases, and Dan had patiently remained good-natured about it when a lesser man might have cracked.

"*Sacre bleu*," John exclaimed when he dropped a cereal bowl on the kitchen floor and watched it shatter into a bazillion pieces.

"*Quel désastre*," John gasped when he spilled a cup of tea on the carpet of his Grandmother Laval's sitting room during afternoon tea. Phillip and Marie were amused and a little puzzled by John's linguistic flourishes. Marie had taught her twin daughters to speak French, but she hardly ever had spoken French around her grandson.

"Where did this come from?" she whispered to Dan.

He shrugged and rotated his palms toward the ceiling in the international signal for "I have no idea". Actually, he had a very good idea, because he had been living with Napoleon

Bonaparte for months since John's debut as Napoleon at the Historical Figures Program.

Napoleon faded back into history, however, on the day a UPS driver delivered to the Dan Hardin house a package sent from Alamogordo, New Mexico by Captain Scott Harrington. John's tenth birthday on the Ides of March was only three days away. The package delivery jangled John's nerves, because kids of that age don't receive UPS packages every day. The fact of the matter was John had *never* received a UPS package before. He knew the driver's name – Chris Gleason – only because he was Corky Gleason's uncle. Chris apparently had been issued a completely different model of thyroid from Corky and Andrew Gleason, because Chris was as lean as a greyhound in his dark brown uniform. Chris left the package on the porch, and John retrieved it before Chris had made it back to his package car. John paced like a thoroughbred at the starting gate until his father came home from the hardware store that evening.

John dispensed with small talk when his father walked into the house, because he didn't think his heart could take the strain of waiting a minute longer to open the package. John presented several arguments in support of opening the package as soon as possible. Conservation – the contents might spoil. Uniqueness – Scott had never sent him a package before. Health – sleep was impossible for John until he knew the contents of the package. The real reason that Dan green-lighted John's immediate gratification was fatigue: Dan was too tired to verbally fence with John about waiting until his birthday to open the package.

John tore into the wrapping as though it were a timed

event. He eschewed the slow, deliberate unwrapping methods used by his Grandmother Marie and Aunt Annette. Their civilized, but agonizing pace irritated John mightily. He overcompensated by ripping the gift box apart like a hyena dissecting the carcass of a gazelle. When the contents spilled out on the floor, John visibly recoiled in surprise and ecstasy. There in a glorious pile lay a coonskin hat and a heavy beige leather jacket with long leather fringes. The raccoon had been relieved of its vital organs, but the eyes, nostrils, and formidable tail were still there. It was a ferocious headpiece.

"It's so real!" John gasped in wonder as he wrestled himself into the leather jacket. He donned the coonskin cap and ran to the nearest mirror to inspect his image. He had been transformed into a frontiersman.

"You look exactly like Davy Crockett," Dan said, discounting John's scruffy sneakers and sweat pants.

That was it. From that moment on, he *was* Davy Crockett. For the next several mornings, John eagerly put on his uniform of the day and it was always the same – jeans, walking boots, sweat shirt, Davy Crockett's jacket, and Davy's coonskin cap. It wasn't a *perfect* replica of Davy's attire at the Alamo, but it was close enough to the real thing for most of the good people of Caledonia to recognize the brave Tennessean as he crunched along on the snow-covered sidewalks around town.

"Morning, Mr. Crockett," Grandfather Phillip Laval said to John as they passed on the crosswalk in front of the Bank of Caledonia.

"Howdy," John said.

Phillip was privately unsettled by his grandson's obsessions, but he dealt gently with John, remembering that Trinette had taken similar flights of fancy. Once, at the age of twelve, she had merged with the persona of Queen Elizabeth I for more than a month. That's a long time to be exposed to hoop skirts, lace, a plastic crown, and overuse of the royal "we" as in, "Papa, we are too tired to clean the dishes tonight." Trinette had spent a good deal of time during her pre-teenage years in parallel worlds of pretense. By contrast, Annette had always seemed content to be *who* she was *where* she was. In Phillip's mind, Trinette had gotten through the fantasy stage and so would John. In the meantime, as his friend Benjamin Hardin had pointed out, John could have fixated on a worse role model – Charles Manson or Pontius Pilate, for example. If his grandson wanted to play at being Davy Crockett, so be it. The flames of his obsessions always extinguished sooner or later.

Davy Crockett ran into his other grandfather the moment the pioneer entered the front door to Hardin's Hardware.

"Holy Zamoly," Benjamin Hardin said, "It's Daniel Boone." The two cashiers nodded to John and smiled at his earnest face surrounded by raccoon fur.

"Davy Crockett," John corrected his grandfather. "I told you yesterday."

"So you did."

John checked in with his father who was in a back room cutting copper pipe to a customer's specifications.

"I left you a ham and cheese sandwich in the refrigerator," Dan told his son. "Eat that before you do your homework."

John left the store to walk the six blocks to his home

on the edge of Lake Tremont. He counted his steps; he didn't lose count until a snowplow almost ran him down in a pedestrian crosswalk on Main Street. He didn't have to avoid stepping on cracks in the sidewalks, because of a hard-packed layer of snow that had covered the sidewalks since December.

John had gone home from school to an unlocked and empty house for his entire elementary school career. He had no memory of his mother Trinette except for her picture in his father's bedroom. If he thought about parents purely from the perspective of information flow, he wasn't as disadvantaged as it may have seemed. From that point of view, most of his peers had three parents – a mother, a father, and the Internet. John had a father and the Internet. He was only thirty-three per cent short of being fully staffed. An absent mother and an empty house caused him no concern.

John found the snack left in the refrigerator by his father. John made quick work of the sandwich before tackling his homework. He followed the same ritual almost every school day. It was uncommon behavior for a fourth grade boy, but John didn't know that. Dan couldn't remember being even half as diligent about doing homework as his son was. To be precise, Dan didn't remember actually doing homework in elementary school, and he certainly didn't hold up his study habits at Princeton as a model. When it came to academics, Dan thought of himself as more of a spontaneous scholar; that is, he was an expert at cramming.

On this day, however, John deviated from his study routine because of an orgy of cannibalism he had witnessed as he walked home past the town docks. After inhaling his ham-and-cheese sandwich, he – that is, Davy Crockett — grabbed his BB gun and headed out toward the town docks where a dozen crows had convened to peck at the corpse of a sea gull.

Gulls were a common sight around Lake Tremont when the ice was out, but, from December through March, when the lake ice often exceeded three feet in depth, sea gulls sought refuge on the Atlantic Coast fifty miles away. Sighting in on a crow, Davy Crockett managed to squeeze off only one errant shot before his hunt was suspended by the screaming approach of a plump man tromping over the snow in L. L. Bean Maine Hunting Boots.

"Stop right where you are, young man!" Andrew Gleason shouted. He was protected from the elements by a Russian fur hat, black leather gloves, and a dark gray woolen winter coat on top of a black suit. He walked right up to John and snatched the BB gun out of his hands.

"That's *my* BB gun," John protested.

"You're not allowed to discharge firearms inside the town limits," Mr. Gleason scolded him loudly. He held the BB gun well out-of-reach above John's head. "I'll give this to your father so he can deal with you when he gets home."

"My father *gave* me the gun."

"Even so, I'm sure he never imagined you shooting it in town." He swatted John away. "Go home," Mr. Gleason shouted. "You're dangerous and you're in big trouble, Mister."

A dispirited John Hardin went home, did the homework he now wished he had done instead of going crow hunting, and waited anxiously for his father's arrival. Sure enough, Dan walked through the door at forty minutes past six with the BB gun in hand. John hunched even more intently over the book he was reading, a desperate act of conflict avoidance.

"Mr. Gleason came into the store," Dan said, hanging up his scarf and jacket and taking off his boots. "He had your BB gun and he claimed you were killing wild life down by the town docks."

"Some crows were eating a sea gull," John said, relying on the Good Samaritan statute as a defense. "I tried to shoot a crow." His father smiled and handed the BB gun over to his son.

"Don't worry about it, John. Mr. Gleason gets excited about trivial things. He doesn't know a gun from his back side." John's relief was apparent. "Just use your gun in the back yard or in the woods from now on. Don't take it around town anymore."

That was it. No trial, no verdict, no punishment. Dan gave his son a hug and headed for the kitchen to make a salad and spaghetti for their dinner. John resolved to do his homework promptly, walk the streets of Caledonia unarmed, and steer well away from Mr. Gleason.

The Davy Crockett phase of John's life had not yet spent itself as the school year came to a close. Flower blossoms were bursting out all over town and trees throughout the village were heavy with buds and new leaves. The May nights were cool, but the days were sunny and occasionally warm. John was fully dressed in his Davy Crockett regalia on Saturday down at the Town Gazebo when Corky Gleason showed up at the park by himself. That's how Corky always showed up – alone.

By an amazing coincidence, Corky also was dressed in a Davy Crockett outfit. Corky's outfit, however, was hideous. His jacket wasn't even leather. It was a heavy brown sweater with white plastic panels sewed to the front. On the plastic panels were riveted two decorative leather medallions with fake leather strips hanging out of their centers. On his left chest panel was an amateur painting of the Alamo, and, on the right, a painting of a long rifle and a gun powder horn. The coon skin hat precariously balanced on Corky's head wasn't really a coon skin or anything resembling a coon skin. It was a ratty blob of gray artificial fur with a stubby little tail no bigger than a key fob. John moved closer to Corky so he could fully appraise the ludicrous outfit at close range. Corky was as embarrassed as he had been playing Robin Hood in the third grade Historical Figures Program.

"My dad gave it to me," Corky said. That explained everything. "I told my mom I wanted a Davy Crockett outfit like yours, and this is the crap he gave me."

John was sympathetic. He couldn't imagine donning the outfit even in the privacy of his home much less wearing it out of the house. A reputation is a fragile thing.

"Why're you wearing it if you don't like it?"

"He made me. He told me to play in the park while he's in a meeting at the bank."

The two Davy Crocketts, one the real deal and the other a forlorn imposter, mulled over this odium without speaking. Corky broke the silence. "John, can I borrow your Davy Crockett jacket and cap for a day? Just a day?"

This was a weighty request. John had never imagined such a request, so he had done no contingency planning to formulate a reason for declining it. He thought of lots of effective responses that night in bed, but at the present moment in the shadow of the Town Gazebo, not a single plausible basis for refusal came to mind.

"For a whole day?" John stalled.

"I can bring it back to you tomorrow afternoon. I promise."

To his own amazement, John began removing his Davy Crockett jacket. He handed the rich leather jacket to Corky and he placed the luxurious coon skin cap on Corky's head at a rakish angle. The jacket was a tight fit, but Corky managed to squeeze into it, and his face lit up in a broad smile.

"It's awesome," he said breathlessly. The fringes swished as he held his arms out wide. He flopped his arms back to his sides. Corky hesitantly offered his low-rent Davy Crockett outfit to John, who declined as politely as possible. Corky thanked him effusively and ran off to his father's car to throw the reviled plastic outfit into the back seat.

"I'll bring it back to you tomorrow afternoon!" Corky shouted over his shoulder.

The exact question John asked himself as he scurried toward the warmth of his home was, "What have I done?" He had just entrusted into the hands of Corky Gleason the coolest Davy Crockett outfit in the Free World. Any kid who saw Corky dressed in John's authentic coon skin cap and leather jacket was bound to know where he had gotten them. The assumption that Corky and he were good friends was sure to follow. In kid algebra, if one friend is goofy, the requirement to balance the equation means that the other friend is also goofy. John's reputation was teetering on ruin. That night, John dreamed he was a circus clown wearing a wig and doing cart wheels. He didn't have to schedule a session with a shrink to figure out the genesis of *that* dream.

True to his word, a cheerful Corky Gleason showed up at the Hardins' front door the next afternoon. In just twenty-four hours, Corky's self-image had improved, and he even managed a smile when Dan answered the door.

"Mr. Hardin, this is for John," Corky said.

"Can you come in for some cookies and milk?" Dan accepted the neatly folded leather jacket.

"I gotta go," Corky said. "Tell John I said thanks…a lot."

Dan took the jacket and cap up to John's bedroom and handed them over to him.

"From Corky," Dan said. "He says 'thanks'."

John took the outfit from his dad and laid it on his bed reverently.

"You let him borrow your Davy Crockett stuff?" Dan asked. John nodded. "Well, that was good of you. It's hard to let go of things we love," Dan continued, "but it means a lot to other people."

"I guess so," John said.

"Corky isn't like his dad. Andrew Gleason is annoying, but Corky's a nice kid."

"He's a blimp."

"No one's perfect," Dan said. "You did a good thing. You're growing up."

John felt elated. His father left the bedroom, and John mentally replayed the compliment. Suddenly he remembered that he hadn't sent a thank-you letter to Scott Harrington. He sat down at his desk to write on white paper with light blue lines.

"Dear Uncle Scott, thank you very much for the Davy Crockett jacket and the coon skin hat. They are awesome. All the kids like them. Also they wish they had them. I let one kid wear them instead of the crappy Davy Crockett stuff he had. It made his day. And you made my birthday with the best gift I ever got in my life. I have the picture of you and your jet on my wall. I like the way you signed it 'The World's Greatest Fighter Pilot.' That's cool. Love, John."

John mailed Scott's letter to New Mexico on Monday afternoon. For the first time in more than two months, John didn't wear the coon skin hat or the authentic leather jacket. He didn't know why, but he no longer wanted to dress like someone else. He didn't need a costume. John had moved on. He wasn't Davy Crockett any more.

Chapter 7

BLIND

DURING SCOTT HARRINGTON'S first semester at Princeton in 1983, the teaching assistant (TA) in his English Composition class gave his students a writing assignment intended to explore satire. The TA used readings from Jonathan Swift, Joseph Heller, Ogden Nash, and Mark Twain to illustrate how ridicule could be used to influence a reader's thinking about a serious subject.

Scott was a ridicule cutting edge finely honed by hours of banal, sometimes caustic chatter with Dan Hardin while fishing the waters of Lake Tremont. As for the serious subject, nothing was more serious to Scott than being a fighter pilot. Fortified with performance-enhancing ingredients — a pitcher of beer and a pepperoni pizza — he wrote his essay.

Brief Essay on the Shortage of Fighter Pilot Candidates

The national defense of the United States relies on effective selection, training, and deployment of a specialized group of combatants – fighter pilots.

Rigorous standards and demographic characteristics of the target age group conspire to suggest that the U.S. will be unable to supply the necessary number of fighter pilots in the future. This may require drastic action by the Department of Defense (DOD) as suggested in the conclusion of this analysis.

Current standards and demographic statistics indicate that not even one person in a random sample of 1,000 twenty-two-year-old men will qualify to be a fighter pilot. Here's how. A poll of ten twenty-two-year-old male residents of Princeton, New Jersey, revealed that 80% had no interest in flying or were scared out of their wits flying even as a passenger. This eliminates 800 of our sample, leaving 200. Nation-wide, only 15% of the male population has both a college degree and the required aptitude for flying, so we're down to 30. Only about 50% of the target group has 20-20 eyesight, further winnowing the number to 15. Some twenty-seven per cent of men of the target age admit to using illegal drugs. The number of candidates dwindles to 11. Eight per cent of the target group is color blind, reducing our number to 10. Serious mood or mental disorders are reported by 9% of the target group; now we're at 9.17. More than seven per cent say they abuse alcohol or are alcoholic: 8.53 remaining. Four per cent are physically handicapped, leaving 8.18. Five per cent are gay so 7.78 remain. Among the target group, two per cent are felons, leaving 7.62. More than two percent suffer from a disease of a major organ or the circulatory system, so we're down to 7.47. One per cent is deaf: 7.39. One per cent has a history of sexually transmitted disease; therefore, 7.32 remain. Historically 50% of Air Force pilot trainees wash out during flying training, so we are left with 3.66 candidates. Fewer than 10% of pilots graduating from Air Force Pilot Training receive fighter assignments, so we arrive at the end of the elimination process with only 0.37 fighter pilots per 1,000 men in the demographic pool.

This year, about 1,650,000 Americans males are twenty-two years of age. At a rate of 0.37 fighter pilots per 1,000 American male twenty-two year olds, we can produce only 610 fighter pilots. The DOD needs about 1,000 new fighter pilots each year. The critical question, then, is what can be done to alleviate this shortfall?

A study group chaired by the author proposes a solution. The single largest disqualifier is fear of flying. Forced cauterization of the portion of the brain controlling judgment and fear reflex among male children at the age of two years would increase the pool of candidates sufficiently to ensure that the DOD satisfies its need for fighter pilots well into the future.

Scott thought his essay was hilarious, as authors often do. He considered his satire *so* hilarious that he asked Dan to review it at what they called "vespers" – a hamburger each and two pitchers of beer down on Nassau Street. Hardly a man of letters, Dan deemed the essay "funny", although not necessarily rising to the level of "hilarious". Dan's judgment was possibly swayed because Scott picked up the tab and, after a reader has chugged a pitcher of beer, even an obituary can pass for high comedy.

The TA grading the writing assignments did *not* think it was funny. By a cruel fluke of fortune, the instructor was a gay pot head who suffered from the chronic passing of kidney stones the size of pea gravel. In other words, he was never going to qualify to be a fighter pilot, astronaut, bull fighter, or any other *macho* thing. He found the essay offensive, and he lacerated the paper with his red pen like a hunter field-dressing a deer.

He concluded, "You have unimaginatively strung together a depressing list of characteristics to make an adolescent point, while stealthily promoting your self-imagined superiority. You've missed the point entirely. I have mercifully given you a grade of *D*."

Ouch. One or two grades like this one might derail Scott's career before it got started, because he had to maintain a *B* average or better to stay in Air Force ROTC. This course was supposed to be easy picking. He swallowed his pride and scheduled counseling time with the TA to ask for his insights and advice. The TA had cooled down considerably by the time they met, and he spent almost an hour with Scott reading aloud essays authored by two gifted students in the class who had "hit the bull's eye".

The first essay was written from the perspective of a bed bug living in the beard of a Muslim cab driver in New York City. The second essay catalogued the travails of a Fortune

500 CEO who, after being kidnapped, is forced to work in one of his own sweatshops in Tijuana. The TA was neither Muslim nor Mexican. Neither of the highly touted literary works made the slightest bit of sense to Scott, but he listened intently and took illegible notes, and, at the end of their conference, he asked the TA if there was a remote chance he could submit a substitute essay. The TA squashed that idea, but Scott left his office on better terms. More importantly, the worst grade Scott received for the rest of the semester was a *B*.

Scott made a pledge to keep his career goals to himself in the future and to improve his situational awareness. To borrow from fighter pilot lingo, Scott learned to "Check Six".

Years later, that freshman experience remained a vivid memory. Scott considered it taboo to talk about flying fighters with anyone but fellow fighter pilots in the same way a husband might refrain from discussing details of his matrimonial sex with anyone but his wife. Boycotting the subject of aviation in conversations with outsiders did non-pilots a favor, too, because they never understood what Scott was talking about anyway. Scott found it sufficient to say that his years of flying F-15 *Eagles* in Arizona, Virginia, Iraq, England, and New Mexico were the best years of his life, and he wanted them never to end.

"Indispensability" is a word that captures the importance of Zorro's mask, Babe Ruth's bat, and a fighter pilot's eyes. Every eye test Scott Harrington had ever taken showed that he was blessed with 20-10 vision, a tremendous advantage in aerial combat where the odds of victory favor the fighter pilot who spots his adversary first.

Scott could see an aggressor F-5 *Tiger* head-on at twice the distance of most of his squadron mates. He frequently "got a tally" on aggressor F-16 *Falcons* high above his formation when they blended into the blue sky indistinguishably to the eyes of his wingmen.

One day during a dissimilar air combat tactics sortie in Nevada, Scott called a "tally-ho" on a pair of Navy F-18 *Hornets* fifteen thousand feet below his two-ship formation. The *Hornets* were flying a sub-sonic low level route barely above the desert floor. Scott rolled inverted, and pulled down to attack from the bogies' high six. Only during the final seconds of the stern conversion did his wingman finally see the adversaries.

Scott's eyes were his indispensable gift. The list of things he would rather lose than his vision was a long list: He would rather lose his Porsche, his girlfriend, or one (and only one) testicle.

In March of 1998, Scott and some friends were enjoying cocktails beside a gigantic fireplace in a ski lodge in Cloudcroft, New Mexico when Scott first noticed a small spot in the vision of his right eye. When he closed his left eye, the spot was even more prominent. At first, he attributed the blind spot to the altitude, because the lodge was situated at more than eight thousand feet above sea level. Maybe, he thought, it was hypoxia, probably histotoxic hypoxia in this case, because he was imbibing his third single malt whisky.

Later that night in his hotel room, Scott opened John Wesley Hardin's thank you letter for two reasons: First, he wanted to revisit the pleasure of knowing that the Davy

Crockett outfit was a big hit with John and, second, he wanted to see if the small blind spot affected his reading vision.

To the first point, Scott knew that John spent a lot of time in his fantasy worlds. He also knew about John's fixation on Napoleon Bonaparte and Davy Crockett. Scott's advice to Dan was not to worry. John was a great kid who was bound to outgrow the make-believe stage. Scott stated his assurances to Dan with confidence as though he knew what he was talking about.

Scott wasn't so confident about the second point – the blind spot. The spot was still there the next morning after a solid night of sleep. He told no one about it, and he didn't arouse curiosity by asking whether anyone else had noticed any visual impairment at altitude. After breakfast he skipped skiing and drove back down to his home in the desert town of Alamogordo. As evening approached, the spot in the visual field of his right eye remained. Scott was scared.

Because his house was at an elevation of just over four thousand feet above sea level, Scott figured he could eliminate hypoxia as the cause of the spot. He was obliged to report any medical abnormality to the Squadron Flight Surgeon right away; however, what if the condition were temporary? All visits with the Flight Surgeon were on the record and one visit might jeopardize his flying career. He agonized over the pending decision around the clock. Fear kept him awake most of the night.

He awoke in the morning to the unwelcome realization that the spot was still there. His pilot training had conditioned him to react promptly to malfunctions or threats, but he reminded himself that, outside of the cockpit, delay was a viable tactic. In the non-flying world, problems sometime resolve themselves with the passing of time. Procrastination in the cockpit could kill; in the non-flying world, delaying a decision could fix a problem or even result in promotion. Scott let a week go by. He flew his normal schedule. The spot was a bother and he couldn't get it out of his mind, but he convinced himself that he hadn't overreacted and unnecessarily ruined his flying career.

By Monday, however, he admitted to himself that stalling wasn't working. The vision in his right eye had not improved, and he understood that he had no way to measure objectively whether it was getting worse. Delaying treatment might be making the condition worse. He made an appointment with an optometrist in El Paso, eighty miles to the south. If his symptoms were inconsequential, his Air Force medical record stayed pristine. If something *was* wrong, he would deal with it even though it most likely involved reporting to the Flight Surgeon.

The optometrist in El Paso was an attractive black woman in her early forties. She told Scott that she could see retinal scars in both eyes that could be the result of a past infection caused by histo fungus spores. She dilated his eyes and told him that she detected active inflammation of his right retina. Then she asked him where he had lived as a child.

"Texas. Abilene and San Angelo. Then, later on, New Hampshire."

"Texas is in the "Histo Belt", she said. "Have you ever heard of histoplasmosis?"

He *had* heard of it, because he had contracted the disease as a child, and his history of histoplasmosis came up every time a physician detected lung calcifications on his chest x-rays. When he told the optometrist about it, she explained that spores can spread from the lungs to the eyes where they remain in the choroid which is a layer of blood vessels that provide nutrients to the retina.

"It's called Ocular Histoplasmosis Syndrome," she told him. "OHS. It's serious, because it can leave scar tissue in the macula. It usually leaves your peripheral vision undamaged, but it can ruin your central vision."

Scott was terrified. He asked, "Is it just the right eye?"

She told him that most likely, both eyes would eventually be affected. Scott was *really* terrified.

"If my diagnosis is right, we need to act quickly. A laser surgery can destroy the abnormal blood vessels at the expense of some retinal tissue. The surgery might cause modest additional sight loss, but it might cut the progressive loss of central vision by up to fifty per cent."

At that moment, Scott knew he had to go to the Flight Surgeon right away. Every day might count. For a second he felt as though he might suffocate. His eyes felt hot. Even his tears felt hot. His career was over and he knew it.

"I'm sorry, Scott. We can't cure OHS right now, but, if we stay on top of it, we can try to slow down vision impairment."

During the lonely drive back to Alamogordo, Scott's mind raced through a dozen scenarios. He wouldn't stay in the Air Force if he couldn't fly. He probably *couldn't* stay in the Air Force if he wanted to because of OHS.

Early in his career, a senior fighter pilot had related to Scott what he called a prophecy: "One day, every fighter pilot wakes up and flies his last sortie and he either knows it or he doesn't know it." Scott was pretty sure he had already flown his last flight, and he hadn't known it at the time. The prophecy was fulfilled.

The Flight Surgeon grounded Scott, and his Squadron Commander assigned him to instructor duty at the training center. Instead of leading flights of F-15 *Eagles* on intercept missions and air-to-air combat sorties, he was giving lectures on offensive missile capabilities and electronic countermeasures. Adjusting to his new handicap was the hardest thing Scott had ever done. He was like a starving man in a glass cell seeing a banquet on the other side of the glass.

He worked to show a positive attitude as he taught his classes and submitted to two laser surgeries by an ophthalmologist in El Paso, but he felt gutted. Every day he faithfully looked at his Amsler grid, one eye at a time, to see if the straight horizontal and vertical lines appeared curved. He stopped drinking alcohol to avoid any chance that alcohol could inflame the retinas of his eyes.

Scott's squadron mates could not have been more supportive, but his interactions with them weren't the same as before. Ninety per cent of every conversation in a fighter squadron is about flying fighters. Avoiding that ninety per cent didn't leave much to be said, and each well-intended inquiry into his health felt like another stab wound. He was bleeding to death from kindness. Scott knew he was on a one-way road. Because there was no remedy for OHS, his days of flying fighters were over.

Scott separated from the Air Force. His confidence was

in tatters. He thought about some of the girls in his life as though such relationships were as trapped in the past as flying fighters.

He had dated a Congressman's daughter while he was flying at Langley AFB. She had gotten serious. He had not.

While stationed in England, he had enjoyed a passionate six-month affair with a Swedish girl he had met at an embassy party in London. That had ended when a fellow fighter pilot in his squadron had begun an even *more* passionate affair with same girl.

One night at a party he had hosted in his home in the foothills of Alamogordo, Scott had met a beauty named Rachel Flores. That intense affair began to unravel one night at the El Paso home of Rachel's parents when Scott overheard Rachel's brother slander him as a *gringo pendejo*. The brother was a boxer with a chip on his shoulder, and Scott's risk-reward analysis indicated that easing out of the relationship was the preferred course of action.

Scott had perfected easing out of relationships. Life had gone his way for so long that he had lost the capacity to imagine life without perfect eye sight and without flying his beloved *Eagle*. Only after losing his profession did he realize that his whole identity was tied to that profession. Without it, he was nothing. He started down a long descending path toward sadness. He felt alone and unneeded. He kneeled to pray for the first time since he was thirteen years old.

"Dear God, you gave me Heaven-on-Earth and, now, you've taken it away. I never thanked you for what you gave me. Help me find a way to make something positive out of this, because, right now, I don't see it."

Scott's thoughts turned to Dan Hardin back in Caledonia. For the first time, he empathetically considered the depth of Dan's disappointment and heartache since Trinette had run away. Scott thought about Benjamin Hardin's loss of his wife as she had given birth to Dan. Both Benjamin and Dan had demonstrated grace in the face of a great loss. Scott knew he had to try to do the same. He wrote Dan his most sincere letter on record. Four days later, Dan called Scott. They spoke only briefly.

"Scott, come home. You've always got a place here." Dan was New England blunt.

Scott had lost his medical certificate to fly, but he still had his New Mexico driver's license, and, as soon as his honorable discharge from the Air Force was complete and his DD-214 was in hand, he pointed his Porsche toward New England for a five-day drive to his parents' home on the shores of Lake Tremont. He was "boomeranging".

For the first time in his driving history, Scott complied with posted speed limits. He no longer felt he was living a charmed life. His swagger was gone. Regrets played over-and-over in his mind like an audio loop recording. His accomplishments seemed irrelevant. He wasn't bullet-proof any more. He drove into Caledonia on the afternoon of July 1, 1998, a beaten, humble man.

Chapter 8

NUMBERS

JOHN WESLEY HARDIN'S eleventh birthday on the Ides of March 1999 was only a week away. This birthday felt different to John from those in the past. For one thing, none of his grandparents could attend. Grandfather Benjamin Hardin and Grandparents Marie and Phillip Laval were scheduled to fly off with Joe T. and Joyce Harrington to Seattle for a cruise up the Alaskan coast. In the past, the Hardins and Lavals always had celebrated John's birthday together at Benjamin's house. Instead, Dan scheduled the party at two o'clock in the afternoon at the Dan Hardin house.

Another difference from years past was the presence of Scott Harrington. After leaving the Air Force and driving to Caledonia, Scott had spent only a few days with his parents before he and Dan worked out a deal that included hiring Scott to work at Hardin's Hardware. Scott also agreed to pay for room and board at Dan's house. Scott's bedroom was on the second floor down the corridor from John's bedroom. Dan was pleased to be working side-by-side with his best friend. Living under the same roof again helped them recapture the closeness of their friendship.

The living and working conditions were a drastic change for Scott, but they mitigated the disillusion and disorientation of losing his career as a fighter pilot. He knew that most OHS patients suffer measurable loss of central vision in the second eye within a couple of months of detecting vision loss in the first eye. Scott had gone through an additional surgery to minimize the progressive loss of central vision in his right eye, and the OHS had so far not recurred in his left eye. This was encouraging to Scott, because his therapist had forewarned him that loss of central vision in both eyes would degrade his life style.

"If it happens, you'll have to use eccentric fixation during conversations with people. We'll test you to figure out how far off-center and in which direction you'll have to align your eyes to use your peripheral vision. You'll eventually learn to see with reduced clarity the eyes and facial expressions of the person you're talking to."

His therapist warned Scott that people sometimes felt uncomfortable talking with a person suffering from OHS in both eyes. The indirect alignment of the eyes signaled disinterest, dislike, or even dishonesty. More seriously, loss of central vision in both eyes would make reading and functioning in the work place difficult, perhaps impossible. Monthly visits to the optometrist was a small price for Scott to pay to keep as much of his vision as he could.

John liked having Scott in the house for lots of reasons. He admired Scott, so having a bedroom on the same floor of the same house as Scott was like being housemate to a rock star. Scott often took John for pizza after cross-country skiing, to a movie, or to the ice skating rink on days off when they could conscript a driver.

Scott's collective name for the three residents of the Dan Hardin household was The Triad. The Triad attended every Thornton Prep home ice hockey game. The Triad even pulled out all the stops and spent a weekend in Boston where they attended a Bruins game Friday night and a Harvard versus Princeton match on Saturday at Harvard's Bright Hockey Center. The Crimson bested the Tigers 5-3 despite avid cheering by John — a thoroughly indoctrinated Princeton fan. The Triad stayed overnight in the Harvard Club on Commonwealth Avenue, courtesy of a reciprocal agreement with their own Princeton Club.

Such escapades were therapeutic for each member of The Triad. The outings took Dan's mind off losing Trinette and they made Scott forget about losing his career. John enjoyed being with his father and his father's best friend. John no longer felt so alone and different from his classmates, almost all of whom lived in a home environment populated by a father and a mother. It wasn't as if he *missed* his mother, because Trinette hadn't been around him long enough for him to miss her; however, when everyone else has something you don't have, you know it. The Triad was compensatory: John had it, other kids didn't.

Dan told John he could invite friends to his party for the first time. This required some contemplation on John's part. Was his father just padding the numbers to make up for the absence of his grandparents? Was this his father's way of encouraging John to make friends because he didn't run in a posse like a lot of fifth graders at Brighton School? Exactly who *were* his friends? After some deliberation, John invited Paul Bruguiere and Corky Gleason to his party.

Both classmates responded as though he had invited them to Disney World. Their enthusiastic acceptances of his invitation surprised John. He had spent most of his childhood alone obsessively reading and role-playing and not much time thinking about his peers, so his peers and their opinions were mysteries to John. One of those mysteries was the fact that most of his classmates were fond of John.

Unfortunately, Raymond Delacroix overheard Corky and Paul discussing the party, and Raymond confronted John and tactlessly informed him that he wanted to attend the party. This bluntness put John in a predicament, because Raymond was about the last guest a sane person wanted to invite to anything short of an ambush. For reasons unknown to John, Raymond had never singled John out as a target, but Raymond had pummeled Corky and Paul at least twice in the past. If John didn't come up with the right answer to Raymond's rude demand, John risked being added to Raymond's list of punching bags. John needed to do some quick thinking to placate an essentially unhappy school yard intimidator. Raymond Delacroix had lots of reasons for being unhappy.

Disorders — physical and mental — were the norm in the Delacroix family. Raymond's father, Richard, had suffered from PTSD – post traumatic stress disorder – since a time when "battle fatigue" was the term most commonly used to describe Richard's condition. Richard had never experienced combat, but, as a teenager, he had been the first basketball player to run off the court and down the gymnasium basement stairs at halftime of one eventful home game.

Being first in the sweaty procession, it was Richard who ran into a man hanging from an overhead pipe by a rope around his neck. The florid head of the Caledonia High School Principal was bloated and his eyes bulged like two Ping-Pong balls. Up until that moment, everyone had assumed that the principal might worry his students to death, so it was a startling irony that the inverse had happened. Richard never shook off the symptoms attributed to his literal brush with death. He told anyone who would listen about the trauma in such detail that some feared contracting *passive* PTSD. Over the years, Richard's PTSD symptoms multiplied logarithmically according to his own testimony, partly because he considered everyone in the village a potential witness to bolster his disability claims.

Raymond's mother, Violette, barely escaped death from a VTE – a venous thromboembolism – that caused her to collapse from low blood pressure on the floor of Raymond's first grade classroom. Although she recovered, Violette lived in constant fear of a repeat VTE. She suffered from cardio phobia. She delegated most of her tasks in life to Richard and Raymond, who soon thereafter developed COPD – chronic obstructive pulmonary disease. The COPD caused Raymond to develop a prominent barrel chest. Had his chest been full of heart, he might have been the bravest boy in Caledonia.

Unfortunately, Raymond's barrel chest was all lungs, and he coughed and wheezed his way through school constructing a thoroughly unremarkable academic record. Raymond's bronchodilator, a device known to inspire sympathy in others, turned out to be his silver lining of the storm clouds of COPD. Raymond learned to dodge punishment by pulling out his bronchodilator as a last-ditch maneuver. Even teachers who previously had seen Raymond's dramatic choking act collaborated with the ploy. Most teachers found it untenable to press an offensive on a young boy turning blue and sucking noisily on a piece of plastic.

Possibly because of this history of ailments, Raymond was diagnosed with ADHD – attention-deficit hyperactivity disorder predominantly inattentive. He was a top-notch procrastinator and he was easily distracted. Those two qualities alone were sufficient to earn bottom grades in the class, which reinforced his negative self-image.

He could have punished himself in frustration and anger, but, instead, he punished others. He became the designated bully in John's class. He couldn't sustain his attention long enough to inflict serious injury on anyone, not even Corky Gleason, his favorite prey. As a result, Raymond was sort of a part-time bully. He bullied as a hobby, not a profession.

John hit upon a capital solution to the dilemma Raymond had caused by inviting himself to John's party.

"There's only one way you can come," John said with authority.

"What's that?" Raymond asked.

"You have to promise never to hit Corky or Paul again."

"No problem." Raymond was a willing negotiator.

"I mean it. You have to promise."

"I promise!"

Raymond, as unlikely a guest as a wolf at a sheep party, was in.

Fortunately, John could count on the attendance of his Aunt Annette. At every birthday John could recall, Annette had baked a cake, acted as a hostess, and helped pass gifts to him in some semblance of order. John kept a list of gifts in his journal, and he had observed that his relatives' choices of gifts fell into categories.

It was hardly shocking that his Aunt Annette's gifts tended to be educational as she was widely regarded as Brighton School's best teacher. Her past gifts included a Monopoly game, a wooden chess set carved in Mexico, and the complete works of Sherlock Holmes stories written by Sir Arthur Conan Doyle. Annette often added thoughtful companion gifts. For example, in addition to the Doyle collection, she gave John a new deer-stalker hat of the kind favored by Sherlock himself and one of Great Grandfather Laval's pipes. John donned the deer-stalker and plugged the pipe into his mouth every time he nested in his father's wing-backed chair for a good read by the fireplace.

John's Grandparents Laval always gave him clothing items such as sweaters and coats. The items invariably were purchased from L.L. Bean and they were colored navy blue, Harvard Crimson, or Dartmouth green. He longed for the surprise of a box of Legos, but the clothing rolled in unabated.

Grandfather Benjamin Hardin's gifts were usually sports-related. Last year it was a new lacrosse stick and helmet. The year before, Benjamin had given John his first new set of cross-country skis, ski poles, and ski boots.

John's father was more unpredictable, his gifts more eclectic. John fondly remembered past gifts like a sling shot made from surgical tubing. Even in the hands of a novice, it was a powerful weapon. It could – and did – take out a window. Another memorable gift was a set of swimming flippers and a top-of-the line snorkel mask. A metal detector, a BB gun, and a magician set were additional examples of his father's past presents.

The Davy Crockett jacket and coonskin cap from the previous year were the only presents John could remember ever having received from Scott. Of course, such a fantastic gift entitled the giver to a multi-year waiver. John found it enticing to speculate about what Scott might give him for his eleventh birthday. The sky was the limit for a patron generous enough to give a Davy Crockett jacket.

As for Paul, Corky, and Raymond, who could guess what the cap on their largesse might be? Thinking about potential loot consumed many of John's waking hours. The extent of Paul's generosity was unknowable. Anything from a five-dollar gift certificate to a chemistry set was possible. Paul had lived with his uncle Thomas Bruguiere, the one-eyed janitor, ever since Simon Bruguiere had skipped town. John worried that Paul's whacky uncle might persuade Paul to give a gag gift like an exploding golf ball.

One exciting fantasy that occurred to John during a sex-education class was that Thomas Bruguiere was secretly a millionaire. This line of thinking opened the door to a number of exciting gifts — a skateboard, for example. The possibility put a huge smile on John's face just as the teacher described in vivid detail the urgent efforts of millions of sperm to reach their goal. The teacher noted John's seemingly lecherous smile among a sea of baffled faces contemplating the fate of millions of little tadpoles fighting the odds in their uphill quest. Rita Fontaine kept the class spellbound by reporting a parental sighting that, if her account was accurate, switched things around to a downhill quest.

Corky Gleason was also a hard read. Andrew Gleason's opinion of John as a juvenile delinquent came through loud and clear during their confrontation by the Town Gazebo, the kerfuffle that John remembered as "The BB Gun Caper". Mr. Gleason's low estimation of John might cause him to veto the idea of a gift. On the other hand, the miraculous redemption of Ebenezer Scrooge came to mind, and John imagined Mr. Gleason undergoing a similar transformation resulting in extravagant munificence on the part of the tubby banker.

John dared not guess at Raymond's gift. Brass knuckles, boxing gloves, instruments of torture all came to mind, but John knew that his imagination was being kidnapped by his negative perception of Raymond.

Just before two o'clock on Sunday afternoon, Corky Gleason's father dropped his obese son from his car at the curb in front of the Hardin house and drove off without a word or even a wave. Paul Bruguiere and Raymond Delacroix arrived on foot seconds later. Aunt Annette was already in the kitchen sticking eleven candles into the cake she had made for the occasion. John answered the door and welcomed the three boys into the foyer where Scott helped them remove their coats and ski hats. Annette left the kitchen to join them, and John served as master of ceremonies by making introductions.

The jazz music that Scott had selected on the compact disc player set what John considered a sophisticated tone for the celebration. Without waiting for an invitation, Corky made a beeline for the cookies. Scott offered Paul and Raymond beverage options of fruit punch, lemonade, and ginger ale. Paul asked for a ginger ale as he put his present on the gift table. Raymond asked for a beer, but it wasn't clear whether he actually expected to be taken seriously or he was just busting Scott's chops.

"How about a lemonade?" Scott wasn't one to risk jail time just to humor a school yard tough guy. Raymond nodded.

Corky was not shy around food, and he popped an entire oatmeal cookie into his expansive mouth and asked if there was any milk around. Milk: Who knew? John sipped a Snapple. Scott, a dedicated teetotaler in defense of his vision, sipped Perrier and Dan poured neat single-malts from a bottle labeled *Sheep Dip*, an exceptional product of Scotland. Annette, a pearl among swine, drank English tea.

Annette asked the three visitors lots of questions, and her former students seemed eager to answer. They felt comfortable right away because of all the days they had spent in her classroom. They laughed easily. The truce governing Raymond's penchant for attack held up. Corky removed most of the mystery of his remarkable weight by raiding the cookie platter repeatedly. After twenty minutes of small talk, Annette emerged from the kitchen bearing John's birthday cake. It was a beauty — chocolate with eleven white candles blazing like roadside flares. Annette started a verse of "Happy Birthday" in F Major. There wasn't an ounce of vocal talent among the chorale of six males, so the cacophony that ensued sounded a little like a herd of cattle in a feed lot. Cookie crumbs flew out of Corky's mouth when he sang the word "happy", and Corky looked around with apprehension until Scott slapped him on the back and laughed. That eased Corky's mind, and he rejoined the chorus in full voice.

Fortunately, the little tune "Happy Birthday" has only sixteen words in it, so the artless recital ended and John blew out all the candles at just the right velocity to extinguish every candle without dripping wax all over the cake. Annette sliced the cake for serving and Dan added vanilla ice cream to each plate. The boys chattered without inhibition as they plowed through two servings of cake and ice cream. When Dan, Annette, and John were out of the room performing cleanup duties, Scott asked Paul, Corky, and Raymond to follow him to his study. The three boys entered Scott's man cave and looked at the paintings of fighters on the wall, models of F-15 *Eagles* and F-16 *Falcons* on the book case, and other assorted mementos of Scott's flying career.

"Can I shoot straight with you guys?" Scott asked them. They nodded assent. "Have a seat on the couch," Scott said. They did. "I really like you guys, so I want to give you the benefit of my observations." The three boys nodded in unison without the slightest idea of where this meeting was going. "First," Scott continued, "I want to establish my credentials. Let me ask you a couple of questions. Why do you guys think every girl who's ever met me has been magnetically drawn to me?"

The boys seemed stumped by this unforeseen lead-off question. None was eager to take a stab at an answer. Could this be sexual abuse? They cast their eyes at one another, but no words came out of their mouths.

"Let me help you here," Scott said. "Do you think it's because of my incredible good looks?"

"Yeah, that's probably it," Corky said agreeably.

"Okay," Scott said, "I won't argue with that." He looked at Raymond. "Do you think it's because of my immense brain power?"

"Yes, I do," Raymond said without hesitation.

"Good, I'll agree with that, too." Scott turned toward Paul. "Could it be my profound spirituality? My trust in God?"

Paul said, "Could be."

"How about my physique, my enormous strength?" The boys defaulted to the head-nodding response mode to this most unusual line of questioning. "I'll tell you why women of all ages find me irresistible," Scott concluded, "it's for *all* those reasons. I am the perfect blend of good looks, intelligence, spirituality, and physical strength...*and* one more thing humility!"

The boys appeared to be relieved that the questioning had ended and the summary was at hand.

"It's a known fact that I am the greatest fighter pilot who ever lived," Scott resumed his oratory. "Enemy pilots surrendered rather than fly against me. Do you get it? Word gets around. I worked at every element we've talked about here today. I didn't just sit around and hope for things to work out. No! I ran every day to increase my stamina. I read a little bit every day to grow my knowledge. I ate healthy food and drank lots of water, sometimes more water than I wanted to drink. I prayed to God every day and thanked Him for his gifts to me. I was born an American and a Texan by the Grace of God. These steel biceps and massive shoulders didn't come out of thin air, I made 'em!"

The boys shifted uneasily on the couch and wondered how long this extraordinary meeting might go on. Corky's idea of a talk with his father was having Mr. Gleason tell him to get a haircut. The closest thing to a chat at the Bruguiere house was when Thomas told Paul to bring him a beer from the refrigerator. It didn't bear contemplating what passed for a conversation between medical emergencies in the Delacroix household.

"Here's my final pitch to you boys," Scott said lowering his voice for dramatic effect. "You have greatness inside of you. I can feel it. But, Corky, I want you to suck in your gut and shave off a few pounds." Corky's eyes got wide. "And, Paul, I want you straighten up your posture. Stick your chest out and pull your little gut in. Right now!" Paul sat up more erectly and pulled his shoulders back. "Raymond, I've heard about you. Stop beating the crap out of everybody and start acting like a man!" Raymond was frozen motionless.

Scott reached into his top desk drawer and brought out six medals. He laid each of them respectfully on the top of his desk.

"I've got some ribbons and these six medals," Scott told the boys. "I want each of you to pick one and take it home with you to remind you of what we talked about today." He stepped back so the boys could gather closer to the desk top. "You go first, Paul."

Paul touched the Air Force Commendation Medal and

then the Air Medal. He held up the Silver Star for examination, but replaced it in favor of the Kuwait Liberation Medal.

"What's this one?" Paul asked.

"That's from Operation Desert Shield and Operation Desert Storm when I was flying out of King Abdul Aziz Air Base in Saudi Arabia," Scott said.

"How about this one?" Raymond asked, as he picked up Scott's Aerial Achievement Medal.

"Same deal," Scott replied. "I got that for flying over Iraq in 1990 and 1991."

"Did you get shot down?" Paul asked.

"Not yet," Scott said. Paul and Corky laughed, but Raymond didn't get it.

Corky chose the National Defense Service Medal because he liked the colors. He thanked Scott for the gift and tried to pin it on his shirt.

"Do me a favor, guys. Don't pin these on your clothes, because they're supposed to be worn only by the recipient in uniform. But save them in a special place to remind you of our deal." The three boys nodded agreement. Scott finished up by saying, "I want you boys doing pushups and sit ups and squats and running and skating – all that stuff – every day. No excuses!" Scott extended his hands for the boys to put their hands on top of his. "It'll change your lives, boys Don't think about it, just do it. 'Just do it' on three." They all recited the benediction, "One, two, three, just do it!" Scott pointed toward the door to the hallway. "Now, go get some more cake and ice cream and have a good time. I'm glad we had this chat, because I believe in you boys."

The three boys scurried from the study back toward the

living room while Scott stayed behind to put away his remaining medals. Scott could hear John ask the lads where they had been.

"Looking at Scott's medals," Raymond, the devious one, answered.

"Scott told me to do some pushups and lose weight," Corky added.

The toilet in the study bathroom flushed and the occupant turned on the bathroom faucet. The occupant of the bathroom wiped her hands on a hand towel. Annette left the bathroom and walked across the study to Scott. She put her arms around his waist.

"You are something," she said.

"Thanks for the compliment."

"Who said it was a compliment?"

"They needed a little boost."

"You really are something, Captain Harrington."

"And, Darlin', so are you," Scott said as he embraced and kissed her lovingly.

Within a few minutes, it was time for John to open his gifts. Annette had devised an ingenious protocol to avoid any possible hurt feelings over the issue of sequence, such foresight being part of the bag of tricks for which elementary school teachers are renowned. She wrote each gift giver's name on a piece of paper and dropped the names into Dan's Boston Red Sox hat. The first name John drew was Annette's. She presented her gift to him and he eagerly shredded the wrapping paper. It was a Scrabble set. The Birthday Boy oohed and aahed appropriately and moved on to the next gift, this one from Paul Bruguiere.

John expressed true delight when he unpacked a set of lightweight ear phones and a small portable radio designed so a jogger could strap the radio on his or her arm for entertainment while exercising. It didn't matter that John didn't jog and it didn't matter that radio reception in Caledonia, nestled in the shadow of the White Mountains, was limited to only four radio stations, the gift had a cool factor to it. Paul accepted John's gratitude shyly but with obvious pleasure.

The next name out of the hat was Dan. John opened Dan's big package and pulled out a new pair of ice hockey skates. He also fished out three hockey pucks and a leather necklace with integrated ice picks for rescuing a skater should he fall through the ice. John had outgrown his old pair of skates, so this was a perfect gift — fun and functional.

"*Always* wear the safety necklace on the lake," Dan said emphatically.

"Okay," John replied.

"Always means *always*," Scott added.

Next on the docket was Corky's gift. To John's amazement, beneath the amateur wrapping was a computer video game. John noted and approved of the sentence on the cover of the game that said, "Recommended for ages eighteen and above." The tight-fitting leather outfit worn by a vixen on the game box suggested to John that Mr. Gleason knew nothing of Corky's choice of gift. Corky had acted on his own, probably with his own money. John thanked Corky with a light punch on the shoulder.

"It's the least I could do for my best friend," Corky replied, punching John on a shoulder in return. John privately asked himself how does a guy with no friends at all have a *best* friend, but it was only a fleeting thought. Corky had said it, and John appreciated his intent.

Raymond presented the penultimate gift, a New England Patriots football jersey. It was an excellent gift, and John praised Raymond liberally, but he didn't punch him on the shoulder for fear of annulling their non-aggression pact.

John opened Scott's box last. Inside were two small gifts. The first was a pocket reference book. It contained a wealth of information in its 768 pages from measurement conversion charts to trig functions to temperature lapse rate tables. John read aloud a sample of the facts between the little book's covers.

"Wow," he said enthusiastically, because it was his birthday, "Page ten...Charles' Law says 'if the pressure is constant, the volume of a given mass of gas is directly proportional to the absolute temperature.' I didn't know that."

"Cool," Corky said, because he knew where his cake was coming from.

"Awesome," Paul added.

"Wicked cool," Raymond chimed in. He seemed to be getting the hang of this personal relationship stuff that had mystified him for so much of his life.

John flipped through the pages, choosing Page 267 at random.

"The area code for Anaheim, California, is 714," John read.

"Who knew?" Corky said.

John opened the second of Scott's gifts. It was a black hand-held calculator that had a somber all-business-no-messing-around appearance. It had keys for squares, cubes, square roots, logarithms, trigonometric functions, and a dozen other functionalities. John punched a few keys.

"What's the square root of thirty," John asked. The three boys, each with traces of chocolate cake around their mouths, exchanged glances of bewilderment. Their life experiences to date, unlike that of the Birthday Boy, had not included square roots.

"About five-and-a-half," Scott guessed.

"About? 'About's' not good enough, Captain Harrington," John teased him. "The answer is 5.47723."

"Get your facts straight, Mr. Math," Dan chided Scott.

Scott's gifts were the catalysts that launched John into orbit on his next great obsession – numbers. John profusely thanked Scott and the others for their gifts, but the gift-giving wasn't over. Dan gave the three young guests a gift-wrapped box each, a turn of events that surprised even John. Each boy removed the wrapping paper containing a game called *Trivial Pursuit*. They thanked their hosts. The adults left the four boys by the fireplace to play *Trivial Pursuit* until almost five o'clock. That was the time set for Andrew Gleason to collect Corky, and if Andrew was known for anything better than his full figure and sour temperament, it was his punctuality. Corky was bundled in his winter jacket and woolen ski hat and ready to dash to his father's car when Mr. Gleason drove up to the curb. Paul and Raymond left at the same time, but Mr. Gleason left them standing at the curb. Paul shrugged and turned to face Dan and John who remained in the front doorway.

"How about a ride?" Dan called.

"No, thanks, it isn't that far to my house." Paul replied.

"No, thanks," Raymond said.

The two boys turned toward the village and trudged away as snowflakes fell silently around them.

John's eleventh birthday had been an unqualified success. Annette and Scott cleaned dishes and put the bag of discarded wrapping paper into the recycling bin. At one point, John walked silently on woolen socks past the kitchen door and saw Annette and Scott embracing one another beside the sink. They touched their noses together, and Annette whispered something to Scott, but John couldn't hear what she said. They didn't notice John, who felt buoyant without completely understanding why.

When the cleanup was finished, Annette put on her ski jacket, hat, and mittens, before kissing Scott, Dan, and John goodbye. She left the house to walk home in the light snowfall as the darkness descended on the village. The Triad watched the final day of a PGA golf tournament on television, snug in the house by the shore of frozen Lake Tremont.

John's new obsession kicked in the very next day. He walked home from Brighton School in six inches of new dry snow, ate a sausage sandwich, did his homework, and started reading the pocket reference book Scott had given him. The first thing he began to memorize was the list of "ten" radio codes. "10-4" meant "message received". "10-23" meant "stand by". "10-12" meant "visitors present". John's daydream included a scene about using the code if kidnappers ever invaded his house and took him hostage. If the police called his house to check on his well-being, he could warn them of the presence of desperados by signing off with a "10-12".

Knowledge was power, and John packed the codes into his memory.

Next on his list of must-know information was the phonetic alphabet. He memorized the phonetics "Alpha" through "Zulu", noting particularly the correct pronunciation of Quebec – "Ke Beck". Morse Code was the next logical step in his fit of memorization. He practiced "dits" and "dahs" for three days in a row until he had committed the code to memory. The mental drain of this flurry of memorization tired him, but he felt "—. —- —- - .." (good).

Next he tackled temperature conversion tables. He didn't try to memorize every single increment, but he did master certain memorable conversions across the atmospheric range. He wrote down the points of equality he chose to memorize: 100° Celsius was 212° Fahrenheit, 28° C was 82° F, 10° C was 50° F, 0° C was 32° F, and -40° C was -40° F.

In school, John had not yet been taught to interpolate, but he had an intuitive sense of how to do it. The way his mind worked, he quickly assessed that 5° Celsius was about 41° Fahrenheit simply by mentally computing the half-way values between the 0° and 10° Celsius lines on his table. For more accuracy, he could use the formula "Degrees Fahrenheit equals 32 Fahrenheit Degrees plus the product of one-point-eight times Degrees in Celsius." He practiced solving the formula until he could convert temperature values in his head quickly. The more he worked with the numbers, the more enchanted he became with them. His curiosity was its own reward, because his memory got sharper with use like a muscle strengthening with exercise.

His final frenzy of mathematical memorization

concentrated on the Periodic Table of Elements. He only vaguely sensed the meaning of most of the data on the table and he had no concept of isotopes or valences, but the order of the table appealed to him. He memorized the first eighty-six elements, including the name, atomic number, and atomic weight of each. He wrote the symbol of each element with an indelible marker on a white plastic poker chip —"H, He, Li, Be, B, C," etc. His practice consisted of drawing a poker chip out of his Red Sox hat and reciting the memory items aloud while standing in front of his bedroom mirror.

"Au, Gold, Atomic Number 79, and Atomic Weight 197.0."

Then he pulled out another poker chip.

"K, Potassium, Atomic Number 19, and Atomic Weight 39.10."

John memorized the elements only as far as Atomic Number 86, Radon, because he noticed that two elements – Ununhexrum (Atomic Number 116) and Ununoctrum (Atomic Number 118) – had been retracted. Retracted? What was going on here? Why bother memorizing something that could be retracted? Additional suspicious elements showed up — Atomic Numbers 113, 115, and 117 were all labeled "Not Discovered". Why give a number to an element that hasn't been discovered? His suspicions of the creators of the periodic table began to grow. When he ran across elements that he disliked, he simply discarded the proxy poker chip. As an example, when he first laid eyes on Atomic Number 58, he knew he was going to exert exactly zero horse power learning anything about it.

"Praseodymium," he mouthed slowly. "I can't even

pronounce it," he told the mirror. "Gone. *Adios. Arrivederci.*" He threw the chip into his trash basket as though he were shooting a basketball. The chip clanked into the basket, and John extended his arms over his head to signify a three-point shot like the referees at Thornton Prep basketball games. The same fate awaited Dysprosium, Ytterbium, Protactinium, and other obscure elements. In summary, John had only a vague idea of what an atomic number was or what an atomic weight was, but he knew how to memorize, and he memorized devotedly. Was this a symptom of *arithromania* (an infatuation with counting things)? Perhaps. A symptom of *pantomania* (an infatuation with everything)? Very likely. John concluded that he didn't have to name what he was; he was just a guy in love with memorizing things. His greatest pleasure came from packing information into his seemingly limitless memory.

Three months later on a Saturday afternoon in June, long after the snows had melted and the ice was out on Lake Tremont, The Triad was gathered on the beach by the back-yard barbeque pit where Scott was grilling steak tenderloins. Dan had poured himself a beer to refresh himself for the task of supervising Scott's grill work.

"Are you intentionally making beef jerky?" Dan asked. "You're burning those things beyond recognition."

"I'm looking for 145 degrees," Scott said, poking each steak with a meat thermometer for the umpteenth time. "A little carbon never hurt anyone."

"Carbon," John said automatically, "the symbol is 'C', the Atomic Number is 6, and the Atomic Weight is 12.01."

Scott-the-physics-major had a casual acquaintanceship with the Periodic Table of Elements himself. Surprised by John's recital, Scott looked up from his barbequing, first at Dan and then John.

"That's pretty good, John," he said. "Know any others?"

"Some."

"How about Sodium?"

"Sodium, Na, Atomic Number 11, Atomic Weight 22.99."

"Where'd you learn this stuff?" Dan-the-economics-major asked.

"It's in the book Scott gave me for my birthday."

One of the most flattering things the recipient of a gift can do is actually use the gift. John had done this in spades. Scott was flattered. Dan was proud. He put his arm on John's shoulder and gave him a hug like he had just knocked a home run over the Green Monster.

"You know, John," Scott said, "My Dad, Old Joe T., is a really good mathematician, and I'm no slouch, but I guarantee you that neither one of us has memorized the Periodic Table of Elements. You, my friend, are a genius."

What son isn't gratified by praise from his father or from his father's best friend? A genius! The compliment made John glow. It was such a perfect moment: Over-done steaks shared with his favorite people in the whole world beside a clear lake on a sunny afternoon in a five-knot breeze with the temperature at 77° Fahrenheit or, if one prefers, 25° Celsius.

Chapter 9

FOOTNOTES
AND GROUPS

UNLIKE HIS CRAVING for food that abated when he ate, John's appetite for numbers grew more voracious with each session of reading and memorization. Powered only by his curiosity, he discovered an array of mathematical functions well before his peers in school. He learned the fundamentals of trigonometry by a kind of reverse engineering after he set out to unravel the mystery of the trig tables in his pocket reference book. Compound interest and mortgage rate tables started him on a similar trail of enquiry before his classmates knew the definition of "mortgage". He read books on capital markets, currency exchanges, and futures markets.

By the end of the summer, he was adept at using his personal desktop computer to call up stock quotes and view real-time equity price charts in a variety of time frames in intervals as small as one minute. His innate ability to visualize what the graphics were intended to convey helped him master chart reading quickly. He sensed that he was different from his classmates. Their cunning was focused on avoiding the work of learning; John's inquisitive mind drove him to want to know more. He wisely kept his obsession for learning private. There was no better way to earn a thrashing at the hands of Raymond Delacroix than by carrying a Wall Street Journal home from school. John knew enough to keep these exciting new discoveries to himself. Despite his efforts, tell-tale signs of his preoccupations occasionally surfaced.

One example of such a breach of secrecy occurred early in his sixth grade year at Brighton School. While reading during the summer, John had fallen in love with footnotes. He liked the scholarly look of a page with three or four footnotes. Footnotes, he believed, gave a page *gravitas*. He observed that the footnotes themselves followed strict rules for ordering the information, so he asked a librarian if she knew of any rules of footnoting. It was the first time in her life that a child had voluntarily asked her how to footnote. She showed John one of several reference books that met his needs, and John dived right in to learn footnoting. What an odd little boy, she thought. For only a moment, she dared to imagine a society made up of children who footnoted properly, ate plenty of raw vegetables, and showed respect for their elders – in other words, a society of John Hardin clones. What a sweet world, indeed.

John didn't have to wait long to employ his newly-developed footnoting prowess. A teacher can't go too far wrong assigning *My Summer Vacation* as a writing assignment, so when John's teacher did just that, John almost quivered with excitement. He decided to write about his trip to Gettysburg, Pennsylvania with his father and grandfather. He expected his paper to be the best, because he was certain the Civil War outclassed swimming at Cape Cod or swatting mosquitoes at some summer camp in Maine. Just to make sure his paper stood out of from the paltry mass of drivel submitted by other students, John peppered his essay with footnotes. He thought the finished product was exceptional, perhaps the weightiest essay he had ever written.

Disaster struck in the early moments of class when John couldn't find page two of his essay. A frantic search of his backpack didn't produce the page of carefully structured footnotes. His fruitless search delayed him, so he was the last student to place his essay on top of the pile on the teacher's desk. He started to explain that his page of footnotes was missing, but he was silenced by the desire to avoid the embarrassment of a public conversation. He didn't want the teacher to say the word "footnote" in her loud voice for all the class to hear.

He said nothing as he left the incomplete product of hours of work naked on top of the pile. He felt deflated. He returned to his seat on wobbly knees. He mentally retraced his steps in the hope of remembering where he had last seen page two. He felt as though he had painted a portrait on a canvas and, at the moment of the unveiling, discovered that he had forgotten to paint the subject's head. What he had turned in was an essay with eleven numbers interspersed throughout the text – in effect, eleven typographical errors.

My Summer Vacation
By John Hardin

It took ten hours to drive from Caledonia to Gettysburg, Pennsylvania.[1] My father and grandfather took me to where the Battle of Gettysburg was fought.[2] The Yankees beat the Rebels. A lot of men died on both sides.[3] If General Lee's orders had been received by soldiers on his right flank, the battle could have turned out differently.[4] My dad says life's like that. You think you've got everything figured out, but things happen and everything blows up in your face. You have to adjust and go on.

The third day of fighting wasn't going too well for the Rebels, so General Pickett led a charge that killed just about everyone.[5] The ground was saturated with blood.[6] The explosion of cannon balls was almost constant.[7] The Yankees fought back and made the Rebels retreat.[8] Confederate General Robert E. Lee felt awful, and he rode his horse among his Rebel soldiers telling them that losing was his fault.[9]

President Abraham Lincoln arrived after the battle to make a speech. We still remember his words today.[10] Two years later, the Confederate States came back into the Union and everybody made up so they could make the great country we have today. Slaves were freed [11] and the country was put back together all because a lot of brave men sacrificed their lives.

You can water ski and swim all summer, but if you want to have a summer vacation that will make you cry and make you glad you're an American, you should go to Gettysburg.

John found the wayward page two sitting in his printer tray at home at the end of the day. He could think of no way to repair the damage caused by his negligence.

John's teacher, who had never visited Gettysburg, didn't know what to make of this most unusual submission. Grading the essays at home that night, she set John's paper aside for a second read. In the end, she wrote on his essay in green ink what she hoped was a note appropriate for the circumstances.

"John, you are very fortunate to have visited such a special place. You have reminded us how lucky we are that our forefathers united our country. The numbers scattered in your essay are a distraction, however, so please wait to experiment with footnotes until we have covered them in class."

John was heartsick when he read the comments the following day. "Experiment!" In his fantasy preview, the footnotes were the best part of the paper, the strawberry on the whipped cream on the shortcake. He had daydreamed about the teacher's exquisite joy when she read the final "Ibid."

When Scott got home that night ahead of Dan, John showed Scott his paper bearing his teacher's comments and he explained his oversight. Scott, who had adjusted to the limitations of OHS by reading with his left eye only, absorbed the paper carefully before offering his opinion.

"Here's the deal, John," Scott said. "First of all, this is a really good paper, and it makes me wish I had been down at Gettysburg with you guys. Of course, it loses its punch without the footnote page. Here's the point: Your teacher hasn't taught you how to footnote, yet, so she thinks you're just padding your essay by using footnotes."

John didn't look relieved or enlightened, so Scott resorted to an analogy.

"A friend of mine was in his first year of law school. His torts professor gave him a no-notice test about a guy being locked in the rest room at a gas station."

"What are torts?"

"Torts are civil actions for things like battery and negligence," Scott said, hoping to keep a lid on his lack of knowledge in this area. "Anyway the professor wanted to know what elements of what torts were possible causes of action with the given facts. So, among several other torts, my friend listed false imprisonment. Well, the class hadn't covered false imprisonment, yet. The only reason my friend knew about false imprisonment is because he had read ahead. So the professor didn't give him any credit for using what the class hadn't covered, yet. Do you see what I mean?"

John thought about it for a minute and, slowly, he nodded his head.

"Yeah, I think I get it. It's okay if I get ahead of everyone else, but I shouldn't show what I know until everyone else catches up."

"Yep. I think that's all there is to it."

So, no matter how frustrated he was about the missing page of footnotes he loved so dearly and how disappointed he was in the teacher's response, John imposed a footnote ceasefire at school. Entries in his journal, however, were exempted from the ban. In the privacy of his own bedroom, he continued to footnote promiscuously.

Footnoting wasn't the only obsession that came to the attention of his teacher. John's fascination with the collective names of animals got him into a similar predicament a couple of weeks later. When John had stumbled on a list of animals and their collective group names the previous summer, he couldn't resist memorizing the list and using as many of the terms as possible as soon as possible. He dropped a few of the collective names at dinner with Dan and Scott, but spoken esoteric words are seldom as impactful as written esoteric words, so John was ready to release his dammed-up store of collective names the moment his teacher told her class to write a paper titled *My Favorite Walk*. Look out, John thought, borrowing a phrase from Scott's lexicon, this is going to roll your socks down.

My Favorite Walk
By John Hardin

It is a Saturday in October. I just want to get away from all the noise. I don't care who's winning the football game between Ohio State and Michigan. The cheering crowd hurts my ears as they jump around like a *flange* of baboons in crazy costumes and blue-and-maize body paint. I want quiet. I don't even want to hear the screeching of a *scold* of jays or the cawing of a *parliament* of rooks.

I bicycle the path that leads from the Old Stage Road to Kennedy's Pond. A *flutter* of butterflies skims over a vernal pool beside my path. The only sounds I can hear are the breeze in the tree tops and the clatter of my rusty chain on its sprocket. I see the tracks of a _posse_ of turkeys. I make gobbling sounds to involve them in a conversation, but they're not that stupid. I don't sound anything like a turkey.

I round a bend in the path and get my first view of Kennedy's Pond. I want to see a <u>prickle</u> of porcupines, but I see only one. He or she (who can tell with a porcupine?) is chewing a pine bough. The look on his or her face tells me he or she doesn't care if I live or die. I ignore his or her indifference. I leave my bike on the trail and walk through the tunnel made by the yellow and red leaves of trees on both sides of my favorite walk.

Once again, John's teacher found herself in the position of liking the guts of John's paper, but having to inform him that he had overworked the collective names for groups of animals like a rented mule. She penned her evaluation of his paper in blue ink, thereby avoiding the stigma of red ink. John couldn't believe that she hadn't posted his essay on the classroom wall as an inspiration to the other students who, in his opinion, couldn't write their way out of a bag. He was incredulous that she had written anything besides, "Excellent." The minute Scott walked through the front doorway that night, John handed him the paper and asked for his input. Scott read the essay slowly.

"Okay, Einstein," Scott said. "I think I get it. When you know more than other people about stuff, you have to be smart about showing your knowledge. You have to let your knowledge dribble out a little bit at a time."

"Why?" John asked, genuinely puzzled.

"It's like dating girls." Scott rarely missed an opportunity to employ a parable. "Let's say I'm in a bar and I walk up to a girl I've never seen before and I say, 'I'm Scott Harrington and I was a wide receiver at Thornton Prep and I ran the 400-meter dash in 49.22 and I went to Princeton and I used to be a fighter pilot and do you want to go out?'" Scott arched his eyebrows and looked down at John. "Do you know what she's going to say?"

"No."

"Neither do I," Scott admitted, "but I'm pretty sure it's not going be good. So, what I do is I ask *her* questions. I get *her* talking."

"You want me to ask my teacher if she went to Princeton or flew fighters?" John asked. He knew better than this, but he didn't want to miss the chance to mess with Scott.

"No. What I mean is you need to let your vast storehouse of knowledge seep out a little at a time or else it gets creepy. It's like if I know how to dribble a basketball between my legs, but I do it every time I bring the ball down court, what are people going to say?"

"Man, that guy sure can dribble?"

"No. They're going to say 'this guy's a showboat'." Scott paused for his wisdom to settle in. It was time for another analogy. "It's like salt on your baked potato: A little bit goes a long way. The point is, you used too much salt on your essay." He referred back to the paper. "Okay, maybe you use only a '*posse* of turkeys'. Or maybe you just say 'I saw some turkey tracks'."

"Okay," John responded to preclude hearing any more

illustrations of the same point.

"You're a really smart guy," Scott said as he patted John on the shoulder. "When you figure out proportion and how to use what you know at the right time, you're going to make a million bucks."

Compared to most of the opinions he freely disseminated, Scott's words were pretty much on-track this time.

Chapter 10
OPTIONS

DURING THE YEAR-AND-A-HALF since Scott's separation from the Air Force, he had steadily adjusted to the loss of central vision in his right eye. Once in a while, however, the loss of his fighter pilot career and the limitations imposed by his visual handicap crowded out every other thought in his mind. Regret repeated like an old scratched vinyl record. At such times, melancholy enveloped him, and he surrendered to self-pity. Such a blue mood had fallen over him on a snowy night in February of 2000. Dan and John had left the house to attend a Thornton Prep hockey game.

Annette came to the Dan Hardin house to eat dinner with Scott. After dinner, she graded papers while Scott cleaned dishes. They started viewing a movie on television, but it was a stinker, so they turned the television off and sat in wing backed chairs by the fireplace watching flames dance in the fireplace. Annette poured a glass of wine and Scott nursed his usual – water neat. Scott admitted that he was in a slump and was feeling depressed.

"That's understandable," Annette said. "You had to give

up what you loved to do prematurely. But it was going to happen sooner or later. A staff assignment. Old age."

Scott listened to Annette thoughtfully.

"We have to deal with life the way we find it. I think about Trinette all the time. We were so close. Now she won't even write to me. I don't want it to be that way, but I have to deal with it the way it is."

Annette looked at Scott expecting a response. Scott just stared toward the fire. "You don't have to work in the hardware store the rest of your life. You can still read with your left eye. You could work in Daddy's bank. You could sell real estate. You could work as a pharmaceutical representative. You could be a stockbroker."

"I've thought about the brokerage thing," he said. He told her that he had registered for an on-line course in preparation for the Series 7 exam. "As long as the left eye holds out, I can do it."

That conversation spring-boarded Scott into action. He bought books on investing and trading and he worked his way through on-line tutorials on his desktop computer all through the winter and into the summer. His enthusiasm faded, however, when he discovered the onset of vision loss in his left eye during his daily Amsler Grid ritual. This raised the distinct possibility that he might lose central vision in both eyes before long. He suspended his flurry of tutorial work, and his investing books gathered dust on his book shelf unnoticed by everyone except John.

John's interest was tweaked one evening in June when he picked up a richly-bound book on options. He thumbed through the book while Scott sprawled on his back on his bed after a day of flattening his arches on the concrete floors of the hardware store.

"What's an option?" John asked.

"An option is a contract agreement that lets you buy or sell a stock at a given price for a certain amount of time in the future," Scott said, simplifying the concept a bit. "Options can give you a lot of leverage. For example, think about Clorox stock selling at $48. I buy forty of the front month $50 Calls for $0.30, an outlay of $1,200. 'Front month' means that a contract – usually for one hundred shares – expires in fewer than thirty days. Say the price of Clorox stock is bid up to $55 in the next two weeks. I sell all forty of the $50 calls for about $5.60 a share. What's four thousand times $5.60?"

"Over $22,000." They were in John's wheelhouse now.

"See? In two weeks you made almost nineteen times your money," Scott said. "Annualize your return by multiplying by 26...."

"Forty-eight thousand per cent?" John reckoned. "Wow!"

"Yeah, something like that. Compare that to buying $1,200 worth of Clorox shares. That $1,200 buys you only twenty-five shares. So when Clorox goes from $48 to $55 in two weeks, you make $175 profit. That's about fourteen per cent, or less than 400% annualized. Got it?"

"Sort of," John said with a curious smile. The part that got his attention was the comparison between the annualized returns of 48,000% for options versus 380% for the stock transaction. John couldn't wrap his mind around it right away. He needed time to work through what he was hearing. He examined the index of the book. Margin, leverage, intrinsic value, time premium, hedges, calls, puts, vertical spreads, calendar spreads, butterflies, and condors, the list went on. He could hardly wait to start reading the book.

"When you grow up, you can do all this stuff," Scott said encouragingly.

John had no intention of waiting until he had "grown up" to start reaping the fruits of options. In his mind, they had invented this stuff just for him. He knew he had a lot to learn. He absorbed the contents of the book like a sponge absorbing water. John found the link to Scott's tutorial web site and he located Scott's password for the site so he could do exercises, often for more than three hours a day all summer long, at no cost. John found a free web site that provided live streaming quotes for equities and options, and he began "paper trading" options at no cost to see how the various strategies played out. He studied historical charts for hours on end. The numbers spoke to him. Chart formations were intuitively meaningful to him.

John's paper profits boggled his mind. His paper trading was so successful that he became cautious about relying completely on the results he was seeing. On one hand, he couldn't wait to start trading for real; on the other, he sensed that what he had learned so far was just a corner of the big picture. In complete privacy, he continued trading make-believe options into the winter of his seventh grade year at Lockhart Middle School. His peers fooled around with football fantasy leagues while John made thousands of dollars of paper money trading options hypothetically. He increasingly reaped most of his daily pleasure in life from his imaginary successes in the solitary setting of his bedroom.

Corky and Paul noticed their friend's withdrawal, but

they said nothing to John about it. Dan and Scott saw that John was spending more time in his room than in the past, but they attributed his seclusion to his age. As Scott noted, it wasn't so long ago that Dan and Scott themselves were "teenage nut jobs".

John had been labeled a genius because of his formidable memory. If he could recall on command that Calcium's symbol is Ca, and its Atomic Number is 20, and it's Atomic Weight is 40.08, could walking on water be far behind? Any problem seemed solvable to a water-walker. John passionately wanted to trade options for real, to replicate in the real world what he was accomplishing in the make-believe world of paper money.

John had overheard his father discussing declining margins at the hardware store. The big-box hardware retailers were steadily increasing their market share at the expense of Hardin's Hardware. Dan had expressed doubts that the store could remain profitable for even five years longer. If the store failed, where would Scott find a job? He had given up on getting his broker's license. Who would employ a blind person? John – a hero straight out of an Ayn Rand novel — believed he could make a difference.

The last traces of infantile omnipotence in a run-of-the-mill teenager – a Corky or a Paul – were all but stomped out by realities such as parental carping, poor academic grades, and bullying by the likes of Raymond Delacroix. Life's hard facts had only infrequently visited John, however, so traces of grandiosity remained.

The absence of John's Grandmother Hardin by death and John's mother by desertion caused his grandfather and father to compensate by reinforcing John's obsessive habits unwittingly. John's family, including his Grandparents Laval, wanted to shield him from life's hard knocks by tolerating his overactive world of dreams in which John reigned as a heroic being. In reality, he was ill-prepared to deal with dangers such as bankruptcy of the hardware store or unemployment of Scott. John's latent infantile omnipotence powered his search for a heroic solution to these threats to his idealized world.

If only John were old enough, he could generate income to solve Dan's and Scott's problems. He believed he had the power. An investor had to be eighteen years old to open a brokerage account. John was thirteen. John's immediate problem was his age. How was the genius going to make five years go away?

The solution came to John like links in a chain. The first chain link presented itself as John was surfing the Internet looking for cheap books on option trading. A pop-up advertisement touting a book on trusts appeared on his screen. It was designed for people who knew nothing about trusts. John qualified. He bought the book and read it cover-to-cover. He found a web site that contained examples of trust documents. The sum of these chain links evolved into a life-changing plan. It was an original though not overly legal plan that John set into motion right after his thirteenth birthday in March.

The first step was a windfall completely outside of John's control. John's Grandparents Laval gave him a birthday gift of a savings account in the Bank of Caledonia. To John's astonishment, the balance of his new account was $5,000. Being a capitalist, John entered in his journal that this $5,000 gift had soared to the top of his chart of coolest gifts ever, bumping his Davy Crockett jacket and cross-country skis down a notch. Over the years, John had accumulated cash savings of more than $1,000 from doing odd jobs like walking dogs, stacking firewood, and washing cars. He rarely spent a dime, so the cash had kept piling up in his secret hiding place – an empty shoe box in his bedroom closet. When John emptied the shoe box and deposited the accumulated cash into his new savings account, his balance soared to $6,250.

The second step in John's plan was to create a revocable living trust. John wasn't trying to minimize taxes or to avoid probate. His only interest in creating the trust was to establish an entity with a Tax Identification Number that could own a brokerage account to enable John to trade stocks and stock options. Once the brokerage account was open and funded, John was able to sign in to the account on-line and conduct trading as if he were Dan, trustee of the trust. As soon as John turned eighteen, he planned to open a personal brokerage account to receive the trust's assets when he terminated the trust. The plan had to work undetected for five years.

Normally, a revocable living trust doesn't file a tax return under the name of the trust, because dividends, interest, and capital gains are treated as though they were received by the grantor. John didn't want to file a personal tax return, however, for fear of focusing a spotlight on his secret. He planned to file a tax return for the trust as if it were an _ir_-revocable trust, thereby paying taxes on trust capital gains. The IRS benefited by receiving taxes at a rate of 35% instead of John's personal rate, a fraction of that rate. An audit might uncover the error, but the result of correcting the error would be a large refund to John (as he served his prison term). By paying taxes at the highest possible rates, John created a disincentive for the IRS to audit his returns.

John styled the trust The Liberty Revocable Trust. John Wesley Hardin was the grantor. He named Daniel Lee Hardin as Trustee and Scott Harrington as Successor Trustee. John named himself as beneficiary and Annette Laval as contingent beneficiary. Of course, Dan, Scott, and Annette knew nothing about these designations.

He planned to loan some of his savings by electronic transfer from the Bank of Caledonia to Tremont Savings and then to the trust's brokerage account. Privacy laws should shield his account balance from the eyes of Grandfather Laval. John planned to repay the loan with interest as soon as he had built up sufficient capital in the trust to constitute the seed money for future options trading. One of the benefits of electronic fund transfers over paper checks was that he didn't need his father's signature as trustee for electronic fund transfers. Even though the plan smelled like fraud, the word "fraud" made John very uncomfortable, so rationalization transported the distasteful concept way out to the back of the parking lot of his mind.

"Forgery" also had an unpleasant odor to John's olfactory receptors, so he devised a workaround that seem slightly less foul. Two witnesses to the grantor's signature were needed on the trust, but John was not required to file the trust in the public record and trust signatures were not required to be notarized. To avoid the heinous crime of forgery, John invented a technique he called "switching". This technique was less like forgery and more like – here we go again, he thought — fraud. Forgery now accompanied fraud out back in the remote mental parking lot created by John's need to justify what he was doing. John further rationalized his actions by convincing himself that Tom Sawyer would have done the same thing.

To enable the switching procedure, John prepared a personal will on 8½" by 14" paper. The page numbers were printed at the very bottom of the fourteen-inch-long paper.

"In the event of my death, I leave all my possessions to Daniel Lee Hardin and Scott Harrington including, but not limited to, the possessions listed herein." The list that filled all the rest of page one was extensive: Lacrosse stick, lacrosse helmet, football, cross-country skis, alpine skis, ski boots, ice skates, tennis racket, books, music collection, CD player, bicycle, etc. At the top of Page Two was a signature block for John to sign and two witness signature blocks for Dan and Scott to sign. He presented the document to them for their review and signature one night after dinner.

"Do you know something we don't know?" Dan asked, as he read the word "will".

"Yeah," Scott asked, "are you taking up sky-diving without a parachute?"

"I don't like loose ends," John answered.

"Really, John," his father insisted, "is everything okay?"

"Dad, everything's fine. I was reading an article about wills. It said you can't be too careful."

In the spirit of good humor, Dan and Scott signed the document.

"Crazy kids," Dan whispered to Scott.

Back in his secret operations center, his bedroom, John then used a paper cutter to reduce the fourteen-inch-length of Page Two to eleven inches. When he ran the trust document through the printer using 8½" by 11" paper, the trust pages showed a sequence of six pages, and the signature of the grantor and the witnesses now appeared on Page Six. John didn't like doing business this way, but he didn't know how else to enable option trading *now*, not five years in the future. John filled out an IRS Form SS-4, and the trust Tax Identification Number came back to him within a week.

John took the third step in his plan on a Saturday morning when Dan and Scott were working at the hardware store. John opened Dan's "Green Book", a notebook packed with Dan's proprietary information and documents such as his marriage certificate, Dan's and John's birth certificates, the death certificate of Dan's mother, Dan's Princeton diploma, and Dan's life insurance policy. John found a reference page containing all of his father's accounts and passwords. Using the information, John signed on to Dan's brokerage firm site. Dan had two modestly funded accounts, a Keogh Retirement Plan and a brokerage account containing an S&P 500 Index Exchange Traded Fund and a short-term bond fund. John printed out his father's account profile page.

John opened a savings account in his own name at Tremont Savings, Andrew Gleason's bank. He withdrew $2,000 from his savings account at the Bank of Caledonia to fund the Tremont Savings account. Next, John went on the Internet to a brokerage firm different from his father's and printed out application pages for setting up a trading account.

He filled out the pages of the application in the name and Tax Identification Number of The Liberty Revocable Trust. He enabled electronic deposits and withdrawals between the brokerage account and his bank savings accounts. He indicated that the Trustee of The Liberty Revocable Trust, Dan, had eight years of options trading experience and he requested the highest level of option trading authority, which permitted him to write naked options, trade complex strategies, and trade exchange traded funds that used derivatives such as futures contracts and swap agreements to mirror index performance. He listed the objective of the trust as "aggressive". Then, John laid low for the month of May.

His seventh grade year was wrapping up and blessed summer was on its way. He stayed awake at night contemplating what to say if his nefarious conduct were unveiled. His intent was not to break the law. His objective was to break the bank. He was more excited about this operation than anything he had done in his life. But he also was fearful that a sledge hammer might come crashing down to splinter his world.

John attended an end-of-school cookout hosted by Joe T. and Joyce Harrington. In addition to his grandparents, Annette, Dan, and Scott also attended. Joe T. made gin-and-tonics for everyone except John and Scott. Joe T. handed John a tonic-and-tonic with two slices of lemon and he poured a glass of water with three lemon slices for Scott. Apparently, in Joe T.'s mind, the less booze in your drink the more lemon slices you got. John felt like just another adult in the conversations that floated like bubbles in the late spring breeze. John sipped his tonic and thought smugly, if only they knew. That thought barely preceded Grandfather Laval's comment that suggested he *did* know.

"Bank deposits are up significantly," he said to Joe T. "Credit spreads are favorable and people are flush with cash." He winked at John. "I think the outlook for banks is good."

John froze. Grandfather Laval knew! The following thoughts raced through John's head in a matter of nanoseconds: Perhaps John could throw himself at his grandfather's mercy. He could face disgrace right there in front of his whole family. He had already kind of forged and created a kind of fraudulent entity, maybe he could kind of lie, too, in a kind of package deal. Deny everything. Or he could admit everything and then lie by claiming to write an article about under-age skullduggery on the Internet. Was it better to confess than to be unmasked? Perhaps he could admit everything and get a plea bargain like on television. Instead of any of those options, John sat still and winked back at his grandfather. Exactly nothing happened.

To John's amazement, June arrived and his world still hadn't collapsed. He signed in to the trust brokerage web site and saw that his $2,000 electronic transfer had been received and was carried as a $2,000 credit balance in The Liberty Revocable Trust's trading account. He moved another $2,000 from his Bank of Caledonia savings account to his Tremont Savings account and, then, to The Liberty Revocable Trust account, so the net asset value of the trust brokerage account was $4,000. It was time for John's first option trade.

He had spent three days reviewing charts and focusing on price action, volume, and short interest before selecting symbol ARUN, a stock that had fallen like a dropped knife for several days. On June 16, 2001, John saw ARUN hit its low for the day at $22.53. When John pulled the trigger on his first trade, his hand was shaking like a tuning fork. He carefully entered the data for the trade and clicked the mouse button. He sold-to-open five July $22.50 Puts naked for $1.50, netting a credit of about $750. Immediately after that trade had filled, he bought-to-open eleven July 25 Calls for $0.60, a net cost of about $660. His second trade was filled in fewer than thirty seconds.

John wasn't sure, but he believed he had established a position called something like a naked ratio risk reversal. It was only a momentary bother that he didn't know the name of the strategy or if it even *was* a strategy. John's immediate feeling was elation. Then a massive wave of worry surged over him. It felt less like inundation and more like drowning. He checked his margin balance and realized that the trade had consumed virtually all the margin available to him. He faced forced liquidation if the underlying stock decreased in value. Everything was at risk.

His entire body was shaking. John felt weak in the legs. His image in the mirror was pale even though it was early summer and he already had a tan from mowing lawns. He didn't know where all the blood in his body had gone, but it certainly wasn't in his head. Feeling sick to his stomach, he lay down on his bed and listened to the pounding of his heart.

Fortunately, ARUN started to *increase* in value. Each day as John checked the streaming quotes, he felt a little more relieved as the price line moved up and to the right. He fed on the excitement. It was the most exhilarating sensation he had ever experienced. Playing Napoleon was nothing compared to this sense of euphoria. On July 7, when ARUN spiked up to $31.10, John closed out the position. He bought-to-close the five Puts for $0.20, netting a gain of about $650. Then he sold-to-close the eleven Calls for $6.25, netting a gain of about $6,215. The moment the orders were filled, he felt ten tons lighter. His exposure to the naked puts was over, and he made a vow to shun naked positions in the future.

John's trust brokerage account had grown from $4,000 to $10,865 in twenty-one days. He idly calculated that if he repeated that kind of gain for the rest of the year, he might be sitting on more than $56,000! Of course, he couldn't do any such thing, but it was marvelous to roll the numbers around in his head and on his scratch pad. As soon as the funds had cleared, he moved $4,000 plus $9.21 interest back to his Bank of Caledonia savings account. If his Grandfather Laval should happen to look at his balance, all he would see is that it had increased from $5,000 to $6,260 plus whatever bank rate interest had accrued. That transfer of funds left about $6,800 in The Liberty Revocable Trust brokerage account. That was his seed money for what he believed was his destiny, to trade his way to riches.

For almost a week-and-a-half, John reverted to working as a cutter of lawns and washer of automobiles. He savored the unforgettable sweet aroma of his first trading success. During his non-working hours, he pored over on-line tutorials and reread the options book. It seemed that he learned something every day. What he loved most about his newest obsession was that no one knew anything about what he was doing. He was a clandestine operative!

The stock that caught his eye next was Beazer Homes, symbol BZH. He made his move on July 18 by establishing a bullish put spread and buying-to-open eight calls, specifically the August $110 calls. He established the position for a net debit of about $2,400. This time, he wasn't naked the short puts; the most he could lose if the stock took a dive was about $5.40 a share, some $4,350. Once again, he was fortunate. BZH climbed as high as $122.40, and John bailed out of the position ten days before expiration, netting a gain of about $5,750.

About the same time, John bought fifty long puts on the stock of Crown Castle International, symbol CCI. He bought-to-open the August $12.50 Puts when the stock was at $15.05; he bought them for only $0.15, or a total debit of about $750. In about a fortnight, CCI dove as low as $9.60. John closed his position when the stock hit $10, and he realized a gain of $13,300. The net asset value (NAV) of his trust account was up to $25,800.

Amazon was in the process of spiraling downward, eventually by thirty-nine percent. John cleared an $11,000 profit going long short-term puts. Priceline.com was in a similar frightening nose dive, and the young options guru nailed down $17,600 in profits in a single trade that he closed in early August. He wrote a closing cryptic note in his journal that night: "NAV $54,400".

In early August, John caught Beazer Homes in a swoon from $128 a share to $99 a share, and he pocketed a gain of $14,300. He made another $16,200 on American Tower when AMT shares dove from almost $16 to less than $10 a share. He rode the decline of Priceline.com in September from $31 to $11 a share, and his net gain was $23,500. Diary entry: "NAV $105,400." It might have been higher, but John abandoned two bearish positions in WTXX and LDNG when they blasted upward on a short squeeze in September. He lost about $5,000 on each position.

John's eighth grade classes were in session at the end of August, so he couldn't devote as much time to searching out stock candidates and entering trades. The only time he had available for business was the last hour of trading from three o'clock to four o'clock. Nevertheless, he rode the wave of descending stocks by establishing bearish vertical spread positions usually for no more than two weeks' duration, and the profits kept piling in. He did put on a few "stinko" spreads, but he was increasingly adept at bailing out before the maximum losses were realized. By Christmas vacation, the trust NAV was over $183,000.

His adventure in options trading had been so successful that it slowly altered the way he saw himself. Frankly, he felt superior to his classmates. His interest in them and their lives had waned as his trading profits had expanded. Corky Gleason and Paul Bruguiere didn't bother to invite him to meet up after school, because John was always busy. His thrilling secret nourished him in a way that no other experience ever had.

John wondered why he should be so fortunate, so special. He had always felt special. His father and grandfather praised him. Teachers praised him. The parents of other children praised him. He could slide in and out of the identities of Napoleon and Crockett because he felt like he was in their league. John felt that he was destined to be a great man.

As Christmas approached, his thoughts strayed to the nativity of Christ. Those thoughts, in turn, raised the question of Christ's return to Earth. Perhaps Jesus was already here among us. Christ's first coming had been under the parental protection of a simple carpenter. Why couldn't Christ return as the son of a hardware merchant? Was it possible that John himself was the Messiah? The concept came to him in a dream, and the possibility left him breathless. Even with odds of four billion to one (assuming Jesus' return as a man), there was a chance.

It required a mighty healthy ego to suggest such a thing out loud, but as long as he kept his thoughts private, he could consider any possibility. John knew he was a good person. A review of the Ten Commandments revealed that he was home free on most of them. Certainly "adultery", "idolatry", "blasphemy", "murder", and "theft" were not a problem. "Deception" was probably a stain on his vestments, so to speak, but he intended to clear that up when he turned eighteen. He was only *renting* the lie.

Among the Seven Cardinal Sins, two were possible thorny areas – "greed" and "pride". Did his obsession with net asset values constitute "greed"? He gave himself a partial bye on this one, because he didn't intend to spend the money on himself. He intended to use it for the benefit of his family. "Pride" could be a show-stopper, because he admitted privately to feelings of grandeur among his peers. He made a resolution to be more humble. He also made a note in his diary to revisit the Ten Commandments and the Seven Cardinal Sins from time-to-time to see how he was measuring up.

John had once asked his father what he thought about the Ten Commandments.

"I'm a big fan," Dan had said.

John had asked Scott the same question as Dan's answer left a little room for expansion.

"I just try to remember that Moses didn't call them the Ten Suggestions," Scott had replied. "My problem is I give myself waivers when it's not convenient to follow the Ten Commandments." The process of working around deception, pride, and greed gave John insight into what Scott was talking about.

An issue that also needed attention was the Scripture verse that says that a camel can pass through the eye of a needle easier than a rich man can enter the Kingdom of God. If he kept making money, that could be a serious problem. Still, he hadn't conclusively ruled out the possibility that he could be the Messiah. He opened a line of questioning with Scott one evening just before Christmas as he and Scott decorated their Christmas tree.

"Scott, you believe in Jesus, right?"

"Yes, I do," Scott answered as he adjusted tiny colored lights on the boughs of the slightly misshapen but completely natural-looking fir John had selected.

"Have you ever thought that you might be the second coming of Jesus?"

Scott looked at John in amazement. "Is that a serious question?" John nodded. "I can assure you that, even though I've had an inflated opinion of myself for most of my life, I've never thought I could be Jesus. Why, do you think *you* might be Jesus?"

After some thought, John said, "I don't think I'm perfect enough."

Scott chuckled to himself before he said, "Well, I'm glad you're close enough to perfect to at least be in the running. You've got me beat on that one." Scott watched John attach ornaments to branches of the tree. This John Wesley Hardin was one amazing young man. The Creator made only one copy of this one, Scott thought.

"I'll tell you something straight to your face." Scott said.

"What's that?"

"You never stop giving me reasons to respect you and to love you, and I always will."

Scott's words had a strong impact on John. A sense of well-being filled him. His eyes moistened as he gazed directly into Scott's face. John didn't find the voice or presence of mind to respond, but he believed that Scott knew that he loved him in return.

John examined his own reflection in the glass display case on his teacher's desk. John's fascination with his own image reminded him of a bird that had perched on the rearview mirror of his father's car for a week the previous spring. John had been unable to determine whether the cardinal was admiring himself or trying to frighten off a perceived intruder, but the befuddled bird had pecked at his image for hours each day. John was as dedicated a narcissist as any cardinal as he studied his reflection in the display case. He thought, what's not to like? His piercing blue eyes, high cheek bones, square jaw, blond hair, and proportioned features led to one conclusion: He was handsome.

John shifted his attention to Rita Fontaine sitting to his left. Rita's jittery bladder days and tardy trips to the toilet were behind her. As far as John knew, her undergarments these days were as dry as the Mojave Desert. In the past, during recesses at Brighton School, Rita had followed John around at a distance. She wasn't exactly a stalker, but she followed him around enough for him to notice.

John carefully observed her stubby nose, flat face, protruding ears, muddy eyes, and thick ankles. She was more plough horse than thoroughbred. Her homely looks and nervous disposition made her a target of ridicule by insensitive classmates like Raymond Delacroix. It seemed unfair to John that Rita should be so short of attractive features and personality while others – himself, for example – were so fortunate. He stole another glance at his reflection in the pane of glass and back to Rita.

In the middle of John's comparative features contemplation, Rita happened to look to her right, directly into his eyes. Surprised and pleased that John's attention was focused on her, Rita smiled as lovely a smile as she could muster. John produced a movie-star quality grin in return. This caused Rita to blush and smile even more widely. It was as close to radiant as she might ever get. John was amazed by the pleasure Rita got from his simple attentions. He brought the subject up at home that night when his father was in his reading chair.

"Hey, Dad, you know Rita, a girl in my class, right?"

"You mean that chubby, kind of plain girl – Fontaine's daughter?" Dan responded.

Maybe his father was the wrong man for this discussion. John decided to wait for Scott to get home.

"What about her?" Dan asked.

"Nothing." Then, because he had to say something, John added, "She doesn't wet her pants anymore."

"That's a good thing," Dan said as he resumed reading his book.

When Scott came home and went to the kitchen to rustle up some food, John followed him and told him how Rita positively glowed when he smiled at her. Scott told John that most people are insecure. Predictably, Scott built a metaphor.

"Insecure people are like boats adrift. To secure a boat, a dock's not enough. You need a line to secure the boat to the dock. You were the line. Good on you."

"Hmmm."

"Sometimes, we go adrift ourselves. Then we need someone else to be the line to secure us."

John pledged himself to be a line to bring security to an insecure world. Making Rita so happy with one simple grin, he imagined the bliss he could bring to the needy if he put a little effort into it!

Chapter 11

RETIREMENT

AFTER CHRISTMAS, THE winds howled steadily out of the northwest across Lake Tremont for three days in a row. Only twenty inches of snow had fallen thus far in the winter season, so the wind had swept the ice clean except for a few mounds of snow, the largest of which had drifted up against the northwestern side of the bob houses on the bay. The ice was transparent, its surface buffed to a fine gloss by the blowing snow. In water depths of up to eight feet, rocks on the sandy bottom of the lake were visible through the ice. When the winds abruptly slackened to calm on Saturday, John invited Corky Gleason and Paul Bruguiere to go ice skating on the bay. The two invitees met at John's house at ten o'clock. Scott and Annette made brunch for the trio of thirteen-year-olds and ensured the boys were layered in wool and fleece before allowing them to troop out the back door.

"Where's your safety necklace?" Scott asked John. "I shouldn't have to remind you."

"I've got mine," Corky said. Corky seized every opportunity to stand out among his peers, because those opportunities occurred so rarely. The twin ice picks at either end of a two-foot leather tether coupled to form a circle – a safety necklace — for ease of wearing around the neck. A skater falling through the ice could separate the two ice picks and use one in each hand to drive into the ice surface to get traction sufficient to pull himself out of the water.

"I don't have one," Paul said.

Scott loaned his necklace to Paul while John went upstairs to find his own. Properly equipped, they exited through the back entrance, across the snow-covered back lawn, and onto the icy surface of Lake Tremont.

Scott poured coffee for himself and Annette and he made fresh pancakes baptized in maple syrup and crowned with wild blueberries. Annette entertained Scott by reading aloud her students' attempts to use similes and metaphors to describe their "study buddies".

"'Jan's eyes are like two blue circles with black dots in the middle.' That's from Bobby Torrington."

"Who's Jan?"

"Jan Dubois, the drama queen of the class. Her motto is 'I talk, therefore I am.'"

"Let me hear Jan's simile description of Bobby."

"'Bobby's cheeks are like two balloons in the Macy's Parade with freckles blasted all over them by a shotgun.'"

Scott laughed. "Ten-year-olds must wonder why we have similes and metaphors. They must wonder why we don't just say what we mean."

"Plenty of thirty-somethings must wonder the same thing," Annette said.

Scott moved close to Annette from behind. He put his

hands on her shoulders and kneaded her shoulders and upper back. He felt the muscles in her upper back relax with his massage.

"The thing I wonder is how I can feel so close to you but never tell you," he said.

"I'm not the easiest person to get close to."

Scott wrapped his arms around her and kissed her neck. Like a score of times previous, Scott left his thoughts unspoken. He released Annette and perched himself on a stool at the kitchen counter. Annette sighed. She wondered if the roadblock to intimate communication between them was a behavior learned more than a dozen years ago while parked in the *War Wagon* as it swayed in rhythm with the back-seat thrashings of Dan and Trinette.

"We had a little drama down at the store yesterday," Scott said. "Andrew Gleason's wife slipped and fell in front of the store."

"Hurt?"

"Don't know. She's got a protective layer of blubber like a sperm whale."

"She's a *big* lady," Annette agreed. "She hatched eleven pounds worth of Corky without a Cesarean."

"She howled like she was being murdered. Dan rode in the ambulance with her to the hospital, and he said she didn't stop screaming until they gave her an injection. He said it was like tranquilizing a rhino on National Geographic." Scott nibbled at the last pancake. "Have you seen how many houses he's bought up around town?"

"Gleason? Over twenty."

"Gleason'll make a fortune. Bankers are supposed to

make money."

Annette made small talk about banking and bankers. She mentioned that her father was retiring in May after forty-two years at the Bank of Caledonia. Scott said that his father also was retiring in about a month. His replacement was an administrator from Connecticut.

"Two old fogies with time on their hands," Annette said. "I wonder what they'll do."

"They can't play pinochle every night."

Annette and Scott sipped their coffees and continued to watch the action on the glassy surface of Caledonia Bay. Scott's view was gauzy; Trinette's crisp and clear. She distinctly made out where the boys' skate marks etched the ice in arcs and decreasing radius curls. Ice shavings at the end of their tracks showed where they had made hockey stops. Three very different body shapes – slender Paul, tall John, and chubby Corky – flew around the ice unpredictably. They used old broom and rake handles for hockey sticks and a tennis ball for a hockey puck. Their game had no goal posts, no side lines, and no discernible rules.

"Annette," Scott asked cautiously, "do you remember the night we were together on the sailboat?"

"Yes," she said. Neither of them took their eyes off the lake.

"Well, I...sometimes...."

"You don't have to say anything, Scott. It was a long time ago." She had mentally previewed this imminent conversation many times.

"Well, I just want you to know...."

Scott was interrupted by Dan who entered through the

front doorway noisily. He flung his coat and hat onto the foyer table and took off his snow boots.

"Greetings," Dan said. "How about some coffee for a working man?"

Scott removed a coffee cup from a cabinet and filled two-thirds of the cup with steaming coffee. He gave it to Dan and pointed to the pancake griddle. Dan shook his head.

"No, I'm all set," Dan said. "We're getting sued."

"For what?"

"For Mrs. Gleason's slip-and-fall yesterday." Dan sipped his coffee. "I saw Andrew Gleason leaving Koeneki's office thirty minutes ago."

Chuck "Canuck" Koeneki was a local attorney of Canadian origin who was well known in town for taking any case that walked in the door, especially a personal injury case.

"It's Saturday," Annette said, "they could be working on a real estate deal or…anything, really."

"Or starting a weight-watcher's chapter," Scott offered. Dan scowled at him, because he wasn't in the mood for snappy repartee.

"No," Dan told them. "There was a kid taking digital pictures of the sidewalk, the street, and Mrs. Gleason's car less than an hour after the meat wagon hauled her sorry carcass off to the emergency room. We're getting sued."

"Why aren't you at work?" Annette asked.

"I'm looking for company insurance papers. Dad said he gave the new policy to me to review two months ago. I have no recollection of it at all. Must be upstairs in my study." Dan looked out the back window at the three boys skating on the ice. "Is that John and his posse?"

"Yeah," Annette said. "Corky and Paul."

"If Corky smacks a puck into John's face, we sue Gleason."

"Don't spend your award, yet," Scott said, "they're using a tennis ball for a puck."

Dan carried his coffee cup up to his study and searched for the company insurance policy for half an hour before giving up. When Dan returned to the kitchen from upstairs, Annette had left the house to go home and Scott was cleaning up.

"Scott, do you remember mailing a company insurance renewal packet back in November?"

Scott looked out at the bay while he tried to remember. "No. I'd remember that."

"I don't remember doing it, either," Dan said. "All I could find in my study was a copy of the policy that expired in November. I'm wondering if Dad got 'em confused." He finished the last drops in his coffee cup. "What if we don't have a policy in force?"

"We're screwed."

During the days that followed, John and Corky remained oblivious to the legal wrangling of their parents. As snow began to accumulate on Lake Tremont, the sons of the litigants and their classmate Paul tried shoveling a sixty-by-one-hundred-foot mini-rink on the lake. The "popcorn" surface of the ice took the fun out of skating, however, so they moved their skating sessions indoors to the village skating rink.

When school restarted after Christmas vacation, John resumed his habitual sprint home at 2:30 each afternoon to squeeze in an hour of trading and an hour of analysis afterwards. He still had time to finish his homework before Scott and Dan came home from the hardware store. Most of the time, John hedged his positions to allow him to bail out of trades quickly enough to avoid severe losses when they turned against him. John answered a telephone call from a representative of his brokerage house on the Tuesday afternoon after January's options expiration.

"This is Dieter Reichart," the broker said. He identified his firm. "May I speak to Daniel Hardin."

Several thoughts raced through John's head simultaneously: Why had he listed the home telephone for the contact number for the trust? Had Dan received a call like this in the past? Had John's trading scheme been revealed to his father? Could he pass himself off as Dan?

"This is Dan," John said.

Dieter asked John for the tax ID number for the trust account as authentication before explaining that some calls assigned the previous Saturday required borrowing shares at a cost of 6.2% if the trustee of the account – Dan, played by John – wanted the brokerage to book the short position. John committed to go online and buy-to-cover the shares right away to prevent having to pay interest on the short position.

As soon as John had filled the order, he expunged the Dan Hardin home land-line telephone number from the trust's brokerage account. He had to ensure that no similar calls got through to his father in the future. As John replaced his home telephone number with his own cell phone number, he wondered how many other details like this one were lying around like land mines waiting to be detonated.

John's investment decisions continued to be rewarded. He remained bearish in all but a few trades, and some of the positions he took resulted in big profits. His best trade on an appreciating stock price was a risk reversal position he established in Procter & Gamble. He benefited from the lion's share of a move in price from $37.38 to $43.92 to the tune of $10,700. As always, he wrote his net asset value in his journal: "NAV $204,422."

He profited nicely on a bear put spread that he established in Merck. The stock fell from $64.89 to $53.75 in less than a month, and he netted a profit of $7,200. When Qualcomm dove from $31.13 down to $15.52, John profited by $26,100. Similarly, Cree Incorporated fell in a major way from $33.32 to $16.32, and John was able to ride the dive into a gain of $28,000. His biggest profit of all came when he bought-to-open 60 front-month Halliburton $10 Put contracts when HAL was at $11.20. HAL fell to $5.47, and John bailed out of the position near the bottom, gaining $30,100.

John found it difficult to control the desire to tell someone how successful his trading had been. He reminded himself, however, that secrecy had been his only viable alternative from the moment he had initiated this quasi-legal scheme. If his relatives, classmates, or teachers detected a bounce in his step or a glow in his complexion, they credited it to good diet or rigorous exercise. John, however, knew that the real reason for his contentment and confidence was the jolt of excitement he enjoyed every trading day. Once again, John made a journal entry, his last in the month of January: "NAV $317,557."

His bearish forecast for the markets had really paid off.

He extrapolated his annualized return on investment, and he came up with staggering numbers: He calculated his worth at $52 million by the time he was twenty-five years old. At the age of thirty-five, he figured he could buy the State of New Hampshire. First, though, he had to make a million dollars. Happiness was a million dollars.

To defend Hardin's Hardware in the negligence action brought against it by Mrs. Gleason, Benjamin Hardin hired a local attorney named Fred Cummings. Benjamin didn't exactly retain Fred, but it had been Benjamin's practice for many years to go to Fred for all of his legal needs. Fred's most distinguishing physical feature was a bright red cauliflower nose that hung onto his ruddy face like a stalactite. His rhinophyma affliction was the most severe and widely-recognized case in the Lakes Region. Scott, a layman in medical matters, estimated Fred's blood pressure to be in the neighborhood of 400 over 220.

During this Era of Correctness, in which smoking cigars and drinking multiple pints of Guinness in local watering holes were frowned upon, Fred did both frequently. He couldn't smoke inside the bars any more, but in his office, where he reigned supreme, the atmosphere was as thick as the exhaust of a coal-burning power plant. As a connoisseur of pints, he was such a regular that his bar stool at the Caledonia Inn justly could have born a brass plaque with his name on it. Despite his high blood pressure and his drinking habits, Fred was a competent advocate.

Benjamin, Dan, and Scott met in Fred's office near the end of January. Benjamin was in a vulnerable mental state, because he, like so many others, had watched his retirement account and equity investments take a walloping when the Dot.com collapse hit Wall Street. Moreover, Benjamin was deeply anxious about the fiscal health of the store. Fred skimmed through the niceties and dove right in to review the facts relevant to Mrs. Gleason's claims.

"Okay," Fred said, "at 10:15 a.m. on the Friday after Christmas Day, that's...uh, December 28, 2002, Mrs. Gleason bought some items in your store, left the store, and walked on the sidewalk toward her car parked in front of the store. She alleges that she slipped on a clear patch of ice on the sidewalk and fell before reaching her car. No witnesses." Fred looked up from his notes. "If anyone has a question or anything to add, interrupt me." The Hardin Hardware delegation nodded.

"The Gleasons had several photos taken about an hour after her fall. We have lots of photos that *we* took about *three* hours the fall, and that's because Benjamin wisely called my office right away and we sent a guy over with a camera. The temperature at ten in the morning was nineteen degrees Fahrenheit and the winds were northerly at fifteen to twenty knots. The sky was clear, no precipitation." Fred paused before continuing.

"The sidewalk had been shoveled and was clear of impediments except for a few icy areas smaller than four inches by twelve inches that appear to be the product of shoes or boots compressing snow onto the concrete surface and then being shaved away by a metal snow shovel. Who shoveled the side walk?"

"I did," Scott said. "The morning after Christmas. It

hadn't snowed since I shoveled."

"Okay," Fred continued, "the street in front of your store had been plowed Wednesday morning, and all that remained was a four-inch berm of snow in the gutter of the granite curb. In other words, the conditions on Friday were about normal for a winter day in Caledonia, even if the winds were stronger than usual."

"How bad was she hurt?" Dan asked.

Fred shuffled through his clutch of papers. "Left shoulder joint pain, left elbow joint pain, left wrist joint pain, bruised fingers on left hand, bruised left wrist, and bruised left forearm, left hip joint pain and bruising, and left knee joint pain," he read.

"No breaks?" Dan asked.

"Apparently no breaks or fractures."

"Now," Fred returned to his outline, "we need to pin this insurance thing down."

"I still haven't found the policy renewal," Benjamin said. "We've had the same carrier for over ten years, so renewal is pretty automatic. I've left three messages with the insurance agent, but he still hasn't returned my calls."

"Do you know for a fact that you *did* have a policy in force?"

"I can't be sure," Benjamin replied. "The old noggin isn't as sharp as it used to be." No one was smiling. "I can't remember returning the packet."

"Well, we really need to know," the lawyer said, "so focus on it."

"Done," Dan said. "You know, I noticed something in the ambulance. The ambulance suspension was pretty rough.

I mean the frost heaves felt like moguls, so things were bouncing around in the back. The stuff in her bag and in her overcoat pocket skidded across the floor along with the receipt. I put them all back into the Hardin's Hardware bag. I noticed that the light bulbs and the two bags of anti-ice salt were printed on the receipt, but the 21-piece drill bit set was not."

"So," Fred asked, "you're saying your cashier didn't ring up the drill bits?"

"No. The drill bits came out of her coat pocket. I think she shop-lifted the drill bits.

Chapter 12
SUMMER 2002

JOHN'S *MOT DU JOUR* through the month of May was "copesetic" – not the easiest word even for John to work into a conversation. Dan and Scott observed with amusement the lengths to which John went to fit "copesetic" into his speech.

"Ready, Einstein?" Dan asked John at breakfast on the first morning of his final exams.

"Copesetic," John replied.

"What'd he say?" Dan asked Scott.

"Yes."

"Good luck in English," Dan grumbled.

Scott had diagnosed John's logomania (infatuation with words) long ago. He and Dan tolerated John's word fetishes patiently as they did his fascination with numbers and collective groups of animals. When John unleashed the first of a barrage of uses of the word "module", Dan and Scott winked at one another. They braced for the stream of "modules" to come.

According to John's journal, May marked the end of another *module* of his life. John exited his Lockhart Middle

School *module* with a record of straight *A*'s, not a single day of absence, and not an instance of tardiness. In Northern New England, where the opening day of moose season is a rational excuse for skipping school, such perfect attendance was a rarity.

Corky Gleason's academic *module* lacked the luster of John's, but Corky was still scheduled to join John at Thornton Prep in August for the start of their new *module* – the ninth grade. Paul Bruguiere's Lockhart *module* was a strong testament to genetic influence on brain power. Not a single *A* grade appeared in Paul's transcript. It was if the letter *A* had been outlawed seconds before Paul's transcript was entered into the Lockhart computer system. Paul was grateful for the pair of lonely B grades he had received during his four-year brush with primary education. Like his father and uncle — Simon and Thomas — before him, Paul was headed for the vocational training program at Caledonia High School.

Labor Day was weeks away, however, and the three pals looked forward to a summer of relaxation. The change was least noticeable to Paul, whose approach to academics charitably could be called relaxed. The boys celebrated the arrival of summer with a sleep-over in John's tent in the Hardins' back yard. They jabbered late into the night comparing their summer jobs and slaughtering the telling of tired jokes.

Paul landed a job working as a grounds custodian at a music camp on an island in Lake Tremont. His duties involved raking pine needles from one spot to another to keep nature looking as natural as possible. He caught the U.S. Mail Boat from the Caledonia Town Docks Monday mornings to get to the island. Then, after raking pine needles and ogling female campers Monday through Friday, he made his way home to Thomas Bruguiere's house by Mail Boat on Saturday morning. He wasn't a slave, so he could choose to stay over the weekend at the camp if he wished. Corky and John agreed that this was a dream job.

"Cosmic *module*," John said.

Corky was delighted not to be looking for a job, because Mrs. Gleason was taking her only son to Italy for the month of July.

"Awesome *module*," John said.

"Italian girls are so hot." Paul pointed out this universally-known fact as a way to flatter Corky even further.

"Wicked hot," Corky agreed

It didn't take long for the three callow, would-be *aficionados* to exhaust their knowledge of the subject of hot Italian girls. Corky theorized that the United States should have annexed Italy as the fifty-first state after World War II to claim Italian girls, Italian cars, and Italian food as spoils of war. It may have been the first geopolitical statement ever to pass Corky's lips. When he got bogged down with the problem of how to arrange fifty-one stars on the blue field of the American flag, he abandoned the hypothetical notion. He promised to report back on any extraordinary hot girl sightings in Italy.

John's summer work schedule at Hardin's Hardware started at noon and ended at 8 p.m. on Wednesdays through Saturdays and at 5 p.m. on Sundays. This gave him ample time to enter his trades all day on Mondays and Tuesdays and from 9:30 a.m. until 11:30 a.m. Wednesdays through Fridays. He traded profitably all through the spring. He got pretty good at managing risk, meaning he avoided most moments of sheer terror at the expense of slightly lower profit margins. John became accustomed to the excitement of trading and he no longer tingled with the desire to tell someone about his big secret. His journal for the end of March reflected a NAV of $344,722. With profits came the duty to pay taxes.

His past experience of watching his father labor over personal income tax returns led John to start his tax research by navigating the Internal Revenue Service web site. His first official act was to file for an automatic extension into late summer of the deadline for filing the trust's tax return. John wrote a trust brokerage account check for $65,000 payable to the United States Treasury and affixed his much-practiced version of his father's signature as trustee.

John was too intimidated to prepare the trust's tax return himself, but he knew that using a tax preparer in Caledonia increased the chances of blowing the cover off The Liberty Trust secret. He needed an out-of-town tax preparer. At fourteen years of age, John was too young to get a driver's license, so driving to another village wasn't feasible. He didn't want to add motor vehicle violations to his list of offenses. The resolution to the problem came to John one Saturday morning in June as he reported early for work at Hardin's Hardware.

As he entered the store through the open front door, one prolonged blast of a boat horn announced the arrival of the *M/S Franklin Pierce* at the town docks. Tourists descended the boarding ramp in droves to scatter around the village buying trinkets they didn't need and consuming beers and fattening foods they certainly didn't need. After boarding new passengers, the *Pierce* was scheduled to cruise back up the lake to its home port of Dartford Parade before returning to Caledonia four hours later. John realized that the *Pierce* was a perfectly acceptable means of transportation to meet with a tax preparer away from Caledonia. John called a Ms. Janet Boyce, CPA, and made an appointment to meet in her Dartford Parade office two weeks hence.

Janet Boyce may not have been Dartford Parade's most successful tax preparer, but she surely was the homeliest. Her red hair reminded John of a frayed scouring pad. She was equipped with three chins — three rolls of fat lodged between her chin bone and her truncated neck. Because of her immense weight, wearing normal-sized clothing would have been an insult to common decency, so she wore a huge yellow cotton blouse the shape of a pup tent and baggy blue Tattersall pants the size of a small bedspread. John wondered only briefly where she found underwear of sufficient size to contain whatever was lurking beneath her pants. Her canvas deck shoes were stretched tight by her swollen feet that bulged over the outside of both shoes like mushrooms on tree stumps.

Fortunately, Janet Boyce's many positive qualities offset these negatives. First, Janet was jollier than St. Nicholas himself. If she had been any jollier, John would have suspected drug use. Second, she didn't ask a lot of questions, and, when she did, it didn't seem to bother her in the least that John answered most of them by saying, "I don't know". Third, Janet didn't ask for a copy of the trust document.

Fourth, Janet didn't ask why Trustee Daniel Lee Hardin was sending his fourteen-year-old son to bring the trust tax package to her office. Fifth, Janet didn't seem surprised at all when John asked her to direct any questions to him personally, because his father wanted him to learn about taxes. Sixth, Janet accepted without question the brokerage bundle containing Forms 1099, accounting of options trades, and statements of capital gains and losses, all of which were short term. Seventh, Janet said, "Wow, this is a high-risk portfolio. But it's clear-cut. I'll take care of this." Finally, Janet said, with a sparkle in her eye, "I see by these summaries that the trust did very well last year."

"That's what I heard."

After Janet finished preparing The Liberty Trust tax return, she called John to tell him that the trust's $65,000 payment more than covered the amount due to the IRS. She credited the modest refund toward next year's tax obligation. Janet was on the telephone when John showed up in her office on the following Monday. That gave him time to examine the completed tax return. He was surprised by its simplicity. He felt certain he could prepare the return himself the following year, using Janet's work as a template.

"How much does my father owe you?" John asked.

"Six hundred dollars."

The figure surprised him. It was three times the samples on the Internet. He didn't show his surprise, however, and he promised his father's payment in three days' time.

Janet was super-sized and she was jolly, but she wasn't stupid. She had been convinced from the time of her first meeting with John that he was not your garden variety teen-age punk. She deduced that he would be willing to pay a premium for heightened confidentiality. Her intuitive sense was confirmed. They shook hands, and John left Janet's office. What an unusual boy, she thought. What a big lady, he thought.

A Boston ophthalmologist performed the first laser surgery on Scott's left eye in the middle of June. Despite having lost almost all central vision in his right eye, nominal central vision in his left eye was lasting longer than predicted four years earlier. He invited Annette to dinner to celebrate the successful surgery. She accepted.

On Saturday night, Annette drove her car to the Harrington house and parked in the circular driveway. She walked across the wide lawn that led to the Harringtons' boat house. Down at the dock closest to the boat house, Scott was ready in his parents' twenty-six-foot runabout for the passage across Lake Tremont to a lakeside restaurant in Stableton Dykes, a village on the west side of the lake. Three-foot waves were not uncommon on Lake Tremont, but on this late June evening, winds were calm and the surface of the lake was placid. The evening run from Caledonia Bay to Stableton Dykes was a pleasant reminder of summers past. The couple exchanged only a word or two during the eight-mile journey to the restaurant. After securing the boat at the restaurant's docks, they walked inside the restaurant. They were among the first to arrive for dinner.

Annette ordered a glass of wine and Scott his iconic glass of water. As the sun arced slowly toward its eventual setting behind the mountains on the west side of Lake Tremont, Annette observed a procession of boats arriving at the restaurant docks. A steady stream of customers disembarked to fill the remaining tables of the restaurant.

"I'm worried about the hardware store," Scott said.

"The law suit?"

"Yeah. Benjamin let the insurance coverage lapse, so the store was uninsured when Mrs. Gleason went down. Fred Cummings showed us some jury awards in similar cases that topped two million dollars."

"Benjamin doesn't have that kind of money, does he?"

"No. Neither does the store. Neither does Dan. Benjamin doesn't seem to be bothered by it, thanks to dementia, but it's taking a toll on Dan."

"Why won't Andrew Gleason just let it go?"

"It's not in his DNA to let go. He's building his empire. He's the real estate king of Caledonia."

Scott ordered their meals and talked about his latest laser surgery.

"To vision," Annette said as she tipped her wine glass against Scott's water glass.

"To hindsight."

Scott could see barely more than a blurred image of Annette as she gazed out the window at sunset's brilliant colors reflected on the calm surface of the harbor, but he found her as attractive now as at any time in her life. Perceiving beauty involves more senses than sight alone, he thought. Annette was a graceful, lovely thirty-six-year-old woman. Her thick, brunette hair fell to her shoulders and surrounded a comely face that seemed little changed over the last ten years. She turned her gaze away from the lake to look directly at Scott's face.

"To hindsight?" she repeated. "What does that mean?"

It was like a word-association game for Scott: "Annette… hindsight." It sounded too much like a Dylan lyric from *Subterranean Homesick Blues* to say it out loud.

"Are you a 'hindsight' expert?" she asked.

"Some days, yeah. Sometimes I spend too *much* time looking backward."

"You're over the fighter pilot thing, right?"

"Mostly. What's the point of thinking about it? I learned that from Annette Laval. And, most of the time, that's exactly how I keep it. But when the memories come back, they come back hard."

"Which hurts most," Annette asked, "the thing that's gone or the longing never satisfied?"

"Dylan?"

"No."

"You remember a Dylan song called *John Wesley Harding*?" Scott asked.

"Sure."

"Is that where John's name came from?"

Annette smiled and nodded.

"You mean Trinette was chilling out listening to Bob Dylan and that's how she named John?" Scott asked.

"Pretty much."

Trinette being Trinette, he thought. They were well into their meals before Scott asked Annette another serious question.

"Have you ever been romantically interested in Dan?"

"I love Dan, of course," she said. "I have deep affection for him, but that's as far as it can go. I can't look at Dan without thinking of Trinette, and I doubt he can look at *me* without thinking of Trinette."

She steered the conversation back to Scott. She asked him if he was content long-term working in a hardware store.

"It doesn't seem like the best I can do, does it?"

"It depends on how you're measuring."

"Princeton's not going to include me on its list of distinguished graduates. I'm happy doing a simple job and living with Dan and John. I love that kid, and I love seeing you with him, too. Maybe this is all I need."

"John thinks the world of you," Annette said. "You're really good for him. If you help just one person the way you've helped John, you've done more in your lifetime than most people."

After their meal, they returned to the Harringtons' boat and cast off. Scott guided the runabout back toward the Harrington house in darkness so complete that the stars seemed to jump out of the sky. Scott laid a towel on top of the illuminated instrument panel to block the backlighting. He knew what 2,000 RPM sounded like without a gauge. Only the navigational lights and elevated aft mast light competed with the stars and lights of houses on the far shores.

Scott believed his night vision was better than his day vision, because his unimpaired peripheral vision was more dominant at night than his central vision. His depth perception was poor, however, so he cruised at a slow speed by setting the engine near 2,000 RPM to keep the hull off-plane but allow for stable steering. Annette backed him up as a look-out for buoys, islands, and other obstacles.

It was almost ten o'clock when Scott secured the run-about to the more easterly of the Harringtons' docks. He walked Annette to her car. Before he opened her door for her, he pulled her to him in a long embrace. When he kissed her, the memory of how she felt pressed against him that summer night fifteen years ago came to life. Annette kissed him gently and then turned to get into her car for her drive home to the Laval house.

"Could you drop me off at Dan's?" he asked.

"I could," she replied.

The Gleason versus Hardin's Hardware suit was shuffled around for six months on the desks of both the plaintiff's lawyer, Chuck "Canuck" Koeneki, and the defendant's lawyer, Fred Cummings. Both attorneys were open to settling the case, but each had reasons to avoid pressing too hard. The two lawyers were content to meet occasionally and to telephone one another a couple of times a month, because billable minutes were billable minutes, and they both believed there was a reasonable chance the case might just go away with no settlement at all.

Benjamin's failure to renew the insurance policy was a great embarrassment to him when he was lucid. On other days, he was unsure of the meaning of the word "insurance". Because of his oversight, the store was not protected from litigation at the time of Mrs. Gleason's unfortunate tumble. Although the absence of deep pockets might cool the ardor of the Gleasons' lawyer, the Gleasons themselves seemed to be undeterred and willing to press their cause of action hoping for a smaller claim against Benjamin's personal insurance coverage or against Benjamin himself.

Benjamin was unnerved by the law suit one day and blissfully unconcerned the next. He relinquished responsibility for all financial and insurance matters to Dan. Benjamin continued working as in the past, but he no longer felt confident in his judgment. Benjamin told his lawyer for the third time that he was willing to pay personally for Mrs. Gleason's medical bills, including the cost of the ambulance service, in the interest of making the whole thing go away.

Mrs. Gleason's injuries turned out to be less substantial than she first believed. No breaks, no fractures, no broken skin. The bruises documented in digital photographs were long gone by the end of January. The fourth time Mrs. Gleason bothered to attend rehabilitation sessions at the clinic in the middle of January was her last time. She was doing fine.

It wasn't absolutely clear that Mrs. Gleason actually had slipped on the sidewalk. During one fair-weather reenactment in front of both lawyers, Mrs. Gleason comically simulated toppling backward trying to step off the sidewalk onto the road surface over an imaginary four-inch berm of snow. Snow removal from curbs and streets was the responsibility of the town. It wasn't unusual for two-foot drifts to pile up on top of the curbs. File photographs from the *Caledonia Reporter* showed mounds as high as five feet in winters past. According to Fred Cummings, the routine methods of snow removal by businesses in the town promised to make negligence in the *Gleason vs. Hardin's Hardware* case difficult to prove.

The two attorneys agreed to a deposition attended by

Fred Cummings, "Canuck" Koeneki, Dan and Benjamin Hardin, Scott Harrington, Mr. and Mrs. Gleason, and Fred's secretary. The secretary turned on a recording device, and Fred began questioning Mrs. Gleason.

"Mrs. Gleason, you told us you bought some items in the hardware store. What items did you buy?"

"Light bulbs," she said looking toward the ceiling to sharpen her memory. "And two bags of salt so I could make our home sidewalk safe. I wanted to prevent any unfortunate soul from suffering a fall like mine." She spoke the last words piously. "I don't think I ever received those items from the emergency response people," she said in the voice of a wronged but conciliatory person.

"You bought nothing else from the hardware store?"

"No, nothing else."

"Did you know that your personal items are still being held at the hospital?"

"No. I've heard nothing." Andrew Gleason shifted uncomfortably in his chair like a man who has received two telephone messages telling him he could pick up his wife's possessions and who promptly forgot both messages.

"We can have those items picked up for you and brought to this office, if you like," Fred offered. Andrew coached his wife with a miniature shake of his head.

"Please don't bother. Andrew will fetch them for me."

Fred laid several pictures on the table in front of Mrs. Gleason.

"These pictures are from the security camera at the emergency room," Fred said as he slid a packet containing duplicate photos toward "Canuck" Koeneki. "Now, in this first one, is this your overcoat?"

"Yes, it is." Her coat was a Nordstrom's purchase, and she was proud of it.

"And this second photo shows light bulbs, two bags of salt, and a receipt, is that correct?"

"Yes."

"Now, *this* page is a magnified copy of the receipt in the photograph," Fred continued. "The packet of four light bulbs and the two bags of salt are itemized, and it shows that you paid for the items with a Visa card."

"Yes, I did." She carried seven credit cards in her purse, and she was proud of them, too.

"Now, this photo of your personal items turned in by the emergency responders shows an additional item, a twenty-one piece titanium drill bit set. Did you buy these drill bits?"

"No I did not." That was Version Number One.

"But Daniel Hardin and a paramedic observed the drill bit set fall out of your coat pocket during the ambulance ride to the emergency room," Fred pressed her as he gave "Canuck" copies of Dan's statement and the paramedic's report.

"They must be mistaken." Then, as if figuring the adverse odds of anyone believing that the two witnesses were both wrong, she interjected. "Actually, I do remember buying the drill bit set." That was Version Number Two.

"Oh, you *did* buy them?"

"Yes."

"That morning, at the same time you bought the light bulbs and the salt?"

"I can't be sure." Playing forgetful and vague always

worked so well with her husband that it was worth a shot here in this conference room with this lawyer sporting what had to be the biggest, reddest nose in Caledonia history. "It could have been from an earlier purchase." That was Version Number Three. Andrew Gleason was not enjoying this line of questioning.

"Here's an inventory of items delivered on Friday morning, that Friday morning, Mrs. Gleason," Fred said as he placed two copies of the inventory on the table. "Canuck" Koeneki took one in his hand and Mrs. Gleason avoided the other as though it were poison ivy. "Friday morning is when Hardin's Hardware replenishes its stocks of items for sale. Each item of any value has a distinct inventory label stuck to it when an employee transfers the item from the shipping box to the distribution cart. I'm going to refer to that one-of-a-kind inventory label as a 'serial number' for simplicity's sake." Fred showed Mrs. Gleason a close up photo of the drill bit set. "The serial number on this drill bit set is the same as this number on the inventory list of items received on Friday morning. The point is this: You couldn't have bought this drill bit set at any time previous to that Friday morning."

"It *was* Friday morning, come to think of it." Mrs. Gleason's face flushed. "I bought it with the light bulbs and the salt, but the cashier must have failed to ring it up on the register." That was Version Number Four. The look on Andrew Gleason's face was the look of a man who was either constipated or in serious need of relocation.

"Did you take the drill bit set from the display case?"

"Yes, I did." That was Version Number Five.

"But," Fred said looking directly into her eyes, "this drill bit set was never *in* the display case. All items going into a locked display case are checked off by the employ when the employee takes the item off the distribution tray and places it in the locked display case. Notice this item is circled, because it never was placed into the display case."

"You're absolutely right. I *did* find it on a tray." That was Version Number Six.

"Next, here's a digital recording from the Hardin's Hardware security camera," Fred said.

"Canuck" Koeneki interrupted. "Could we recess for twenty minutes?"

Fred consented, and the secretary turned off her voice recording device. "Canuck" and his clients adjourned to the coffee shop next door. When they were gone, Benjamin turned to his lawyer and said, "Fred, the only security camera we have is in the garden center. We don't have a camera at the cashier counter."

"Yes, I know that," Fred said. "But, apparently, they don't."

Benjamin, Dan, Scott, and Fred waited for more than thirty minutes before the telephone rang. Fred took the call from "Canuck". Benjamin made a motion with his wallet in an attempt to remind Fred that he was willing to pay Mrs. Gleason's medical bills. Fred waved him off. When he hung up, Fred turned to his clients.

"'Canuck' wants to get back to us on this. I told him that'd be fine." He motioned toward the door and suggested they go down to the town docks for lunch. He stopped before they walked out of the conference room. "I don't want to get ahead of ourselves," he said, "but this is what a case feels like just before it goes away."

Benjamin sighed audibly.

"Ben, do you have an insurance policy in place right now?" Fred asked.

"Yes. Dan worked it all out."

"Good," Fred told him as he slapped him on the back, "keep it that way."

During the last week of June, it was the Harringtons' turn to host pinochle night. Joe T. didn't enjoy the group's card nights like he once did because of Benjamin's mental decline. Joe T. was a mathematician, and most of the pleasure he derived from pinochle was memorizing the cards played so he could predict which cards each player held in their hands. Benjamin no longer played the game competently. Several times during each game, he failed to follow suit, and that required all players to fold their hands, reshuffle, deal, and replay the hand.

"It's too much like work," Joe T. told Joyce while they were dressing for the evening. "I'd rather just sit and drink and talk."

"If you're the Joe T. I married, you'll do whatever it takes to make Benjamin happy," Joyce said. "Benjamin loves his pinochle, even if he can't really play anymore."

"It grates on my nerves," Joe T. growled.

"Stop being a mathematician and keep being a friend," Joyce soothed him with a hug. "If you two were switched, Benjamin would do it for you."

Phillip and Marie Laval arrived a few minutes late, because of Phillip's volunteer work on the Bank of Caledonia's float for the approaching Independence Day Parade. For forty-one years in a row, Phillip was proud to have marched, waving an American flag in each hand, for the entire two-mile-plus parade route. Joe T. met the Lavals at the front door. He presented each of them with a tall, frosted gin-and-tonic.

"*Merci*," Marie said to Joe T. as she gave him a peck on each cheek. "The perfect drink for a warm evening." Phillip accepted his gin-and-tonic gratefully, shook hands with Joe T., and took a sip right away. Joe T. led the Lavals to the back porch where Joyce and Benjamin sat nursing their own drinks. The sun's rays were weakening now that the sun was low in the sky. A fresh breeze blew in from the west over Caledonia Bay and up the green lawn to their elevated porch.

The old friends hardly remembered a time when they *didn't* meet for snacks and cards. As always, they grazed on vegetable trays, crackers, and cheese. They had a good chinwag before sitting down at the card table inside the house at sunset. The village clock bells struck eight o'clock. They each gathered a glass and a plate of food and trooped into the living room. Joe T. refreshed their gin-and-tonics. Joyce brought a tray of cucumber sandwiches to the card table.

"We can't play pinochle if we're famished," she said. She changed the subject without a transition. "I saw Annette and Scott together the other night when they went to Stableton Dykes for dinner. They make a lovely couple."

"Yes, they do," Phillip agreed. Marie smiled, but didn't respond.

"So, Joe T.," Benjamin asked, "how does retirement agree with you?"

"I've finally found what I'm good at," Joe T. replied.

"Don't listen to him," Joyce said. "He's still consulting. He's going over to Vermont next month to work with a prep school that's in financial trouble."

"Believe me," Joe T. said, "I'm ninety per cent retired." He turned to Phillip Laval. "Ask Phillip; he just bailed out two months ago." Phillip smiled placidly.

"Ask me," Marie said. "He's in my way ever since he retired. I can't get anything done."

Joe T. brought two decks of cards to the table and he separated the jokers and tossed aside the twos through eights and began shuffling the decks together.

"We're fortunate people," Joe T. said. "We're not hungry. We've got good kids. Ben and the Lavals have a wonderful grandson. And we've got each other." The five friends raised their glasses in a wordless toast.

"Today is Helen's birthday," Benjamin said unexpectedly. "She died more than thirty-six years ago."

"Do you think of her often?" Marie asked.

"Yep. How can I forget an angel?" Ben asked rhetorically. "She was an angel to me in life and now, I do believe, she's an angel in Heaven."

Joyce kissed Benjamin on the cheek and gave him a one-armed hug. "Helen's real proud of you Mr. Hardin."

"When will *you* retire, Ben?" Phillip asked.

"Well, I'm halfway there. I resigned from the Thornton Board of Directors the same time you two did and I've turned over all financial and management decisions at the store to Daniel. I'm going to retire when I turn sixty-five – that's in 2004. In the meantime, I'm just another pretty face drifting around the hardware store."

"Time to deal 'em out," Joe T. said. The four players seated themselves at the table and Marie retired to a reading chair with her book. As on many other similar nights, they chatted the evening away in the warm ambit of their friendship. Benjamin failed to follow suit often, and some of his choices of lead card were pretty awful. As many times as it took, Benjamin's friends folded their hands without comment and played the newly-dealt hand. Joe T. placed his big hand on Benjamin's shoulder and gave him an affectionate squeeze. Benjamin practically purred.

"I'm sorry," Benjamin said when he failed to follow suit.

Joyce always covered Benjamin's breach of the rules by saying something like, "I didn't like the hand I was dealt anyway." When Benjamin's speech faltered because he couldn't think of a noun, Joyce supplied it in her sweet way.

And, each time, Benjamin said, "Thank you, Helen."

Chapter 13

SHOCK

JOHN WATCHED THE Independence Day Parade from the lawn of the Caledonia Post Office at the two-mile mark on the parade route. The route to that point was downhill, so the military formations, floats, and bands had a lot of kick left in them when they reached the Post Office for the last half-mile uphill.

Corky approached John from behind and thrust his knees into the back of John's knees which made John's legs buckle. This adolescent prank had been amusing idle adolescent minds since as far back as the Stone Age. John's quick reflexes prevented him from falling to the ground like a sack of potatoes. Corky punched John on the left shoulder.

"It's me," Corky said. He was vigorously licking soft-serve chocolate ice cream in a cone to preempt it from melting all over his hand.

"I know it's you," John said as he punched Corky solidly on the right shoulder. "Thanks for the ice cream."

"I didn't know you'd be here, or I would've got you one."

"Right."

"*Really*," Corky insisted.

A drove of teenagers from the music camp where Paul was working for the summer approached the Post Office. The campers plodded by in an approximation of a formation. Dressed in khaki shorts, red golf shirts, and white tennis shoes, they constituted more of a walking group of musicians than a marching band, because of their failure to march in step or to play in key. More than forty of the youngsters shuffled along comically out-of-step while mutilating an indeterminate Sousa march.

"Look," Corky pointed at the head of the group, "there's our own Paul Bruguiere. He's a-prancin'-and-a-dancin'!"

John yelled out Paul's name, but there was little chance of Paul seeing or hearing him among the throng packing the parade route five deep. Paul wore a big smile on his face as he carried the music camp flag.

"He's grinning like they made him Parade Marshall," Corky said through a glob of ice cream in his mouth.

"He's not grinning now."

Paul and his merry pack of musicians were following the riding club horses from Spokeworthy Stables. One horse's stern receptacle bag had malfunctioned, so the path of the horse's passing was not litter-free. Paul's powers of observation failed him at a crucial moment, and his wide grin was replaced by a look of dismay. The crowd cheered sympathetically as Paul tried to drag horse manure from his shoe.

Paul's Uncle, Thomas Bruguiere, was his usual inapt self as he flounced beside the youngsters shouting, "Left, right, left right!" Not surprisingly, his shouts were opposite to his own steps, so his contribution to the order of the procession was marginal. Thomas had wrapped his eye patch in red-and-white striped paper and his shirt was dark blue peppered with white stars. On his head was an oversized sombrero.

"Thomas thinks it's *Cinco de Mayo*," Corky observed. As annoying as Thomas was to the residents of Caledonia, he was a big hit with the tourists, many of whom had flocked off the *M/S Franklin Pierce* in the mood to cheer, and they gave him a big round of applause.

"Thomas is like a rodeo clown," John said, "he's funny the first time you see him, but once is enough. Don't encourage him." This wasn't the only negative critique of Thomas' contribution to the parade.

"Lock him up!" shouted Raymond Delacroix who was standing among a small group of Caledonia High School thugs. Thomas continued to cavort joyfully alongside the music campers.

"Hey, John Boy," Corky said between ice cream licks, "I'm flying to Italy tomorrow. My Mom and I are catching a Friday-night flight out of Logan." He licked furiously at a breakaway lump of chocolate ice cream that threatened to collapse onto his hand like an iceberg calved by a chocolate glacier. "I'm gonna sleep the whole way over so, when we get there, *voila*, I'll be all set."

"*Voila* isn't Italian," John said.

"It doesn't matter. Italians speak everything. They're known for being multi-multi-lingual. That's why I didn't bother looking at that Italian language book my mother gave me. Anyway, I gotta go." He punched John on the shoulder, and John shoved him off in a patent *macho* teenager move.

"*Arrivederci*," John said.

"*Ciao.*" The oversized twit *had* been practicing Italian after all, John thought.

John waved at Phillip Laval as his grandfather walked beside the Bank of Caledonia float, but Phillip didn't see John among the dozens of people on the Post Office lawn. Immediately trailing the nine-member American Legion Band, the Caledonia Walkers Precision Drill Team came along. About fifty marchers strong, the primarily senior-aged team piggy-backed on the music from the American Legion Band as they smacked their aluminum walker crutches on the ground smartly. They folded the hinged legs of their walkers in unison, pumped them in the air over their heads, and performed exquisite about-faces and side steps to the delight of the crowd.

At the head of the Drill Team was the choir director from the Episcopal Church. He wore an ornate drum major outfit and held aloft a scepter bigger than Queen Elizabeth's. Judging from his strut, he was the most over-stimulated man in Caledonia. The crowd loved his antics, and they gave him a big hand. John remembered Scott's First Theorem of Social Behavior: "To gain notoriety, act like a maniac."

John spotted Grandfather Benjamin Hardin, in the sixth row of the Drill Team. The team was dressed in all white — shirts, trousers, and tennis shoes — and blue baseball caps. Benjamin flung his walking crutches around in perfect time with his drill teammates. Smack! Smack! They slapped the aluminum frames against the asphalt. John waved to his grandfather, but, of course, Benjamin didn't see him. John recalled Scott's Second Theorem of Parade Behavior that stated, "If you're not in the parade, you're invisible."

John left the parade well before it was over, because he had been on the clock since the town clock tower bells had struck noon. He walked the two blocks back to the hardware store to resume washing windows, a chore that didn't require a lot of headwork. That was fortunate, because John needed all the free brain power he could muster to worry about his latest dilemma.

He had established an options position on Monday that had troubled him from the moment he had clicked the mouse button to submit the trade. He had broken his vow never, *ever* to write naked calls or puts. In this trade, he had done both, and, as the position moved against him, the frightening specter of financial extermination threatened John's over-developed sense of grandiosity. His prevalent mood had switched from confidence to chronic anxiety.

Lean.com was a start-up Internet company that had gone public during the height of the initial public offering frenzy back in 2000. Trading under the symbol LEAN, the company's stock was bid up from an opening price of $28 to $34 the very first day. Anyone taking more than a cursory glance at the company fundamentals recognized that barriers to entry for competitors were almost non-existent. Momentum buyers ignored the fundamentals.

Lean.com's business plan worked like this: A client who wanted to lose weight signed up on-line for a one-time charge of ten dollars. The client entered the food and drink items she consumed each day into an eForm diary on the web site. Lean.com's computers assigned calories to each item and calculated the client's intake. A daily morning email to the client told her how many calories she had consumed the previous day. If she was over-plan, her Electronic Demerit Balance was debited at a rate of one penny per ten calories over-plan. For example, one hundred calories over-plan cost the client ten cents worth of demerits. At the end of the month, the sum of the client's demerits for that month was electronically transferred to Lean.com's coffers.

According to television advertisements, the good news for a client was that, if she adhered to the program and stayed *under*-plan by restricting her calories, she would lose weight and look marvelous. Her friends would rave about her incredible new shape. Strangers would seek her out for dates. She might get a part in a movie. All of this for only ten dollars.

Not included in the television advertisements was the somewhat neutral news for a client who went *over*-plan; her Electronic Demerit Balance grew at the same pace as her eating and drinking transgressions, but she could opt out at any time by writing a letter that guaranteed the return of ninety per cent of her Demerit Balance within ninety days. Ninety-in-ninety was the catch phrase in tiny print at the bottom of advertisements.

To be candid, what was needed to make this concept work was a bountiful supply of overweight dupes. Fortunately for Lean.com, the Internet provided access to a world-wide target client base numbering in the hundreds of millions. If current trends of fast-food joint proliferation continued in India and China, there were potentially billions-with-a-"b" of overweight international clients to enrich Lean.com and its investors.

The good news for Lean.com was that for every

knucklehead who signed up and paid by credit card on line, an immediate cash infusion of ten dollars accrued to the company. Later, as the demerit credits began to pour in at a high rate for truthful people and at a somewhat lower rate for liars and amnesiacs, the money thus credited to company coffers remained there and grew to the benefit of the company. Furthermore, focus groups had demonstrated that the people who were most likely to sign up for such a plan were most *un*likely to write a letter for any reason, so most of the balances in dead accounts went unclaimed. Even in the minority of cases where clients actually wrote a letter to opt out, the company was able to retain ten percent of their Demerit Balances.

Hypothetically, even assuming a high churn rate, each million clients were predicted to generate ten million dollars in initiation fees, an average of about seven million dollars a month in Demerit Balance deposits, an average of two million dollars a month in unclaimed Demerit Balances, and an average of $450,000 a month retained from Demerit Balances of clients opting out.

More really good news for Boston-based Lean.com was that the firm had only four employees. The President and CEO was a thirty-five-year-old graduate of Dartmouth College's Tuck School of Business. The six-man board of directors was made up of the CEO's friends with *MBA*s from Dartmouth, Cornell, and Columbia. He hired a knock-out secretary from Charlestown, an Information Technology guru two years out of Tufts, and an accountant who, five years after graduating from Boston University, still lived with his mother.

The firm operated out of a nine-hundred-square-foot rented office in Allston. The CEO's permissive work dress code allowed his employees to wear tee shirts and shorts in the summer and ski attire in the winter. He provided an antique pinball machine in the office to amuse his employees and himself during moments of sheer boredom. He also stocked a vending machine with eight kinds of trail mix and a theater-style popcorn machine. These perks promoted good eye-hand coordination and exemplary bowel habits among his employees.

A Boston newspaper ran a feature on the company as soon as its initial public offering was announced. The story included a picture of the four employees on Segways. The photo was completely misleading, because Segway travel in the tiny office was nearly impossible, but it implanted an image in readers' minds of a group of enthusiastic employees darting around efficiently on motorized wheels.

Lean.com's first quarterly report showed earnings of $0.34 per share. The stock soared to $44 resulting in a projected price-to-earnings ratio of 32. The CEO increased annual salaries to $70,000 for the secretary, $210,000 for the IT guru, $250,000 for the accountant, and $800,000 for himself. Directors maintained their current rate of compensation, $4,000 per quarterly meeting.

The 10-Q for the second quarter reflected earnings of $0.38 per share. Then, in the third quarter, Lean.com earned $0.48 a share. The accountant suggested that the company reduce its cash account and short-term bond holdings by investing in equities as a way to increase the return on the company's cash hoard. The board members – all suffering from Dot Com Fever — agreed. It was done.

A financial magazine published an interview with the CEO on the one-year anniversary of Lean.com's public offering. A picture of the CEO on a rented Segway in a plush office rented for the photo shoot supported the notion that the company was on the express elevator to the top. Moving its investment portfolio from government bonds to equity positions in Nails.com, Abs.com, and Zen.com rewarded Lean.com with enormous investment income in the fourth quarter. Assets soared, and earnings came in at $0.59 a share. With the stock at $57, the price-to-earnings ratio was only 31, so an analyst quoted in a large publication predicted a mid-term stock target price of $80.

Unfortunately, when tough times fell upon Lean.com, bad news followed like disease following an infestation of rats. First, the secretary filed a paternity suit against the CEO for a child she delivered out-of-wedlock late in 2001. Next, Nails.com and Zen.com filed for bankruptcy and the common stock of both companies dropped like a rock to $0.01 a share. The accountant suggested the company buy oil futures to make a fast killing to make up for the enormous losses realized with the failures of Nails.com and Zen. com. At several times in history that might have proved to be excellent timing, but that was not the case in the first half of 2002. Then Abs.com went out of business. Clients began drifting away from Lean.com faster than new ones joined up, and initiation fee income started a precipitous decline.

Three new privately-held competing on-line copycat firms appeared. As the general economy declined, members lied even more pervasively about their over-eating, and Demerit

Balances fell into the tank. In the 10-Q released by Lean. com on June 27, the company reported earnings of minus $0.03 a share and a decrease of more than sixty-two per cent in assets on the balance sheet. Lean.com stock plummeted from $62 to $30 in one day. The next day, LEAN opened up a dollar to $31, before resuming its nose dive to $13. LEAN's next close was at $9.50. On the fourth day, LEAN closed at $6.05. That's when John got in on the action.

John did almost no fundamental research. He had discovered LEAN by running a scan to identify stock options with inordinately high ratios of time premium to stock price. LEAN jumped off the page. John had never seen such rich time premiums. The front-month at-the-money calls and puts on this $6.05 stock were selling for one dollar each. He could sell short the $6 naked straddle for $2 in premiums, thereby collecting a third of the price of the stock in a premium that could decay to zero at expiration in only fourteen trading days.

Commit, he told himself, have some guts and commit. So, commit he did. He sold short two hundred naked July $6 straddle contracts and collected $40,000. The transaction used up a boat load of his margin, and it left him very little wiggle room if circumstances moved against him. He had to rest his hopes on the stock price remaining near $6 for the next three weeks. He would break even if LEAN climbed as high as $8 or descended further to $4. He would start losing money if LEAN climbed above $8 or fell below $4. The most he could gain from the high-risk position was the $40,000 he had collected by writing the calls and puts. The most he could lose if the stock rebounded half as madly as it had collapsed was…everything.

On the Monday afternoon before Independence Day, just a few hours after he had written the straddles, LEAN closed at $6.15. So far, so good. After market close, John sat on his boat dock and fished for sunfish and small mouth bass. The fish had gone deep with the warming of the lake water so the fishing was slow. John's brain, however, was *not* slow. Calculations careened off the walls of his mind uncontrollably.

He considered one possible disaster after another. What if the stock shot up to $20? He would lose $240,000. What if it fell to $2? He would lose $40,000. His pulse stuttered each time a new method of measuring the risk occurred to him. What if the stock price climbed to $8 at expiration? He would break even, but his nervous system would never be the same. What if the stock price shot back up to $34 – the closing price on the first day of trading? He would lose $520,000. He didn't have $520,000 to lose. Sleep came to John reluctantly that night.

Tuesday was another day off from work for John. By market open, Dan and Scott had left the house, so John could fire up his television and his computer in privacy. To his horror, LEAN opened up seventy-five cents to $6.90 within three minutes of the opening bell. John felt his heart shudder. He felt weak in the knees. He felt panic trying to force its way into his mind. He could buy-to-close the $6 puts for $0.30. Should he do it and eliminate half the risk? The problem with that was, if the stock kept climbing, he would have thrown away $6,000 needlessly. What if he bought-to-open $8 calls for $0.55 to hedge his losses against a runaway increase in the stock price? The problem with that was, if the stock fell back in price, he would have thrown away $11,000 needlessly. He finally made the decision to hold fast. He had made a commitment. He was sticking to it. He needed a diversion.

John rode his bicycle for a four-mile jaunt around Caledonia Neck. He stopped at a public beach along the way. Watching the capers of carefree children at the water's edge reminded John of how burdened by anxiety his life had become. His inability to foretell the future of financial markets was an agonizing torture for John.

His gaze fell on Raymond Delacroix, the quasi-fascist life guard designated to prowl around the beach purportedly as insurance against drowning. Raymond, who was wearing only his sun tan, whistle, and a pair of red life guard shorts, was putting his best moves on the daughter of some unsuspecting summer resident. What a surprise! Raymond, the former bully of Brighton Elementary School, had graduated to being a ladies' man. Why can't I be a stupid lunkhead like Raymond, John thought. In his entire life, Raymond will never suffer the way I'm suffering now, he thought. The agony isn't worth the aggravation, his internal monologue continued. He vowed never, ever, *ever* to write naked options again. John rode his bicycle home in time for the end of trading in the regular market at 4 p.m. LEAN closed at $7.18.

After a night of fitful sleep, John woke up Wednesday morning and shared breakfast with Dan and Scott. They were reading sections of the *Boston Globe*, so they exchanged only necessary phrases such as "pass the butter". Near the end of the meal, as John collected dishes to wash, Dan looked up at John and broke the silence.

"John, you look tired. Are you alright?"

"Yeah, I'm all set." If his father could read minds, his cover was as good as blown.

"I don't think you're getting enough sleep."

"I'm good, Dad."

Scott and Dan left the house and John ran upstairs to have the television selected to a business channel by 9:30. No big news to report. He logged on to his brokerage web site and checked the bid/ask for LEAN at the open. It was $7.20 bid, $7.28 asked. The knots in John's stomach tightened. By the time John left for work just before noon, LEAN had last traded at $7.07. Please go to $6 and stay there, John whispered, despite his knowledge that the market didn't care about his needs or desires.

That afternoon, LEAN closed at $6.92. Markets were closed the next day for Independence Day. Friday was another trying day for John, but, by market close, LEAN was last traded at $6.57. Ah, reversion-to-the-mean, he thought, things are falling back into equilibrium. John enjoyed his weekend. Paul Bruguiere didn't return to the island with the music campers after the July Fourth parade, so he joined John and Scott for fishing and swimming on Saturday morning before John went to work. Such weekend distractions alleviated some of John's suffering.

By Monday morning, John's mind was consumed with contingencies for bailing out of his LEAN positions if things went horribly wrong in the last ten trading days before options expiration. He wasn't enjoying life anymore. He decided to record his feelings in his diary for the last ten days of the drama he had created. Monday night, after LEAN had closed at $6.11, John wrote, "LEAN $6.11 feeling good."

Tuesday: "LEAN $5.88 feeling real good."

Wednesday: "LEAN $5.94 feeling like a genius. Why do I worry so much?"

Thursday: "LEAN $5.68 feeling OK."

Friday: "LEAN $5.30 feeling OK, but I hate to see $0.70 get away, that's $14,000 taken away from my $40,000 of premium."

Saturday and Sunday were work days for John, and his anguish had abated partly because of a growing rationalization that he never had expected to profit by the entire $40,000 in the first place. He could only wish LEAN to be the dullest stock in America for the next five days so he could get out of his position with his pants on.

LEAN was not destined to be dull. The slow deterioration of Lean.com accelerated on Monday when the United States Attorney's Office for the District of Massachusetts filed criminal charges against the Lean.com accountant. The charges accused the accountant of "front-running" — buying shares of Zen.com in his personal account before running the price of Zen.com shares up with Lean.com purchases and immediately selling his personal stake when the company buying was finished. John's daily diary entries memorialized the agonizing implosion.

Monday: "LEAN $4.12 feeling scared. Hope for a bounce tomorrow. Accountant may be a crook."

Tuesday: "LEAN $3.64 feeling awful. I'm down $7,200."

Wednesday: "LEAN $3.10 I'm dying. Down $18,000."

Thursday: "LEAN $0.30 feeling sick. Trading suspended.

I've lost $80,000. I can't eat. I just want to evaporate. I will never write naked options again. *Never*".

There was no Friday entry. John had lost $80,000 dollars, about a quarter of his net asset value, in a few miserable days. During the ascendancy of his good fortune, he had longed for the whole world to know of his success. Now that he had suffered this huge loss, he hoped that no one would ever discover his failure. He walked around like a grieving survivor for a full day until Saturday night when relief came from an unexpected quarter. John and Scott were talking down by the beach while Scott made kabobs on the grill.

"You seem a little down of late, Hoss," Scott said to John.

"I'm okay."

"Two things you can count on, *Amigo*," Scott said, "when a woman tells you 'it's nothing', it's *something*, and, when a teenager tells you he's 'okay', something's *wrong*." Scott let his wisdom settle in. "Making the transition to high school isn't easy, John. You've got all those hormones beaming around in your body and girls start looking real good and school gets tougher. It's a lot to figure out."

"Yeah," John said. Even though the genesis of Scott's sympathy was off the mark, it was sympathy none-the-less, so John was grateful. He wondered at Scott's reaction if John told him the truth, as in, I lost $80,000 this week. In a perverse way, it struck John as funny and he smiled. His father got in on the conversation.

"Scott's right," Dan said, "he was nut job in the ninth grade. I saved him."

The Triad enjoyed some good laughs and some overcooked kabobs. As subsequent days passed, the pain of John's beat-down by Lean.com slowly subsided. It occurred to him that no one knew about his stupidity. His failure had gone unobserved.

Napoleon's loss at Waterloo could have been a small bump in the road if he had stifled news of the defeat. Similarly, if General Robert E. Lee could have hidden the fact that he had been hammered at Gettysburg, his latter years might have been considerably more carefree.

That was it. A tree had fallen in the forest, but no one was in the forest to hear it fall except John. And John wasn't talking to anyone. He ended the boycott of his journal the following Friday: "NAV $256,844."

Three weeks later, John had worked through the worst of the tremors and intestinal distress brought on by the Lean. com setback when he received a post card from Corky bearing some of the most intricate stamps John had ever seen. Italians, it seemed, were experts not only at cooking spaghetti and creating sexy cars, but designing stamps, as well.

"Italy is great!" Corky wrote. "The girls really are amazing, although I haven't actually talked to any of them. I'll tell you about this beach Mom and I went to when I get home. I haven't learned any Italian words, yet, because I haven't needed to talk. I've lost two pounds if this scale is right. I hope you're surviving without me. *Ciao.* Corky."

Chapter 14
SUMMER 2003

SCOTT HARRINGTON HAD learned how quickly adversity can turn a hero into a philosopher. During the five years since Scott's initial OHS diagnosis, he had known that surgery most likely could only mitigate – not prevent — blindness. He could hope for the discovery of a miracle cure within the next year before all of his central vision likely deteriorated, but such a cure had not been forthcoming in the last 5,000-plus years of recorded human history, so the odds didn't favor such a conveniently-timed miracle. Because he refrained from complaining about his misfortune, he felt entitled to render sage, unsolicited observations, and he passed along his philosophical tidbits with increasing frequency.

"'Water is the only drink for a wise man,'" Scott advised John as the youngest member of The Triad poured a can of Pepsi into an iced glass. "That's from *Walden*."

"That wasn't your tune back at Princeton," Dan quipped as he passed through the kitchen for a cup of tea on his way to his favorite reading chair in the living room.

"I didn't have time for Thoreau then," Scott

counterpunched, "I was a busy boy."

"Just so," Dan mumbled.

"A Pepsi a week won't kill me," John said in defense of his indulgence.

"Do you know what that stuff does if you soak a nail in it?"

"Yes. That's why I insist on serving my nails on the side."

Scott's philosophical offerings often came out of the blue, and the link between the philosophy and the event that inspired it was often obscure. When John complained about Raymond Delacroix planting his fist in Corky Gleason's face in violation of the non-aggression treaty, for example, Scott chimed in with a quote from Ralph Waldo Emerson.

"He is but a weed. 'A weed is a plant whose virtues have not yet been discovered.'"

"You think Raymond's a weed?" John asked. "He's a jerk."

"We used to cover guys like that with a blanket at night and beat the snot out of them," Scott said, momentarily straying from the path of the philosopher. "Of course," he added hastily, before the seed of the idea could germinate in John's fertile mind, "such violence is inappropriate in these more enlightened times."

"You actually did that?" John asked. John couldn't visualize Scott as Sergeant Bilko.

"We *talked* about doing it," Scott replied, as much as admitting that he had embellished history a tad. "How's Corky's face?"

"Swollen," John said. "Like the rest of his body only redder. Raymond promised me he'd leave Corky alone, but then he goes and whacks him anyway. I told Raymond I'd smash his bronchodilator if he did it again."

"Good move. Hit 'em where it hurts." When revenge was involved, Scott was more of an eye-for-an-eye man than a follower of Gandhi.

Later in the same conversation, John lamented that most of the international and out-of-state students at Thornton Prep were more sophisticated than John and his Caledonia pals.

"Just be yourself, Stud," Scott advised. "Ralph Waldo said we should see through pretense. The less you try to impress people, the more they'll be impressed by you."

"Is that last part Confucius?" John asked.

"No, that's Harrington," Scott said. "Here's the deal, Grasshopper: When you're honest with someone, he trusts you and wants to be your friend. He doesn't care whether you're from London or from a little village in the sticks."

"Like Dad. He doesn't change to please other people." Dan was in the living room pretending not to hear the compliment.

"Bingo. That's why he's been my best friend for twenty-some years. You're lucky to have Dan Hardin for your father." Scott couldn't leave it at that. "And you're certainly one lucky juvenile to have *me* around," he said, demonstrating that philosophers can be self-serving.

Three days later, on one of Scott's days off, the philosopher walked over to the Laval's 1883-vintage Queen Anne style house to meet Annette for a hike up Mount Reverence. The Laval home featured bay windows, a large turret, a fish-scale slate roof, and a porch big enough to accommodate the entire Garden Club Beautification Committee. Annette's mother answered the door and invited him in.

"Annette's not home from the market, yet," Marie said. "How about a coffee while you wait?"

"Just a glass of water, thanks."

Scott followed Marie into the kitchen and sat on a stool beside the island counter. Marie knew a lot more about Scott than Scott knew about Marie. Annette had talked to her mother about Scott ever since Annette and Scott were freshmen at Thornton. Also, Scott was Joyce Harrington's favorite subject, so Marie had listened to Joyce's reports on her son while he was at Princeton and while he was flying fighters in the Air Force. Joyce had even read some of Scott's letters aloud to Marie over the years.

On the other hand, Scott couldn't say he knew Marie well at all. Marie had always seemed aloof to him. That puzzled Scott, because he was so accustomed to women responding eagerly to him. He suspected that, at least in the past, she had viewed him as a self-centered fraternity boy involved in too many sports, social diversions, and girls. Marie's subtle traces of asexuality more than her reserve or detachment made him uneasy.

Scott knew that Marie was a controlling person. On a ten-point Control Scale, Scott rated her a "ten". By contrast, he graded himself a "seven" and Marie's husband Phillip a "four". For all the years since Scott had first met Marie, she had kept a tight rein on her twin girls. She had packed so many activities into their lives that it had taken a girl with a will of iron to find the time and to expend the energy to defy her mother's wishes. It had taken a Trinette. Scott and Marie had been in the same room with other people many times before, but Scott had never spoken with Marie alone.

"I'm glad you've gotten on with your life," Marie said, jumping right into the deep end of the conversational pool by addressing his vision loss. She wasted no time with pleasantries, because she might never again have the chance to speak privately with this seemingly over-confident, self-content, yet appealing young man. "Did you know that Annette's had a picture of you on her bedroom wall since prep school?"

"No. But I think a lot of Annette, too."

"Apparently not enough to keep you from chasing after Congressman Szabo's daughter and that Swedish girl and that girl from El Paso." She handed a glass of water to Scott.

Scott's mother presumably had leaked these episodes drawn from his robust romantic history. He was grateful that he had shared with his mother only a sampler of his affairs over the years. He speculated that Marie must have an industrial-strength memory to enable her to retrieve details of events that had occurred in his life more than a decade ago.

"I didn't really chase after them," Scott said defensively.

"Oh?" Marie arched her eyebrows sarcastically. "You're so dashing that they chased after *you*?"

"I didn't mean that. I mean, there was no chasing."

"Well," Marie exhaled, "Scott always got the girl."

"Why so critical?"

"I'm not criticizing. I'm just cross with you because you can't seem to see how fond Annette is of you."

"Marie, I'm really close to Annette."

"You're *geographically* close to her. She's too convenient for you, Scott. You play with her emotions because it doesn't take any effort on your part."

"Marie!"

"Annette's thirty-seven years old, Scott. Her sister was married sixteen years ago, and you've taken Annette for granted for all of those sixteen years!"

Scott couldn't think of a way to de-escalate the conversation other than by withdrawing from it. He had never been spoken to like this. He considered apologizing to get out of his predicament, but he didn't think he had anything to apologize for. He shifted the focus clumsily.

"Dan didn't take Trinette for granted," Scott said. His words didn't make much sense to him, and they certainly confounded Marie. He hoped to use Marie's AWOL daughter as a diversion from Marie's inquisition.

"I think about Trinette every day," Marie said. "I love her so much. But she made herself unapproachable to me. If I tried to get close to her, she'd pull away. Maybe I demanded too much of her. Annette coped, but Trinette couldn't."

"You've still got your grandson. John loves you and Phillip."

"John's such a sweet boy," Marie sighed. She had tears in her eyes.

"Yesterday," Scott said, in search of catharsis, "John told me that Dan drives him insane because of the way he loads the dish washer. John sorts the cutlery by putting only knives in one compartment and only forks in another. And the plates have to be ordered in the bottom drawer smallest toward the center and largest toward the sides of the drawer."

Marie blotted a tear and laughed. "What did he say exactly?"

"'Dad makes me crazy.'"

"What'd you tell him."

"I told him that I'd get back to him on the dishwasher outrage as soon as I fixed world hunger."

"And?"

"He said, 'Why do I even bother telling you stuff?' And I told him if he didn't tell me he'd be talking to himself."

Marie smiled thoughtfully.

"Marie, you have a wonderful grandson."

"Oh, I know. I know. The decisions we make...."

Scott left his stool and walked around the kitchen island to wrap his arms around her and hug her gently. She didn't feel asexual anymore.

Marie held Scott firmly as she felt release, even pleasure in his strong arms.

"Don't blame yourself for what's happened," Scott whispered. "You've done a remarkable job." Scott let go his hold on Marie because his instincts told him to. Marie blotted her eyes on a napkin. Scott walked from the kitchen to a deck off the kitchen where he settled into a wicker chair. He looked with his marginally operative left eye northward at the view of Mount Tremont. He heard Annette walk through the doorway from the mud room to the kitchen.

"*Bonjour,*" Annette said lightly, unaware of Scott's presence. She didn't notice her mother's teary eyes.

"*Bonjour, ma petite,*" Marie said, pressing her face against Annette's.

Annette announced that she was going to make deviled eggs for her hike with Scott. Marie nodded toward the open door through which Annette could see Scott mountain-gazing. Annette blushed ever so slightly and waved to him.

Within an hour, Annette and Scott had parked at the trailhead and started their hike up Mount Reverence. They climbed steadily upwards on the yielding, leaf-strewn floor of the forest. Shielded from the sun by the thick summer foliage of conifers and hardwoods, they scaled steep rocky faces and passed silently over flat sections of the trail on a carpet of pine needles. When they reached the top of Mount Reverence, they sat on a great stone left by glaciers on the eastern crown of the mountain. They surveyed the wide expanse of Lake Tremont. The blue surface of the lake was crisscrossed by the white wakes of boats from Dartford Parade in the north to Oxbridge in the south. They watched the boats travel in and out of the harbors at the other lakeside towns – Stableton Dykes, Stone Haven, and Caledonia.

After eating the six deviled eggs and drinking a bottle of water each, Annette and Scott picked blueberries in a patch on the western side of the Mount. They picked until their bottles were full. They returned to their rocky throne and spent part of the dreamy afternoon eating blueberries and gazing at the lake and mountains beyond.

"I talked to your mother about Trinette," Scott said. He had no intention of telling Annette what Marie had said about him or his faults.

"How'd that go?"

"She was emotional about it. She blames herself for Trinette's disappearance."

"Mummy's a realist. She knows we all love Trinette, but Trinette wanted more than we could give her. She's gone, so we go on."

Scott threw a blueberry toward a chipmunk.

"I think Mummy has a little crush on you, Scott Harrington. I've watched her watching you."

"I doubt it." His thoughts were occupied with the notion of not taking Annette for granted.

Scott lay down on his back on a patch of pine needles that formed a miniature bed on the crown of the mountain. Annette lay on her side and rested her head on Scott's chest. She listened to the rhythmic beat of his heart. Scott flicked the luxurious locks of her hair out of his face and gently stroked her back along the track of her spine. The sun warmed them and the westerly breeze cooled them.

"Sweet-and-sour," he said. "Yin-Yang."

"Captain Harrington – Master of Paradox."

"You know I've become a philosopher."

"This country's in desperate need of more philosophers."

"Hmmm."

They talked intermittently until Scott dozed off. While he slept, Annette listened to the concert issuing from his thorax — heart on percussion accompanied by a gastric duet powered by deviled eggs and blueberries. She wondered if her eavesdropping on his abdominal growls and grumbles constituted invasion of privacy. When Scott stirred, Annette resumed their indolent conversation.

"I love seeing John with you and Dan," Annette said. "You two have made him very happy."

"He's a great kid," Scott said. "He's smart, he works hard, and he's a genuinely good person. There is no guile in that boy."

John's clandestine option-trading scheme had prospered

in the year since his near nervous breakdown over the Lean. com disaster. He had suffered several modest setbacks, but he had hedged his positions carefully, thereby defining his risk at the outset of almost all of the adverse trades. He had a few big winners to celebrate.

His first big score was set up when he shorted Citigroup – symbol C — in July of 2002. With C at $363, he bought-to-open 10 of the September $340 Put contracts for $7.00. Two months later, when C dove down to about $260, John sold-to-close his 10 contracts for $72.90. In fewer than sixty days, he had profited by $65,900.

His second noteworthy gain came in October when he predicted that Lexmark (LXK) was ready to break out to the upside. With LXK at $42.43, John bought-to-open 50 of the November $45 Calls at $0.28 for an outlay of $1,400. He closed out the position when LXK reached $64.90, making $98,100 on the trade.

His third stellar profit came when he spent $6,000 to buy-to-open 80 Home Depot (HD) June 25 Calls at $0.75 in February of 2003 when HD was at $21.10. In less than four months' time, HD climbed to $32.90, so John sold-to-close the calls for $7.90, a gain of $57,200.

Finally, the trade that produced the highest annualized return on investment for the year was a trade in symbol USG. In May, John spent $1,920 to buy 48 of the June $6 Calls at $0.40. A little over a month later, USG had shot up in share value to $17.10, so John closed his position at $11.00 for a gain of $49,920. The annualized ROI was over 27,000%. Not bad for a Caledonia hayseed in his freshman year in prep school, John thought.

At the end of trading on the June day when he closed out the long call position, John wrote in his diary, "NAV $633,558". And that was net of paying $144,000 in taxes for 2002. John had prepared the trust's taxes on his own this year, using Janet Boyce's 2001 return as a template. He forged his father's name on the tax return and on the trust check he used to make the payment. John still hated the word *forgery*. It was beneath him.

John went for a swim off his father's dock. He floated on his back and gazed at seagulls soaring in the dark blue sky. Looking back on his success at managing The Liberty Revocable Trust reinforced his confidence. In just two years he had increased the trust assets from almost nothing to over $600,000. He was sharply focused on his goal to make a million dollars.

John's growing confidence wasn't confined to financial matters only. The aura of his financial success projected to his social life. He no longer pretended to be a character in one of his complex daydreams. Napoleon and Davy Crockett were whimsical memories of his past. He had learned to take a place in the real world. He found that he made friends easily when he gave his attention to *them* instead of the constant stream of ideas that crowded his mind. Among all the Thornton students he got to know, one special girl stood out above all the rest.

Andrea von Bergen was the Austrian girl who transformed John's algebra class from the dullest place on earth to a place where any eighth-grade boy in his right mind wanted to be. She was about four inches shorter than John. She wore her blonde hair short, and, as far as he could tell, she wore no makeup. She didn't need to wear makeup. Her pretty face enchanted not only Thornton Prep boys like John but the algebra teacher, too.

Although Andrea spoke English as well as any other student in the class, the teacher – an "old codger" at twenty-eight years of age – sucked in his belly and smiled brightly when greeting Andrea with a hearty *"Guten Tag, Fraulein von Bergen"* almost every time she walked into the classroom. It was an embarrassing scene to witness, in the opinion of Corky Gleason.

Andrea was gracious about it, however, and she returned his greeting politely, *"Guten morgen, Professor Hayden."*

"Professor, my ass," Corky grumbled from his seat beside John in the back row of the classroom. For an undisclosed reason, this *"morgen"* business bothered him mightily.

"Are we here to learn algebra or German?" Corky whispered to John, who shrugged and ignored Corky, because John didn't want to take his eyes off of Andrea.

It came out at some stage that Mr. Hayden had lived in Graz for a year while he was in university, and he had fallen in love with all things Austrian.

"Including Freshman girls," Corky complained well out of earshot of the teacher.

John spoke briefly with Andrea once when they were both waiting for a student council meeting to start. Walking into the room, John knew – almost to a certainty – that every eighth-grade boy in the room wanted to sit beside her. But the chair on either side of Andrea was empty. John sat in the chair to her right, because he fancied that the left side of his face was superior to the right side especially in light of a lethal pimple – on the verge of going septic — just below his right ear.

"Hi," Andrea said.

"Hey," John replied with the careless air of a man bored out of his skull from a lifetime spent sitting next to Austrian beauties.

"You're called John?"

"Yes, I am." He extended his hand to her. "Nice to meet you." Their handshake was not the most coordinated handshake in history, and John clasped her hand for the extra millisecond required to make his face flush slightly.

"I've never talked with you before," she said.

"No. You're always surrounded. You attract boys like the President attracts Secret Service Agents."

"I think it's my accent."

"It's more than your accent." Most of the moving parts of his body, including his vocal chords, were melting into pools of plasma (figuratively). He was saved from the heartbreak of *inarticulitis* when the student council sponsor waddled in to start the meeting. John spent the whole meeting thinking of fascinating things to say to Andrea after the meeting.

He jotted down memory-boosters:

"Field hockey" meant "when's the next girls' field hockey game"?

"Lacrosse" meant "our boys' lacrosse team is playing Oxbridge Prep on Friday".

"Where" meant "what town in Austria are you from?"

"Out" meant "do you want to go out for a hamburger". "Out" could also mean "pass out", which he felt he might do if he actually tried to deliver the invitation. He was so involved in his plan to walk Andrea to her dorm and charm her with his word play that he jumped a little when the sponsor asked, "What do you think, John."

"I agree," he stammered.

"With what?" the sponsor pressed. It was time to wave the white flag. He could feel the heat rise in his neck.

"Please forgive me," John said, unaware of his reputation for guilelessness, "my family has experienced a tragedy recently, and I'm not myself today."

"I'm so sorry," the sponsor said softly. Her big brown eyes turned very sad-looking, and that made John feel terrible.

John had become so accustomed to secrecy and dubious dealing, he thought, that lies just rolled off his tongue like…like…lies rolling off his tongue. The fabrication got John out of his immediate predicament, but it put him off his stride enough that he missed his chance to walk Andrea to her dorm. As he was gathering his books into his backpack, Andrea was whisked away by a small group of girls, experts at talking simultaneously. On the positive side of the ledger, Andrea did look back at him and wave as she left the room.

John's next chance to talk to Andrea, not counting the unremarkable "hi's" they exchanged in algebra class was at a lacrosse match a week later. Forgetting the barely-healed zit near his right ear, John had the look of a star athlete. Andrea considered him muscular, handsome, and well-proportioned. John recognized the truth, however, that he had a long way to go to reach stardom on a lacrosse field.

John had run around like a beheaded rooster for about five game minutes of uninspired play when his helmet was ripped off by a burly Stone Haven Prep player. Seconds later, a lacrosse ball traveling at about Mach Ten hit him in his right eye and slapped him to the ground like a beanbag. John's eye turned purple and very large very quickly. The Thornton coach removed John from the lineup and asked him if he was okay.

"I'm all set," John said. He stood on the sidelines holding an ice bag on his right eye and ruefully considered that the Hardin household might now be the domicile of *two* blind guys – Scott *and* John. At that moment, Andrea appeared by his side. She put a hand on his left shoulder.

"How bad are you hurt?" she asked.

"Not bad," John said when he had recovered from the surprise. He maneuvered to ensure that she could see only the left side of his face. His right side was now marred not only by a semi-healed zit but a black eye the size and color of an eggplant.

"How are you?"

"Okay," she said. "I don't have a bag of ice on my eye." They both chuckled at that one. "I was watching you before you got hit. You're very fast."

"Thanks," John said, "I'm pretty quick, but I never have a clue where I'm going."

She liked that, and John did, too. It had the right flavor of self-deprecation to suggest that he might be a rising lacrosse star. He was relieved that she wasn't a first-hand witness to his mediocrity on a lacrosse field. Then the throbbing began. He stayed until the game was over, because, for all he knew, this might be his last chance to enthrall Andrea. When they said their goodbyes and she left his side to rejoin her friends,

John was pretty sure that no enthralling had occurred.

He decided to walk two blocks to the Laval house to tell Annette about his wound. Also, he was hungry, and Marie never failed to treat him to cookies, cake, or a slice of pie. The cars of Annette and Marie were both gone from the driveway when John reached the Laval house. He went in through the mudroom door and started a one-armed cookie hunt. His right hand was still holding the ice bag over his right eye. Unless Marie had devised a new hiding place, there wasn't a single cookie in the house. He decided to inspect the damage to his eye, so he walked into the bathroom in the hallway.

The moment John removed the ice bag from his eye was the most sickening moment of his short life, including the day he lost $80,000 on Lean.com. In the place of his right eye was a tennis-ball-sized purple mass of tissue swollen as tightly as a drum skin. When he forced the swollen eyelids open with his fingers, he was even more horrified. Apparently all the blood in his body had migrated to his right eyeball. It was a crimson, hideous mess. He felt sick to his stomach and he wanted to heave or lie down, but he was too fascinated by the freaky, bloody mass attached to his face. Perhaps his right eye could be saved if he could get to the emergency room of the hospital right away. He was on his way out of the mud room when Annette parked beside the garage. When she saw John holding the half-melted ice bag over his eye, she jumped out of her car and ran to inspect the injury.

"What happened?" she said breathlessly.

"A lacrosse ball hit me in the eye." It was easier to be

brave with another person at his side.

"We're going to the emergency room right now," Annette said.

The doctor inspected the eye and predicted John's recovery with no ill effects.

"Great sport, lacrosse," the doctor said. "I played a year at Andover and two years at Amherst."

It was clear to John that he would have gotten more sympathy from a female physician than from this nostalgic lacrosse stud. The doctor gave John pain medication and a first-rate bandage that wrapped around his head and bulged impressively over his covered right eye. The unmistakable message of this bandage was, "This is no trivial injury".

Annette took John home to a hero's welcome at the Hardin house. Dan and Scott asked for a detailed play-by-play, and even Benjamin arrived to see the traumatized athlete. Dan ordered delivery pizzas, and John's family turned the occasion of his maiming into an impromptu party.

While he wore his professional-looking bandage to school for ten days, John basked in a notoriety that his skill at lacrosse never had merited. Corky wanted to sign the bandage with a magic marker, but John finally convinced him that the autograph convention was for casts only. Paul Bruguiere came by the Hardin house one afternoon after his vocational school let out and very thoughtfully offered to loan John an eye patch belonging to his Uncle Thomas. John didn't voice his opinion that this was the most distasteful offer he had ever received.

The highlight of all the condolences and offers of assistance that he received during his fortnight of fame was when

Andrea asked if he wanted help with his algebra homework. Of course, he did. They worked on assigned problems for almost an hour a couple of times each week until he retired the bandage. On those days, John didn't get home in time to trade options, and he didn't care.

Andrea von Bergen trumped Wall Street through the end of the school year and the start of summer marked by Andrea's return to Austria. With Andrea gone, John concentrated on working at the hardware store and trading options throughout June and July. His string of successes continued.

Corky returned in late July from another vacation in Italy with his mother. The morning after his return, Corky stopped in at Hardin's Hardware to see John. He asked John whether he wanted to go fishing after work. John negotiated an early release from work. Shortly after the town clock chimes had struck seven o'clock, John and Corky pushed the runabout away from the Hardin dock. Corky, a skilled procurer of edibles, had brought two Pepsis and two submarine sandwiches with him, so they anchored the boat near a small island a mile outside Caledonia Bay and ate before they made a single cast. Corky couldn't stop talking about Italy. He seemed different from the Old Corky. He was less inhibited. He kept talking about an Italian teenager who worked in the gardens of the house where they stayed. In fact, he talked about him so much that it annoyed John.

"Did you have a thing for this Antolini guy?" An uncomfortable pause followed. Corky wasn't laughing and he wasn't protesting. "So?"

"He's a good friend," Corky said. He wasn't telling

John everything. John didn't know what to say next, so he concentrated on fishing for a while before resuming his questions.

"So, does Anthony speak English?"

"*Antolini*," Corky corrected him. "Yeah."

"A gardener and a linguist?"

"Hey," Corky said defensively, "don't slam a guy you haven't met!"

"Whatever."

"Anyway, we used to swim together in this swimming pool on the mansion grounds." Corky seemed driven to get the words out. "When we swam together, we swam in the nude." Corky watched John carefully, assessing the effect of his words. John still didn't get it. "It was so cool. No one else was around. We could run around the gardens in the nude and swim in the nude, and it was so awesome." John had never experienced a conversation like this one, and his feelings were suspended somewhere between curiosity and revulsion. "One time in the pool, Antolini touched...."

"Whoa," John interjected. "That's all I need to hear, Corky. Why don't you cool your jets and catch a fish?"

"I'm just trying to tell you about Italy," Corky said. He seemed hurt.

"I don't have to hear every minute detail about Italy," John said attempting to assuage any insult to the loquacious world-traveler.

Corky rested for a while. The sun had set behind the mountains and the lone cloud in the western sky was bright red with magenta edges. John turned on the running lights and the anchor light.

"Do you want to go swimming?" Corky asked.

"Not right at the moment."

A third of the way into August, Paul Bruguiere invited John and Corky over to Thomas Bruguiere's house for Chinese food. Paul wasn't famous for his generosity, so the invitation aroused their curiosity. As it turned out, there was no reason for suspicion. Paul was spending Sunday and Monday with his Uncle Thomas before returning to the music camp on the island, so he seized the opportunity to show his two old pals his secret creation.

Thomas, already privy to the secret, was in an expansive mood. He ladled out huge portions of fried rice and pork and sweet and sour chicken with chunks of pineapples as big as dominoes. He served green tea so hot it could melt the fillings in one's teeth. Thomas put on quite a clinic on eating with chopsticks, but after a few moments of amateur chopstick fumbling, all three boys asked for forks. It was a tasty meal, and it lasted long enough for Thomas to pound down two Australian beers.

"Do yourselves a favor and don't drink when you get older," Thomas said. Apparently, Thomas was more inclined to serve as an advisor than an example. "Now, Paul has something he wants to show you."

Paul got up from his dining room seat, walked out of the house by a sliding glass doorway, and stood like a television game show host beside a large object covered by a tarpaulin. Thomas, John, and Corky followed in his footsteps.

"This mysterious object took me a year to build," he said. "And you guys are the only people besides Uncle Thomas to ever see it." The technique used by magicians to uncover surprises like ladies sawed in half, etc., is the technique Paul used to whip the tarpaulin off the object to reveal the most exquisite canoe either boy had ever seen.

"Awesome," Corky said as he ran his hand along the finely finished gunwales.

"The rails and thwarts are spruce," Paul said, "and the ribs and planking are northern white cedar. I got the wood from Maine."

"It's the most beautiful boat I've ever seen," John said. "The stain and finish are perfect."

Paul was obviously pleased. He lightly passed his fingers over the inlaid accent pieces on the bow deck plate. "I got the plans for $50 over in Maine, too. It took me ten months to build it and a month to apply the finish."

"It's priceless," Corky said.

"I think I can get $8,000 for it."

Thomas was clearly proud of his nephew. He assured John and Corky that he had never seen finer workmanship. Thomas pulled the tab on another pint of Aussie beer after the three boys had moved back into the house so Thomas could serve them each a huge slice of store-bought cherry pie and a glass of milk. John looked around the small house more carefully than he had before. It was sparsely decorated, but every surface was immaculately clean. The wooden floors were as highly polished as the lanes of a bowling alley, and there wasn't a speck of dust anywhere. John pointed to a thick book on the birds of New England. Thomas said he was reading it. This Thomas Bruguiere was a hard man to figure out, John thought.

Long before sunset, John and Corky took their leave from the Bruguiere house after thanking Thomas elaborately for his hospitality and after another round of praise for Paul's boat-building skill. John could tell that Paul was genuinely flattered. As they walked down the narrow streets toward the town docks, Corky discoursed on the theme of artisanship and on the wondrous works by skilled artisans he had seen in Italy.

"I saw great statues and awesome buildings and I thought how could they make these things," Corky said. "And then I see Paul's canoe and I think the same thing."

"Yep."

"That was cool. I'm glad we went to Bruguiere's house," Corky said.

"And I'm glad you didn't ask Thomas and Paul to go swimming in the nude," John said as he punched Corky on the shoulder.

Corky snorted and punched John back on the shoulder. Right then he knew his obliquely disclosed secret was safe with his friend John.

Andrew Gleason added six more houses to his growing inventory of renovated rental properties in Caledonia that summer. John searched the Internet and found a list of twenty-two such rentals owned by Corky's father. John asked Corky about the properties, and Corky told John that his dad just wanted to make money. That was understandable. This was America. Andrew Gleason had been named to the Board of Directors at Thornton Academy in July. He retained his place on the Brighton School Board. He was a man of influence.

Thornton Prep invited past members of the Board of Directors to attend the installation of the new Board. Phillip Laval, Joe T. Harrington, and Benjamin Hardin drove together to the induction ceremony in the Thornton Chapel. The ceremony was brief, so the present and former directors were happy to mosey over to the complimentary bar as the day was warm and Thornton buildings were not air-conditioned.

Andrew Gleason ordered a dry Martini. Phillip Laval asked for a glass of white wine. Joe T. Harrington ordered a gin-and-tonic. Benjamin Hardin got a rock-and-rye mixed with ginger ale. Joe T. left a nice tip for the bartender.

"How long have you been sipping those sissy drinks?" Joe T. asked Benjamin.

"Decades."

Phillip and Joe T. had seen Benjamin's mental state slipping at a faster rate during the past six months. At first, it was nouns. Benjamin often couldn't think of the names of things.

"I left my...thing for starting the car," he said once. "Key" was the word he couldn't locate in the filing cabinet of his mind. Another time, Benjamin told Marie that she had left her "frisbee" at his house. He meant "pie plate". The next data to be erased from Benjamin's mental hard drive were peoples' names. He said "Dan" when he meant "John". He called Joyce by the name of "Helen" frequently. It became increasingly hard for Benjamin to keep track of the thread of dialogue, and he sometimes blurted out incongruous phrases just to be part of the conversation.

Joyce Harrington called Dan to ask if he had noticed.

Dan told her it had started about a year earlier when his father had begun forgetting to do repetitive tasks he had done from memory over the years. He had forgotten to renew the insurance policy on the hardware store. He had often lost his car keys. He had left his credit card on the counters of at least five different establishments around town. Dan assured Joyce that Benjamin was getting expert medical attention.

"Dan," Joyce said, "we're going to take care of that precious man, your father. He has been a loving friend for all these years and we love him like family!"

Dan told Joyce that he had tried to persuade Benjamin to come live in the Dan Hardin house. So far, however, Benjamin was reluctant to leave the house he had bought with Helen so many years before.

"It doesn't make any sense for him to live alone anymore," Dan said. "I'm afraid he'll turn his house into a bonfire."

"I know you'll do what's right for your father," Joyce said. She seemed satisfied that Dan was sufficiently protective of his father's well-being. "Joe T. and I will try to put a bug in your dad's car about moving in with you."

At one point in the cocktail reception in the Thornton Chapel Annex, Andrew Gleason arranged to be alone with Benjamin. Andrew had noticed that Benjamin's mental capacity was declining, and he wanted to tell him something while Benjamin could still comprehend it.

"Ben," Andrew said, "can I speak with you about a private matter."

"Yes."

"Some time ago, my wife fell and hurt herself outside your store, do you remember that?"

"Yes, I do."

"Well, I'm not proud of my actions back then. I was worried that my wife had hurt herself seriously, and I stormed around making quite a fool of myself."

"A husband wants to protect his wife."

"Well," Andrew said, "some things came out in that deposition that were, frankly, very disturbing. I've sought help for my wife's problems and she's made great strides. Gossip damages reputations. You didn't gossip, and I want to thank you." Andrew shook Benjamin's hand.

"There's not one of us without fault, not a single one," Benjamin said softly. In previous times with full mental capacity, Benjamin might have been suspicious of the new, mellower Andrew Gleason. Now, however, Benjamin was as trusting as a child. Andrew patted Benjamin on the shoulder and walked back toward the bar.

After the reception, Phillip dropped Joe T. off at the Harrington house and then dropped Benjamin off at the Dan Hardin house so Benjamin could join The Triad for hamburgers. Scott served the overdone hamburgers straight off the grill.

"Nice hockey pucks," Dan said. Scott scowled at him.

"I like hockey," Benjamin said.

The banter continued around the table until Benjamin suddenly spoke up in a moment of clarity.

"Andrew Gleason thanked us for keeping our mouths shut about his wife's thing," Benjamin said, referring to Mrs. Gleason's slip-and-fall.

"No harm done," Dan said, although he added less generously, "I'm still not convinced that Andrew Gleason is anything but a manipulator."

"What happened?" John asked.

"Just some complications about Mrs. Gleason's hospital care when she fell outside the store two winters ago," Dan said. He didn't want to get into details in view of John's friendship with Corky. "It's all squared away now."

"That's right," Benjamin said, his clarity fading, "it's all squared away now."

"Done?" John asked.

"Done," Dan replied.

"Done," Benjamin parroted.

Chapter 15

SOPHOMORE

JOHN'S SOPHOMORE YEAR at Thornton Prep was a year of transformation. His interests switched from solitary pursuits like reading to more social activities like sports, specifically, running. The genesis of John's obsession with running occurred near the end of his freshman year as he dawdled beside the Thornton Champions Trophy Case. John had heard autobiographical tales of Dan's and Scott's prowess on the ice and on the football field, but he had heard nothing about their running laurels.

On display in the trophy case were gold and silver medals from the 400-meter run at the 1982 New England Prep School Track Meet. A display card read, "Scott Harrington's gold medal (49.22) and Daniel Lee Hardin's silver medal (49.33) were generously donated after their graduation from Princeton University." Neither his father nor Scott had ever mentioned these medals to John. He mistook their incomplete memories for modesty. John asked his father how he had learned to run so fast. Dan set aside his customary verbal frugality to talk for fifteen minutes about interval training.

After a lengthy search, Dan found his books on diet and sprint training and he gave them to his son.

John took up running with his typical singularity of focus. He trained arduously all summer long. He lowered his 400-meter time from 54.20 seconds to 51.45 in ninety days, but he knew he had a long way to go to be competitive. He used a cloth tape measure to record the diameter of his thighs and his calves, and he was amazed by increases in muscle size. Running became such an important part of his daily ritual that he felt out-of-sorts if he missed a day. He felt healthier, slept better, and ate more conscientiously when he ran. His goal was to break 50 seconds flat by October and to turn a 48-second-flat time by track season in the spring.

John's physical conditioning improved his lacrosse play, as well. In the past, he had felt like an electron propelled by an invisible force in an unstable two-dimensional orbit around the ball. He was all speed and no direction. During autumn intramurals, however, he flitted around the pitch on a powerful set of legs and a maturing mental discipline. He was quicker, so his defense was vastly improved, and he began to grasp concepts like spreading the offense and predicting ball movement better. He scored goals in three off-season friendly matches – Oxbridge Prep, Stone Haven Prep, and Inverness School. No one ripped his helmet off, and neither of his eyes was smashed into a swollen eggplant.

He gained confidence socially. He no longer felt like a provincial among his classmates from Toronto, Taipei, and Amsterdam. He discovered that the big city kids owned a set of doubts and flaws just like him and his fellow Caledonia "townies". Like the "townies", rich kids from around the world also nibbled at their nails and tried to hide their zits with medication that dried to the consistency of wood putty. It seemed that each student – international or "townie" – showed at least some trace of insecurity. Awareness of his peers' lack of confidence reinforced his own sense of self-worth.

John joined in conversations with other students more readily than in the past. He was still more likely to listen that to speak when in a group, but he felt more engaged in peer conversations than in previous encounters when episodic day-dreams often transported him miles away. When he did speak, his classmates paid attention, because they liked his sense of humor and his easy-going manner, mainly plagiarized from Scott Harrington.

He scanned the quadrangle during one such cluster-talk on the first day of class in his tenth grade year and his blood pressure spiked when he spotted Andrea von Bergen. His inner ears buzzed and his breathing became shallower as he watched every move she made. When she saw John, she left her gaggle of girlfriends and hurried over to him and hugged him hard enough to squeeze the air out of his lungs and to set his heart pounding. When she initiated the European double-cheek-kiss routine, John was ready for her, because he had practiced during the summer using a football as a proxy for Andrea's head.

"John, I'm so glad to see you!"

That was music to John's ears. He had carefully selected his first day's outfit with Andrea in mind. He had inspected himself scrupulously in his bedroom mirror before leaving for class. He wore prep school boilerplate — slightly worn

Weejuns, no socks, khaki shorts, a white button-down oxford shirt with school tie loosely knotted in a half-Windsor, and a school blazer. Admiring himself in the mirror, noting with approval his dark sun tan and muscular runner's legs, he entertained the thought that a girl would have to be stark-raving insane to resist his charms. He deduced by Andrea's reaction that she was not stark-raving insane.

"You look ravishing," he said. The phrase had sounded perfect in front of his practice mirror, but now, in an actual game-time situation, he worried that "ravishing" was too suggestive or a word not in her vocabulary, so he added, "and healthy and happy". He felt that a guy had to be flexible about his choice of words when he was talking to a girl who was possibly the most attractive sophomore on the East Coast. They talked for only a couple of minutes because class beckoned.

"Meet you for lunch at the town docks," Andrea said as she held his hand extended until her departure separated their fingertips. It was a dramatic move, and John wondered if she had practiced the move in front of her dormitory room mirror. She hustled back to join her friends in their migration toward their next class.

John's two colleagues standing next to him wore smiles of awe with a touch of envy. Nuo, a kid from Shanghai, beamed as he said, "You lucky, lucky dog."

Corky Gleason said, "I think she likes you."

Corky, suntanned and slightly thinner than last year, had just returned from Italy, and he was in a perpetual state of good humor. He showed his new optimism by over-decorating his conversation with Italian phrases. It was a little more difficult for him to show his alleged weight loss. Does a bean bag look thinner after the loss of ten beans? John accepted Corky's weight loss claims in good faith. Apparently, running around the woods and swimming in the nude with Antolini was just what Corky needed to shed a pound or two.

John borrowed one of Scott's coined metaphors to describe the benefits of Corky's cavorting in the buff: Romping about in the nude with his gangly Italian companion seemed to "stabilize the gyro of his soul". John liked the phrase because it blended the scientific with the idyllic. It suggested a collaborative pastoral image that could have been inspired by Albert Einstein and Emily Dickinson. Time ran out on John's in-depth analysis of Corky, and the three sophomores moved on to class.

Not only did Andrea join John for lunch, she agreed to go fishing with him on Saturday. John horse-traded a day off from his Saturday work schedule at the hardware store. He collected Andrea at her dormitory at ten o'clock, and they walked the three blocks to the Dan Hardin house.

At John's request, Dan, Scott, and Annette were all present and busy making breakfast in the kitchen. John wanted a full panel of judges for the introduction of Andrea. Annette received Andrea with a handshake, which surprised John, because he assumed that women routinely embraced complete strangers as in movies he had seen. Dan also shook hands with Andrea and he welcomed her to his home. Scott's greeting, of course, was wordier and more flamboyant than Dan's.

"*Guten morgen*," Scott hailed her cheerfully. Scott's lingual armory contained two words, and *only* two words, in ten languages, and he liked to use his ammunition early. Andrea shook his hand and played along by replying in German. He had no idea what she had just said to him, so Scott said, "*Ja, ja*," and he returned to his cooking duties.

Breakfast went well. Dan asked Andrea about Salzburg, and her description was neither too long nor too short. Scott wanted to know about universal conscription in her country. She said that when her cousin was issued a U.S. Army surplus helmet for his mandatory service in the Austrian Army, the cousin's great uncle told him that he had spent two years of his World War II service shooting at Americans wearing the identical helmet.

Andrea threw a bone to the chef by raving about Scott's omelets. Scott reacted as though he had invented the omelet. Dan would have said, "Thanks." Scott commenced a tutorial on how to make an omelet.

Annette packed a cooler with sandwiches, fruit drinks, and cookies, and she left the cooler beside a plastic container of worms sitting on a bench on the back deck. John and Andrea carried the provisions to the dock. John uncovered the runabout, warmed the engine, and stowed the worms, fishing rods, food, and towels. Within five minutes, John and Andrea had reversed away from the dock and were onplane to traverse the width of Caledonia Bay. Annette joined Scott and Dan on the back deck to observe their departure.

"Is it just my imagination," Scott asked, squinting to watch their departure through his left eye, "or is our John Wesley Hardin an unusually cool dude?"

"Just so," said Dan, a big Kipling reader since his own prep school days.

"I hope she brings him happiness, not misery," Annette said distractedly.

Scott accused her of stealing her depressing lines from a soap opera.

"Don't mess it up!" Scott called. Of course, his voice could not be heard across the lawn or over the waves or over the noise of the inboard motor.

OHS was obscuring Scott's vision as slowly and as surely as dementia was eroding Benjamin's mental capacity. Scott was more acutely aware of his own impairment than Benjamin was of his. Scott rarely made any reference to his flying days, but he frequently had vivid dreams about flying. When he awoke from a flying dream, his initial sensation was one of immense well-being and of desire to hold on to the vision. As sleep released its hold on his brain, however, melancholy drifted in like a fog, and he had to work to block it, compartmentalize it, and tuck it away. His antidote was to get up from bed, do sixty pushups, sixty crunches, fifty deep knee bends, and take a shower. A hot shower locked the door of the vault where flying was stored. He continued working for Dan at Hardin's Hardware, and he no longer looked for other jobs.

Dan persuaded his father – Benjamin — to retire completely from working at the hardware store. Symptoms of dementia had caused some awkward misunderstandings with customers and a lot of misplaced merchandise. In one instance, Benjamin had unpacked an entire box of toilet float balls and stocked them in the nautical section next to the plastic boat fenders and rubberized buoys.

"It's a marvel how the brain works," Scott observed.

"Or not," Dan said.

Dan had a more difficult time persuading Benjamin to sell his house and to move in with The Triad at the Dan Hardin house. The Benjamin Hardin house was a Colonial style brick home built in 1822. Benjamin had been born there, and he had lived there for sixty-five years. Its symmetrical windows were topped by solid lintels made of New Hampshire granite. Benjamin had ensured that the large chimneys on either end of the house were professionally swept every year since 1963, the year he had bought both the house and Hardin's Hardware from his father. Benjamin's identity was mortared into the bricks of the house, and getting him to leave was going to be difficult.

Benjamin made a habit of buying lunch for tourists and giving out twenty-dollar bills to strangers. He did so with such sincerity that strangers didn't know how to react. Benjamin lowered the volume and tone of his voice as he presented a crisp twenty-dollar bill to a surprised tourist.

"I want you to have this to make your stay in Caledonia a pleasant one," Benjamin said. He was like a one-man Chamber of Commerce. His conduct was baffling to visitors from Hartford, Boston, and New York – cities where people attempted to *take* one's money, not give theirs away.

When a waiter at the café closest to the town docks informed Dan of his father's cash-dispensing habit, Dan confiscated his father's debit card, credit card, and personal checks. Benjamin had always carried a roll of cash in his pocket, and he claimed to feel naked without such a roll. Dan's solution was to photo-copy some ten- and twenty-dollar bills to re-place the legal tender in his father's pocket.

Before long, the phony bills started showing up all over town. Compassionate friends returned the bills to Dan when they visited the hardware store. They asked after his father's health and wished him well. As the funny money made its way back to Dan, he could piece together the tracks of his father's meandering travels and calculate how much Benjamin might have given away without the improvisation.

Dan discovered that his father had applied to get a re-verse mortgage on the Benjamin Hardin house. Benjamin had contacted Andrew Gleason at Tremont Savings to help him convert the equity in his home to cash, presumably so he could hand it out to strangers in the restaurants of Caledonia. At some risk to himself because of privacy laws, Andrew Gleason alerted Dan to Benjamin's intentions.

Partly in gratitude for Andrew's help, Dan worked out a deal to sell Benjamin's house to Andrew to add to the Gleason inventory of converted rental apartments. It took two months to get Benjamin to go along with the agreement and another two months to remove all of Benjamin's posses-sions from his long-time residence, but Gleason could afford to be patient, because Dan had agreed to a discounted selling price to facilitate lenient terms of timing and vacancy. Dan used the proceeds from the sale of Benjamin's house to re-tire debt on the books of Hardin's Hardware. Dan effectively took control of Benjamin's modest assets except his Keogh IRA and his Social Security income.

Benjamin drifted in and out of long bouts of confusion

interrupted by short interludes of clarity. Dan spent most of his days off from work taking his father out of the house to stimulate his mind. Dan chauffeured Benjamin to all of his medical appointments. In the height of winter, Dan cross-country skied with Benjamin on weekdays when the trails were relatively free of other skiers. He took him alpine skiing once a week when conditions were good. These activities delighted Benjamin, because he could depend on a lifetime of muscle memory to give him confidence on skis and skiing didn't require speaking.

Scott entertained Benjamin on his days off, too. Scott and Benjamin paddled their kayaks all around the perimeter of Caledonia Bay in warm weather. When autumn came, Scott enlisted the cleaning girl, Lisa, to take him and Benjamin to the indoor ice rink during hours set aside for public skating. Scott and Benjamin skated laps for an hour without exchanging more than twenty words. Lisa returned to pick them up for the ride back to the Dan Hardin house, and Benjamin tipped Lisa generously with counterfeit bills. Benjamin stayed physically strong and avoided the worst of insomnia symptoms. Scott was always patient with Benjamin, and when Benjamin babbled incoherently, Scott responded in a normal conversational voice, having no idea whether he was on or off point.

"The ice thing can't, uh, eat the nets with lawnmowers," Benjamin said as he skated beside Scott on lap umpteen.

"Yeah," Scott said, "they take the goals down so the Zamboni can dress the ice."

After John got his driving license in March of 2004, he was even more help with Benjamin. On weekends, John used Dan's car to take Benjamin along with him and Andrea to watch the Thornton Academy hockey team clash with their prep school rivals. Benjamin especially liked away games. At the Stone Haven Prep arena, John and Andrea left Grandfather Benjamin to block three seats while they went to the concession stand to get popcorn and soft drinks. Benjamin tried to force a counterfeit ten-dollar tip on John, but John refused, telling his grandfather that the treat was on him.

When John and Andrea returned with the snacks, Benjamin had left his seat in the stands and was nowhere to be seen. John left Andrea to guard the snacks, and he started an arena-wide search for his missing grandfather. John found him in the middle of a droll business transaction near the home team locker room. Benjamin was trying to buy skates so he could get out on the ice. Amid the din of hockey pucks slamming into the boards as the two teams warmed up for their match, Benjamin was offering a Stone Haven Prep junior varsity hockey player thirty dollars to rent his skates. The amused youngster and his teammates were laughing and trying to explain that Benjamin couldn't skate at the moment because a hockey game was about to begin.

"I can skate rings around those kids!" Benjamin said. "Here, take *forty* dollars."

John arrived in time to distract Benjamin. He pointed to his head so the boys understood his grandfather's limitations, and he told Benjamin he couldn't skate right now, because the teams had reserved the ice.

"I've got popcorn for you, Granddad," John said, as he guided Benjamin back toward the seats Andrea had saved for them.

"Popcorn?" Benjamin asked. "I like popcorn."

"I got you a Coke, too."

"Coke?" Benjamin said, as enthusiastically as a five-year-old, "I like Coke."

Back in the Dan Hardin house, life with Benjamin settled into a kind of normalcy. John discovered that physical contact comforted Benjamin, so John often sat on the couch beside his grandfather and put his arm around Benjamin's shoulders.

"You're a good boy, Dan," Benjamin said without fail.

John also bathed Benjamin's feet in a warm tub of water and clipped his toe nails once a month. Somewhere in the back of John's mind was the notion – probably Biblical — that washing the feet of a person was a way of showing respect, so John washed and massaged his grandfather's feet, hoping Grandfather Benjamin comprehended that he was loved and respected. John also brushed his grandfather's hair and laundered his clothing to keep him fresh at all times.

"You're a good boy," Benjamin said.

Andrea had joined John one Saturday in April in the height of "mud season" to walk with Benjamin over sidewalks lined with melting snow down to the diner at the town docks for breakfast. Friends of Benjamin's came by their table to greet him. They were careful to state their names for Benjamin's sake, because he couldn't possibly remember them. Benjamin called John by his father's name – Dan – most of the time.

"Benjamin," Fred Cummings said as he approached their table, "Fred Cummings here. How are you?"

"Fred," Benjamin beamed, "you old rascal. How are you?"

"I'm good." They shook hands. "I see you're with a beautiful girl as usual," he said, as he shook hands with Andrea.

"Yep, yep. You know Helen, of course."

"Of course," Fred said, as he patted John on the shoulder and moved away. "Take care, Benjamin."

"You too, you old rascal," Benjamin said. When Fred was a good distance away from their table, Benjamin added, "He does book things."

"He's a lawyer," John said.

"He's a lawyer," Benjamin repeated.

John and Andrea walked Benjamin home past the town docks. "Ice out" had been officially announced, and the *M/S Franklin Pierce* was back in service cruising the waters of Lake Tremont between Stableton Dykes, Dartford Parade, and Caledonia.

"She's a beautiful...." Benjamin couldn't think of the word.

"She's a beautiful vessel," John said. He was holding hands with Andrea, and she squeezed his hand when he said the words.

"She's a beautiful vessel," Benjamin echoed. "Helen, I've taken Dan on that vessel many, many times."

Having returned home, John and Andrea walked Benjamin upstairs to his bedroom and helped him lie down still in his walking clothes before covering him with a lamb's wool throw.

"Enjoy your nap, Granddad," John said.

Andrea kissed Benjamin on the forehead.

"Enjoy your nap, Helen," Benjamin said to her.

John squeezed his grandfather's hand and tucked it under the throw.

"You're a good boy, Dan," Benjamin said, and he closed his eyes like a child.

John closed the door after he and Andrea had exited the bedroom. Andrea faced him and wrapped her arms around him, inclining her face to give John a long kiss. John held her tightly.

"You *are* a good boy," she whispered.

The tears in John's eyes embarrassed him, but Andrea's long embrace did not.

Dan had hired Lisa Sullivan as a cleaning lady after Benjamin's move into the Dan Hardin house. She was a pleasant twenty-five-year-old divorcee who had left with her three-year-old son from Kennebunkport, Maine to live with her mother in Caledonia. Her mother had worked as a cashier at Hardin's Hardware for more than twenty years, so Dan was quick to hire Lisa when he found out that she needed work. Lisa cleaned the Dan Hardin house from nine o'clock to three o'clock on Mondays, Wednesday, and Fridays. She vacuumed, dusted, cleaned windows, and ironed. Perhaps as importantly, she was an extra set of eyes to watch over Benjamin while she was in the house. Occasionally, Lisa brought her toddler with her, and the little guy entertained Benjamin for hours, or vice versa.

On a school day in late April, John darted home during the lunch hour to pick up his track shoes. Lisa Sullivan's car was parked in the driveway. John entered the house through the mud room as quietly as possible to avoid interrupting his grandfather Benjamin's nap. Just as he silently opened the glass-paned door that separated the mud room from the kitchen, John saw his father holding Lisa tightly as they shared a long kiss. Neither Dan nor Lisa had heard the door open or detected John's gasp of astonishment as he stood frozen with one hand glued to the door knob. Dan's left hand brushed Lisa's long auburn hair away from her eyes.

"I shouldn't have done that," Dan said. "It's been a long time."

"It's been a long time for me, too," Lisa said.

They released one another then, and they fortuitously turned their backs on the mud room to look out on Caledonia Bay. John silently closed the mud room door and backtracked to the door leading from the driveway into the mud room. He closed the door audibly and dragged his boots on the throw rug to scrape every last grain of sand off his boots. He walked to the door that led from the mud room to the kitchen and opened it noisily. He walked into the room as Lisa and Dan turned around to face him.

"Hi, guys," John said. He headed for the refrigerator to reconnoiter as he always did.

"Hello," Lisa said.

"Do you want some tuna?" Dan asked him.

"Thanks, no. I already ate. I just need to get my running shoes."

John stealthily climbed the stairs, glided by his grandfather's bedroom, entered his own room, and found his track shoes. Whew, he thought, I dodged a bullet. Until the moment he had seen his father kissing Lisa, John had not seriously thought about how lonely fifteen years without

Trinette must have been for his father. John had been too focused on himself, his own life and his own obsessions, to have more than a passing thought about his father's life and his needs for affection. When John returned to the kitchen, Lisa had already moved into the living room with a duster in her hands. His father was spreading mayonnaise on a tuna sandwich.

"See you, Dad," John said as he walked out the door to the mud room with the shoe laces strung over his neck like a Hawaiian lei.

"See you, Champ," Dan said.

John had a lot to think about as he stretched and ran a pattern of alternating quarter-miles of 65-second and 90-second laps. The eighty-minute workout seemed to last for only five minutes so intent was he on thinking about his father and Lisa.

Lisa surprised John again about a month later when he walked into his bedroom on a Friday afternoon at just before three o'clock. The Thornton Invitational Track Meet had been cancelled for rain, so John was home earlier than expected. His footsteps on the stairs were muffled by the constant downpour of rain on the gabled roof of the house.

As he walked into his room, Lisa was standing beside a floor lamp with a book in her hands held close to the light to make reading easier for her. The book she was holding was John's diary. His entry into the room startled Lisa, and she jumped with alarm and clasped the book to her chest. Her face reddened and she spluttered a garbled apology.

"Oh, John, I…oh, I'm so sorry. I'm so embarrassed. This is so wrong."

Lisa was deeply distressed. She held out the diary to him.

"I was cleaning, and I, oh, there's no excuse for what I did. I should never have opened this book. Please, I hope you can forgive me."

John took the book and he looked down at the open page. The text that jumped out at him was "NAV: $927,275 net of 2003 taxes!!!" Lisa was embarrassed almost to the point of falling prostrate on the floor.

John was embarrassed, too. Had Lisa read his thoughts about Andrea? Had she decoded his secret Kissing Evaluation System where a "5" was an average kiss and a "10" was the best kiss known to mankind? Had she read about his quest to save Hardin's Hardware from bankruptcy and to keep Scott off the dole? Had she discerned the meaning of the steadily increasing NAV figures in the pages of his most secret of all books? He blamed himself for not hiding the diary better.

"John, I apologize from the bottom of my heart. I really need this job. I hope you can forgive me." She kept pleading as if her heartbeat depended on it. "I don't blame you if you're angry with me."

"Lisa, can you forget everything you read in my diary?"

"Yes, right now. It's done," Lisa said, waving her hand in an arc as though casting a spell or erasing a chalk board.

"A lot of stuff in my diary is meaningless. I mean all those numbers, they're just a game I play with some friends, kind of like football fantasy league."

"I thought so," said the woman who had just professed to have already forgotten the contents of the book.

"Then, let's forget about it. I know you didn't mean any harm."

"Thank you very much, John." Lisa's shoulders slumped in relief. She awkwardly moved toward him as if to give him a kiss, but she ended up squeezing both of his biceps in her two small hands. "I'll never forget your kindness. And I'll keep my nose out of your business in the future. You can count on it." Lisa released her grip on his arms and folded her arms across her breasts as she walked past him toward the door. Lisa worked like a dervish for an extra hour that afternoon, and she didn't charge extra for the overtime.

John's new diversions – running and Andrea von Bergen — altered his habit of hurrying home at 2:30 each school day afternoon to seek out money-making opportunities in the last hour-and-a-half of trading. As stock market indexes climbed steadily from August 2003 through the summer of 2004, he refined his chart-reading skills and hedged his portfolio more carefully. The option trades he put on tended to be of longer durations.

For example, in July of 2003, before the start of his sophomore year, he had established a bullish put spread using Ingersoll-Rand (IR) July $21 and $24 Puts. The forty IR July $24 Puts were assigned to him before their expiration at a cost of $96,000. He had established the put spread for a net credit of $1.40, so his cost basis was $22.60 a share. Rather than sell the 4,000 shares and go on to another trade, he decided to hold the shares because he liked IR's continued bullish price pattern. In November, he sold-to-open the December $33 covered Calls for $1.33. The Calls were exercised in December shortly before expiration, and John received the $132,000 in proceeds from the sale and he kept the $5,320 premium from the sale of the Calls. In about five months, John had netted $46,920, better than a hundred per cent annualized return.

John managed a $38,300 profit when J. C. Penney (JCP) stock ran up from $18.50 in August 2003 to $33.88 in March 2004. He fared even better on a trade in Monsanto; MON climbed steadily from $11.40 in August 2003 to $17.85 in March 2004, and John profited by $43,600. His best return on investment came near the end of the spring semester in 2004. In April, when New York Stock Exchange stock (NYX) was just below $20, John paid about $3,600 to buy-to-open eighty of the (NYX) May $30 Calls for $0.45. A little over two weeks later, when NYX leaped to $31.17, John sold-to-close the calls for $11.35, realizing a profit of $87,200. John's diary entries that Spring were more often about Andrea von Bergen and about his lap times in the 400-meter run than about stock options, but he underlined the April 30 entry: NAV $927,275 net of 2003 taxes!!!" That was the entry that Lisa Sullivan had read and promised to forget.

John ran his season-best four hundred meters in a time of 49.89. That proved good enough to win in the dual meet with Inverness School, but not good enough to qualify for the New England Prep School Track Meet. He had fallen short of his goal. Dan and Scott soothed his feelings by assuring him that he would break his goal of 48 seconds easily next year if he kept training. Andrea's tonic for John's disappointment was a kiss and the words, "I don't care if you qualified. You *ran!*"

Andrea and John celebrated the end of final examinations

by joining friends for a food orgy at a village pizza house. Between bites of thin-crust pizza, one boy talked about returning to Houston for his summer job caddying at a country club. An international student from Mexico described the music camp in Michigan where she was scheduled to spend the summer. A girl from New York had landed an internship for the summer which entitled her to work like a dog for free at a fashion design firm in New York City.

Nuo, the boy from Shanghai, said something that wasn't completely understandable, but as always, everyone laughed heartily. Nuo had an impish smile glued to his face constantly, so people were disposed to laugh with him, no matter what he said. Nuo claimed that his name meant "graceful" in Chinese. If so, it was obvious that his parents had dubbed him "graceful" at birth before seeing him stumble over curbs and entrance thresholds all over the Thornton campus.

John asked Andrea if there was any chance she could stay in New England, specifically Caledonia, for the summer. This was not a new question from John's lips. As in previous conversations, she told him she had to go back to Salzburg.

The group of six made their way to the Thornton boat house complex. They sat on one of the docks in a line like a colony of sea gulls. They bantered about trivial things, anything worthy of a good laugh. Andrea and Nuo planned to share a limousine to Boston Logan the next day. John couldn't stop thinking that three months was a long time to miss touching Andrea's soft skin, hearing her laugh, and kissing her supple lips.

The students left the docks at sunset, and John walked Andrea to her dormitory main door for the last time that school year. In deference to school rules, John tuned down the intensity of his farewell. He kissed Andrea lightly on the left check and told her, "You know how I feel." Andrea cried and returned his kiss before walking hastily through the front entrance. John walked home in the dusk to the Dan Hardin house.

When Andrea passed the dormitory monitor's desk, the monitor looked up and called out her name. Andrea retraced her steps to the monitor's Dutch window. The monitor handed Andrea a note with a telephone number starting with "43", the country code for Austria. Andrea recognized the telephone number.

"I took the call at about four o'clock," the young woman said. "The caller didn't say who she was, but she did ask whether final examinations were finished. I told her that exams were over as of today."

Andrea expressed her thanks and went to her room. She was still emotional over parting with John, so she waited for a while to compose herself before calling her mother. When she went down the hallway to the visitors' lounge, she had another wait before she could get into one of the two sound-proof telephone rooms to call home. When she finally got through, her mother picked up the telephone on the second ring, even though it was 3:30 in the morning in Austria.

It didn't take long for Andrea's mother to deliver the crushing news. Andrea left the sound-proof room in tears. She returned to her first-floor room. Her roommate had left with her parents that evening for the ride to her home in Rhode Island. Andrea was alone, and she guaranteed staying that way by locking the entry door. She fell onto her bed sobbing uncontrollably. She had to see John.

Andrea waited to crawl out of her window until 11:25 p.m., half an hour after the lights had extinguished in the window of the dormitory monitor. She used a judo belt to tie back the curtains on both sides of her window to prevent the curtains from flapping in the breeze and drawing attention. She dropped from the granite window sill four feet to land lightly on the fresh spring grass below. She would need John to give her a boost back through the open window and into the room before daylight. Andrea made her way through a line of maple trees to mask her passing. She squeezed through a gap in the hedge around the lacrosse field to reach the road leading three blocks to the Dan Hardin house.

The only light on in the house was a spotlight in the kitchen. Andrea knew from previous visits that the Hardins didn't lock their doors at night, so she was confident she could enter through the mud room and into the kitchen. She knew that climbing the stairs to the second floor posed the greatest threat of being discovered. A simple pretext occurred to her – a plausible story to tell anyone other than John who might discover her in the house.

First, she had tried to call John, but his cell phone was turned off. Second, the house phone was an unlisted number, and, even if she had known the house number, she would not have wanted to awake the household. Third, a knock at the door or ring of a doorbell would have disturbed Benjamin, Dan, and Scott. Finally, she was upset. Upset girls do crazy things. Andrea was sure that no one in the Hardin household would give her grief over what she was about to do. She opened the outside door to the mudroom and made her way silently into the kitchen. She went up the stairway stealthily. She opened John's bedroom door without making a single creak or thump.

Inside John's bedroom, she maneuvered by the light of the distant street lamps down by the town docks. John lay on his back breathing light, shallow breaths. Her instinct was to lie down beside him and to cuddle against his body, but she didn't know how John might respond to being awakened from a deep sleep. Instead, she laid her hand gently onto John's mouth. He awoke and tossed his head to one side. His eyes bulged as though he had been electrocuted. Two seconds passed before he recognized his visitor, and he sat up in bed with a confused look on his face.

"I have to talk with you," Andrea said. "This is serious."

"Let's go to the basement." He slid out of bed dressed in only a ragged Red Sox tee shirt. He found a pair of khaki pants to pull on, and he led her quietly from his room down two flights of stairs to the basement. He turned on a lamp and took out two cans of apple juice from the refrigerator in the billiard room.

"Why're you here?" He sat beside Andrea and put his arm around her shoulders and kissed her on the cheek.

"I can't come back to Thornton next year. I just found out."

John could see tears in her puffy eyes. "Why not?"

"My father's business has failed. My mother called to tell me. She's known for three days, but she didn't want to distract me during finals."

"But, can't he get another job?"

"He's the boss, the owner of the company. His money

is tied up in the business and the business was closed on Tuesday. My family hasn't the money to send me here again next year."

John seemed confused.

"It's complicated. My father's a proud man. Appearances are important to him. We're not even supposed to use the 'von' in our names since the war, but Father insists on hanging on to the 'von' and to the past. This will crush him," she sobbed.

Andrea had more reasons than she was willing to tell him. She was in love with John, and she didn't want to tell him anything that might threaten their relationship.

"I'll pay your tuition," John said.

"It's over thirty thousand dollars. You can't get that kind of money."

"Yes, I can."

"No you can't. Be reasonable. My parents wouldn't accept it."

"Stay here with us. You can work over the summer, and we'll find a solution."

"No, John. My parents want me home right away. I couldn't leave without talking to you. Also, my mother told me to send home all the things I was going to store here for the summer. She waited so long to tell me that I don't have time to do that."

"I'll do it for you. Just give me the key to your storage room and the shipping address of your family, and I'll take care of it."

They rehashed the problem until it became clear that Andrea was going home the next afternoon and nothing could change her mind. They gave mutual promises to write regularly and to call one another from time-to-time. John wanted to tell her about his trading success so she would take his offer to pay her tuition seriously, but he knew he had to keep his secret. It was after one o'clock when Andrea said she had to get back into her room at the dormitory. John put on a fleece and his topsiders to walk her back to campus. He borrowed a three-step stool from the mud room to make the climb into her window an easier task.

The next afternoon, John sat in the shade of the ancient maple tree that still bore scrape marks from his father's careless parking job twenty-two years ago. Andrea had asked him to let the previous night's parting be their final goodbye. John munched trail mix while he waited for the limousine to arrive to pick up Andrea and Nuo. A black limousine drove up to Andrea's dormitory entrance. The driver helped Andrea and Nuo load their bags into the trunk. In misguided efforts to help, Nuo opened and closed doors and generally interfered with the driver's bag-loading routine. Nuo couldn't believe his good fortune of sharing the next two hours with this lovely girl from Salzburg.

The driver closed the door behind the two students after they were seated. The driver slid into his seat, started the engine, and the limo pulled away from the curb. John couldn't see through the tinted glass. He was fairly certain that Andrea hadn't seen him, either, as he sat beneath the maple tree tossing sunflower seeds to a gray squirrel. John thought of sentiments he wished he had expressed to Andrea. He had been too occupied with convincing Andrea that he was good enough to deserve her love to simply tell her how he felt about her. Now, it was too late. Tears welled in John's eyes as the limo turned southbound onto the road to Boston.

Chapter 16

CALAMITY

JOHN'S DIARY MEMORIALIZED the important events of his junior year at Thornton Prep and in the Dan Hardin household. John recorded several high points in his precise block-letter printing.

"Paul Bruguiere's pumping iron like a maniac. Wants to join the Marine Corps."

"Took Granddad Benjamin cross-country skiing. He can't think straight, but his skiing is as good as ever."

"Won the 400-meter run at the New England Prep School Finals in 48.36...that beats Dad's and Scott's times!!! Scott called me a *thoroughbred*."

"Paul Bruguiere sold his canoe at the boat auction for over $6,000. Amazing!"

"Lacrosse season ended today...won 11, lost 3...not bad for a bunch of knuckleheads with Attention Deficit Disorder."

"Straight *A*'s again...genius."

"NAV: $1,311,768!!!"

John made lots of dismal entries, too.

"Received tenth letter from Andrea. Emails are too ordinary. Miss her big time."

"Granddad Benjamin doesn't make sense any more. Joyce Harrington comes by a lot to visit Granddad...she loves him so much...she's the kindest person ever...Granddad calls her 'Helen' all the time."

"Paul Bruguiere says he wishes he'd never sold his canoe."

"Corky Gleason got caught in bed with a Thornton sophomore guy from Saudi Arabia...looks like he's playing for the other team, now. His father went nuts on him, so every day is hell for Corky. He talked about committing suicide. I shook him so hard his sunglasses fell off. I told him 'Never!' He cried like a baby."

"Over a month since I got a letter from Andrea. Emails don't seem as personal as letters. Tried to call, but the time zones mess things up."

"Scott's forward vision is almost gone now...he doesn't read books or watch football on TV anymore."

It was Joe T. Harrington's turn to plan the annual vacation trip by the Lavals, Harringtons, and Benjamin Hardin. Joe T. had been unusually secretive about his plan, and, because he was the host of the monthly pinochle night in May, he gave notice that he planned to start the evening off by revealing the mystery vacation he had booked. He invited Annette, Dan, Scott, and John to come by for cocktails before the card playing started at sunset.

Marie Laval had taken Benjamin's place at the card table many months before when dementia became too much of a roadblock for Benjamin. Even Joyce had given up lobbying on Ben's behalf, because playing with Benjamin in the four-some was like playing cards with a three-year-old. When he started calling the Jack of Diamonds a "bullet" and identifying spades as "hearts" he had to come out of the lineup.

In the new order of things, Benjamin was happy to mess around with a Scrabble board on an adjacent card table making words like "EOQRMTG" with his seven letters just so he could draw a fresh seven tiles from the drawing pool. Keeping score was out of the question for Benjamin, but he still announced imaginary scores when he laid down his seven tiles anywhere he wanted to lay them on the Scrabble board.

"Thirty-six," he said aloud. The four card players at the nearby card table acknowledged his stellar play. Joe T. wished he could stifle Benjamin, because his Scrabble capers interfered with Joe T.'s memorization of the cards that had been played.

"Good work, Sweetheart," Joyce Harrington said to Benjamin as she coldheartedly trumped her husband's trick-winning Ace of Spades. Joe T. called her the "Loving Assassin".

"She calls Ben 'sweetheart' the second before she puts a bullet in my skull," Joe T. said. He had lost count of the number of spades that had been played because of Benjamin's stream of interruptions.

Even Marie had rounded off the corners of her semi-formality in her sixty-seventh year, and, at the previous pinochle night in April, she had sat close to Benjamin on the couch during cocktails. He had kissed her on the cheek and wrapped his arm around her shoulders.

"Helen, you're the best looking chick in the joint."

"You got that right," Phillip Laval had said.

"Richard, you old rascal, how have you been?"

"Just fine," Phillip had replied.

The Harringtons and the Lavals loved their friend of forty-five years regardless of what he called them.

Annette was fixing the traditional gin-and-tonics for everyone when The Triad arrived on the appointed May evening with Grandfather Benjamin in tow. She passed a gin-and-tonic out to everyone, including John.

"*Pour moi?*" John asked. Annette simply nodded her head and batted her eyes.

"You're the best cook in the joint, Helen" Benjamin told Annette when she handed him his tall frosted glass.

"One tries," she said airily.

"The reason we invited you to our very private card festival," Joe T. addressed the younger set while tapping his tumbler with a pen pointer, "Is so we can brief you on our top-secret summer trip."

He unrolled a large map of Labrador and used unopened decks of cards to weigh down the corners on the card table. Everyone gathered around the table to view the chart like a general's staff studying an invasion plan. Judging from the dearth of contour lines, Labrador was as flat as a billiard table with a gazillion small lakes scattered about like blue confetti.

"Let's all synchronize our watches," Scott said, dusting off his military humor. He couldn't read the map, but he could stay invested in the group dynamic by spouting pithy commentary.

"Okay," Joe T. began, "On July 3, my lovely wife Joyce and I along with Benjamin and Phillip and Miss Marie are flying out of Boston at 10:50 in the morning to Montreal then to Halifax then to Goose Bay, Labrador! We'll land at 6:50 that evening."

"There's an airport in Goose Bay, Labrador?" Annette asked.

"*Certainment*," Scott said. "We used to get air refueling tankers out of Goose Bay when we were taking fighters across the pond to Europe."

"Save the war stories for later," Joe T. said authoritatively. "Yes, there's an airport in Goose Bay. We'll spend the night at a lodge near Goose Bay, and the next morning, while you Caledonians are at the Fourth of July Parade, we'll be flying in a sea plane from Goose Bay out to a remote fishing camp. We'll be there in the middle of nowhere roughing it for ten days. How do you like that?"

"Wonderful!" Joyce exclaimed in the voice of a perennially chipper cheerleader.

Marie remained silent. She wasn't fond of wrestling with mosquitos or co-mingling with the heads of dead animals mounted on rough-hewn wooden lodge walls. Her idea of "roughing it" was a river cruise on the Rhine or staying in a *gite* in the French countryside. She wondered if it was too late to work out a compromise with Joe T.

Joyce put an arm around Benjamin. "Isn't that wonderful, Benjamin?"

"Can we fly on the sea plane now?" Benjamin asked.

"Not until July Third, Honey," Joyce told him.

"Could I speak with you privately?" Marie asked Joe T.

Joe T. looked puzzled, but he put down his pointer, picked up his glass, and followed Marie into the kitchen.

"This isn't going to work," Marie said when they reached the kitchen.

Joe T. was taken aback. "Why not?"

"The problem is Benjamin. The camp's too remote. There's no hospital within miles if something goes wrong."

"We're only there for ten days," Joe T. said. He had considerable skin in the game, because he had already made deposits and reservations at both lodges, and he had made a non-refundable deposit on the bush plane to fly them into the remote lake.

"You should have coordinated with the rest of us."

"I thought you'd all love the idea. I still think it's a perfect location for us."

"It's not too late to change the plan," Marie insisted. "It'll be too hard with Benjamin."

Joe T. stood his ground. "It'll be perfect for Benjamin. We'll have to take care of him no matter where we go."

"I won't be part of it."

"Marie, please. You and Phillip are planning next year's vacation, and you can pick any place you want."

"I won't go."

"Will you at least leave it alone for tonight and let us talk about it tomorrow, just the Harringtons and the Lavals?"

Marie agreed to say nothing that night in the interest of domestic tranquility. Nevertheless, she was convinced that the Labrador trip was a bad idea. She would insist on a substitute vacation plan no matter how much money Joe T. might lose to cancellations.

At the end of the evening, before retiring to bed, Marie told Phillip about her objections and her talk with Joe T. Her husband was mortified that Marie had thrown a wrench in the gears of Joe T.'s plan.

"Marie, Joe T. did all that planning and has spent a good deal of money on this vacation. Don't be petty."

"I'm not being petty. I know in my heart that this isn't right for our group. You know I rely on my intuition."

"Please reconsider," Phillip begged her.

"Joe T. had no right to surprise us this way. It's his own fault."

"Perhaps he should have been more collaborative," Phillip conceded, "but please compromise just this once. People make concessions for their friends."

After another couple of days of haggling, Marie agreed to go on the trip, but she refused to get excited about it the way her four travelling companions were. Joe T. promised not to surprise her in this way ever again. Marie reminded Joe T. more than once that she was doing him a big favor and she voiced her objections to Annette to the point of irritation. Annette tried to soothe her mother's angst

"Mummy, take plenty of books and insect repellant. It's only ten days."

"It feels like a life sentence," Marie moaned.

Early in June, Andrew Gleason came by Hardin's Hardware at day's end when he knew John was normally there alone. Andrew knocked on the front door and John left his broom in Aisle Nine to open the door for him. Andrew wasn't in top form. His shirt needed to be tucked in properly.

He hadn't taken his belt in by even one notch in years. He walked through the doorway and asked if they could sit down to talk for a moment. John took him to the office, and they sat down on straight-backed chairs that fronted a wooden table.

"John, this isn't easy for me, so bear with me." Andrew readjusted his massive body so he could lean on the table in front of him. "Corky's left home. His mother and I pleaded with him to stay, but he wanted out so bad he said he couldn't stand it one more day."

"Where is he?"

"He's already gone. He left for Italy yesterday."

"He didn't even come by to tell me," John said.

"He was too ashamed after that scandal at Thornton. It was all we could do to get him to finish his junior year. I don't think he could face up to you after all that happened. He liked you a lot, John, and I don't mean that in some perverted, sick way."

"He's a good pal. Is he coming back for his senior year?"

"He says 'no' right now. Do you know about his friend over there?"

"I think so," John said without committing.

"Antolini?"

"Yeah."

"My wife's told me about their stunts over there during the last couple of summers. I didn't know what to do. Can you imagine my monster of a kid chasing around butt-naked with a scrawny Italian teenager? Can you see them frolicking nude in a swimming pool like a couple of demented dolphins?"

Actually, John *had* visualized such a scene more than once, but he had shaken it out of his imagination as a precaution against brain hemorrhage.

"My wife is frantic. She won't talk about anything else. I've got her medicated just to quiet her down. The sense of failure is overwhelming. I can't get it out of my mind. I just don't know what'll become of Corky. I gave him a credit card and some cash to keep him safe."

The silence was heavy in the small room. Andrew sighed gloomily and removed a sealed letter from his inside suit pocket to give to John.

"Can I read it now?"

"Certainly," Andrew said. "You don't have to tell me what's in it, but, maybe you can tell me if Corky is likely to hurt himself." John opened the letter.

"Dear John, I'm outta' here before I get any goofier than I already am. I don't know for sure what I want, but I'm pretty sure that it's not in Caledonia. Thanks for not turning your back on me after that stupid thing I did with that kid from Jeddah. Believe it or not, it was his idea, not mine. Anyway, I couldn't bear seeing people smirk at me anymore. I mean, that's been my whole life anyway with the exception of you and Paul Bruguiere. You guys were good friends, and I'll always laugh out loud when I think of you. Tell Paul what I said and tell him not to get shot in the Marines. Anyway, I hope you understand why I'm leaving to be with Antolini. He's the only person I know who understands me. He speaks English like a baby, but he's a good-hearted, simple guy who makes me forget that I'm a fat, uncoordinated slob. My Dad doesn't understand me, but he's helped me a lot with money and stuff so I'll be okay. And, no, I'm not going to commit suicide. I'd probably screw that up, too. So, goodbye, John Wesley Hardin. I'll always remember you out on Lake Tremont soaking up the rays with your blond hair blowing in the breeze and you laughing about your latest obsession while I would do *anything* to be you but I know that I can't ever be you, and all I can do is love you. Corky."

The letter brought tears to John's eyes, and, for a moment, he didn't have a voice.

"Well?" Andrew asked, his face showing his desperation.

"Corky's not going to commit suicide, Mr. Gleason. Corky's going to be all right."

"Thank you, John." Andrew rose to his feet and fastened a button on his suit coat. "Let me know if I can ever help you with anything."

They shook hands, and Andrew Gleason left by the front door into the twilight.

Preparations leading up to Independence Day 2005 were logistically more complicated than in years past. The Triad and Annette helped pack their parents' van for their early-morning July 3 departure for Logan Airport. Judging by the number of fly rods in the van, the fish in Labrador were destined for perilous times. Joe T. drove out of the Harringtons' circular drive with a hearty wave. They left as near to six o'clock in the morning as they could so they could be in place for the 10:50 a.m. flight to Canada. Benjamin was so excited he could hardly sit still. He waved through his open rear-seat window at The Triad and Annette.

"We're going fishing, Helen!" he shouted.

"Have a good time!" Annette called out.

"Get some pictures!" Dan said.

"Leave the native girls alone, Joe T.!" Scott shouted.

"*Ciao*," John said, because all the quality lines had already been used.

The following morning, the Triad woke early again just because they had gotten up so early the previous morning. The Labrador Explorers were flying out to the fishing camp today. This was only the second Caledonia Fourth of July Parade in the past forty-five years that would be conducted without a Hardin, Laval, or Harrington marching in it. Dan and Scott were working in the hardware store. John went with Annette to his favorite spot on the Post Office lawn to watch the two-hour procession. The day could not have been more perfect – sunny, seventy-six degrees, and a southwesterly breeze blowing in off Caledonia Bay.

The *M/S Franklin Pierce* disgorged her throng of tourists, swelling the ranks of spectators along the parade route. Marching bands, veterans' color guards, and trucks bearing blue grass, country, and rock bands passed by the flag-waving, cheering crowd. Tractors pulled wagons with young lovelies touting the names of the organic farmers who sponsored floats.

The choir director of the Episcopal Church discharged

his duties as drum major for the Caledonia Walkers Precision Drill Team. Once, when his huge drum major's hat became dislodged as he arched his back and blew his whistle to execute a brilliant maneuver right in front of the Post Office, he caught it in midair, fast as a whippet, and he placed it back on his skinny head. He got a standing ovation from the appreciative crowd.

"The Patriots need a wide receiver with good hands!" Chuck "Canuck" Koeneki shouted with his booming voice. John wondered if "Canuck" attended the parade to harvest personal injury clients. "Canuck" often said liability is in the air. Flags flew from every light pole on the main street of the village, and at least half the people in the crowd were waving American flags and clapping. Surely "Canuck" could find a plaintiff with an impaled eyeball before the day was over.

Paul Bruguiere no longer worked at the music camp on the island, but he had finagled a position on the float belonging to the antique boat auction. He was seated in a kayak displayed on a flat-bed trailer. He was naked from the waist up, and the sun accented the rippling muscles he had developed in the past year of weight-lifting. The Marines would be getting their money's worth when they got Paul. His paddles were red, white, and blue, and he kept a steady paddle cadence, dipping the tip of each paddle into a tub of water on either side of his kayak. Water splashed out of the tubs when he paddled or when the driver of the pickup truck pulling his trailer stopped too abruptly, so the tubs were hand-refilled by an elementary school boy dressed in the costume of a rainbow trout.

The theme of the parade was "Let Freedom Ring".

Neither John nor Annette could figure out the connection between Freedom Ringing and Paul paddling. They clapped enthusiastically as he passed by their vantage point. Paul smiled constantly. He was thoroughly enjoying his moment in the spotlight.

Paul's uncle appeared later in the parade marching beside a swarm of about twenty-five Little Miss Muffet Day Care Center clients. The five-year-old tykes were dressed in Statue of Liberty costumes the color of oxidized copper and a similarly colored foam crown on each of their heads. Thomas Bruguiere wore a teal bed sheet to represent Lady Liberty's gown and a foam crown like the children's crowns. His eye patch was the color of oxidized copper, too. John commented on Thomas' legs protruding beneath his gown like bleached celery sticks covered in thick mohair.

"That's the whitest skin I've ever seen in my life," John said to Annette. "Look how hairy his legs are. He's like the missing link."

Annette admitted that Thomas made a fascinating anthropological case study.

Thomas grasped a worn Bible next to his chest with one hand, and in the other he held aloft an object representing a torch. One of his sandal straps had broken and it flapped on the asphalt street surface like a diving fin.

"Left, right, left, right," Thomas called out just as he did every year, and the children kept putting down their left feet and their right feet whenever and wherever they desired quite independently of his commands. The crowd cheered wildly for the straggling Miss Liberties as they passed by.

The parade ended when trailers sponsored by various

politicians moved by on the way up the hill to the terminus at Thornton Academy. The crowd dispersed in all directions by foot, bicycle, motor bike, car, kayak, canoe, and power boat. Scores of power boats that had tied up to the town docks for access to the parade exited the harbor and headed for their homes on the islands or on other mainland shores. An even larger flotilla would return six hours later, carrying spectators to attend the eight o'clock concert in the Town Gazebo.

Between these nautical goings and comings, John and Annette walked to the Dan Hardin house to lie in the sun down by the beach where they dozed peacefully and recaptured hours of sleep lost to two early-morning wakeups in a row.

The Triad and Annette left the Dan Hardin house at 7:45 p.m. for the walk to the Town Gazebo. Power boats had already tied up beside every available foot of space at the town docks. Clusters of boats anchored in the harbor within hearing of the amplified speaker system. The mild breeze blew their sterns toward the gazebo, so the boat cockpits could trap the amplified music like oversized ears.

What the boat spectators lacked in proximity they compensated for in perks like alcoholic beverages, which couldn't be consumed in the park. The landlubbers were proscribed from consuming cocktails in the park, but there was no ordinance restricting soft drinks, ice cream, cotton candy, popcorn, or hot dogs, and vendors of those commodities were doing a brisk business. The Triad and Annette arrived in the park in time to claim a spot on the lawn about halfway back from the gazebo, and they opened their lawn chairs up and arranged them in a row a decent distance from the row of lawn chairs in front of them. Dan – the designated hunter/gatherer – stood in line to buy popcorn at a concession stand.

The choir director at the Episcopal Church, who was the drum major with the sure hands, was also a town selectman, and he used a band member's microphone to address the crowd.

"Good evening," he said. "Welcome to July Fourth Under the Gazebo!" Everyone who wasn't licking an ice cream cone clapped. "Before we get started with tonight's concert, we have an important announcement." Fire department volunteers bearing plastic buckets ringed the great lawn. They were poised to conduct a collection. "As most of you know, George LeMond was seriously injured this week when he fell out of the tree he was topping. He's in a lot of pain, and he's confined to bed while his back heals." People either nodded that they knew about LeMond's misfortune or they raised their eyebrows if they hadn't heard about it yet.

"As you know, a lumber jack isn't much good in bed." This got a lot of laughs from the crowd. The choir director was an unintentional comedian. "What I mean is, you can't make a living in bed." This got some more laughs. It was doubtful that the choir director had spent a lot of time preparing this speech. "You know what I mean," he finally concluded. "George and his family need help, so give what you can."

The fire fighters came through the crowd and people threw bills of various denominations into the bucket. Dan and Scott each tossed in a twenty. John couldn't see what

Annette put in the bucket, but he palmed a single dollar into the bucket. A number – the latest entry in his diary — flashed in his mind: "NAV $1,455,728". He felt ashamed to be so cheap, but he was new to the millionaire game. He vowed to do better next time.

The choir director thanked everyone and encouraged members of the audience to silence their cell phones. He introduced the cover band, an energetic group dressed in sequined jackets and black bow ties. They manned their instruments and immediately tore into *Proud Mary* with an explosion of sound that got the joint rocking. Grandmothers danced with grandchildren on the lawn. Boaters left their boats to dance on the docks.

Annette nudged John and pointed toward a covey of dancing girls from one of the lake's summer camps where, apparently, a girl could be a camper only if she were trim, blonde, and a finalist in the Miss Teenage America Contest. John nodded approval. It was a joyous way to start the concert, and it only got better. The band kept the audience rocking by covering a sampling of favorite rock-and-roll songs as darkness descended on the village. The Fourth of July made John's spine tingle.

The band had just started playing a James Taylor song when Dan's cell phone vibrated. He walked over to the edge of the docks to take the call to have a fighting chance of hearing the voice of the person calling. He put a finger in his free ear, moved further away from the gazebo, and plugged his ear piece so far into his right ear that surgery might be required to remove it.

John saw Dan's shoulders slump. About two minutes

later, Dan closed his cell phone and looked out toward Caledonia Bay, his back still turned toward the great lawn and the gazebo. When Dan returned, he bent over to speak individually into the ears of Scott, Annette, and John.

"Fold your chair and follow me. We have to leave."

They folded their lawn chairs and exited the great lawn for the walk back to the Hardin house. The band continued playing *Fire and Rain*.

On the main street away from the crowd, Annette started to ask Dan what was going on. He asked her to wait until they got home. He had to think, he told her. It was a dreary seven-minute walk to the Dan Hardin house. Each person imagined the worst. Annette couldn't stand the dread any longer. She pulled Dan's arm to make him stop walking.

"Tell us what's going on!" she insisted.

"I can't." Dan said. He was crying. "Don't make a scene. We have to get home."

Annette grasped Scott's hand and fell into step as the foursome resumed walking to the house. Amplified music from the gazebo echoed off the walls of the houses they passed. They entered the mud room from the side door and went in to the kitchen. Dan led them to the living room. His eyes were red. His voice cracked.

"Guys," Dan said, "I'm probably not doing this right, but the Royal Canadian Mounted Police called. Our parents' plane went down."

Annette appeared to go into shock. She visibly trembled and lunged toward Scott, who held her in his arms with a look of disbelief on his face. Dan moved beside John and locked him in his arms.

"Did they make it out?" Scott asked.

"Nobody made it out," Dan said, and he sobbed violently. John squeezed his father for reassurance. They eventually released their holds on one another and they sat down in a huddle of crushed hopes and aching hearts. Scott poured white wine into two glasses, and he gave one each to Annette and John. Then he poured two huge tumblers of *Sheep Dip* for himself and Dan.

They talked for a long time, through the concert and the entire fireworks show that reverberated over the bay. The group of four mourners barely noticed the pyrotechnics. The faint smell of cordite wafted into the open windows of the house. Scott refilled their glasses. Their talk diminished. The town clock tolled ten bells, the last hourly bells of the evening.

A Royal Canadian Mounted Police Inspector had promised to call with more details, but neither the house phone nor Dan's cell phone rang. By eleven o'clock, the grievers had selected Dan to fly to Canada to escort the five urns of remains home to Caledonia. Annette was chosen to arrange a memorial service with the help of a local funeral home. She hoped to reserve a priest at Saint Paul's Catholic Church to conduct a funeral mass for all five of the deceased – Catholic and Protestant. Annette volunteered to arrange for burial plots beside one another in the cemetery on the hill north of town. That was the plan they agreed to, barring contrary instructions in any of the wills of the deceased. They had to talk to bear the grief. They had to be together to endure the pain.

Dan called Lisa Sullivan's mother, a long-time employee

at his hardware store. He apologized for the late hour and said, "I want you to run the store while I'm away." Mrs. Sullivan asked why he hadn't chosen Scott. "I'm choosing you," Dan said. "It could be a week or it could be longer, but you're the right person to run the store. Scott won't be in, either, so cover however you have to." She wanted to know what had happened. Dan told her that Benjamin had died. He promised to tell her details when he could.

Dan called to make reservations for his flight the next day to Goose Bay. They agreed to leave Benjamin's bedroom unoccupied, so Annette commandeered Scott's room. Scott slept on a couch down in the billiard room. Dan escorted John to his bedroom. He put his hand on John's shoulder and asked, "Are you all right?"

"I feel numb," John said. "Everything's switched around. One minute I was so happy and now...," his voice trailed off.

"I think that's how it's going to be for a while, John. We're going to have to put one foot in front of the other and keep going. Do the best you can. Don't go to work until I get back."

John had hardly spoken in the last three hours. He had just cried and watched his expanded family grieve and wondered what was next. He lay in bed for a long time unable to sleep. The light from street lamps at the docks illuminated patches of the walls of John's room. The armada of power boats had dispersed. The band had packed up their amplifiers and gone home. The gazebo lights were extinguished. The sea of lawn chairs had been folded and taken home by the townspeople celebrating American Independence. John heard Dan answer the telephone long after midnight. Dan talked on the phone for an extended time. He heard his father's footsteps on the stairs and in the hallway as he went to his bedroom. John longed to have Andrea lying beside him to hold him and rock him to sleep.

John pictured the faces of each deceased person. He visualized Grandfather Benjamin laughing innocently and calling out to him, "You're a good boy, Dan." He saw the quiet serenity in the face of Grandfather Laval. He saw the dignified features and knowing smile of Grandmother Marie Laval. He could see Joyce Harrington doting on Grandfather Benjamin, "Here's some apple pie and ice cream for the most handsome man in New England," she said. "What about me?" big, strong Joe T. Harrington asked playfully. That's the way John imagined them. That was his lasting memory of them. A loon called mournfully from the bay.

When John woke in the morning, the first thing he did was walk down to his father's bedroom. Dan was gone.

Dan spent a week in Goose Bay. The Mounties told him the sea plane had gone down in heavy fog in a remote location in Central Labrador. An eye witness at the camp estimated the pitch attitude was fifteen degrees below the horizon with a left bank of twenty degrees when the airplane impacted the trees. The left wing hit the trees first and that induced a violent left yawing moment on the aircraft in the split second before the right wing sheared off from the fuselage. Fuel from the ruptured fuel tanks ignited instantly. All six occupants of the aircraft were immobilized – and probably killed – by the impact, so they were unable to escape the flames that engulfed the downed aircraft.

Dan coordinated delivery of dental and medical records to facilitate identification of the burned bodies by Canadian authorities. He also obtained the consent of powers-of-attorney so all five bodies could be cremated. He returned to Caledonia as escort to the ashes of the deceased on July 11.

Dan, Scott, Annette, and John muddled through the days that followed. Annette slept in Scott's bedroom for the duration. She talked a lot about her parents and the regrets she had. All her life she had tried hard to please her parents; now that they were gone, were her efforts for naught, too? She was haunted by the memory of her mother's objections to the trip. Dan and Scott were non-responsive most of the time. They listened to Annette and they lay beside her in the grass in the back lawn of the Dan Hardin house at night, but they rarely spoke. John was almost mute. On a warm afternoon, he reclined on the couch where Annette was sitting, rested his head on her thigh, and stayed there motionless, wordless.

The four occupants of the Dan Hardin house did only what was required of them in the near term. They attended their parents' memorial service and the burial of their remains. Dan contacted Fred Cummings, the attorney used by both Benjamin Hardin and the Harringtons. He assured Fred that he and Scott would meet with him when they felt competent to do so. Annette called her father's attorney in Concord and did the same.

The Dan Hardin house seemed vacant and still even though the four occupants spent more time there than ever before. Dan unplugged the house telephone line. All four of them turned off their cell phones for hours at a time, because answering well-meaning telephone calls was too painful. Flowers arrived on the front porch. Acquaintances left meals on the porch beside the flowers. Annette spent hours each day responding to such acts of kindness with thank-you cards. The second week dragged by as slowly as the first.

John, like Dan and Scott, had not gone to work since the plane had gone down. He stayed in his room most of the day and night. The only time he went outside was to lie in the hammock in the shade of the maple trees during the warmest time of the day. He didn't want to be observed doing his usual sun-bathing or swimming at their beach. The only time he and the others swam was at night, when there were no witnesses. The cool waters of the bay lowered their core body temperatures and enabled them to sleep in bedrooms that had baked all afternoon in the summer sun. Air-conditioning wasn't normally needed or installed in Caledonia's older houses, so, on warm nights, cooling off in the lake before bedtime made sleep come faster.

John had lost his keen interest in options trading. Making money seemed pointless in the aftermath of the tragedy. Nevertheless, out of habit and a sense of duty, he went on-line for a few minutes each morning to adjust positions as necessary. Although he knew he shouldn't make decisions during this time of mourning, he made a mistake of both the "fat finger" and the "poor judgment" varieties that threatened his financial ruin and encumbered him with anxiety for many weeks to come.

When John noticed Amgen stock surging in price from $60.71 to $69.69 in about five days, he succumbed to an impulse to sell-to-open 50 contracts of August $65 Calls <u>naked</u>.

Not only did he sell the calls naked, he inadvertently typed in "500" contracts instead of "50". He sold the calls at $7.80, so he expected to receive a credit of $39,000. He didn't notice that the credit posted to the account was $390,000, nor did he notice that his margin account contracted dramatically. Grief had distracted him to a point that he made compounding errors.

John's befuddlement had placed him in jeopardy of losing everything. Every day, the AMGN stock price climbed higher and John's margin account shrank by large chunks each time the stock price went up. By the expiration date in August, the stock had climbed to $85, and the 500 calls were assigned. The assignment resulted in a position of 50,000 shares he had sold short for $3,250,000. The cost of closing the position was $4,250,000. His imprudence had exposed his entire account balance to liquidation.

John became irritable. He couldn't sleep for more than three hours at a time. He spent most of his days in bed. He got no exercise. He saw no one outside of the house because he didn't leave the house. He hardly spoke to Annette or Scott or even his father. In only six weeks, he had put at risk everything he had worked months to earn.

On top of feeling foolish, he felt disloyal to the Lavals, the Harringtons, and to his Grandfather Benjamin. How could he have even thought about money while mourning their passing? For the first time in his life, John truly loathed himself. He wondered if this was the realm of endless regret and mental anguish inhabited by Corky. Worst of all, he couldn't talk to anyone about it.

By the first week of August, the men of the Dan Hardin house – The Triad – had gone back to work. Invitations to dinner had been politely refused. Dishes had been washed and returned to the kind people who had gifted them with meals. Mail that had piled up for three weeks had been opened and letters answered and bills paid. John had cut the lawn. Annette had returned to the Laval house to resume sleeping there, but she still came to the Dan Hardin house in the evenings for dinner and companionship.

On one particularly pleasant evening, Annette, Scott, Dan, and John played Scrabble for two hours. They bantered and, for the first time since July 4, they laughed. During the following week when the upstairs rooms of the house were too warm for sleeping, the four of them motored in the runabout to a small island five miles away. They drank beer and swam in the shallow waters of the island's sandy beach until midnight. A kind of normalcy was returning to their lives. It was time to turn their attentions to insurance payments, wills, disposition of possessions and houses, and inheritance assessments. It didn't seem profane to think about such things anymore.

Annette received Trinette's letter on August 24. It was post-marked in Belgium.

"Dear Annette, I got your letter about the plane crash. I was away in Holland so I didn't get it sooner. It's so sad to think of Mummy and Daddy being gone. Forever. How did Grand'Mere take it? I want to come home, but I don't have any money. Can you help me out? I will really appreciate it. Love, Trinette."

Annette sent $2,000 to Trinette within three days. The prodigal daughter was returning home.

Chapter 17

REUNION

SIX WEEKS AFTER attending the funerals of his grandparents, John scarcely could remember even salient details of the ceremonies. He felt as though he were living in a fog bank, unable to see where he had been and too disoriented to see where he was going. He felt remote from his friends and out-of-sync with his family. He had a lot on his mind, and, given the choice to advance or retreat in the face of the issues dominating his thoughts, he would have preferred retreat every time.

First, he was depressed over the deaths of his grandparents. Reminders of their absence visited him every day, and he gradually came to realize how much he had depended on them for his sense of security and identification. Every time he walked by the granite steps leading up to the Bank of Caledonia, John imagined his Grandfather Phillip Laval elegantly descending the steps dressed in his dark blue banker's suit. He couldn't pass by the front of Hardin's Hardware without the image of Grandfather Benjamin Hardin looking out through the front window at him. When anyone in the village used the term "The Caledonians", that's who they were referring to – his Grandparents Laval, the Harringtons, and his Grandfather Benjamin Hardin, gone to his eternal rest with his beloved Helen.

Second, Trinette – the mother of whom he had no memory – was flying from Amsterdam to Boston the very next day. He had a pretty good idea of what his mother would look like, because he had studied the photograph in his father's bedroom a hundred times. He figured that Annette was a reasonable proxy for his mother's physical appearance. He had overheard enough conversations over the years, however, to expect that his mother's personality was very unlike his Aunt Annette's. He knew about Trinette's drug and alcohol abuse. He knew about her temper. He knew she had left his family abruptly to go to live in Brussels with some Belgian yahoo. With benefit of all of this knowledge, John concluded that his interest in his mother was more curiosity to see her in the flesh than desire for a relationship with her. He didn't need a pen pal.

Finally, Amgen was not cooperating with his interests as its share price continued to grind higher. Every trading day threatened his financial ruin. With that peril hanging over his head, John's forecast for his senior year at Thornton Prep was bleak. Andrea was gone. Corky was gone. John didn't sign up for autumn conditioning for the lacrosse team. He didn't train for track anymore, either. His teachers and classmates were confounded by how glum he had become. He resented even their smallest efforts to resume their former relationships with him. Eventually, they stopped trying. They left him alone.

Dan tried to resuscitate his son's spirit, to revive his enthusiasm for life.

"Your last year in high school is like the last one-hundred meters in a 400-meter race," Dan said. He had never been able to express his love for his son in words, and his inability shackled him now. "You feel like you're running in deep water, but you have to switch into a higher gear."

"I don't care anymore," John said. "Nothing seems important." He couldn't say anything about the foreboding he felt every day when he checked the bid/ask on Amgen stock to see whether he was wiped out or left to fight another day. The constant worry made his head ache. Over a million dollars of his assets had been wiped out in the space of two weeks. John was ashamed that he thought more about losing money than he did about losing his grandparents. He felt more anxious and less grandiose than at any previous time in his life.

"You're goal has to be an *A* in every advanced placement class," Dan said. "The prize for reaching that goal is that you can get into just about any college you want."

"I'll try," John said, but he didn't sound convincing. They were two people talking on two different levels, and no real benefit came from their conversation. John felt like the captain of a rudderless vessel in jeopardy of sinking. Dan had tried to render assistance but had been rejected.

Scott's attempt to snap John out of his funk had more of a buddy-buddy tone to it. Scott drew a parallel between his vision loss and John's loss of his grandparents.

"The hardest thing about my blindness is I can't look deep into someone's eyes anymore to see the spark of their soul. I can't see the flash of interest in a girl's eyes the first time we meet when everything is fresh and boundless. I can't see that she understands what I just told her. I can't see the look in her eyes that says she wants to know me better. All I can see is out-of-focus shapes and motions." Even as he spoke these words, John's face was just a blurred image to him. "And that's how your grandparents are going to be for you now, John. You won't be able to see their souls distinctly anymore. Your memories will have to do."

Scott put his arm on John's shoulders as John lowered his head and cried softly.

"Your grandparents are gone," Scott continued. "My *parents* are gone. Gone physically. But they'll always be right here in our minds." Scott pointed to his temple. "They want us to press on. Always press on."

John imagined how much better his life would be right now if he had stopped trading options when he got close to two million dollars in net worth and had simply bought a basket of dividend-paying large-capitalization stocks. Instead, he had to admit that, as soon as he hit two million, he would up his goal to three million or even four. That, he now realized, is how greed works.

Every time John tried to focus on honoring the memories of his grandparents, his mind involuntarily switched to the financial debacle that threatened to take him down. John disliked himself for his selfish thoughts, and he felt unworthy of the affections of Dan and Scott.

"I'm trying to press on," John said.

"I know you are, Champ. And so am I." Scott paused. He considered himself anything but a model for bravery in the face of adversity. Scott had done his fair share of whining about losing his eyesight. He could have been a more inspirational example for John. He chose a different angle to pursue.

"If you start running again…right now…I know you can beat forty-eight seconds flat. You can blow past those pansies from Connecticut and Massachusetts and win the New England gold. You have all the tools."

John wondered what the bid/ask was on Amgen at that very moment. He pursed his lips and nodded with token determination in response to Scott's words. John had lost over a million dollars. He didn't trust his instincts any longer. What a huge beat-down, he thought. He felt defeated. He felt remorse for his past arrogance and pride.

"There are a billion guys who wish they could be you, John. You're special. You're destined for greatness. Don't throw it all away."

As in John's talk with his father, Scott's and John's threads of conversation were not even close to intersecting. John couldn't focus on what Scott was saying. John had never guessed that his desire to make money would interfere with his communication with the people who mattered most in his life. Movement in the price of Amgen was now controlling him, and he didn't have the courage to close the position, take the losses, and stop feeling like a victim.

John thanked Scott for taking time to encourage him, and he went up to his room to brood for an hour before dinner. He checked the closing share price of Amgen and calculated that if it climbed another seven dollars, he was wiped out. The thought made him sick. He just wanted to sleep. He had never been so miserable in his life.

Annette came up to John's bedroom before dinner.

"Can we talk?" she asked. John got up from his bed and sat on the edge of the mattress where Annette joined him. She put her left arm around his waist. "John, I don't feel like I've done much to help you get through the last few weeks. I've had my hands full trying to get through them myself."

John didn't know what to say. He was so depressed he was speechless.

"In school, I see little children hurting every day. I see them when they're scared because of a mean parent. I see them when they're frightened because of a family illness. And I ache for them when they can't keep up with other kids or when they're misunderstood. Even though I hurt for them, I can't take the hurt away from them. And I can't take the hurt away from you."

"Yeah." He couldn't control the flow of tears in his eyes.

"Life doesn't work out the way we think it will. Imagine how your dad felt when your mom went away. He had to go on."

John nodded and blotted the tears that were hot on his cheeks.

"And think about Scott," she went on, hoping that her words were helping him see that his hurt would eventually recede over time. "Scott's dreams were crushed by tiny little spores that he breathed into his lungs thirty years ago. Our lives have cruel twists, and we have to switch our plans around just to survive."

"What about you?"

She couldn't tell him the cruelest twist of all, so she said,

"I know I'm not special enough to have the man I want to share my life with. And I have to watch myself grow older, knowing I'll be living another year all alone."

John had never thought of Annette this way. She had always been so supportive of him. He had taken her for granted, perhaps more than any other person in his life. He touched his head to hers, and she squeezed him tightly. For the moment, he forgot his looming financial collapse, and he thought about this gentle woman who was trying to console him.

"We have to get on with our lives for each other as much as for ourselves," Annette said. "I need you to be your normal self. I won't feel better until *you* feel better."

"I could manage if Andrea were here." He had never expressed out loud – in or out of Andrea's presence – how much he needed her.

"You're probably right," Annette agreed, "but she's *not* here. You've just got us. We've got to do the best we can for one another."

"I'll try," John said.

They sat together on the edge of the bed, too lonely to move and too wretched to speak.

"Your mother will be here tomorrow. Leave your mind open and try not to set up any expectations." Annette felt as though she were giving advice to herself. "Just let her be whoever she is and be willing to forgive, if that's what it takes."

"I'm nervous about meeting her," John admitted.

"I bet she's nervous about meeting you, too."

Annette had arranged to be free from teaching on the following afternoon when Trinette was scheduled to arrive in Boston. Annette parked her car in short-term parking and waited in the International Terminal at the portal where Customs and Immigration discharged weary travelers just arrived from overseas. Long after the first Amsterdam passenger passed through the portal, Annette continued to wait for her sister.

Had Trinette missed the flight? Was she huddled in a corner of the Schiphol Airport in a drug-induced coma? Had she been intercepted by Customs trying to smuggle drugs into the country? Had she decided not to come? Had she walked right past Annette and Annette hadn't recognized her? They were identical twins, Annette thought, how could that happen? Annette pulled a compact mirror out of her purse and examined her own face. There, she thought, that's the face I'm looking for.

"They stuck me in the back of the plane," Trinette said as she approached Annette from the right. Annette jumped with fright, but recovered in an instant. They embraced one another and executed the Euro-kiss maneuver flawlessly.

"You look beautiful!" Trinette exclaimed with enthusiasm that appeared genuine.

"So do you!"

In fact, Trinette wasn't a carbon copy of Annette anymore. She was still an attractive woman at the age of thirty-nine, but her skin wasn't as clear as Annette's, her bottom eyelids were puffy, and her hair seemed brittle compared to Annette's silky hair.

"I'm so glad you could come back home after all this time."

"Thanks to you. I'll pay you back," she said as an afterthought.

"Forget that," Annette told her. "That was a gift. I haven't given you a gift in fifteen years, so that's a catch-up."

"Let's get a drink for the road." Trinette pulled Annette toward the bar to the right of the portal.

"Go ahead," Annette said. "I'll be the designated driver."

"Still Annette."

There it was again – Trinette's need to point out all the ways they were different from one another: Prim Annette, flamboyant Trinette.

The twins stopped halfway home in Portsmouth for dinner near Strawbery Banke. Trinette asked a lot of questions about the plane crash, establishing that Annette knew surprisingly little about the details.

"Ask Scott. He knows all about the airplane stuff. The accident report won't be out for months."

Trinette drank a Martini and two glasses of wine. Annette took one glass of wine with her meal. Trinette volunteered next to nothing about her life in Brussels. Annette asked questions about her job and her friends, but Trinette concealed her life behind a veil. Trinette asked about Dan and John and, in time, Scott. Annette warned her that Scott had lost most of his forward vision and that talking with him might be a little unnerving, because he had to use eccentric fixation to see, so his pupils would point toward her chin so he could get the best image of her face.

"My God!" Trinette exclaimed. Physical abnormalities

of any kind made her queasy.

Their conversation continued sporadically as they drove toward Caledonia. Annette told her sister that John hadn't fully recovered from the shock of the accident. "He's kind of moody now and he mopes around most of the time."

"Life is hard," Trinette said. "He'll just have to buck up." She cringed to think of how many times Laurens – her Belgian boyfriend – had spoken those words to her.

The comment bothered Annette, because she didn't feel Trinette had earned the right to pass judgment on John. The twins had left a lot unsaid over the years on the subject of John. As in the past, Annette retreated to a sanctuary of silence. As they drove into Caledonia, Annette broke the silence to ask Trinette if she wanted to visit the grave sites of their parents.

"Time enough tomorrow," Trinette said airily. Annette's efforts to dictate her schedule annoyed Trinette. Trinette was already calculating how long she could tolerate this inconvenient disruption of her personal life. "I just want to have a drink, take a shower, and go to bed. It's three in the morning my time."

That bothered Annette, too. Every word and deed of Trinette's was centered on Trinette – what *she* wanted, what *she* needed, how she felt, what *her* opinion was. Perhaps Annette was being overly sensitive. It had been a hard time for everyone. Trinette needed to rest. Annette parked the car in front of the Laval house. Trinette allowed Annette to carry her suitcase to the room Trinette had slept in for almost nineteen years from the time she was a child. Trinette helped herself to a glass from a kitchen cupboard. She opened the refrigerator, grabbed a handful of ice to fill the squat glass, and poured gin over the ice. She carried the glass up the stairs following in Annette's footsteps. Trinette entered her bedroom and looked around at the room décor that was frozen in time.

"Still the same," Trinette said. She felt debilitated just walking into her bedroom of so many years. The cynicism in Trinette's voice depressed Annette.

Dawn brought a beautiful New Hampshire day — blue skies and a gentle breeze from the west. Trinette missed the dawn part, because she slept until the sound of the town clock bells woke her up. She counted their striking. Ten. She located her watch on the bedside table and adjusted the time piece from Brussels time to Caledonia time. She stretched luxuriously and left her bed. She smelled the aroma of coffee wafting up the stairs to her room. Wearing only her linen gown and an old pair of slippers she had found in the bedroom closet, she headed downstairs toward the origin of the coffee aroma. She found Annette in the kitchen reading the *Boston Globe*.

"*Bonjour*," Trinette said. She had coached herself to be lighthearted and cheerful. She had business to conduct. She hadn't come four thousand miles to upset everyone and return to Belgium empty-handed.

"*Bonjour, ma cheri*," Annette replied. The sun had chased away her misgivings of the previous evening, and she was in the mood for rapprochement. She left her counter stool and hugged her sister. "*Crêpes?*"

"*Oui*," Trinette said. "*Et café, café!*"

They talked about how the town had changed during Trinette's absence. Trinette asked if Dan knew she was coming. Annette assured her sister that he did.

"I told only family that you were coming." Annette cleaned the griddle and accessories after serving Trinette. In the past, Annette had not resented cleaning up after Trinette, but, this time, Annette could feel the sting of indignation as she dried the dishes. "Did you say you've seen Grand'mere recently?"

"Last year. I visited her in France. I was going to spend three days, but she didn't know who I was. I mean, she was *way* out there." Trinette rolled her eyes and gestured with her arm toward Vermont to indicate how out-of-touch her grandmother was. "So I left the next day and spent two days in Paris on the way back to Brussels. I met this incredible guy in Paris."

"You're still with…?"

"Laurens," Trinette said, cutting off that leg of the conversation. "I'll spare you the details." She sipped her coffee. "So, I guess I'll go see Dan. We didn't part on very good terms. Is he okay?"

"He's fine," Annette said. She didn't know how much to say without stirring up Trinette's emotions of what? – jealousy, regret, possessiveness, criticism? "He's a little more serious now than the Dan you used to know. He's got a lot on his plate right now."

"Gotta peddle those light bulbs and power tools. Poor Dan." Trinette paused to look at her sister. For a second, she wondered if Annette and Dan had ever slept together, two small-town survivors comforting one another. "He doesn't know does he?"

"No," Annette replied. "You and I are the only ones left who know."

"Dan had already taken over the hardware store?"

"Yes. Benjamin was slipping into dementia, and he couldn't deal with inventories or even customers very well near the end. He called every woman he met 'Helen' and…it was just too hard to keep track of him. He was giving money out all over town."

"Dan should have put him in a retirement home, one of those full-care facilities." Trinette was a firm believer that aged and infirmed relatives should not be a burden on healthy, active, younger family members. Caring for incapacitated people was society's obligation, she believed, not a liability for people like her to shoulder.

"Dan took him into his house on the lake…where you guys lived." Annette believed that guardianship was a family duty. "Dan sold the Benjamin Hardin house and put whatever money he cleared from the sale into the hardware store."

"Good old soft Dan. More heart than brains."

"He made it work really well," Annette said defensively. "Between the housekeeper and Scott and John and me – I went by to look in on Benjamin a couple of times a week – I mean, we all pitched in. Benjamin loved his life."

"*Tee*-dious," Trinette sighed. The thought of baby-sitting an older man with dementia gave her the creeps. She handed her empty plate to Annette. "Thanks, Baby Girl."

"Do you want to visit Mom's and Dad's graves?"

"We can do that later," Trinette said waving off the idea. If Annette brought up visiting the cemetery one more time,

Trinette would blow a gasket, she thought. "I want to shower and clean up. I suppose I can find Dan down at the hardware store?"

"I think it's better if you call him and arrange to meet somewhere else." Annette's tone was an annoyance to Trinette. She nodded affirmatively, but she knew full well she was going to do it her way. Before leaving the room for her shower, she asked Annette to call Dan and tell him to meet her at the Town Gazebo at 11:30 that morning. Annette told Trinette to call Dan herself, but Trinette said she didn't want to talk to him until they met in person. Annette complied with her sister's wishes. Trinette got her way.

Dan sat on a bench in the Town Gazebo until 11:50. He was about to give up the wait and go for lunch at a nearby café when he spotted Trinette walking that walk of hers through the crowd of people who had just disembarked from the *M/S Franklin Pierce*. Boy, he thought, doesn't that bring back a memory? For only a second, a vision of his wedding day flashed across his mind. On their wedding day, he and Trinette had climbed into a limousine parked at the exact spot where she was walking now. She was still lean and shapely, and she turned a lot of tourists' heads as she made her way toward the gazebo. Dan walked toward Trinette – his wife. He took her in his arms and hugged her.

"You look great," he told her. Her embrace felt formal, perfunctory.

"You, too, you big stud," Trinette said playfully. She wanted neither to encourage him nor to turn him off. She didn't mind refreshing his memory of how she could attract the interest of men without really trying.

"I'm so sorry about your parents," Dan said.

"And I'm sorry about Benjamin," Trinette said. She had always thought of Benjamin as a bit of a slow-thinking, small-town bore, but he *had* always been nice to her. They sat down on a bench looking out across Caledonia Bay.

"Your mom and dad were wonderful people," Dan said awkwardly.

"Yep, they were okay if you're big on drill sergeants."

"You're dad wasn't a drill sergeant."

"I wasn't talking about my dad." She wiggled her toes at a duck that waddled by their bench looking for a handout. "Did they slander their wayward daughter?"

"Never once. And neither did I, Trinette."

"Good of you, Daniel." A benefit of living in Brussels was that she didn't care much one way or the other what Dan said about her. "Have you been all right?"

"I'm all set," he said.

"Ah, New England Boy," she teased him. "You don't hear 'all set' in Belgium."

"Habits, I guess." They looked out over the glistening wavelets. The *Pierce* cast off, issued three blasts, reversed, and set off on its jagged giant slalom course around dozens of islands on its way back to Dartford Parade. "Have you seen John, yet?"

"No. I wanted to see you first."

"He's the real deal. Big and strong, straight *A*'s, and he beat my time in the 400-meters last year. He's got the whole package."

"Jealous?"

"Proud."

After another long pause, Trinette said, "You know I'm just here to pay my respects to my mom and dad?"

"I figured that," Dan said. He watched two ducks paddle by in the water beside the docks. He had heard that ducks were monogamous for life.

"I think we should get a divorce, Dan."

"We don't have to if you don't really want to," Dan said, as much as admitting that he had no interest in marrying anyone else. He focused on remaining composed. He was uneasy talking about divorce after dodging the subject for fifteen years.

"No, I want to," she said. "I can go see 'Canuck' Koeneki this afternoon."

"You're going to use 'Canuck'?"

"What's wrong with him?"

"Nothing." "Canuck" was a personal injury hack, Dan thought, but it didn't really matter in an age when you could print drafts of divorce papers off the Internet.

"Dan, I'm going to be blunt, so don't be offended." Trinette needed to say this right, and her body language needed to match her words. "I've had sort of a tough time, recently, so I need to know whether your dad left you an inheritance of any size."

Dan was instantly put off by the question, but, deep down, he knew he should not have been surprised. He had met with his father's attorney, Fred Cummings, so he had a pretty good idea of the answer to her question. He decided to be completely straightforward in his reply.

"If you add up his insurance, his Keogh, and his

investment account, it's in the neighborhood of $145,000."

"So, can I count on half of that?" she asked. She had hoped the windfall might be much higher.

"I think it's better to ask your lawyer," Dan said. "I don't know enough to answer that question."

"Has Annette told you what my parents left for her and me?" Trinette asked.

"No," he replied. If this line of questioning was Trinette's idea of "paying her respects", her definition was a long way off from his. He took a long look at his wife. Any soft edges she may have had in the past had been hardened by her fast-paced lifestyle and poor decisions over the past fifteen years. Her eyes were swollen and her skin was not a healthy color. Compared to the sensuous young woman he had married, she seemed tense and nervous. There was no pleasure for Dan in sitting beside her on this bench by the bay.

"Can I come by to meet John tonight?"

Dan told her that she was welcome. He was relieved when she stood up to leave. He couldn't bring himself to hug her, but he put his hand on her left shoulder and squeezed gently, a non-committal affectionate gesture. She didn't appear to be disappointed. He wondered if he would ever see her again, because he planned to evacuate the house before she arrived that evening.

When Trinette left Dan at the town docks, she went directly to Chuck "Canuck" Koeneki's office, and "Canuck" let her walk right in off the street and into his office as she had predicted. He agreed to take her case in the divorce proceeding. She told him she had talked to Dan and she was quite sure he intended to create no barriers. "Uncontested,"

"Canuck" wrote on his yellow legal pad. He asked her about her history since the birth of her child, and Trinette was happy, even eager, to tell the last fifteen years' worth of her life story. She couldn't share her life with family for fear of being judged, but she could spill her guts to a stranger, because she didn't care what a stranger thought.

"How much is this going to cost?" she asked "Canuck".

He gave her a ball park figure but emphasized how variable the figure could be if things got dicey. She assured him that things wouldn't get "dicey". She left his office for the walk back to the Laval house past Caledonia High School students escaping their encounters with education like hamsters from their cages. She walked past Thornton Preppies swarming the ice cream vendors for cones to while away the rest of the afternoon in the town park. When she arrived at the Laval house, she could hear china tinkling in the kitchen. Annette was home from school, and she was making afternoon tea. Trinette joined her on the back porch.

"How's Dan?" Annette asked.

"He's Dan."

"Was it hard?"

"He's agreeable to a divorce," Trinette said, surprising Annette. "I got a lawyer, and he said it should be a simple deal." Trinette shifted in her wicker chair, sipped her tea, and paused before speaking again. "Annette, I have to ask you a question, because things have been hard on me recently. I'll cut to the chase. My question is how much can I expect from Dad's will?"

Annette was embarrassed by the question, the question she had dreaded since the moment she found out Trinette was coming home. She felt unprepared to answer it.

"Daddy's lawyer knows the details."

"You mean that skinny guy who wears the welding goggles in Concord?"

"Yes. He can tell us the details, but I'm almost sure you'll receive an insurance payment and the value of some of Dad's investment account."

"What's the value?"

"I'm not sure," Annette said. Trinette looked unsatisfied, so Annette felt compelled to say more. "I think Dad's retirement account goes to me and this house goes to me."

Trinette's face clouded over. "That's crap!" she shouted. "Why should you get the house? We're twins, for God's sake!"

"Wait for the lawyer to explain it to us," Annette pleaded.

"Why should you get the house, Annette? You've been living here for free for years while I've been out on my own scratching and fighting for a place to live!"

"Maybe Mummy and Daddy put a value on my being here."

"Oh, God, Annette! You're such a saint!" Annette's use of their childhood names for their parents drove Trinette wild. "You're saying that you're such a dream to be around that they paid you to be here? Doesn't that make you a whore?"

"Trinette, please...."

"You lived here for free. No wonder you have eight thousand dollars in your checking account. You never had to pay rent like the rest of the world!"

"How do you know how much is in my checking account?" Annette asked, her mouth open in astonishment.

"Here's your debit card. I used it to get some cash, because I'm broke."

"Trinette!" Annette was shocked and offended. "You took it out of my purse?"

"I'll pay you back."

"You don't even know my PIN!"

"The teller at the bank thought I was you, so she helped me reset your PIN. Don't freak out!"

"That is *wrong*, Trinette!"

"Your new PIN is '4567'." Trinette was accustomed to conflict. Nothing Annette could say would bother her.

"I sent you two thousand dollars!"

"I ran out," Trinette said. "I'll pay you back. I'll get what's coming to me and I'll pay you back." Desperate for a rationale, she referred to their unmentionable pact, their secret agreement entered into long ago. "I helped you when you were in need," Trinette said, "now, you can help me."

Annette simply stared at her twin sister. She was too emotional to say a word.

Trinette rejoined her criticism of her parents' will. "Speaking of 'wrong', giving this house to you instead of splitting it between us...*that's* wrong."

"I was *here*, Trinette!" Annette was as angry as she had ever been in her life. Years of accommodating Trinette's selfishness and years of acceding to her mother's wishes and Trinette's desires had pushed her beyond the limits of her patience. "They knew I'd be here to take ownership of the house."

"This is disgusting. If 'Mummy' and 'Daddy' were so fair-minded, why did they try to manipulate us? Why'd they

pay you for staying and punish me for leaving? It's not fair!"
She put down her tea cup abruptly and stormed off the back
porch in the direction of the village.

Trinette walked into a pub by the town docks and sat at
the bar.

"Annette?" the bar tender asked as he looked up from
washing beer mugs.

"I'm not Annette," Trinette snapped. "Give me a Martini
straight up."

"Trinette?" the bar tender squinted in the reduced light-
ing of the pub interior. "Is that you."

"Yes, you hick," Trinette growled. "What's your name?"

"Rambo Johnson," he said with a smile. "Don't you remember me?"

Trinette broke into a laugh. "Oh, yeah, yeah. You were
that meatloaf…you went to Caledonia High, right?"

"Yeah, baybeee! You remember Old Rambo. That night
on the Mail Boat?"

"Oh, God," Trinette laughed. "And why did they call you
'Rambo'?"

"I lifted weights big time," he said. He flexed his biceps
and smiled broadly as he remembered the night on the Mail
Boat.

"I see you gave up lifting weights a long time ago unless
that thing hanging over your belt is a muscle."

"Occupational hazard," Rambo admitted as he patted his stomach bulge affectionately. "Here's your Martini,
Beautiful."

Trinette took a powerful gulp from her Martini. Rambo

made the mistake of asking where she lived, and she sat there describing Brussels for the next hour.

"Brussels sounds awesome," Rambo said. "I should move there."

Trinette knew that he'd never get as far as the Massachusetts border. At the end of her lengthy monologue on the benefits of living in Brussels, Trinette got up to leave. She pulled a fifty dollar bill out of her skirt pocket.

"Get outta here," Rambo told her. "No charge. No charge!"

"You're the best, Rrrrambo," she purred. She planted an enormous kiss on the barkeep's cheek in time to be observed by two of Rambo's regular patrons who had just walked into the bar. If Rambo had smiled any wider, the bottom half of his face might have fallen off. Trinette walked by the newcomers and said, "This guy is an animal!"

"Give me two of whatever she's drinking," the first patron said.

Rambo was still smiling when the door closed after Trinette.

Trinette had just presented a two-hour summary of her life to Rambo. She had anesthetized her brain for free in the company of a man whom she barely could remember, a man she was unlikely to see again. She had shared intimate details of her life to impress a small-town barkeeper, but with her family, the people who loved her, she shared only rudeness and insult.

She walked down the main street to a café on the town docks. She ordered a Panini and a glass of wine, which she took out on the deck overlooking the harbor. She had already made up her mind to see Scott and John within the hour. She had to return to "Canuck" Koeneki's office in the morning to sign paperwork. If that went as fast as she hoped, she might get out of Caledonia by eleven o'clock. By going directly to the airport, she might be able to change her ticket to a departure that evening, three days prior to her original schedule. If the airline couldn't amend the departure date of her flight, she could stay in Boston for the intervening days. She could try to contact a couple of McGill girlfriends who would be happy to meet up with her on short notice for a few drinks. Laurens had given her five thousand Euros for the trip, so she could stay in a comfortable hotel down at Copley Place. A girl had to be flexible. But a girl didn't have to be miserable, and Trinette knew she had to get out of this one-horse town.

Two men, who were brothers-in-law, sitting at an adjacent table struck up a conversation with Trinette. Their homes were in New York City, but they came up to their father-in-law's camp on one of the islands on Lake Tremont every summer after Labor Day for a two-week vacation. They bought Trinette a glass of wine after moving over to her table to make conversation easier. They talked about skiing in Europe and Utah and they talked about Broadway shows and they talked about their jet skis that were bobbing like corks down by the town docks visible over the deck railing. The town clock tower bells announced seven o'clock. She said she had to go. They asked where she was going. She pointed across the harbor to the lake side of the Dan Hardin house. They offered to take her by jet ski on their way back to their island. She accepted the offer.

As the jet skis approached the Hardin dock, Trinette

could make out a tanned figure with cotton-colored hair fishing from the end of the dock. He was wearing tan top-siders, a baggy aqua-colored bathing suit, a white tee shirt, and a navy Boston Red Sox baseball cap. She recognized the way he moved and the shape of his body. It was Scott Harrington. He put down his fishing rod when the jet ski drew abeam the dock to discharge Trinette.

"Temptress of the Seas!" Scott called out as he extended his hand to boost her onto the dock. Trinette thanked the jet ski operator and waved goodbye to his brother-in-law. She weaved a little but found her balance.

"Look at you!" she squealed as she hugged Scott and made a big deal out of squeezing his biceps and patting his tight stomach. "Still the jock!" The jet skis roared away toward the northwest.

"Good to see you again," Scott said. "You look awesome." Trinette noticed that his eyes weren't aimed directly at her just as Annette had warned her.

"You, too."

"Sit down for a while," he said. "Dan's working late, and John's running on the indoor track at the Thornton field house." He pulled two plastic bottles of water from a cooler, and he handed one to Trinette.

"Thanks," she said, "I'm dehydrated." She eyed Scott as she mentally compared his muscular build to Laurens – pale, self-indulgent, rich Laurens.

"It got up to over eighty degrees today," he said after swallowing a gulp of water. "I guess that's twenty-seven degrees to you."

"Something like that," she said. She noticed again that

he wasn't looking directly at her, and Scott noticed that she noticed.

"Bother you?" he asked.

"No. Annette told me you can't see straight ahead. I'm really sorry, Scott. It must be horrible for you."

"I'm okay," he said. "It does creep people out a little, though."

"I couldn't stand it!"

"Maybe that's why it was laid on me," Scott said. "I can."

By sitting side-by-side on the end of the dock, they could avoid the unsettling eye non-contact issue and just talk. The sun was low in the sky over Caledonia and the light breeze made their reunion physically comfortable even if not every topic they discussed measured up to the same standard.

"Did Dan tell you that we talked today?"

"No," Scott lied.

"Yeah. Dan and I are getting divorced."

"Wow! Are you sure about this?"

"Why stay married? I've been gone for fifteen years."

Dan had said pretty much the same thing while preparing John for his first meeting with his mother since his infancy. For years, Dad had told John that Trinette hadn't left town to get away from her son; she had left to escape her depression, her Caledonia Blues. There were three reasons for Trinette's visit. First, she wanted to pay respects to her parents. Second, she wanted a divorce. Third, she wanted to see her son all grown up.

His voice was deeper than Trinette had expected. She felt the vibration of the dock under his approaching steps. Scott stood up and extended his hand to help her to her feet.

She turned and looked up directly into John's eyes. He was lean and muscular and strikingly handsome.

"What a hunk!" she said. She smothered John in a tight hug.

"Hi, Mom," John said to the top of her head. He had practiced that line several times standing in front of his bedroom mirror. He had tried *"Bonsoir"* and "Hi, Mother" and "Hello, Trinette" and "Hello" without any name at all. "Hi, Mom" seemed best under the circumstances.

"He called me 'Mom'," Trinette cooed. "I'm so glad for the chance to see you grown up to be a man." They released their embrace and stood facing one another.

Trinette didn't look as much like Annette as John had expected. She certainly didn't look as fresh as the photograph in his father's bedroom. Scott told them to sit on the end of the dock while he went to the house to make gin-and-tonics for them. When Scott reached the house, he called Dan at the hardware store to summon him to the house.

"I think John can use some backup," Scott said.

"Can't do it," Dan said. "I don't want to lay eyes on Trinette ever again."

"Yes, you *can* do it, Hero. John needs some help."

"I can't stand to look at her face," Dan insisted. "It hit me today. All those wasted years."

"You need to put on your man suit and get down on that dock," Scott pressed.

"Nope. I'm done with her. She hasn't got any soul left, and I don't have anything left in my soul to give her."

Scott hung up the telephone and started building gin-and-tonics.

John and Trinette sat beside one another on the end of the dock. Trinette spoke first.

"Dan told me you're a track star."

"Dad gives me more credit than I deserve." He smiled. He couldn't think of anything to say.

"So, any girl friends?"

"One. But she's not here this year."

Trinette didn't pursue the subject. John's toes skimmed the surface of the lake as he swung his legs slowly.

"I'm sorry about your mom and dad," he said. "Grandmom and Granddad were really nice."

"Yes, they were. It was a real shock. I guess you can't believe they're gone, either."

"Dad says it'll take a while," John said. They both swung their feet, John's toes tipping the water and Trinette's missing the surface by six inches.

Sitting next to John made Trinette question her desertion of her baby for the first time in years. She felt a stab of regret when she considered how she had missed out on the life of this strapping youth by her side.

"Did your father tell you that he and I are getting a divorce?"

"No," John lied, as he had been instructed to do. Lying was easier than usual for him, because he was acting on a command from a higher authority. Dan had told John to let Trinette do the talking on this one.

"I have some problems to work through," Trinette said. She didn't want to give the impression that she was severing the bond capriciously. "It's just easier for all of us this way. I know I haven't been a very good mother."

John let her words hang in the air while he thought, you haven't been a mother at all. Again, he kept the thought in a cage. He wasn't a personal relations expert, but he knew that he couldn't get words back once he had spoken them. His mother had just lost her parents and father-in-law, so she didn't need to hear about his low opinion of her mothering instinct. More leg swinging.

"So, what's your girlfriend's name?"

"Andrea," he said. "She's back in Austria this year. She had to drop out of Thornton."

"Why?"

"Her father's business went bust."

"Uh, oh," Trinette said, trying to be jovial, "you broke the first rule. Only date the rich ones!"

That's annoying, John thought. Of course, most everything was annoying to John of late. Amgen was hovering in the eighty-dollar range and every afternoon as he walked into the house from school he expected the hammer to have dropped. If it got to $92, he was finished, cleaned out. He guessed at his mother's response if he told her that a month ago he had been worth $1.7 million? Do I still need a rich girl friend now?

Scott walked toward the end of the dock and gave them each a tall glass containing gin-and-tonic with a wedge of lemon. Scott returned to the house.

"Do you drink normally?" Trinette asked.

"Twice a year," John said truthfully. The tonic tickled his tongue.

"It's twice a day for me," Trinette said. It was intended as a joke, if the truth can qualify as a joke.

"Well," John said, "you're a European now and everybody knows Europeans are bombed out of their skulls half the time." That was supposed to be a joke, also. Trinette laughed, so John guessed she took it the right way.

"You sound like Scott talking," Trinette said.

"He's a cool guy," John said. "You never know what he's going to say. He gave me quite a briefing when we thought Andrea's parents were coming over from Salzburg for Parents' Weekend."

"What'd he say?"

"'Look 'em right in the eye. Squeeze the father's hand until his knuckles pop. Pay close attention to the mother's every word. Keep asking the parents questions. They can't ask you questions if they're busy answering yours. And don't throw your arm around Andrea and yank her to your side the way you do, because they'll think you're a wife-beater. Be humble. Andrea's parents won't like a cocky American prep school punk telling them how great he is.' I mean, he went on for twenty minutes."

"Reasonable advice," Trinette said.

"Yeah, but," he looked at his mother inquisitively, "do I look like a wife-beater?"

"I see your point. Still, Scott's always got a lot to say... you know, all that macho stuff he comes up with."

"You should've been around when he was a fighter pilot. It was 'wounded wombat' here and 'shoot 'em in the lips there'. He's a lively dude."

"So what did *Dan* say about Andrea's parents coming?"

"He said, 'Here's a hundred dollars. Take 'em to lunch.'"

"That's Dan," Trinette sighed.

John asked Trinette about Brussels, but she clipped it short by saying that all big cities are the same. She asked him about Thornton, but none of the teachers she remembered were still there. Dan had warned John that Trinette wasn't reentering their lives, so he shouldn't get his hopes up. He probably wouldn't see her again. They talked until the town clock tower bells chimed eight times.

"I have to go," she said. John got up and helped her to her feet. They left the dock and crossed the back lawn to the back porch. John called for Scott, but there was no reply. After scolding Dan for not facing up to Trinette, Scott had gone AWOL, too. John offered to walk Trinette to the Laval house, but she declined his offer. Every moment with John reminded her that she had abandoned him, and she didn't want to deal with the guilt.

"I know my way to the Laval house in my sleep," she said. And it's still daylight, so Caledonia's mad rapists aren't out, yet." John opened the door for her to leave. Trinette turned to embrace him.

"John," she said emotionally, "I love you very much. I'm sorry for...."

John cut her off, and they were both glad for it.

"I love you, too, Mom," John said, just the way he had practiced. That got Trinette started bawling, and she looked at him through her tears before loosening her grasp on his hand and hurrying away down the street.

When Trinette entered the Laval house, Annette heard the door close. She was prepared for the worst when Trinette walked into the kitchen. Trinette walked over to her sister and embraced her.

"Annette, I'm so sorry for all the things I said!"

Annette could tell Trinette had been drinking and crying. Annette had gone through identical make-up scenes scores of times in the past, and she wasn't in the mood to be manipulated anymore.

"It's in the past," Annette said.

"I don't know why I can't control myself. Why do I say the things I say?"

"Because it gets you what you want," Annette said, repeating what her sister had told her twenty years ago. They laughed ruefully.

"Seeing Dan and then John, it's taken everything out of me," Trinette said. "I'll take my tea to my room. I have to sleep."

Again, everything Trinette said was about herself. Annette resented how she had been such a pushover for Trinette for so many years. Annette resented her mother, too, for manipulating them both. Annette said goodnight to her sister, went to the living room, sat on a couch, and pretended to read.

Annette had left for school long before Trinette awoke the next morning. Trinette showered before walking into the village center to "Canuck" Koeneki's office. As he had promised, the divorce documents were ready for her signature. After affixing her signature and receiving her copies, she paid the lawyer's fee in cash and accepted a receipt for her payment. "Canuck" assured her that any subsequent details could be managed by fax and telephone or by electronic

documents and email. He wished her well and sa~
front door.

Trinette left the law office and walked to a restaura..
by the old train station. The town clock tower bells announced twelve noon. During lunch, she ordered a car for
a two o'clock pick up to take her to Boston. Annette didn't
normally get home from school until almost three o'clock,
so Trinette could avoid seeing her again and having to go
through a long explanation of why she was leaving early. She
could avoid a long, boring goodbye.

Annette came home early. The limousine hadn't even arrived at the house, yet. Trinette palmed the note she had left
on the kitchen table and braced for the inevitable conversation about why she was leaving after only one night back in
town. Trinette emphasized that it was all too sad for her to
stand another day. She begged for Annette to be fair with the
distribution of their parents' inheritance. Annette, sounding
very legalistic, told Trinette the lawyer was compelled to en-
force the will of her parents. Trinette got testy again, and she
started repeating herself. Near the end of their conversation,
after the limousine had driven in to the Laval drive way,
they were both wishing Annette had stayed late at school.
Annette looked out the hallway window at the limo driver
who was waiting for Trinette.

"But you haven't gone to the cemetery," Annette said.

"Annette, I didn't have time to go to the graveyard. Will
you get this through your head: Our parents are dead! It
doesn't matter who visits their headstones and it doesn't matter who puts flowers on their graves. They're gone, and that's
all there is."

She stomped toward the front door where she paused. She motioned through the glass for the limousine driver to open the trunk. "I can't even hug you goodbye right now, Annette, you're too depressing!" She slammed the front door after her and carried her bag to the rear of the limousine. The driver, who had been sunning himself in the front garden, hustled to take her luggage. The driver placed her suitcase into the trunk and closed the lid. Trinette got into the rear seat of the limousine without looking back toward the house. She longed to get away without a moment's delay.

Annette stood on her parents' front porch — her front porch — and watched the limousine head out onto the road to Boston. Her mind was a muddle of resentment and loss and sorrow. Annette wept.

Chapter 18

FALSE RECOVERY

UNKNOWN TO ANYONE among his family and friends in the autumn of 2005, John had suffered calamitous unrealized financial losses since July when Amgen stock prices had spiraled crazily upwards, putting immense strain on his short position. Fear told him to close out the position and accept the loss of over $1,700,000. Greed told him to hold on and hope Amgen shares might decrease in value to a point where he could close out his short position and break even. Greed won the debate, and John held on and gritted his teeth.

Testing his thesis, Amgen stock shot up to over $83 on July 22, putting John's 50,000-share short position teetering on the threshold of collapse. He was only a few thousand dollars away from receiving margin calls. A few more dollars added to Amgen's stock price would bring complete ruin.

Through trial-and-error, John discovered that he could relieve his chronic stomach cramps by avoiding carbonated soft drinks and sipping a brilliant pink liquid antacid potion at bedtime. He had a long way to go to reach eighty years of age, but Amgen was cruelly introducing him to some of the symptoms waiting for him when he got there.

He thought he could tolerate the agony of Amgen if he could tell someone what he was going through. Secrecy had heightened the thrill of making money, but, now, with his fortunes in decline, secrecy was a giant weight on his chest. He inhaled deeply and sighed mournfully dozens of times each day. His longing to confide in someone to dilute his suffering even invaded his dreams. In one dream, Corky walked toward him beside a swimming pool. Corky, naked as the day he was born, waddled ever closer to where John stood, exposed and afraid.

"Corky," John's dream voice said, "I've lost everything."

"Let's go swimming," Corky said in the dream. John never had to find out what such a swim might have entailed, because, mercifully, he woke up in a sweat and took a sip from his antacid bottle.

John considered talking about his tribulations with Paul Bruguiere. A chance meeting down by the Town Gazebo revealed what a serious mistake in judgment that would have been. Paul's body was so reshaped by months of body-building that he cut a formidable figure even in street clothes. Unfortunately, his Uncle Thomas' influence had left Paul with the fashion sense of a gypsy. Late one afternoon, while John was returning home from a mail run, he encountered Paul who was wearing flip-flops, old-school shorts, a tank top, and a rapper-styled baseball hat worn sideways. John took his old pal aside to the privacy of a park bench beside the gazebo.

"What are you doing?" John hissed.

"What?"

"You look like an Albanian pimp!"

"What's a...."

"Look," John said, as he fumbled to open an L.L. Bean catalogue he had just retrieved from Dan's Post Office mail box, "look!" He opened the catalogue to a page of khaki walking shorts. Then he found a page of golf shirts. Then, sandals. "Don't wear anything that's not in here...please!"

"What's the point of having muscles if I can't show them off?" Paul asked.

"What you're wearing is below low-class. It's sub-human. Chimps in the circus wear better stuff. Wear normal clothes. People will know you have muscles without you running around in your underwear." John was unrelenting.

"Jeez."

"And for God sake, wear a baseball hat like a man – straight, not sideways like some loser on the streets!"

"All right, all right. I just don't get this stuff, you know, how to dress. It's all random."

"Just pick someone and copy him," John said. "Pick *me.* Just dress like I do and you'll be fine. You're not a loser, Paul, so don't dress like a loser."

The pressure was getting to John. In the past, he hadn't made such a big deal out Paul's eccentric attire. Goofy attire was Paul's birthright. They left the gazebo with an unwritten understanding, a kind of dress code. Paul was to copy John, just as John copied Scott.

John tried to imagine sharing his financial ordeal with Paul. John: I lost two million dollars. Paul: Bummer, Dude. How do you like my triceps? John vetoed the idea.

Fortunately, the Amgen stock price ticked lower during August and early September, and John dared to believe he might be spared financial Armageddon.

Scott had once told John that a fighter pilot always has to neutralize his most immediate threat. If a missile is tracking his aircraft, he has to defeat that missile before going counter-offensive on the enemy fighter on his tail and before dealing with the ground-to-air missiles that haven't launched yet and before solving his low fuel state and before recovering to his base in zero-zero weather conditions. If he gave his attention to his threats out of order, he was dead meat. Scott illustrated life lessons in fighter pilot analogies, so most of his advice to John was adorned with such colorful imagery. The analogies helped John remember the lessons.

John's most immediate threat in August had been his pending financial devastation. His most immediate threat in September had been the pending meeting with his mother. His hyperactive imagination had dreamed up a number of rosy scenarios in advance of her arrival.

In one scenario, his mother shrieked and fell faint in his arms, overcome by the emotion of meeting her beloved son.

In another less gratifying scenario, his mother, appalled by his provinciality, promised to tutor him in the ways of European sophistication.

In still another, his mother's love for Dan was rekindled, and his blissfully reunited parents pledged to reestablish their family and commit their lives to the adoration of their son.

In the aftermath of actual events, John had to marvel at the excesses of his optimism.

What he actually had experienced after walking down

to the dock to meet his mother on that sunny afternoon was a hug from a slightly inebriated, gushy middle-aged woman. She had looked a lot like Annette, but the similarities had ended there. Trinette had seemed unsubstantial to John like a fern growing in shallow soil in a crevice of a boulder. She had giggled foolishly while praising him obsequiously and then, in the next breath, insinuating something sexual between him and Andrea. She had fished around as though wanting to hear about their intimate times together. Meeting his mother had been a huge anticlimax. Disillusioned, John put his mother out of his mind. He felt relief that she had left prematurely, because he had bigger worries to deal with.

Amgen turned against him again. On September 23, the first margin call was issued by the brokerage. John stared horrified at the computer monitor. Amgen shares had climbed back up to $86.90, and the brokerage demanded an infusion into his account in the amount of $46,000 by September 28. John felt ill. A shiver ran through his body like an electrical pulse, and he felt like vomiting. What if AMGN spiked to $90? It could be the end. All he had secretly worked for was vulnerable to destruction. Gone from his mind were such minor threats as advanced placement calculus, a pimple over his right eyebrow, his mother's visit, even Grandfather Benjamin's empty bedroom down the hall. He signed off the web site and fell onto his bed.

He rocked and groaned miserably. He began a serious negotiation with God. He acknowledged that he was just an ant on the surface of a giant sphere hurtling through space. He asked forgiveness for his recent arrogance when he was worth almost two million dollars. He beseeched the Lord to forgive him for feeling superior to his adolescent classmates who were mired in a world of relative poverty and cell phone texting and football fantasy leagues while, he, John the Magnificent, scored victory after victory trading options. At one point, John made a fantastic offer to God: If God would smack Amgen stock down to $50, just for a day, John would donate ten per cent of his annual proceeds to the Protestant church across the road from the Caledonia Inn. If John were God, he would have taken that deal in a heartbeat.

"But, wait, there's more!" John thought as a trite television commercial came to mind. John contemplated what a pathetic case he had become. He considered how amusing God must find John's absurd proposals. John asked forgiveness for the way he had asked forgiveness.

John was stuck in a miserable prison of his own making. He would have to gut it out, get through another day without puking, hoping AMGN would come off its new high. Fortunately, AMGN *did* begin a steady downward trend in price so that, by October 21, it had fallen to $73.13. If John bought-to-cover the 50,000 Amgen shares now, he would have lost only $17,000. The decision of whether to close the position – Fear — or hang on for a capital gain – Greed — tormented John. He did nothing: Greed 1 – Fear 0 in a nail-biter.

John fell back into the Swamp of Regret when Amgen stock started another upward trend. Every day, another $30,000 to $60,000 disappeared from his net worth. The downward spiral in his financial position continued without pause for a solid month. John felt sick again. On the positive side, he found a coupon in the mail box good for buying two bottles of antacid for the price of one. What had he been thinking? He had missed an opportunity to get out of this leveraged position from Hell with only a minor loss.

Once again, he tried to strike a deal with God for one more chance to get out with his shirt. On November 18, AMGN hit $84.35. John was on the doorstep of disaster again, and he wasn't handling it any better than he had before. He couldn't sleep well at night. He was preoccupied by day. He had begun running, largely because of his father's pleading, but, now, faced by doomsday, he ran to punish himself. He sprinted until his lungs burned and his sides heaved as atonement for his stupidity. The pain of running became a form of flagellation without the visible scars. He had always been an obsessive counter — he counted each time his foot struck the ground. Now, he chanted a cadence, not "left, right, left, right" like Thomas Bruguiere in a parade, but "I – am – stu –pid, I – am – stu – pid."

This autumn of John's severe discontent wasn't much better for Annette, Scott, and Dan. The weeks after Trinette's two-night stay in Caledonia — which Scott called a "Nuclear Boomerang" — was a dreary period for them, too. While their days were filled with sadness, October arrived in glory for everyone else, it seemed. Tourists on buses from North Carolina, Oklahoma, and Maryland stopped in Caledonia to photograph the vibrant yellow and red trees that surrounded the village's lakes and streams. The *M/S Franklin Pierce* deposited hordes of additional tourists onto the town docks every day during Leaf Season. When the buses came at the same time as the *Pierce*, the restaurants of Caledonia were filled to capacity with seemingly carefree people. The visitors vanished as surely as the flamboyant colors of autumn faded to brown marking the end of Leaf Season.

"We knew it had to end," Scott said. He told John that Leaf Season was a reminder that John's grandparents had died during the autumn of their lives when the rich colors of their goodness were at their vibrant peak. He told John to let Leaf Season remind him that the deaths of his grandparents meant they never had to face pain and decline of capacity in the deep winter of their lives.

As the last of the brilliantly-colored leaves fell in November, the town became enveloped in a serene quietness. The forests turned brown, accented with the green boughs of pines. A sea of orange and brown leaves covered the whole county. Lake waters turned colder with the passing days, days that had shortened from sixteen hours of sunlight to only nine. Summer visitors had boarded up their cottages and returned to their primary residences for another six months. The aroma of oak burning in fireplaces permeated the air. It was a solemnly tranquil season, and the survivors of the three families had a lot of work to do in consultation with their lawyers before the wills of the deceased had been executed.

Annette had suffered more than anyone from the effects of Trinette's short visit. Trinette's words had cut her deeply. Trinette's greed and lack of respect for their parents bewildered Annette. Annette was named executrix of the estates of her parents. The routine personal effects audits that she painstakingly performed in the evenings after school revealed even more reasons why Trinette should have shown gratitude toward her parents instead of scorn. Her parents' Bank of Caledonia records went back for only seven years, but an audit of more than eighty monthly statements showed bank drafts drawn quarterly in the amount of five thousand dollars. Annette found photo copies of the bank drafts themselves made payable to Trinette Laval. There was more evidence of her parents' generosity. Her father's personal checking account records showed monthly electronic transfers of two thousand dollars payable to Grand'Mere in France.

Phillip Laval's life insurance policy paid a cash benefit of $50,000 each to Trinette and Annette. Annette used her cash to buy certificates of deposit and two-year U. S. Treasury Bonds. She had no idea what Trinette did with her cash, because the only communication from Trinette had been a letter containing the wire transfer address of her Brussels bank and an apology for her behavior during her stay with Annette.

In the months that followed, the Concord attorney guided Annette through the liquidation of Phillip's brokerage account, transfer of Phillip's 401(k), and sale of the Laval house. After settlement of these transactions, Annette realized an inheritance of more than $700,000. Annette wired half the value of Phillip's liquidated brokerage account about $40,000 — to Trinette.

In return, she received a letter complaining bitterly about not receiving anything from the sale of the house, which Trinette had discovered in an Internet search. Trinette's claim for a share of the proceeds was calculated as though Annette had received cash in the amount of the entire gross sales figure. Annette's lawyer advised her to send Trinette only amounts specifically called for in the wills of her parents. When all taxes had been levied and the dust had settled, Annette could always make a gift to Trinette of some additional amount if she wished to do so.

Annette rented a small two-bedroom apartment from Andrew Gleason's rental company. She sold most of her parents' home furnishings in an estate auction, but she retained a few precious items to furnish her new dwelling. On the advice of a certified financial planner, she invested more than $700,000 in high quality corporate bonds and an S&P 500 Index Exchange Traded Fund. Her modest income from teaching at Brighton School was sufficient to pay rent and living expenses, so Annette felt financially secure. The Concord lawyer eventually engineered a solution to Trinette's campaign to wrangle money out her parents' estate. In exchange for a letter from Trinette waiving all future claims against Annette or the Laval estates, Annette sent $110,000 to Trinette.

Dan also was a target of Trinette's avarice. The Triad continued living in the Dan Hardin house, even though "Canuck" Koeneki asserted a claim for half of the assessed value of the house on behalf of Trinette. She also listed a claim for $75,000 cash in her divorce petition. Respondent's attorney, Fred Cummings, negotiated with Koeneki to craft a final divorce settlement under which Dan wired $87,000 to Trinette. When the conflict was resolved, Dan realized a net benefit from Benjamin's estate of little more than $50,000, barely enough to pay for John's senior year at Thornton and, perhaps, his first semester in college.

It was a sad ending to a long, painful journey for Dan.

He had known Trinette for most of his life, and he had seen her mutate from a high-spirited, carefree girl into a self-centered harpy. Between her alcohol and drug abuse, she might be unrecognizable in ten years. He removed her photograph from his bedroom table. In the aftermath of the divorce process, he preferred *not* to see her or her image again. Nevertheless, he didn't criticize Trinette in front of John. Trinette was John's mother, Dan reasoned, and any complaint against Trinette was, in some way, a complaint against John. Dan's only confidant in the unpleasant process of dealing with Trinette was Scott.

Through all the sadness of burying his parents and executing their wills, Scott continued to live in the Dan Hardin house. Scott and Dan consoled one another on many a long autumn night as they adjusted to their lives without their parents. Scott also had retained Fred Cummings as his counselor in the execution of his parents' wills. The sale of the Harrington house and liquidation of their financial assets yielded an inheritance of more than a million dollars.

Scott opened a brokerage account in the same firm his father, Joe T., had used. He put the management of his assets into the hands of an experienced financial planner and consciously willed himself to forget about it. Thinking about money profaned the memory of his parents. Scott and Dan talked often about John, and they "tag-teamed" him in an effort to support him as he dealt with the loss of his grandparents, the absence of Andrea, and the pressures of his senior year at Thornton. John didn't always reward their efforts with gratitude.

After hovering near $85 for five days like a punted football at the zenith of its trajectory, Amgen stock began a steady decline lasting eight weeks. Mercifully, the trend that started on November 25 continued all the way through Christmas and the New Year so that, on Friday, January 27, 2006, John bought-to-cover all 50,000 shares of Amgen at $70.90. He had leveled the position for a $90,000 gain and he was free. He was released from his financial shackles. He trained for the 400-meter run with new energy. He smiled again.

Although John reneged on fulfilling his prayer contract with God for saving his bacon, John celebrated his salvation by taking his father, Annette, and Scott for a pizza dinner Friday evening. His dinner guests were delighted to see the "Old John" back in form. They erroneously ascribed his re-discovered happiness to the passing of a season of mourning, not knowing that the real reason for John's return to normalcy was his successful avoidance of being squashed like a bug financially. They split up outside the pizza joint to walk to their respective homes under clear, starlit skies. John kissed Annette good night and whispered thanks to her for the support she had given him during his darkest days.

Back by the fireplace in the Dan Hardin house, The Triad talked and laughed over beers. Scott wasn't a strict abstainer anymore. He had shunned alcohol because it might make him blinder faster. Now that he had lost all of his central vision and, in his words, become a "bat", he was back to enjoying an occasional drink. Their conversation ranged from the hardware store to running the 400-meter dash to football – which is to say the New England Patriots. In a game of

Charades, Scott acted out the name "Thomas Bruguiere" so comically that John laughed until his stomach shook and his eyes teared, something he hadn't done since learning of his grandparents' deaths.

John made a long entry in his diary before turning in for a blessed night's rest. He made another in a lengthy line of promises to never, ever, *ever* write naked calls! Ever! "NAV: $1,810,023!!!" John the Obsessor, John the Genius, John the Magnificent had prevailed! He poured the contents of the pink antacid bottle into his sink, wrote a long letter to Andrea, and went to bed at peace with the world.

Chapter 19

SACRIFICE

THE MORNING AFTER John's liberation from the bondage of his short position in Amgen, he awoke to a bright, crisp winter's day. He was the first of The Triad to enter the boundaries of the kitchen, so he made coffee and laid out ingredients for Western omelets in accordance with Rule 7. Scott was the author of The Rules of the Triad.

> Rule 1 was "Seize every opportunity to praise Scott Harrington."
> Rule 2 was "Better to die than look bad."
> Rule 3 was "Make your bed within ten minutes of rising."
> Rule 4 was "Never laugh at your own joke. (*See* Rule 5.)"
> Rule 5 was "Always laugh at Scott's jokes."
> Rule 6 was "Bravery consists of hanging on for one more second."
> Rule 7 was "First man in the kitchen makes breakfast for everyone."

And so on. The rules were Scott-centric. Because Scott

had authored the rules over dinner or while fishing, their order was random, so a common mortal might have difficulty memorizing the rules. John was an uncommon mortal, so, in the words of Scott, John's memorization of the rules was "a low hurdle for a high-stepper".

John laid out the *Globe* for Dan and Scott, who arrived only five minutes after John. Exploiting Rule 7 was a common practice among The Triad. A skillfully-timed entrance to the kitchen allowed one to read the paper while someone else performed chef duties. They all knew the drill. Dan and Scott had to be at work before nine o'clock, but John didn't have to go in until one o'clock on Saturdays. Rule 7, for all its faults, worked. John was still cleaning up the kitchen when Dan and Scott walked through the kitchen on their way to the hardware store.

"See you, Son," Dan said.

"Later, Dad," John called as he turned from the sink to watch them go.

"Who's the World's Finest?" Scott called out.

"I am," John said.

"That is correct, Grasshopper," Scott said as he popped a mini salute in John's direction. Dan and Scott walked out through the mud room into the sharp morning air.

John went upstairs and scoured his bathroom toilet, shower, sink, and floor. He put a load of laundry into the basement washing machine. He did some pushups, crunches, and leg stretches. He studied calculus for thirty minutes. Then he shaved and showered. Two hours remained before his work report time at the hardware store, so he put on his cross-country ski pants, two layers of fleece pullovers, and his ski hat. He walked in snow boots down to the dock where he changed into his hockey skates.

The surface of Caledonia Bay was uncharacteristically free of snow so near to the end of January. Winds had sculpted snow dunes on the ice, but about half of the surface was completely clear of snow. John skated about a mile out toward the middle of the bay. He greeted fishermen lounging outside their bob houses to soak up the morning sun on their mid-winter pale faces.

John had forgotten to wear his safety necklace and he wished he had worn his heavy mittens. The gloves he wore were, at best, liners for his mittens. He wriggled his fingers to increase circulation and warming. He stepped up the pace of his skating to heat his body from the inside out. Instead of doing tight turns and hockey stops, John established a steady pace, and he cruised in a straight line out of the bay and northerly toward a cluster of small islands. When he neared the islands, he turned around to skate back toward the village.

Two snowmobiles accelerated down the ramp at the town docks and skimmed across the water for a hundred feet before reaching the ice. Electric bubblers prevented ice from freezing around the town docks, so, even during the coldest temperatures, a band of open water surrounded the docks for a thousand feet of shoreline. The two sleds reached the ice and roared away at over sixty miles an hour, leaving clouds of snow particles when they powered through mounds of dry snow.

John skated closer to the deserted town docks. The Town Fire Boat and the Mail Boat were away in dry dock.

Fire-fighting duties fell to all-terrain vehicles in winter and mail delivery to the islands was suspended when the lake was iced in. As he neared the edge of the ice where the band of open water began, John could hear bells in the town clock tower begin to strike twelve. Then John heard another sound, a low-frequency buckling sound.

Instead of maintaining his speed, John hockey-stopped to listen, and the ice under his skates gave way with a sickening crack. He instantly slid into the shockingly cold waters beneath the ice. His legs flailed frantically. His skates sliced through the water, giving him almost no propulsion at all. His fleece jackets quickly became saturated and weighed him down. His thrashing arms barely kept his head above water. His most strenuous efforts barely moved him toward the edge of the ice.

Dan Hardin grabbed the arm of Fred Cummings to stop him abruptly in midsentence. From the vantage point of their table in a dockside restaurant, Dan saw the skater fall through the ice. He had recognized the skater's posture, his fleece jacket, and his ski hat. When the skater went through the ice, Dan knew in a flash that he had only a few seconds to save his son's life.

Dan ran out the lake-side entry door to the right of the town docks where the ice was solid all the way to the shore. As he ran across the snow covering most of the back yard of the property adjacent to the restaurant, he broke the mast of a Sunfish free from the crust of snow on the boat deck, and he carried the mast with him out onto the ice. He ran toward the hole where John floundered. Without a safety necklace, John had no ice picks to try to gain a grip on the ice to extract himself. Dan ran to within five feet of the hole where John still fought to keep his head above water.

"John!" Dan shouted, "I'm here!"

John's eyes widened in panic as he fixed his desperate gaze upward on his only chance of rescue – his father. Dan laid the sailboat mast across the center of the hole in the ice like a bridge. John looped one arm over the pole and the other arm onto the edge of the ice, but the cold water had increased his weight and robbed him of his strength. He was unable to pull himself up onto the ice. Dan stepped feet-first into the water near John. He surfaced blowing water out of his nose and mouth. Dan grasped the pole in his right hand for leverage and he hoisted John with his left arm up toward the edge of the hole.

"Climb up on the ice!" Dan screamed.

With another boost from Dan, John pulled himself up onto the mast and the ice. He kicked his feet as he turned onto his back and rolled away from the hole. One of his skate blades slashed across Dan's face. The force of the kick drove Dan's head underwater. John rolled away from the hole for another ten feet before he tried to stand up. His muscles had gone stiff in the freezing temperatures. He was shaking un-controllably and he could barely stand on his skates. The wet blades quickly froze to the ice.

"Dad!" John shouted. He couldn't see any trace of his father in the water except for blood near the surface. People on the shore were shouting and waving. The only motion in the water was the bobbing of a few chunks of ice floating in the hole. John broke his skate blades free of the ice and stiffly skated on numb legs toward the people on the shore. Two men ran towards him from the growing throng. They carried a heavy rope as they scrambled clumsily across the ice.

"My Dad's in that hole!" John shouted to them.

"We know!" they shouted back without slowing down. "Go to shore now!"

John collapsed before he reached the shore. Two men reached him on foot just as a snowmobile arrived from the bay behind him. One man cut the laces of John's skates with a knife and struggled to pull the skates off John's feet. When he had removed the skates, the two men lifted John onto the sled right behind the driver. They secured John to the driver with a rope, and the sled accelerated away back toward the center of Caledonia Bay to avoid the water belt and then altered course for the Thornton campus and the hospital beyond. The sled sped over the ice, across the campus fields, across people's lawns, over snowplowed streets, into the hospital emergency entrance and right up to the door to the emergency room.

Two days later, Scott was sitting beside John's bed when John regained consciousness after surgery. John had been delirious or sedated all through Saturday and Sunday. His hands were swollen, but all his fingers were intact. The two smallest toes on his left foot had been amputated. John asked about his father immediately upon regaining consciousness. Scott wanted to protect John from the truth, but he faced up to the inevitable. John had to be told, and Scott was the one to do it.

"Your Dad is dead," John. "He drowned."

John hadn't reached a state of full capacity, yet, and

Scott's words seemed only partly real to him. He groaned and closed his eyes tightly.

During the past two days, memories of Dan had dominated Scott's thoughts just as his twenty-six-year friendship with Dan had dominated his life. Scott had shared every success and every failure with Dan for so many years that he couldn't imagine a life without his confidant, his friend. Scott felt ashamed to wonder whether his job was secure at the hardware store now that Dan was gone. Where would he live when the Dan Hardin house was sold?

Scott feared for John's well-being in the wake of losing his father so soon after the deaths of his grandparents. Scott touched John's face with his hand as if to steady him. John began shaking his head, slowly at first, then more vigorously. Scott squeezed the button to summon the nurse. She entered the room and checked John's vital signs. She injected a sedative into his intravenous bag port, and John slowly relaxed and found relief from his agitated state.

Annette joined Scott by John's bedside while he slept. She leaned on Scott's shoulder for comfort as she cried. Thinking back on John's long adjustment after losing his grandparents, she worried that Dan's death was an insurmountable obstacle for him to clear. She wondered where John would live if the Dan Hardin house was sold. Should she take him in? She could use part of her inheritance to pay for John's college expenses. She sobbed when the thick bandage on his left foot reminded her that two toes had been taken from this boy whom she had loved so deeply for his entire life. The amputations had been necessary, but they defiled his perfect body and hurt Annette as much as if they had been cut from her own body.

When John was alert enough to start dealing with the loss of his father, he began talking through the guilt and regret that permeated every thought. He replayed "if only" conditions in his mind. If only John had run on the indoor track instead of skating. If only he had not skated so close to the edge of the ice. If only he had worn his safety necklace. If only his father had not gone to that particular restaurant that day to see him falling through the ice. When he had exhausted the "if only" coping process, John graduated to the bargaining phase: "Dear God, if you will undo this...bring Dad back, I'll do...."

"I killed Dad," John cried as he talked with Scott.

"No, John. It was an accident."

"I never told Dad I loved him," John said through his tears. He closed his swollen eyes and sobbed. "I didn't deserve to be rescued by him."

"He loved you without conditions," Scott said. "You didn't have to earn it."

Annette was crying, too. "If you had fallen through the ice a thousand times, he would have saved you every single time."

John moaned and gasped for breath between sobs.

"John, you were his delight." Emotion had constricted Scott's throat to the point that his voice was little more than a whisper. "He died in your place. Accept his gift."

Confined to bed, John couldn't attend the funeral or the burial of his father. Dan was buried adjacent to Benjamin Hardin, and Dan's head stone was an exact replica of his father Benjamin's stone, which was an exact replica of his father Richard's stone beside it. The engraving on Dan's stone read, "Daniel Lee Hardin 1966 to 2006," simple and brief. Dan's way.

While others gathered to memorialize his father's life, John lay helplessly in his hospital bed. For all his conditioning, John knew that his own strength had been insufficient to save himself that day. He vividly recalled the panic of his last seconds in the water. At the last possible moment, John's father had lifted him up from certain drowning. John remembered believing that he was dying. He knew that he had been saved only because of his father's ultimate sacrifice.

Chapter 20
TRUTH

SCOTT RODE WITH Annette to the hilltop cemetery for Dan's burial on February 2. Dan's ashes were laid to rest beside his father and grandfather on a hillock overlooking Caledonia. Fewer than thirty people attended the brief grave-side ceremony held in gently falling snow. Andrew Gleason offered his condolences to Scott after the service. Andrew hugged Annette and offered his help should she need it. Seeing this aspect of Andrew's personality in contrast to the contentious man she had faced at Corky's parent-teacher consultations was as surprising as a first view of the back side of the moon. How much simpler life could be, she thought, if angelic people could be counted on to be angelic in all matters and if cads behaved like cads consistently. The unpredictability of people in real life meant no one could get a life-time free pass and no one could be written off forever, either. Annette thanked Andrew for his courtesy.

Rather than return to Annette's apartment or to the Dan Hardin house after the service, Annette drove Scott out of town so they could have an early dinner away from chance meetings with acquaintances in Caledonia. In the village of Bristol Heath, twenty miles distant, they were unknown and able to dine without interruption by well-meaning towns-people. By the time Annette parked her all-wheel drive car in the restaurant parking lot in Bristol Heath, three inches of fresh snow had fallen since morning. Annette and Scott entered the two-hundred-year-old brick edifice, hung their coats on a rack, and settled into a booth near one of the crackling fireplaces. Annette ordered a glass of wine and Scott a single malt Scotch neat. The Bristol Heath clock tower bells chimed four times. Snowflakes as big as popcorn continued to fall in the loaming outside the window by their booth. Annette rested her head on Scott's shoulder for a moment and sighed.

"The minister captured Dan's essence ," she said. Sitting beside Scott instead of directly across from him in a booth or at a table was a comfortable configuration for Scott, because his periphery could form an image without resorting to the eccentric fixation techniques he had learned in low vision rehabilitation.

"A man of few words and big deeds'," Scott agreed. "That was Dan." Scott paused to calculate. "I knew him for twen-ty-six years," he said. "They seated us alphabetically the first day at Thornton...Hardin...Harrington. If he'd been Dan Archer and I had been Scott Zilinski, maybe we'd never have gotten together."

"You were destined to be together."

When their drinks arrived, they sipped them as they cuddled and reminisced about dances at Dartford Parade and double-dates in the *War Wagon*. Scott said it was paradoxical that Dan and Trinette, the two rear-seat contortionists, had divorced while he and Annette were still close friends. He suggested off-hand that maybe it was because they knew when to stop. He said this as if he had ever done anything voluntarily to put the brakes on their kissing and groping. Annette laughed at his mischaracterization. Their conversation lapsed while they individually thought back on the one exception, that one night on Lake Tremont, the night of Dan and Trinette's wedding.

"Scott, I need to talk to you about something, a talk that's been a long time coming. The way things are, now, I think it's time." Scott assented, his curiosity stirred. She continued, "Did you know that Trinette had a miscarriage?"

"I had no idea."

"Because of complications from that, she was never able to get pregnant again."

Scott looked confused. "This is after John was born?"

"No. It was during our junior year at McGill. I don't know if Trinette even knew who the baby's father was."

"I assume it was Dan"

"You don't know how promiscuous Trinette was back then. I suppose it doesn't matter now."

"Okay," Scott said slowly, "John was born *after* Trinette's miscarriage, so the doctors got it wrong when they said she couldn't get pregnant."

"The doctors weren't wrong," Annette said. Scott squeezed Annette's thigh and turned toward her a little. "Trinette wasn't John's birth mother."

Scott considered this for a few seconds. Did this mean that Annette was John's birth mother? The implications were obvious. In almost twenty years, Scott had never once considered any possibility other than Trinette getting pregnant while she and Dan were on their honeymoon in Paris.

"Who *was* John's birth mother?"

Annette placed her hand on top of Scott's. "*I* was."

Scott exhaled and used both hands to rub through his hair, forehead to crown. Then, he thought, who was John's birth father? Dan? Not likely. He could think of no one besides himself with the opportunity to be with Annette around the time of Dan and Trinette's wedding.

"Am I John's father?"

"Yes."

Annette had grown accustomed to the countenance of third graders hearing an amazing piece of information for the first time, but Scott's face was as astonished as any face she had ever seen in her classroom.

"But, why did you wait until now to tell me?" He instantly felt derelict in his paternal duty. "I don't understand why you waited almost twenty years to tell me. Imagine how I feel right now!"

"It was Mummy," Annette said, tears flowing down her cheeks. "Mummy wouldn't hear of an abortion. Neither would I."

"Surely Trinette didn't care."

"There's no right or wrong with Trinette," Annette said woefully. "With Trinette, all that matters is what's convenient. She has the morals of a snake. She never did understand why Mummy and I were so against aborting my baby."

Scott's mind was tumbling. He felt foolish for never once considering any possibility besides Dan and Trinette being

John's birth parents.

"Mummy was very protective of Daddy's status as president of the bank. She was active in Caledonia society, and, as far as the people of the town knew, she had two perfect daughters. Mummy wasn't about to let anything discredit our family image if there was any way out."

"So, it was all fabricated?"

"Mummy had already decided to take us to France. She insisted that we cooperate. Trinette played the part of the pregnant wife, and I played the part of the supportive twin sister. I followed the script. I cancelled my trip around Europe to be with Trinette."

"Your Grand'Mere had a stroke," Scott said, his memory jostled. "I remember Dan telling me that all three of the Laval Gals were going to France to take care of Grand'Mere, and they wanted to travel early in Trinette's pregnancy."

"Mother wanted to travel before I started showing."

"Didn't Dan know whether his own wife was pregnant?"

"Dan didn't have a clue. At fewer than twelve weeks of pregnancy, *you* wouldn't have had a clue, either."

"So, did Grand'Mere even have a stroke? Did Marie make that up, too?"

"Grand'Mere didn't have a stroke," Annette said. "At least not then. She did have serious symptoms from atrial fibrillation, but Mummy invented the stroke to make our departure credible."

"Did your father know?"

"Daddy knew."

"So Trinette's morning sickness was a lie, too."

"The closest Trinette got to morning sickness was a

hangover now and then. She even had a fling with the son of the vineyard owner next door to Grand'Mere's house."

Annette's resentment was showing. She had always harbored unexpressed anger at her sister for cheating on Dan at the same time she was scripted to be with his child. She also carried a grudge against her mother for coercing her daughters to go along with the fiction. And she was mad at herself for not standing up to either one of them.

Scott put his arm around Annette's shoulders. "You went through all of that and never told anyone."

Scott was stunned by the audacity of the lie. He grasped why Marie had been motivated to get her two daughters out of the country so she could orchestrate the switch and control the information flow. Like anyone left out of the information loop, though, Scott felt slighted. He could understand that, once the lie was established, it had to be perpetuated to protect Dan and others from being hurt even worse by revealing the truth. He could also see why Dan's death finally freed Annette to tell him the real story.

Annette began to cry softly. She had hoped for relief by owning up to the subterfuge, but the more she thought about the effect on Scott, the harder it was for her to untangle the web without losing control of her emotions.

"How did Marie falsify John's birth certificate?"

"The locals couldn't tell the difference between us Laval twins. Grand'Mere simply gave Trinette's name as the birth mother, and the paperwork all supported that version. Honestly, Grand'Mere and Mummy acted as though they actually believed the cover story while it was playing out. Grand'Mere often called me Trinette, especially when I was nursing John."

"And the name – John Wesley Hardin?"

"That was Trinette's doing. The baby was Trinette's in Mummy's reality, so Trinette gave him his name."

"I can't imagine what it was like for you to be around your own son living as someone else's son."

Annette sobbed. "It was so hard, Scott. So hard. I slept in Baby John's room in Dan's house for a few weeks before I started teaching in Boston. It was hard to hold our baby in my arms but pretend to be his aunt. As hard as it was to leave John in Caledonia, it was good that I moved to Boston before I cracked up." She dried her eyes with her linen napkin. "It wasn't fair to John, either. People should never hide a secret like that from a child. It was really, really hard."

Scott kissed her cheek. "And Dan never knew?"

Annette sniffed and shook her head. "No one else but Trinette and Mummy and Daddy knew. I mean Grand'Mere knew, but, then she actually had a stroke, and I don't know whether she could remember, but she couldn't talk after the stroke, so it didn't matter anymore."

"And now, Phillip and Marie have died, so only you and Trinette know?"

"Plus you, now. I stayed away from town for a while. After Boston, I taught school in Portland before John started elementary school. That's when you were flying out of Langley and Saudi Arabia."

Annette examined Scott's face to see if he was surprised that she knew his career moves. She wanted to tell him how much she had longed for a letter from him, something besides a Christmas card.

"You didn't come back to Caledonia for a long time. You went to England and then you transferred to New Mexico. By then I was teaching at Brighton School. I had always spent a lot of time with John during the summers. I sometimes wondered if I hovered around him too much to keep the secret."

"Apparently not."

"John was a student in my third grade class. Can you imagine having your son in your class every day, but you can't tell anyone that he's your son, and you can't go home with him?" She sniffed again and nodded her head at the waiter when he gestured toward her wine glass. Scott ordered another Scotch. "That's the year that I knew for sure that John was a gifted boy. Even today, he's special. The word 'special' isn't strong enough."

"Extraordinary!" Scott said.

"Yes," she agreed, "he's always been extraordinary. Did I tell you about his Napoleon phase?"

"Oh, yeah. I heard about that one. John even told me about it, so I've heard multiple versions."

"I mean, if you just could have seen how his mind developed. He still amazes me today."

The waiter delivered their reinforcement drinks and took their dinner orders. Their faces were warm from the glow of the fire. Outside in the darkness, the snow fell steadily. It stuck to the window muntins and framed each dark pane with a pure white border.

"So," Annette said, "John thinks he has no parents with Dan dead and Trinette gone, but, in fact, he *does* have parents. He has *us*."

"John is *my son!*" Scott said as though the fact had just sunk in. "I can't get used to the idea. It blows me away." He thought about it for a while. "Maybe I should have been more suspicious. How many times have people 'mistaken' John and me for son and father? Perfect strangers saw what I couldn't see."

"You don't hate me?" Annette asked.

"No, I don't hate you. I just don't understand why you didn't tell me."

"Mummy.... "

"She was a control freak," Scott said as he squeezed her to him and gave her another kiss on the cheek. "I love you, Annette. I realize now that I've taken you for granted, but I love you."

"I've been in love with you for a long time. Mummy knew it, too, because I told her when I was pregnant with John that this wasn't some casual encounter with a stranger. I told her I loved you, and I wanted to tell you that I was pregnant. But Mummy said 'no'. She demanded that I not tell you. She said that, if I did tell you, you might ask me to marry you, but I'd never know whether you would have proposed if I *wasn't* pregnant." She waited for a while for Scott to say something, but he didn't speak. "*Well?*"

"I don't know." Scott was trying hard to remember his life eighteen years ago. "It's easy to say 'yes' now, but I honestly don't know." He speculated what his life in the Air Force might have been like with Annette as his wife and John as his son.

"John's not ready to hear this," Annette said. She had thought about it a lot. She had tried to imagine what it was like for John to think he was the last in a long line of Hardins and then to discover that he was actually the last in a long line of Harringtons. "He's had too much grief in too short a time to cope with any more upset."

Scott agreed. "I'm not sure *I'm* ready for it," Scott admitted. "We need to decide what we're going to do. We've been sidestepping around each other for almost twenty years. Today we've both admitted we're in love. If we decide to commit to one another, we need to ask some hard questions."

Scott knocked down the last of his Scotch. Annette gazed intently at Scott's profile.

"I'm not the same guy you had a crush on in prep school, Annette. I'm legally blind. I have to pinch the top of a tea cup to know when to stop pouring from the tea pot. When I scald my thumb, I stop pouring."

"I don't care about that."

"You've always had a load on your back," he said. "You don't need to be stuck carrying me, too."

"I've wanted to be your wife for half my life. If you think your blindness changes that one *iota*, you don't know me very well."

Chapter 21

SECRETS

WHEN JOHN WAS released from hospital late in the afternoon three days after Dan's funeral, Annette drove him home. Lisa Sullivan was driving out of the driveway just as they arrived and she waved self-consciously. Lisa worried that her employment would end after Benjamin's death, but Dan had assured her that her job in the Hardin house was secure. Scott knew about Dan's promise, so at Dan's funeral he made a point of telling Lisa that she had a job as long as John and Scott lived in the Hardin house. He made the commitment even though his own income was hard-pressed to cover mortgage payments, taxes, and maintenance expenses until he could dispose of Dan's home.

Lisa had faithfully maintained the house throughout the ordeal of Dan's death and John's hospitalization. She had cleaned and vacuumed that day, and she had set the zone heating rheostats at sixty-three degrees Fahrenheit to make the house comfortable for John when he arrived from hospital. John limped across the threshold on a cast that protected the stitches and surgery site on his left foot. These rooms that had contained so much happiness for so many years felt like an empty shell to him. Annette turned on a satellite music channel to relieve the void. John settled into a recliner in the living room to elevate his left leg. Annette went to the kitchen to make snacks.

For almost twenty years, Annette had been a prisoner in a cell of convention. Her fear of being discovered a fake had kept her from taking risks of any kind. She had nurtured the favor of everyone she knew as if storing up good will against the day when she might be unveiled as a pretender. She wondered how different her life might have been had her mother Marie not sworn her to protect the secrecy of her motherhood. Annette also wondered whether Trinette might have lived in harmony with Dan all these years but for the pressure of keeping the secret. Keeping such a secret could drain vitality out of a person for a lifetime. Had Trinette's resentment against her mother been so strong that it eliminated any chance of finding contentment in Caledonia?

Annette had been conflicted between loving her mother and resenting her mother for two decades because of her mother's insistence on sticking with the cover story. As saddened as she was by the death of her mother, Annette felt released from confinement. Now, the death of Dan Hardin was another restraint removed. Dan had been an unwitting pawn in the lie, but, for as long as Dan was alive, Annette could not have been freed from the bondage of the lie. The last step to freedom was telling the truth to John.

John's feet still throbbed with pain. He didn't speak. Guilt had silenced him. Remorse had made him mute. Surely, he believed, everyone in Caledonia knew that his recklessness had killed his father. He had skated without a safety necklace and he had skated too close to open water. He had relived the terrifying moments in the water so many times that he wondered if he could ever turn the memory off. He remembered the shock of the freezing water and the weight of his saturated fleece dragging him down. He recalled the numbness in his hands as he tried to grasp the mast that spanned the hole in the ice. And he remembered the sickening thud of his skate blade against his father's head as he scrambled to pull himself out of the hole and onto the ice. In the past eight days, he had rarely spoken except to answer questions from nurses and physicians. John's empty stare, his red eyes, and his occasional uncontrollable sobs pained Annette. She sat on a chair near John's and surreptitiously watched him eat his snack. When tears began to flood her eyes, she returned to the kitchen.

Scott came home from Hardin's Hardware at 7:15 p.m. For eight years, Scott had walked in from the mud room calling out one of his stock greetings — "Attention on deck!" or "Pound the Adjutant's Balls!" — a quaint distortion of the drill command "Sound the Adjutant's Call!" On this night, however, he hung his ski jacket and hat on a rack in the mudroom and quietly entered the kitchen. He walked into the living room and found John and Annette sitting silently, John with his left foot elevated on the footrest of a reclining chair. Scott knew that John's skin was still sensitive from frostbite, so he momentarily laid his hand gently on the top of John's head.

Scott bent to kiss Annette on the cheek before he sat down beside her. He read the signs and he knew that no words were appropriate for this moment. Silence hung in the Hardin house like a heavy fog. Music was the only sound that could partially displace the oppressive silence in the room. Annette went to the kitchen to make meals that she served to John and Scott in the living room. When he had finished eating, John thanked Annette and said goodnight to Scott. He haltingly climbed the stairs to go to his room. He lay on his bed without removing his clothing. Annette followed with his pain medication. She covered him with his duvet up to his chin.

"I love you, John."

John couldn't reply. He lay motionless. His feet throbbed. From lack of exercise, his legs felt as though ants were crawling all over them just below the epidermis. He had suffered anxiety for weeks, his Amgen short position threatening financial obliteration, and, then, the day after that burden had been lifted, a worse fate had befallen him – his father had died. What an irrational God this was who pulled the strings this way. If there was a God. Tears filled his eyes.

John started rehabilitation two weeks later, the same week he returned to classes at Thornton Prep. By the first week in March, John could walk normally using a protective shroud around the skin graft sites where his two toes used to be. He had caught up with homework and papers in all of his classes. His classmates had been scurrying for the past four months to apply to colleges. John had applied to only one school – Princeton. He had intended to follow up with applications to a couple of back-up colleges, but events had quashed those efforts, and John didn't have the will to follow through.

Paul Bruguiere came by to visit John after Paul's classes had ended at Caledonia High School and after he had finished cleaning floors and classrooms at Brighton School. Paul wasn't as sophisticated as the adults who paid visits, but his uninhibited chatter helped relieve John's depression. Paul bragged about how many pounds he had bench pressed that morning. He showed off his muscles to John. More than once, Paul inspected the stubs on John's left foot where his two smallest toes used to be.

"Does it feel weird?" Paul asked.

"Big time. I feel like I want to bend my toe joints, but there aren't any toe joints to bend. And the missing toes itch."

"Bummer." Paul shifted conversational gears back to his favorite subject. "I'm going into the Marine Corps this summer. I've got it all set up with the recruiter."

"They don't let fairies into the Marines," John said. They prattled on "busting chops" for an hour some evenings, and, if Paul were still there when Annette came to the Hardin house to make dinner, she invited him to stay for the meal. Paul never turned her invitation down. John talked with Paul more than everyone else combined. The hospital helped rehabilitate John's foot and Paul helped rehabilitate John's mind. Paul asked John if he was still going to try to break 48 seconds in the 400-meter run. John said, "No chance". He doubted he could cover 400 meters in less than four minutes.

In private, John began to ratchet up the frequency of his option trading. He felt off-balance, so he opened small positions at first. For example, in his first trade since his father's death, John established a bullish call spread in Merck shares that lost $3,420 in less than a month. He was still smarting from the weeks of nausea and fear brought about by his naked, fat-fingered Amgen trade, so he reviewed every trade twice before hitting the "submit" button.

He clandestinely compiled the information he needed for The Liberty Trust tax return. He drove Dan's car to the mailbox every day so he could filter the incoming mail. Scott offered to relieve him of his long-standing mail duty, but John insisted on doing the routine chore. He didn't want Scott or Annette to discover the thick envelope from the trust brokerage firm with Forms 1099 and other information enclosed. John forged Scott's signature as successor trustee on the tax return and on the $178,000 check issued by the trust to pay taxes due on its 2005 capital gains. Even after paying taxes and despite the small number and size of John's option trades, he entered a familiar one-liner at the end of his diary entries for March 14, 2006: "NAV $1,746,344".

One of John's first tasks when he turned eighteen the following day was to open a personal brokerage account now that he was of legal age. He also opened personal checking accounts at both the Bank of Caledonia and Tremont Savings, as he no longer required an adult co-signer. By the end of March, he had enabled electronic transfers between all his bank accounts and his new personal brokerage account. He began transferring funds in chunks from The Liberty Revocable Trust to his personal account. The first transfer was for $101,000. The second was for $102,000, and so on. John thought back on his passion to make a million dollars. Once he had reached that goal, he had instantly switched his goal to *two* million dollars. He wondered how he would alter his goal when he reached two million. Would his new goal be three million or four?

On May 20, as Annette, Scott, and John finished a late dinner, the doorbell rang. John answered the door and invited Paul to come in and join them at the dinner table. Paul was bursting at the seams to tell them his news.

"I'm leaving for Parris Island tomorrow!"

"Outstanding!" Scott said. He shook Paul's hand and left the table to get a round of celebratory beers. John slapped his old pal on the back and gave him a man hug. Annette offered him a plate of casserole and salad, and Paul surprised no one by accepting. Paul alternately ate and briefed them on the details of his fantastic adventure. Scott asked Paul how his Uncle Thomas felt about this move, and Paul said his uncle had told him to "get out of this burg." Paul stayed for two beers and would have happily stayed for a third. Paul's talents lay in canoe-building, not reading social situations, and he almost always needed a little prodding to get out the door. Scott cast his magic spell and told Paul it was time to go without hurting the feelings of the muscle-bound future Marine.

"Go get 'em, Marine," Scott exhorted Paul as he shook his hand goodbye.

"See? I listened to you," Paul whispered to Scott. Paul opened the palm of his hand to reveal the Kuwait Liberation Medal Scott had given him seven years earlier. "I look at this almost every day." Paul said. "It reminds me of what you told me – to suck my gut in, stick out my chest, and start acting like a man." Paul's fist closed over the medal and he held it over his heart. "This'll be with me until the day I die!"

"The credit's on you, Marine," Scott said, as he wrapped his arm around Paul and hugged him affectionately. It was a touching moment for Scott, as he remembered his chat with Paul, Raymond, and Corky so many years before.

"Pace yourself, Paul," Annette said. She had seen enough movies and heard enough of Scott's yarns to suspect that Paul's eagerness might wane after a few early-morning runs through swarms of hungry South Carolina mosquitos. Paul hugged Annette and held her in his iron embrace for a little longer than etiquette required. They all understood that a guy leaves for Parris Island for the first time only once.

"Email me," John said as he hugged his childhood friend goodbye.

"*Semper fi,*" Paul said.

Right after Paul left for Parris Island, Annette told Scott that she thought it was time to tell John who his parents were. She thought it would help with the healing process. Scott was skeptical. He believed that it was too soon and he lobbied for more time for John to adjust. Another reason Scott pleaded for the delay was his ongoing negotiations with two potential buyers in a deal to sell the hardware store. John had made it clear he wanted no part of being future owner, and Scott was obligated to fulfill the terms of Dan's will. Scott had retained Attorney Fred Cummings to represent John's interests in the sale, and Fred sat in on every session with the two interested parties. Scott, in his role as executor, also was preoccupied with trying to sell the Hardin house in June, when real estate buying interest normally picked up. Scott depended on Annette to read obscure contract-for-sale documents to him.

"I don't want to wait too long," Annette said, restating her interest in talking to John as soon as possible. "Trinette's a loose cannon. I know her. She'll write a self-serving letter to John one of these days."

"Ouch!" Scott said, cringing at the prospect.

"She'd do it!" Annette knew that her sister was an expert at getting other people to shoulder her responsibilities. "She'd preempt every version of the story with her own. It's her way of tossing the hot potato."

"Just give me a little more time."

"Soon, Scott. Please!"

Andrew Gleason was one of two bidders for the purchase of Hardin's Hardware. Scott was suspicious of Andrew throughout negotiations. When the other bidder mysteriously withdrew, Andrew began chiseling away at his bid price by emphasizing every discrepancy identified by the property inspector. Scott heard a rumor that Andrew had made a cash payment to the other bidder to entice him to go away. The nature and sequence of events made Scott uneasy, but the sale to Andrew eventually netted the estate of Dan Hardin more than $400,000.

Andrew assured Scott that he was keeping the name of the store unchanged in honor of John's father and grandfather. The courtesy cost Andrew nothing. Scott wondered if Andrew kept the name to compensate for the concessions he had squeezed out of Scott in the process of lowering the eventual selling price.

"You have your job as long as you want it," Andrew told

Scott. The plain meaning of the words were reassuring, but Scott sensed a more nuanced interpretation: "Move on."

The sale of Dan's residence took longer. The house was situated on prime water-front property on Caledonia Bay, but the house was neither an Eighteenth Century master-piece nor a modern dream house. Its bathrooms were small, its accessories were dated, and it needed a new roof. Andrew Gleason emerged as the buyer of the house. Even though the land by itself was worth over a million dollars, when Andrew got through wringing out one concession after another, Scott felt fortunate to net over $300,000 at closing. Scott added the proceeds to the escrow account of which John was beneficiary. The balance was more than $700,000. A week after closing on the house, Andrew hired a new manager for the hardware store. The new manager's first administrative action was an across-the-board ten per cent cut in employees' pay, including Scott's.

Scott complained about his dismal performance in the two negotiations with Andrew, but Annette said, "It's only money. You did the best you could."

After confirming that John was moving in with him, Scott rented a two-bedroom upstairs apartment from Andrew Gleason's rental company — not because Scott wanted to further enrich Andrew, but because Gleason's Rentals constituted the only game in town. Scott put most of Dan's household goods into a local storage facility, keeping out just a few pieces – beds, bureaus, and chairs – to furnish the apartment. Scott transferred the title of Dan's car over to John. As Scott's "to do list" got shorter, Annette pressed harder to have their talk with John.

"It'll be a new start for John. We need to explain it all to him soon."

"I'll do everything I can to support John, including adopting him," Scott said, "but I want to do things in proper sequence. Let's get our engines started before we try to take-off." Of all the issues Scott wanted to resolve before telling John about his parents, only one remained. "Just one more thing to do, and then we'll tell him."

Annette consented to a delay reluctantly. Scott reached into his trousers pocket and pulled out a small black object.

"The most important thing of all is *this*," he said as he extended his arm to reveal in his palm a black velvet box. Annette accepted the ring in the velvet box delicately. The day she had dreamed of for almost twenty years had arrived.

Scott and Annette were married on July 8, 2006 on the bow of the Harringtons' sailboat as it lay at mooring by a small island seven miles north of Caledonia Bay. Annette was willing to have the wedding performed by a Protestant minister with only seven people attending. Scott guessed that John's misleading birth certificate and that side-stepping a trip to a confessional kept her from insisting on a Roman Catholic priest. A fellow teacher at Brighton School served as Maid-of-Honor, and John served as Best Man. When the ceremony was complete, John left the sails reefed, cast off from the mooring, and motored to a restaurant on Lake Tremont in the harbor at Stableton Dykes. The minister, who had parked his car at the restaurant, was needed at another wedding, so he left the wedding group as soon as they docked. The remaining party of nine joined in a three-hour feast in a private room looking out on the mountains to the northeast. It was a simple, joyous celebration, and the bride and groom were delighted when John rose to discharge his Best Man duty of toasting the couple.

"I have loved Annette for as long as I can remember," John said. "And I have imitated the words and actions of Scott since I was ten years old. I admire them both, and I don't think there's a more perfect couple anywhere. A child of Annette and Scott will be the luckiest kid in the world!"

The celebrants said, "Hear, hear."

Perhaps, Scott thought, the talk with John will turn out to be easier than he had presumed.

"Soon," Annette whispered to Scott, and he knew exactly what she meant.

After the wedding, Scott moved in to live with Annette, leaving John by himself in the two-bedroom Gleason's Rental apartment.

John opened the Hardin mail box in the post office and extracted a bundle of mail. A letter confirmed that The Liberty Trust was closed. John was required to file one last tax return for a part of 2006, but that would be the last sign of the paper trail revealing that the trust had ever existed. As soon as the trust's 2006 taxes were filed the following spring, John planned to destroy the forged trust documents. The "dog-ate-my-homework" defense to enquiry would have to suffice. John had paid a great deal more in taxes at the trust's thirty-five per cent rate than required at his own personal rate, but the benefit now was that the IRS had no motive to audit the returns. John was enormously relieved to see the trust recede in his rear-view mirror.

The first things John noticed about the last envelope in the pile were the unusual stamps. Belgian stamps. John withdrew to a remote corner of the post office before opening the letter from Trinette.

Dear John,

I was glad to meet you in New Hampshire last September when I was there to pay my respects to my parents. It was a difficult time. Now I have heard about Dan's drowning and your narrow escape from death. I know you must be devastated. You are very brave to carry on in the face of all these events. I'm sorry that illness prevented me from attending Dan's funeral.

By this time, you no doubt have learned the identity of your true parents. You know by now that I am not your mother. My sister Annette is your mother. Scott Harrington is your father, not Dan Hardin.

My mother — your Grandmother Marie Laval — freaked out when Annette, who was single, became pregnant by Scott. I was the married twin. I was married to Dan, who wanted to have a baby, but I was unable to have children. So Marie made Annette and me go to France with her so we could create the illusion that I was pregnant. The family avoided the shame of Annette having a baby out of wedlock and Dan and I were blessed with a baby that I wasn't able to provide for Dan.

This revelation has to be very painful for you, but

in the long run, you will know how lucky you are to have a mother like Annette and a father like Scott. I guess I was sort of your adopted mother, and I wasn't a very good one. I have a lot of personal faults that I'm not proud of. I couldn't really take care of myself, much less a baby.

Now you're old enough to be on your own, so I hope you can deal with what we did to you eighteen years ago. None of us wanted to hurt anyone, especially you. I was mad at Annette for a long time for not getting an abortion. She stuck to what she believes, and now I'm glad she didn't get an abortion, because you are a wonderful young man and you'll have a wonderful life.

I hope you can forgive me for the part I played in this deception.

Love, Trinette Laval

P.S. Please let me know if anything is coming to me from Dan's will. XOXOXO

The contents of the letter smacked John across the head harder than any sledge hammer. The story Trinette told seemed impossible. How could such a secret remain hidden for so many years? John thought about what these alleged facts meant to his life. He vacillated between anger and shock. How could so many people be involved with such a lie? John's hands began to tremble. Was Trinette insane? Was she trying to hurt her sister? Was she trying to hurt him? He telephoned the hardware store and asked the cashier to transfer him to Scott.

"Scott," John said, his voice trembling, "I need to talk to you."

"What's the deal?"

"I got a letter from Trinette. I don't know...."

"John, go to Annette's apartment. I'll leave work now and I'll be there before you get there." Scott inhaled deeply. All along he had doubted that Trinette would spill her guts to John. She had removed herself from John's life for the last eighteen years, why would she intermeddle now? Whatever her reasons, Scott knew he had to limit the damage right away.

"I want to talk to you alone. Will Annette be there?"

"She's probably there now," Scott said. "I think it's better if all three of us talk."

In John's mind, that statement made it more likely that there was at least some truth in Trinette's letter. John's mind was reeling. He told himself to hold his emotions in check until he knew if her facts were true. He agreed to go directly to Annette's and Scott's apartment.

"Tell Jim I can't make it in for work tonight," John said. Scott agreed. John closed his cell phone, pushed the mail into his khaki pocket, and left the post office. He walked on cobblestone pathways five blocks to Annette's and Scott's apartment. Scott answered the door. When the front door was closed, John passed the letter to Scott. Annette wasn't in the room.

"You'll have to read it," Scott reminded him.

When John had finished reading the letter, he asked Scott, "Is this true?"

"Pretty much true. I didn't know anything about it until

the day of Dan's funeral. I guess I know a little bit about how you feel."

"I don't think so, Scott. No one lied to you about your parents. You knew Joe T. was your dad and Joyce was your mom."

"But I *didn't* know I was *your* dad," Scott said.

Annette walked into the room and approached John, who half-turned away from her and motioned her away.

"You knew about this all along!" John shouted.

"Yes," Annette replied, tears collecting in her eyes. "Mummy made us switch roles, because it solved everyone's problem." This wasn't the calm start she had imagined in her mental dry runs.

"It didn't solve *my* problem!" John said angrily. "Benjamin Hardin wasn't even my grandfather, and I called him Granddad for all those years! Joe T. was my real granddad, and I barely knew him."

"John," Scott interrupted, "Joe T. and Joyce never knew I was your father. Benjamin Hardin never knew that Dan *wasn't* your father. Neither did Dan. And neither did I."

"Do you have any idea what it's like? You played around with my life. You made a phony birth certificate. I don't even have the right name. The woman who isn't actually my mother named me after a friggin' murderer, and she shouldn't even have had the right to name me. What were you doing?" John shouted at Annette.

"I was having you," Annette sobbed.

"My name should be *Harrington* for crying out loud." John was shaking and his face was livid with rage. "My whole life is a lie!" He turned toward the door. "Well, I don't need this crap! I'm outta' here. You can shove Caledonia...."

"Wait, wait, John," Scott pleaded with him. "Stay here so we can talk it through. We want you to be our son."

"You had a son!" John screamed. "But you didn't want him. You gave him to some nut job who likes booze better than babies. And all those years your child was right there under your nose...in your own classroom and you didn't claim it! You didn't claim *me*!"

"John, please, be fair to Annette," Scott said, reaching out to John.

"I'll be fair to her like she was fair to me! I was too inconvenient, so her *evil* mother brainwashed her and made her give up her own baby! It makes me sick!"

Annette cried openly and tried to walk toward John again.

"Don't!" he cautioned her. "No way! You can't have secrets in a family! You have to be honest! And you haven't been!" He walked to the door and grasped the door knob in his hand. "How long do I have before I go blind, too?"

"It's not genetic," Scott said, trying to assuage John's rage.

"How do you know? Is that a lie, too?" John shouted the words in a final salvo as he opened the door, stormed out, and slammed it behind him.

"That was horrible," Annette sobbed as she embraced Scott and buried her face in his chest.

"Let's give him a little time to recover from the shock. I'll talk with him again tomorrow. Just me and him. A new day. He'll come around."

What neither Scott nor Annette could foresee, however,

was that John was so traumatized by events that he felt driven to leave Caledonia right away. Back in his apartment, he read Trinette's letter again in the hopes of finding something he had misunderstood, something to stop him from carrying out his decision to leave. He didn't.

He filled a backpack with clothing and loaded a hand grip with his laptop computer, cell phone, diary, driver's license, passport, charge card, and $2,000 in cash. He slammed the front door of his apartment after him and drove his car toward Portsmouth. He was glad he had applied only to Princeton without exploiting his status as a legacy applicant. He was glad they had rejected him. He didn't want to go to college. He didn't want to do anything that Scott or Annette had done. Most of all, he wanted to distance himself from them and their lies.

In Portsmouth, John caught the scheduled bus to Boston Logan Airport. The flights to Germany had already departed by the time he reached the international terminal, so he checked in at the nearest hotel he could find. Using his computer in his hotel room, he bought a one-way ticket to Frankfurt for the following day. He planned to catch a train from Frankfurt to Salzburg to find Andrea.

Chapter 22

ANDREA

JOHN RECALLED TALKING with Dan about contrails in the spring of his sixth grade year while practicing lacrosse passes on the Caledonia High School pitch under a cloudless blue sky. The last traces of snow were almost completely gone; only in shadows on the north side of rock walls and in places where snow plows had left banks of snow did reminders of the past winter remain. Caledonians' spirits blossomed with the daffodils. Lacrosse sticks sprouted with the daffodils. High overhead, contrails — long and undisturbed by wind shears — etched east-northeasterly.

"What makes contrails?" John asked.

"Condensed water vapor from the exhaust of jets."

"Where are the planes going?"

"They're headed for the North Atlantic Tracks to Europe," Dan said.

"Tracks?"

"Lines of latitude from the Maritimes to Ireland. The planes fly parallel courses at different altitudes all at the same speed to keep their separation. These planes probably took off from Miami, Charlotte, Washington, Philly, Baltimore, Atlanta, Orlando, or New York." Dan padded his answer with a long list of cities on the East Coast, because he had quickly approached the limits of his knowledge on the present subject.

"How do you know that?" John asked out of intellectual curiosity, not skepticism, because he believed his father's word in all things.

"Scott told me. You can tell it's smooth up there because the contrails are so perfect. When it's bumpy, the contrails are roiled."

"Flying over the ocean seems dangerous," John said, displaying a twelve-year-old's myopic view of risk. By a sixth-grader's calculus, a safe activity was skateboarding down Caledonia's Main Street surrounded by cars bearing New York and Massachusetts license plates. Slamming an ice hockey opponent into the boards at full speed was safe. By John's reckoning, however, it was this flying straight-and-level in smooth air six miles over an ocean infested with sharks that was dangerous.

"It's a lot safer than things you do every day," Dan assured him. He tossed the lacrosse ball to his son. "There's a better chance of having your eye taken out by that ball than going down in an airliner in the Atlantic." (His words preceded the nasty incident in the Thornton versus Stone Haven Prep game when a supersonic lacrosse ball turned John's right eye into an eggplant.)

Seven years later, here was John – aged nineteen — sitting in the aft section of a Lufthansa jetliner, thinking about contrails and his father and life expectancy as the jet carried him toward Frankfurt, Germany. John peered out the right side window and saw no definable object, just a flat ocean that stretched to the horizon. He didn't know whether the jet was making contrails, but, if so, he knew they weren't smooth. The continuous light turbulence had started as they climbed through twenty-five thousand feet and persisted as they leveled off at Flight Level Three Five Zero. That's what the Lufthansa pilot said in an accent so American that only his *W*'s gave him away. The pilot had a deep, resonant voice like Moses, so people believed whatever he said. A deep, commanding voice was vital in these situations. John doubted the Israelites would have ventured very far into the Red Sea if Moses had sounded like Groucho Marx, for example, or Burl Ives. The pilot with the Moses "pipes" oozed authority, and, if he said the flight attendants were suspending meal and beverage service because of light-to-moderate chop, then no rational passenger was going to complain about it.

John hummed as deep a note as he could to try to match the pilot's pitch, but he stopped when he noticed the man in the adjacent seat scrutinizing him suspiciously. The guy smelled like the Thornton Prep locker room, and that was not a compliment. If John were king, airlines would force passengers to pass through an "aromameter" on the way to the plane. If the alarm buzzer went off, the offending passenger would be separated from the hygienic passengers. The aromatically-challenged prospective passenger would be thoroughly scrubbed before being allowed to board the aircraft. John wasn't king, however, so this was going to be a long flight.

John thought a lot about Andrea. Ever since he had first met her, he had been fascinated by her beauty, her gentle manner, and her enchanting smile. So many girls her age were self-conscious or self-absorbed to the point of making themselves quite unlovely. John wondered how Andrea had been inoculated against arrogance. He contemplated the most puzzling question of all: What did Andrea see in him? He had to admit that, at the moment, he felt pretty unlovely himself.

After spending a full day and night in Frankfurt, John caught a morning train to Salzburg, a journey of less than six hours. John watched the countryside roll by out the left window for so long he got a crick in the left side of his neck. He pivoted his head to the right to compensate. He gazed for a few seconds at a teenage girl dozing across the aisle from him. Her features were angelic, and her hair had the consistency of corn silk. Her navy blue cotton sweater barely moved with her slight breathing. Her shapely legs were crossed at the ankles. John examined her for so long he got a crick in the *right* side of his neck.

Had this lovely girl ever experienced hardship or disappointment? Had the order of her life been disrupted by deceit? Could she bear the strain when a terrible secret in her life was revealed? How could it be that one such perfect specimen of humanity could exist so untouched in a world populated by hungry, deformed, ignorant people? Why should she be so immune to the sufferings born by so many others? John turned his head back to the front and closed his eyes to ponder his own misfortunes.

The train stopped in Munich, and John saw the girl pull

her backpack out from under her seat. As she stood to leave, she looked fully into John's face and she smiled radiantly. As she turned to leave through the rear of the coach, John was astonished to see that the girl's right arm ended about ten inches below her shoulder. Her surprising disability was a jolt to John. He remembered Scott's words after Dan's death: "We're not much use to anyone besides ourselves until we've been broken."

It was almost three o'clock when a taxi deposited John at the curb in front of a *Gasthaus* not far from Andrea's mailing address. After checking in, he left his computer and backpack in his room and walked westerly to a small park called Hans-Donnenburg. His limp was gone, and walking caused only mild pain at the site where his toes had been amputated. He hiked almost every trail in the woodland. Walking was John's antidote for restless leg symptoms.

He considered how English has a name for conditions of even the smallest importance such as restless leg syndrome. Blackhead, whitehead, papula, pimple, and pustule were all words for the common zit, of which John was glad to be rid. He wanted to look his best for Andrea. The reason his mind was sauntering around from toes to restless legs to pimples was that he was sick-to-death of recycling the revelations in Trinette's letter. If he thought about who was and who wasn't his mother, father, or grandparent one more time, he thought the top of his head would blow off. It helped to be in a country where puzzling over *umlauts* and *Eszetts* could distract a worried mind.

John found Andrea's house, and he walked by it on the opposite side of the street. He settled on an innocuous pace, not as slow as a burglar casing the joint and not as fast as a sexual predator on the prowl for a victim. His steps were the steps of a righteous passer-by.

Andrea's home was sandwiched between other homes in a configuration similar to townhouses in America. The main entrance to the two-story home was at ground level unlike some of the elaborate steps leading up to neighbors' doors. He could see a light illuminated in the front room on the first floor, but he detected no motion as he continued his reconnaissance patrol. He thought it best to stage his reunion with Andrea on the following day after he had rested for the night.

Ten o'clock seems a late waking hour, but John calculated that on "his" time, it was actually four o'clock in the morning. After showering, he descended to the host's parlor for a breakfast of heavy bread and little finger-sized fish. He wondered how fine a net would be needed to catch fish of this size. Preparatory to what he hoped was going to be a record-breaking kiss, he brushed his teeth twice, added a molecule of expensive cologne consistent with procedures in the Scott Harrington Official Grooming Manual, and set out for Andrea's house.

When he was only two hundred feet from her door, he saw a girl emerge from the doorway pulling a boy in a wheelchair out after her. She closed the door and began pushing the wheelchair toward the park. John followed. He didn't want to be rude by seeming to spy on her, but he didn't want to scare the wits out of her, either, so he followed at a healthy distance.

In the park, the girl parked the wheelchair beside a bench

facing into the morning sun. John stopped beneath a tree to watch her. She rubbed lotion from a tube onto the boy's face as his head bobbed around unpredictably. He could hear the boy moaning. The girl cooed to him and tapered the lotion near his eyes. The boy's arms jerked around, but the girl calmed him.

John squinted for positive identification. The girl sat on the bench beside the wheelchair, and she opened a book to read. John moved a little closer until he knew for certain that the sun-lit face was Andrea's. He wanted to walk right up to her and sit beside her on the bench, but he figured that was a recipe for inducing a heart attack, so he kept his distance and called out her name. She didn't look up. He called her name again louder, and Andrea lowered her book and looked toward him.

It took a moment for Andrea to absorb the image of the flaxen-haired boy wearing top-siders, khaki walking shorts, and a navy blue Thornton sweater. She quickly recognized who the figure was by his dress and his posture. He raised an arm slowly as a greeting. Andrea could not have been more surprised. John had said nothing in his last letter of weeks ago or in subsequent emails about coming to Austria. She lay down her book to run toward him. John walked toward her, and the two met in a tight hug. John swayed her back and forth, and then they kissed. Andrea had tears in her eyes as she looked up at him in disbelief.

"You're here!"

"I had to see you. I was afraid you had a boyfriend or your father had a shotgun or...I was afraid of lots of things."

"Who has time for boyfriends?"

Her accent was stronger than John remembered, but he figured that was natural, because she hadn't been around any *Gringos* for almost three years, as far as he knew. Andrea led him back to the park bench. She introduced her younger brother Karl who sort of half-smiled as his arms twitched and his head bobbed around precariously. Andrea kissed the boy on the head and told him that John was her friend from America. Karl moaned.

John kneeled down beside the wheelchair so his eyes were on the same level as Karl's and he held one of Karl's atrophied hands in his own. Karl's fingers writhed, but John held on gently. Karl seemed to smile, but it was fleeting. John wished his strength could transfer through their touching hands and heal Karl's malady. He wished he had the power. Andrea told John to sit beside her on the bench. She said Karl didn't mind if they talked, that it was all the same to him.

Andrea explained in more detail why she had dropped out of Thornton. When her father lost his company, the family could no longer afford their expensive home. Her father found a new job and her mother began working so they could afford the rent on their substitute townhouse. Their salaries were insufficient to pay for the full-time nurse they had formerly employed, however, so Andrea had returned to care for her brother. She admitted that she hadn't told John the whole story for fear of frightening him away.

"You know," she said, "never date anyone with bigger problems than your own."

"Rule 18." Then he had to explain the Scott Harrington rule system. And that got him started telling his story.

Andrea was astounded by the revelations.

"Switched at birth," she said.

"Except the baby wasn't switched. The mothers were switched."

They talked about it for a long time. John wasn't shy about letting his anger out. He cried when he described how Dan had died, and Andrea consoled him with a hug. Her brother never interrupted them during more than an hour of steady conversation. John wondered if he could understand what they were talking about. They were talking as though Karl weren't present. It was well past noon, and they had plenty more to say, but Andrea said she had to take Karl back to the house for his lunch. Karl rolled his head and moaned. He apparently knew what "lunch" meant.

"When can I see you?" John asked.

"Tonight. I'll come out at eight o'clock. My mother will be home to mind Karl, and I'll come to your *Gasthaus*."

"I could pick you up."

"Not now. It's too soon for introductions. My father's blaming himself for losing everything. He can finally admit that he enrolled me in Thornton as "von Bergen" instead of "Bergen" because he wanted Americans to be impressed with the title."

"Wasted effort. We Yankees don't know what the 'von' means."

John and Andrea used the beer garden as their meeting place for three nights in a row. Andrea suggested they go to John's room. John confessed that he wanted to be with her more than anything in the world, but he said to look at where that had gotten Scott and Annette.

"That's where all my problems started."

"There are ways around that," Andrea teased him.

"Yeah, but right now is the wrong time."

John was of two minds about fulfilling his desires with Andrea. He wondered if he was the only male in Austria who wouldn't jump at Andrea's suggestion. He didn't need to add any more layers of worry on top of the problems he was dealing with now.

"My little Puritan boy. I love my Puritan boy."

"I love you, too," John said for the first time in his life.

The third night was a three-beer night. Andrea and John had talked through each of their situations so thoroughly that there wasn't much more to say. Andrea had to stay to care for her brother for the foreseeable future. The idea of John moving to Salzburg didn't gain much traction with Andrea. John wasn't overly sold on the idea, either. How far could "*Ja*" get you in Austria? John made it clear that he wasn't going back to Caledonia, a place populated by lies and pretense. He intended to move to Florida. He wanted to tell Andrea that he was a millionaire, but it wasn't prudent, and she wouldn't have believed him anyway. Here was a boy who not so long ago thought he was Napoleon Bonaparte and who had only recently given up on the possibility that he was Jesus Christ come again, obsessions he had admitted to Andrea, and she was supposed to believe that he also had $1.7 million sitting in an account somewhere? John had made some real boneheaded moves in his life, but he avoided this one.

He did, however, offer to pay for a full-time nurse for Andrea's brother so Andrea could join him in Florida.

Andrea looked at him as though his imagination had stampeded. He said he was serious, but she cut him off again. He left the subject alone. John told Andrea of his decision to catch a train to Rimini to see Corky Gleason, so Andrea gave him recommendations on how to make the journey.

"What's Corky doing in Rimini?" she asked.

"He's living with a guy named Antolini. They're sort of like an item."

"I understand."

"He ran away from home because he couldn't run away from himself. I just want to see how he's doing."

"Or *what* he's doing?

"No, *how*."

"Do you speak Italian?" she asked as a joke.

"*Ja.*"

At the end of their night, just before she left the beer garden to go home, Andrea got serious. She said how happy it made her that he had come all this distance to share his misfortunes with her. And she was pleased that he was taking a break from his problems to go down to see Corky.

"Sooner or later, though," she said, "you have to go back to Caledonia, because you have some important things to do."

"Like what?"

"Like, first of all, realize that your mother and father – Annette and Scott — love you very much. I knew they loved you before I even knew they were your mother and father. And then you need to *forgive....*"

"Never!"

"In Matthew's gospel, Peter asks Jesus how many times

he should forgive someone who has sinned against him. Do you remember that?"

John answered "no" truthfully. There was a great deal in Matthew's Gospel that he didn't know or remember.

"The Jewish law said you had to forgive someone three times. Peter asked Jesus if he should forgive his brother *seven* times, and Jesus said 'seventy times seven times'…an infinite number of times. There has to be no end to our forgiveness, otherwise we stay locked up and love can't flow."

"Are you a nun?"

"No," Andrea said with a laugh, "I'm just a Catholic girl who was so angry at her father for going bankrupt that she didn't want to live anymore."

John gazed at Andrea. He was an angry young man being counseled by a compassionate young woman. He knew how fortunate he was to have met her.

"I went to a priest. He told me about the power of forgiveness. He told me it's one of the hardest things we ever have to do, but it's also one of the most richly rewarding."

"I guess so," John said without much conviction.

"Read the eighteenth chapter of Matthew," Andrea said. "I read it again this morning on the park bench just to remind myself."

John thought about what an odd twist this conversation had taken, this conversation with a beautiful girl sitting beside him citing the Gospel of Matthew in a beer garden a few minutes after suggesting they go to bed. You think you know someone, he thought, but you don't really know them until things start going wrong.

"John, when your heart is ready to forgive, forgive

yourself first. You didn't kill Dan. An accident happened. Dan loved you so much that he made the ultimate sacrifice for you. Give thanks to him by forgiving yourself; then, forgive your mother."

John began to cry. He intuitively knew she was right, but he didn't know if he had the courage to act on her advice.

Chapter 23

CORKY

THE TRAIN RIDE from Salzburg to Rimini was scheduled to last about eleven hours. The man in the ticket line ahead of John was a drunken Czech with a six-day beard and precious few teeth. John bought a first class ticket to eliminate the chance of sitting within smelling distance of the slovenly Slovak. A millionaire had to be careful. John reminded himself of his financial status more frequently now. I don't need anyone, he thought. I'm rich enough to take care of myself, to fix my own problems. Money was an insulator against the world's misfortunes.

John noticed that the American Preppy Look had not caught on in Italy, so, during a delay in Bologna, he bought clothes to help him blend in with the natives. The Euro clothes apparently worked. Two teenage Slovenian boys who were seated across the aisle from him kept giggling at private jokes and sizing him up from across the aisle. They finally asked, "*Deutsch?*"

"*Ja,*" John said. Satisfied that he had blended, he turned his head away from the boys, closed his eyes, and pretended to sleep as he tuned his mental image selector back to one of his favorite daydreams in which he solved the Bergens' financial problems and brought Andrea to America. If he could fixate on his role of hero to Andrea, he could crowd out images of blood and ice and he could blunt the twinges radiating from the site of his missing toes.

Corky had warned John via email that a heat wave had descended on Rimini. Corky's email also had told John he could easily identify his host in his yellow suit, purple wing-tips, white hat, and a blue carnation. John was almost certain that these idiosyncratic fashion details were products of the unshackled wit of Corky Gleason.

It was almost two o'clock in the afternoon when John prepared to step down from the train coach to the platform that led to the center of the station at Rimini. When the heat of the July afternoon engulfed John as he walked along the platform, he was *positive* Corky wasn't going to be attired in a suit of any color, because only a pathological masochist could bear wearing a suit on such a day.

The dreadful heat and humidity were only a blip on John's personal Richter Scale compared to the effect of the figure in dark sun glasses holding the sign with "Caledonia's Finest" neatly printed in black indelible ink.

"Corky?"

Corky laughed hugely and held out his arms to receive his newly-arrived guest. Corky wore a wide-brimmed white hat on his head as forecast, but, in place of the advertised yellow suit, Corky wore an off-white linen shirt, pale yellow walking shorts, and leather sandals. He had lost at least thirty pounds and he was as sun-tanned as well-done hash browns.

"John Boy," Corky called out. "Get over *heah*!" A touch of New England in Italy.

John gave the completely renovated Corky a monster hug. It was the first time John had laughed out loud in a long time. He stood back from Corky and inspected him up-and-down.

"I'm not just saying this, Corkster, you look amazing!"

"One year and counting. I've lost forty-four pounds!"

"Are you pumping iron?"

"Are you insane? I just cut out junk food. I go to the beach in the day time, and I work a night shift loading trucks. And this is what you get."

Corky led John out of the train station to hail a cab. The taxi was as hot as a toaster, so both boys lowered their windows to get as much ventilation as possible as the driver steered southward toward San Marino. The driver mumbled something, and Corky translated.

"He said 'it's very hot.'"

"He's a taxi driver *and* a weatherman." John's attempt at urbanity sounded more like sarcasm, even to himself.

"Whatever," Corky defended the driver. "You expect him to ask about the Red Sox?"

Just before the *Autostrada Adriatica*, the driver stopped on a narrow street bordered by three-story apartment buildings. Corky paid the driver and led the way up three floors in a narrow stairway to the world's smallest apartment.

"Heat rises, right?" John asked as they walked into a warming oven disguised as a sitting room.

"It's not usually like this," Corky said defensively. "The high is usually only thirty."

"Euro dude," John said. Corky knew John was just busting his chops.

"You'll be sleeping — or sweating — here on the couch tonight. We have a fan."

John accepted the invitation, although the thought occurred to him to reveal his millionaire status and inform Corky he preferred to sleep in an air-conditioned hotel. He knew better than to do that. Friends take offers as they are tendered, he thought.

John examined a photograph of a handsome, though skinny, Italian boy posing like a Ralph Lauren model on the wall. "Antolini?"

"That's Antolini. He works days, so we mostly see each other for a late dinner during the week."

Corky told John to leave his backpack and computer on the couch while they escaped the close air of the apartment by going to the seashore.

When John and Corky got to the beach, Corky took the lead and ordered two *Campari-sodas*. This was Corky's turf. He led John over a wooden walkway so they wouldn't cremate their feet in the brown sand, heated by the sun to just below the temperature of molten lava. Corky selected two beach chairs in the shade of an umbrella. He laid his walking shorts and towel on his beach chair. He unbuttoned his shirt and dropped it on top of the towel. That left Corky – completely tanned for the first time in his life — standing there as brown as an overcooked pancake and clad in a black Speedo. A year earlier, a disrobed Corky would have seemed a caricature, but now, two inches taller and forty pounds lighter, he looked better than ninety per cent of the similarly clad men on the beach. The transformation was remarkable.

"Don't stare," Corky said.

"Sorry," John mock whispered.

Corky motioned for John to drop his pants, so John pulled off his new Italian shirt and trousers and dropped them on the towel on his beach chair. He drank a satisfying mouthful of his *Campari-soda*.

"You don't need the boxer shorts on this beach," Corky said disdainfully.

"Yes, I *do* need boxer shorts on this beach."

"You're such a prude," Corky laughed. "The only reason I'm wearing the Speedo is because you're here. You know, out of respect for the *Americano*."

John looked around the beach to take a census of nudists. He didn't see many, and, when he did, they were usually the very people who could have most benefitted from wearing a swimsuit.

"A textile-free zone?" John asked.

"Correct. You're the only guy in the zone wearing baggy boxers with blue anchors printed on them. How nautical."

Never in his lifetime had John expected to receive fashion tips from Corky Gleason. They ran over the hot sand to the edge of the Adriatic and dove into the clear waters. Corky motioned to a stone breakwater, and the two Lake Tremont veterans swam out to the rocks and back.

John couldn't get accustomed to the new Corky. Not only was his body reasonably fit, but his manner of speech had changed. Gone was the hint of a stammer that afflicted him sometimes when the going got tough. Gone were the corny jokes that he had purloined from the Internet. He talked like a normal person, not an adolescent waiting to be whacked on the back of the head by his father.

They stood chest deep in the water and let the gentle swells lift their feet off the sandy bottom rhythmically. Corky told John about Antolini and how well the two of them got along.

"He's a little too effeminate for you, Hardin."

"I like my men *macho*," John growled sarcastically. "About the Hardin thing, I've got a story to tell you." John related the whole astonishing story about the Hardins, Lavals, and Harringtons. He finished his monologue by telling Corky about his visit with Andrea.

"So, the deal is…you're John Wesley Harrington?"

"No. I'm still John Wesley Hardin. But do you see how hard this is? How freaked out I am?"

"It's really strange. I always thought the world was your *enchilada*. I wanted to be you so bad that I would've made a deal with the Devil. Anyway, now I find out they've pulled a switch on you and you're as weird as the rest of us."

"Well, it's too weird for me," John said, as he splashed water on his head for relief from the heat of the late afternoon sun. "I'm outta' there. I'm moving to Florida."

"To do what?"

"I don't know."

"Give Annette a chance," Corky advised. "Go back to Caledonia and work it out with Annette and Scott. Let them be your mom and dad. You'll be leaving home soon enough. Do it for them."

"She never did it for herself or me, why should I do it for

her? How can I live with a mother who never claimed me in eighteen years?"

"Have you thought about what this was like for Annette? She had to do what her mother told her."

"No, she didn't. She could have told her mother to back off, and she could have married Scott, and I'd be their son!"

"You're wrong, John. She couldn't tell her mother to back off any more than I could tell my *father* to back off. I know. I lived in fear of that prick for my entire life."

The wave action nudged them toward the beach.

"You don't know what it's like to be bullied, John. Your father and grandfather were gentle with you. They never ridiculed you or criticized you for not being good enough. Give Annette a chance. You've got to forgive her just like Andrea says."

John seized the initiative. "How about *you*? How about forgiving *your* dad?"

"I'll tell you the truth, John Boy — my dad is *not* a nice man. He'd be even more miserable than he is now if I were there."

John told Corky that he thought he was wrong. The debate ended without resolution. They left the sea to lie down in the shade in a row of umbrellas a quarter-mile long. There were rows and rows of beach-goers seeking refuge in the shade all around them, and every one of them probably had personal problems as gargantuan as the boys in the Speedo and the anchor boxers, but no two persons on the beach were thinking harder about their problems than Corky and John.

Antolini joined Corky and John at a dive of an outdoor

restaurant well after nine o'clock in the evening. A blessedly cool breeze played with the fringes of the worn umbrellas that sprouted like mushrooms around the plaza. Antolini seemed a little unsure about the reason for John's visit and his English was sketchy, so Corky did most of the talking. He told some "fishing-on-Lake-Tremont" stories, but Antolini never seemed to get the point of the yarn.

John shifted their alleged conversation into a different phylum, asking Antolini about where he grew up. Either this was a sensitive subject or Antolini wasn't a big talker, because it was an unproductive branch of the conversational tree. John insisted on buying dinner, which put Antolini in a better mood. When he had finished eating, Corky gathered his towel and a little bag containing his work shoes and socks and left the plaza in time to report to work at midnight. Antolini and John caught a taxi to the apartment. John paid for the taxi.

The apartment had cooled by at least ten Fahrenheit degrees, but John estimated the room temperature still to be an uncomfortable eighty-five degrees Fahrenheit. Antolini pointed to the couch: "Your bed," he said. John nodded. "It is hot," Antolini said, in a fit of loquaciousness. "I sleep now."

"*Buena sera*," John said. Antolini nodded at him indifferently and went into his bedroom, and, in answer to John's prayers, stayed there.

The air cooled to a temperature reasonable for sleeping about an hour before Antolini got up to shower. Antolini shaved, groomed himself, and left without having to say a word, because John pretended to be sleeping contentedly. In less than an hour, Corky showed up looking a little frayed and ready for a nap. John waited for him to shower. John brought his backpack and laptop with him as they went downstairs to the street and turned right to walk to Corky's regular café.

Breakfast consisted of coffee as thick as syrup and croissants as light as clouds. John thought he knew how Corky had lost weight: Starvation really sheds the pounds. Neither of the former Thorntonians was in the mood to talk. They had exhausted all the junior high school prank stories and the goofy prep school gag stories the previous evening. They each had given advice to the other that neither seemed inclined to accept. Their lives seemed headed in very different directions, so their common ground was fixed in the past. By the end of the second croissant, it seemed like the right thing to do was to go their separate ways.

"John, thanks for coming over here. Honestly, you've always been my best friend, and you gave me a lot to think about."

"Thanks for taking me in." Concerned that thanking Corky for a sleepless night in a sauna might seem insincere, John added, "I'm proud of you, Corky. You're healthy, you're happy, and you're making your own way."

"Thanks, John." Corky was glad he was wearing sunglasses.

John stood up to leave. Corky hugged him like a non-swimmer clinching a life jacket, and John squeezed him back. Corky let go with a sigh. John grabbed his computer and shouldered his backpack. He punched Corky on the arm.

"Do something about that Speedo," John said as he turned to walk away.

"Lose the anchor boxers!" Corky called out after him, busting John's chops for possibly the last time.

Chapter 24

FLORIDA

JOHN BOUGHT A ticket for the Rimini to Rome train departing at just past noon. The day was milder than the preceding scorcher, so it was pleasant for John to loiter around the station waiting for departure time. He surveyed a film festival poster heralding Federico Fellini, a home-town Rimini boy and winner of five Oscars.

John studied a huge wall map of Italy. He noted that Rimini was located on about the same line of latitude as Caledonia. That could come in handy if he ever competed on a television trivia show, he thought. The nice thing about maps in a foreign country, it occurred to him, is that he already knew what the cities were called in English, so translation was a breeze. "Roma" was "Rome". "*Molto bene!*" he thought, employing most of the Italian bullets in his linguistic magazine.

John thought a while about the Tower of Babel and what a fiasco that had turned out to be. He imagined how simple it would be to live in a world where everyone spoke English. He imagined improvements in productivity. He also imagined understanding among peoples entering a golden age. Wars might come to an end, although speaking English as a common tongue hadn't helped much during the American Revolution or the War of 1812. John's daydreaming was under full sail, which is why he almost missed the train to Rome, because the departure was announced in Italian. He managed to get on board with seconds to spare, but, if the whole world spoke English, it wouldn't even have been close.

In fewer than five hours, John was at the *Aeropuerto Internazionale Leonardo da Vinci di Fiumicino*. No airport on earth needed a three-letter identifier (FCO) more than this one, he thought. He found one of the few restaurants in the vicinity that wasn't decorated and lit up like a hospital emergency room, and he ate heartily and drank liberally. He checked into an air-conditioned hotel and slept like a baby.

The non-stop flight to Boston arrived in time for John to catch the three o'clock bus to Portsmouth where he had left his car. He was on Interstate Ninety-five headed south toward Florida by five o'clock. He didn't have an exact destination in mind; he was headed for a concept – sun, waves, and beaches. He skirted Boston to avoid rush-hour traffic, drove abeam Worcester and on to Hartford before fatigue overpowered alertness. He stopped at a hotel for his first night back, as he saw it, in the Land of Round Door Knobs and Soft Toilet Paper. Exhaustion from crossing six time zones helped him fall asleep.

Two full driving days later, John crossed the line from Georgia to Florida. He saw no need to drive any further south, so he took the first Florida exit he came to, a four-lane road lined with tall pines and oaks from which Spanish moss hung like Halloween props. He crossed the bridge to Amelia Island and found a hotel just off the beach.

Across the road right on the beach was an outdoor restaurant where he ate a basket of fried shrimp fresh off the shrimp boat and downed a pitcher of ice-cold Southern tea. He sat alone in the cool breeze off the Atlantic and watched the rednecks at the Tiki bar hoot and holler. John liked their Southern accents, because he could stay ahead of them. Up north, he had to think fast, as he saw it, because Yankees' brains were going a thousand miles an hour. A guitar player was just finishing up a wrestling match with an *Eagles* tune, and when he said, "Thank you very much" in response to the applause of the crowd, he sounded exactly like Elvis Presley. John was Down South.

John had plenty of money, but he decided to get a job while he figured out what he was going to do about college. His only college application had been rejected by Princeton. His ACT and SAT scores were in the 98th percentile, and he had made virtually all *A*'s in prep school, so he believed he could get into any but the most elite colleges. His plan was to get a job to pay for his apartment and food, and he wanted to get to know some people – his posse, his network. Corky and Paul or Dan and Scott were as close as John had ever come to having a posse or a network. It was time to change all that.

The next morning at breakfast, he confided to his waitress that he was new in town. The waitress was the kind of person who had everyone's best interests in mind. She was a problem-solver. John guessed that she had solutions to problems that didn't even exist. Using her telepathic powers, she deduced that John was looking for a job, so she laid a "help wanted" clipping from a newspaper down on the place mat next to his plate. A local resort was hiring.

"Nice place," she whispered confidentially, as if to prevent any unemployed eavesdroppers from getting an advantage on John in his quest for a job. She didn't make a big deal of it. She was just spreading the sunshine. John left her a generous tip.

John scheduled an interview for two o'clock that afternoon. He drove to a men's clothing store to buy a suit, shoes, shirt, belt, socks, and silk tie. Scott had advised John to dress appropriately not just for the job in question, but for the job to which he wanted to be promoted. Scott's exact words were, "If you want a job as circus clown, go to the interview dressed like a ringmaster." Sometimes, John questioned whether Scott knew what he was talking about, but, most of the time, John accepted Scott's words as Gospel.

John ate a light lunch before returning to his hotel room. He used a brand new razor blade to shave, because bloodletting of any kind, even a nick, might ruin his image. He wore out an emery board trimming his fingernails. He had showered and was looking fine by one o'clock when he drove south down the island's main road to the resort. Scott had always stressed that promptness was a virtue appreciated by every employer. "If you're early, you're on-time," Scott used to say, "and, if you're on-time, you're late."

John remembered more of Scott's guidance as he sat in the human resources waiting room. What came to mind was Rule 17: "Always look people straight in the eye unless you're blind." Scott always laughed when he recited that one. John longed to hear Scott laugh. And how he missed Dan! These were exactly the wrong thoughts to entertain seconds before being interviewed.

It was as bad as looking at a nurse just before the doctor checked you for a hernia. That had happened to Raymond Delacroix when he was getting his Caledonia High School football physical exam. He was naked as a Jay bird when the nurse walked by, which got his blood pressure in a bother, which resulted in the doctor looking up from his hernia exam and saying, "Son, you seem to like it here."

Luckily, the memory of Delacroix's penile exhibition got John's mind off of Dan and Scott, so his tears were replaced by a stifled laugh that lasted a little longer than he desired as he entered the office to meet his interviewer. The human resources representative across the desk was a graduate of the Gomer Pyle School of Southern Accents. He liked to talk, and, when he laughed at his own jokes, his Adam's apple jerked up and down like a fishing float when a sunfish messes with a worm. When his Adam's apple bobbed, the knot of his polyester tie exaggerated the action. It could have been a carnival act.

At first, John couldn't believe the man wasn't doing it on purpose. Then, he realized that this affable, well-meaning gentleman had no idea how funny his Adam's apple was, and that made it even funnier. John thought he might die from an aneurysm trying to suppress his laughter. The stakes were high. John wasn't coming off the rolls of the unemployed if he couldn't keep a straight face. Fortunately, the interviewer thought John was laughing at the joke he had just told, so the interviewer hee-hawed a little longer. That, of course, set his

Adam's apple to dancing again.

John's stomach actually shook at one point, and John faked a cough to disguise the fact that he was about to rupture his spleen fighting to control his laughter. The impulse to giggle was so strong that John resorted to an emergency day-dream in which he imagined himself being tortured by North Korean prison guards. He forced the image to stimulate his amygdala and to awaken his left prefrontal cortex so a wave of sadness would drown his urge to burst out laughing. These cranial high jinks made him perspire, though, and the interviewer noticed it.

"Now, young man," the man drawled, "no need to worry about this interview. It's completely straight forward, and I won't ask any question that I'm not glad to answer myself." He smiled goofily, and that almost got John cranked up again, but John willed the second laughing impulse away with his vivid imagination of the North Korean cruelty scenario.

"Now," the man with the acrobatic Adam's apple said, "I know that you are a resident of New Hampshire by your driver's license. My, that's a long way away!"

"Yes, sir." Scott had told John that people outside of New England showed respect by saying "sir". John had been practicing saying "sir" since he crossed the Mason-Dixon Line.

"Now, it says here that you are a graduate of Thornton Academy, is that right?"

"Yes, sir."

"Is that a military school?"

"No, sir. Just a normal prep school." He could see the interviewer write down "normal prep school" on his interview sheet.

"I couldn't enlist in the military on account of flat feet," the man admitted. John had to fight the laughter urge again. The road to hysteria can be a very short journey for a person with a really good imagination.

"Are you a felon?"

"No, sir."

"Have you ever used illicit drugs?"

"No, sir."

"Well you certainly aren't stupid," he said, chuckling at his own humor in violation of Rule 7. "You'd be amazed at how some people answer that one." He asked several more questions. "What's your work experience? Are you a team player? Describe your work habits."

"I believe in arriving early, working hard, and respecting my employer."

"My, my," the man said, "you certainly are an attractive candidate. I can tell you right now, that you are the best-dressed candidate I have interviewed this week."

John could believe it, because he had seen first-hand some of the rustically attired candidates in the outer office.

"I'm going to take a most unusual step," the man continued, "I'm going to offer you a position right on the spot. Don't be alarmed, I can do that, because I'm Manager of the Human Resources department."

"That's very decent of you, sir. Which job do you have in mind?"

"Valet," the man said confidently. "The first person most of our clients see when they drive up to our five-star resort is a handsome, smiling, articulate valet! Valets work from noon to midnight in six-hour shifts, five days a week."

"Very good, sir."

"Do you want to know about the pay?"

John answered in the affirmative, although he privately was thinking, I'm a millionaire, you countrified schmuck.

"Ten dollars an hour plus tips! We pay the best to get the best." He shuffled his papers and asked John directly, "Will you accept our offer?"

"I'm happy to accept."

"That's my shortest interview on record. You'll be a great addition to our family. Oh, I forgot to ask you what your goals are."

"I'd like to make money for college."

"I mean, your goals. What are your *long*-term goals?"

"To someday be qualified to hold your job." John sometimes split infinitives on purpose to avoid sounding highfalutin. As for the blarney, Scott had told him that it often worked.

"I like your spunk, young man."

John found a furnished one-bedroom apartment off the beach the very next day, his first day at work. His fellow valets were generally good guys. One exception was a twenty-year-old lummox from Waycross, Georgia named Sid. He was over six feet, four inches tall topped off by flaming red hair. The oozing scabs on his shins suggested that he had fallen into a blackberry patch that morning. Being a valet parking attendant isn't nearly as restrictive as being a horse racing jockey, but excess height is no more of an asset for climbing in-and-out of Japanese sedans than it is for riding thoroughbreds. Sid complained bitterly about banging his knees and head getting in-and-out of compact cars.

Sid had a serious, literal view of the world. He seldom smiled. When he finally did smile, John hoped he never would again because of the misalignment and color of his teeth. Sid seemed to be carrying a heavy psychic burden. John failed to see how Sid reflected anything on the resort except doom and gloom. Sid complained and boasted as naturally as he breathed. Every day, he insisted on briefing his colleagues on the details of his alleged sexual conquest of the previous evening.

"I got laid again last night," Sid said in a coarse whisper. He looked at John to see if he had heard. John nodded casually showing zero interest. Sid continued, "You know the blonde down at the *Broken Beak*?"

"Yeah," John replied.

"It wasn't her," Sid said. John wondered what kind of mind thought this way. "You know the brunette down at *Givenchy's*?"

"No."

"It was her," he drawled. He furrowed his brow as he transitioned to the evaluation stage of the story. "One very, *very* hot young lady," Sid intimated.

"Well, I don't know her, so...."

"That's why I'm telling you, Man." Did Sid think he was doing John a favor? "I mean, get yourself a golf ball and a garden hose, and...."

"Sid, that's your private life. I don't want to invade your private life, so keep it to yourself."

"I don't mind," Sid said.

Another valet named Brad agreed with John. "Yeah,

keep it to yourself, Sid."

Sid regarded them sternly. "I think you boys are a little jealous."

John scanned Sid's shins and calves. Some of the scratches had turned into sores. Could it be an early stage of leprosy? Diagnosis uncertain, John thought.

"Jealous? I don't think so," Brad said.

"Maybe just a little bit," Sid teased, still frowning.

A steady diet of Sid was hard to take, but John remembered Rule 33: "It's always something".

September flew by. John's shift was from six o'clock in the evening until midnight Saturday through Wednesday. It was a perfect schedule for options trading. He could research and trade during market hours from 9:30 a.m. until 4 p.m. He picked up the pace of his trading. He was going to make two million bucks or more. — break the bank. His success didn't have to be a secret anymore. He was of legal age. He switched his trading activity into overdrive.

John's imagination remained active. The only way to go back to Caledonia was driving a Ferrari or a Lamborghini. He didn't want to flaunt his wealth, but he'd show Caledonia what a winner looks like. He intended to share his wealth, too. He wanted to hire a full-time nurse for Karl Bergen, bring Andrea to America, and buy a fancy house for her. That's how he would make the hurt go away, by showing the people who hurt him that he was too rich to care!

On October 1, 2006, John bought 100 American Express December $55 Calls for $1.35. When the stock hit $60 the week before expiration, he sold-to-close the Calls for $5.20.

His profit was $38,500. On October 6, 2006, John bought-to-open 90 Boeing December $85 Calls for $0.85. Boeing climbed to $91 on November 21, and John closed the position, selling the Calls for $7.40. His profit was $58,950. He enjoyed profits in several other lesser transactions and managed to limit his losses satisfactorily. Option trading had regained the dominant place in his thinking, crowding out concern for others and even crowding out loneliness most of the time.

He thought about Annette and Scott just about every day, but he made no effort to contact them even though his anger had cooled over time. Denying them knowledge of his location was a big part of the punishment he was hoping to inflict. He was consumed with a desire to make a ton of dough, so he focused all his brain power on that one objective. His posse wasn't even in the early stages of forming, and his network was not expanding in any measurable way.

Andrea was the only passion he had outside of trading. He exchanged emails with her three or four times a week. John had built Andrea up in his imagination to an abstract concept of every quality he admired in a woman. He refined his mental image of her every day – like adding a layer of lacquer to a fine piece of furniture — so her memory became perfection itself. She became more of an ideal than a person in his mind.

The resort offered John a promotion giving him a thirty per cent pay raise, but he stayed with the valet job, because the valet schedule let him analyze and trade almost seven hours a day. On Thanksgiving Day, John entered only one line in his diary: "NAV $2,046,335." He decided to go for *four* million. He began to increase the size of his positions.

John had turned bearish just before Thanksgiving. The S&P 500 had recorded many months of steady price appreciation and John had become obsessed with the notion that a correction was long overdue. He bought-to-open 200 Home Depot January $35 Puts on October 18, 2006, when HD was at about $36. He paid $112,000 to establish the position. Instead of falling as John had predicted, the HD stock price rose steadily toward $40.

A couple of weeks later, John bought-to-open 300 General Electric December $35 Puts for an outlay of $67,500. Rather than lose value, GE stock slugged slowly higher, reaching $37 by expiration. In the middle of November, John bought-to-open 300 American Telephone & Telegraph January $32.50 Puts for $102,000. The stock price traded in a range and slowly climbed to $34 by expiration. He stuck with every position all the way to zero at expiration.

John stuck to his bearish bias despite the S&P 500 Index's grinding climb higher. He was afraid to go long the market, because he was convinced that a big correction could occur at any moment. He had never lost such a large percentage of his assets in such a short time. The result of three months of grueling trading was a loss of more than $400,000. He wrote in his journal: "NAV $1,624,177."

Money meant everything to him now. Strangely, he was greedier now in pursuit of revenge than he was when his motives were altruistic. He was so consumed with making money that he spent very little time on the beach, and he almost never joined the other valets anymore for a midnight beer after they got off work. He didn't need anyone, and he didn't care whether they needed him.

He lay in bed and sighed deeply. The thought of losing so much money so quickly shook his confidence. He felt a nervous tremble in his legs and chest, a sort of nervous leg syndrome of his entire body. John decided to fly back to Caledonia for a clandestine visit at Christmas. He planned to leave a token gift each for Scott and Annette at Annette's door. He wanted them to know that he was okay, but he didn't want to let them off the hook of guilt completely.

He needed this trip to get his mind off his financial bleeding. He assured himself that he could stem the tide when he returned to Florida.

Chapter 25

CHRISTMAS

JOHN HIRED A limousine for the trip from Boston Logan to the Caledonia Inn where he had reserved a room for two nights. The limo driver was of Middle-Eastern origin – recent origin – and, in John's opinion, his body language and attitude had "Terrorist Sleeper Cell Leader" written all over them. John thought himself a mainstream, up-to-date, right-thinking American, however, and he steadfastly refrained from publicly profiling, gallantly accepting the chance that the driver was banded with sticks of dynamite. As John saw it, the risk of being blown to smithereens in an act of holy *jihad* was outweighed by the possibility of insulting an innocent immigrant by choosing a different limo driver.

As the limo driver saw it, his client was a jet-lagged, irritating twit who probably had more money than brains. The driver had traded shifts with another driver thinking that no one in his right mind wanted to hire a limo to drive to a place such as the wilds of New Hampshire during a major snowstorm. His plan had backfired, so, instead of huddling in the comfort of his home with his family, he was stuck chauffeuring a self-indulgent teenager on this bleak, snowy night. The two men were in the same limo breathing the same air, but their perspectives were so dissimilar that their communications were destined to be brief.

Snow had been falling all day, and, for four solid hours in light Sunday traffic, the limo slipped and slid dramatically in the hands of a driver who clearly had missed the class on steering *into* the slide. One particular hair-raising near-collision with the right guard rail gave John an "*atria-bonk*", which, by Scott's definition, was "a cold shot of urine to the heart". For possibly the first time in history, four hours passed without a word being uttered by a Boston limo driver or his client. As the limo slid sideways onto the shoulder at the border of Massachusetts and New Hampshire, John considered breaking the conversation embargo to ask the driver whether he had ever driven in snow in Iraq, but John's better judgment kicked in, and he remained silent. Obviously, the driver had *not* driven in snow anywhere on earth and John imagined that the question might have been the camelback-breaking straw that triggered the detonator.

John tipped the driver extra when the limo stopped in front of the Caledonia Inn, but he didn't go overboard. No amount of tipping could balance the scales in the mind of the disgruntled driver. The look on the driver's face as John said, "Good luck", conveyed the message of "don't leave me out here all alone". The Boston television evening news made no mention of a death on Interstate Ninety-three, so John presumed that the driver had slipped home safely, possibly by midnight.

John checked into his room, donned his heavy winter

coat, pulled on an old ski hat, and left the Inn to walk to Rambo Johnson's pub down by the town docks. Six inches of snow covered the sidewalks of the village. It had been dark since 4:30 p.m. The streets were almost deserted but for the Christmas Eve bustle of families going to church services and tourists crowding into restaurants and taverns for a taste of New England holiday cheer. John recognized a few of the locals he passed on the street, but their gazes were downcast to prevent snowflakes from falling into their eyes, and no one recognized him. John entered the pub and moved directly away from the bar toward a quiet booth in the rear of the room. He slid into the booth out of sight of the other customers. Rambo Johnson left his station behind the bar and approached John's booth.

"John?" Rambo asked tentatively.

John looked up at the barkeep. "Rambo, I'm not here, okay? You never saw me."

"Whatever, Secret Agent Man. You okay?"

"I'm all set, but I don't want to see anyone. How about a burger and a pitcher of Sam?"

"Seasonal?"

"Boston Lager."

This set into motion a complicated protocol. The Rambo method for serving alcohol to clients below the age of twenty-one was, first of all, to see that they were seated at a private booth in the rear of the bar. The next step was for Rambo to ring up a Coke on the register and put the glass of Coke in front of John. Rambo also drew a pitcher of beer that he did *not* ring up on the register, and he put the pitcher and a glass on the opposite side of John's table. The fiction was that the beer belonged to Rambo. The reality was that John could pour beers from the pitcher into the glass, take a drink whenever he wanted, and replace the glass on "Rambo's side" of the table. Rambo and the client kept track of the pitchers of beer so payment could be an "off-register, on-tip" transaction. A skeptic might call it an honor system among dishonorable parties. The long New England winters provided plenty of time for developing these kinds of protocols to meet the needs of the citizenry.

John listened to the jumble of conversation from the regulars at the bar. New England Patriots this and the Boston Celtics that and the Boston Bruins the other thing. Rambo refreshed the pitcher, and John remained in his booth long after the dinner patrons had left the pub. Rambo turned the bar over to his trusty sidekick and brought a fresh pitcher of Samuel Adams to John's table.

"Can I join you?"

"Sure."

"What's going on with you?" Rambo sat in the booth opposite John.

"I'm living in Florida, now."

"You like it?" John nodded affirmatively. "I should move down there," Rambo said sincerely enough that a stranger might actually believe that Rambo had any inclination to ever move anywhere.

"Do you remember Corky Gleason?" John asked.

"The fat kid whose dad runs the bank, right? Sure, I remember him. He never came in here, though."

"He's living in Italy. He's all set over there."

"Italy?" Rambo thought about that and chugged a third

of his glass in one deft motion. "God, they have beautiful women over there. Italian chicks are *beeotiful*. Until they turn thirty-five, then they blow up like balloons." Rambo considered himself an authority on women of the world even though no one could remember Rambo ever dating any legally competent woman more than once.

"And Corky's not fat anymore. He's taller and skinnier than any of these schmucks in here."

"Yeah," Rambo said motioning toward the bar, "well, come on. None of these guys are built for speed. We're talking boozers, here. They're built for comfort."

"Corky's looking good." John put a period on it. He didn't mention Antolini.

"I should move to Italy," Rambo said. He thought for a moment and chugged another draught of his beer. "Hey, you were in school with Thomas Bruguiere's nephew, right?"

"Yeah, we hung out."

"He got bagged in Afghanistan."

"Paul! No!"

"Yeah, Thomas was in here getting sloshed and he told me. The kid had only been in-country two weeks. Friggin' Taliban. Thomas is over the edge. They fired him at the boat yard, because he didn't show up for work. He's a mess. I'm surprised he's not in here getting bombed tonight. He's done, I'll tell you that. Stick a fork in him, he's done."

John could see Paul's face vividly in his mind. He remembered Paul unveiling the canoe and how proud he had been. He remembered him pulling in a two-pound bass and making a big deal out of it like he was landing a sailfish. He remembered Paul's frenzy of weight-lifting. John didn't want to imagine Paul lying in the sand with the life blown out of him.

"He was a good guy. He was so proud to be a Marine," John said.

"We're throwing away the lives of a lot of good kids for nothing. Those camel jockeys don't understand democracy. It's a waste. They treat their women and children like they treat their camels. They're not worth one single American life. Friggin' Taliban."

"I gotta go," John said. Rambo said it was on the house, but John insisted on paying, and he left a big tip on top of that. "I wasn't here."

"I know that," Rambo said.

Outside in the falling snow, John took refuge in a recessed entrance on the main street and called the Gleason residence on his cell phone even though it was past nine o'clock on Christmas Eve. Andrew Gleason answered the phone. John didn't apologize for the late hour of his call; if John didn't call then, he might never call. John told Mr. Gleason that he had heard about the death of Paul Bruguiere and it started him thinking about how awful it must be for any parent to lose a child or not to know the whereabouts of a child. Andrew's voice got very tense, and he asked John if he was telling him that Corky was d.... John quickly interjected, wishing he had phrased his words more artfully.

"No, no. Corky's great. I just wanted you to know that I saw him in Italy."

"He never calls," Andrew said.

"He looks terrific. He's very happy, and loves you and

Mrs. Gleason very much."

Corky hadn't actually voiced the last sentiment, but the beers had mellowed John and his message, and John was striving for goodwill toward men, a hallmark of the season.

"I just wanted you to know that," John said in the hopes of truncating the conversation. He doubted that Corky would approve of his phone call to Mr. Gleason.

"Thanks for letting us know. Merry Christmas, John."

Andrew Gleason owned a third of Caledonia, but he didn't have his son.

John walked through eight inches of fresh snow past the town clock tower and down a side street too narrow for parking cars. The snow covered everything on the street, and the scene was straight out of the Eighteenth Century. The only signs of modernity were power lines strung overhead. The Bruguiere house was a small Cape Cod style shake-sided house built in 1785. A couple of shutters were skewed on their hinges from neglect. Thomas had not shoveled the snow around his house in days, and light from a single living room lamp cast a glow on the two-foot blanket of snow snug up to the front door.

The town bells had already tolled nine o'clock, but John didn't want to wait to talk to Thomas Bruguiere for the same reason he hadn't wanted to put off the call to Andrew Gleason. John banged on the front door with a gloved hand. When he didn't hear any response to his knocking, John removed his right glove and banged his knuckles against the ancient door. Heavy footsteps approached. Thomas cracked opened the door and peered out into the darkness with a solitary red eye.

"Whaddayuh want?" Thomas croaked.

"It's John Hardin, Mr. Bruguiere." Thomas continued to stare at the figure in the ski cap standing on his front stoop. John removed the ski cap from his head, and snowflakes fell off his cap onto his face. "Remember? Paul showed me and Corky his canoe?"

"John," Thomas slurred as the round peg suddenly fell into the round hole of his memory. "Get in here. Get in here where it's warm."

Thomas smelled like a microbrewery. His hair was tossed wildly about, and John was willing to bet he hadn't showered in two days. The tiny, formerly immaculate house was still clean but littered with bedroom pillows on the couch and piles of clothing on the living room floor. It was as if Thomas had set out to do a load of laundry and decided a quarter of the way through the job to take a sabbatical.

Thomas trudged to his refrigerator and took out two beers, giving one to John. "Take off your coat and sit down, John." Thomas pointed to a padded arm chair as he twisted off his bottle cap and put it in his pocket. John kept his coat on as he twisted off his bottle cap and put it in his pocket, too.

"I'm so sorry about Paul," John said.

"Yep. Yep." Thomas sighed deeply like he was trying to fight back a sob.

"Paul was a great friend." Thomas brushed a tear out of his good eye and swiped below his eye patch, too. John didn't know what was behind the eye patch, and he surely didn't know that whatever was there could make tears. "Paul always talked about how good you were to him."

"Yep. I tried. His father was such a dick. I tried."

"He was really proud to be a Marine." John had tears in his eyes, too.

"Yep. He muscled up and filled out that uniform pretty good." John saw a picture of Paul in his dress uniform on the fireplace mantle. "I wasn't that good for him," Thomas blurted out. "I could hardly hold a job...I wasn't much better than his father."

"Yes, you were, Mr. Bruguiere. You meant everything to Paul. He was very protective of you. He used to defend you when someone made a remark about the silly crap you used to shout out." John's phrasing left a lot to be desired.

Thomas howled laughing. "He did? He was running interference for his old uncle?"

"Big time. You did a good job with Paul."

"He sure could make a canoe," Thomas mumbled before taking a pull from his beer bottle.

John removed his check book and a hotel pen from his inside coat pocket. He made a check payable to Thomas Bruguiere for twenty thousand dollars, signed it, and gave it to Thomas.

"What?" Thomas inhaled and his single eye bulged.

"Don't say anything. Paul was a great friend to me, and I want you to have it, and that's it."

"You don't have to do this."

John chugged the last of his beer and put the bottle on a side table.

"Yes, I do. I want to." John donned his ski cap. He extended his hand to accept Thomas' calloused paw in a firm handshake. "I'm probably never coming back to Caledonia,

Mr. Bruguiere, so this is goodbye. Good luck."

"Mind yourself, John."

Big, fluffy snowflakes skimmed John's face as he retraced his footsteps in the deepening snow. Thomas closed the front door, held his beer bottle up to his lips, and tilted his head back to let the last of the bottle's contents drip down his throat. His words slurred as he mumbled aloud, "Twenty thousand bucks, ha! Passing out good intentions just like his Grandfather Benjamin. Crazy mixed up kid...lost his dad, lost his granddad, now his best friend's gone." Thomas tore the check in half and tossed it to the floor. "Friggin' Taliban."

Another four inches of snow fell during the night. The storm had passed the village by ten o'clock in the morning and the sky was a brilliant blue dome over a pristine white layer of fluffy snow that covered everything in the village. John ordered breakfast brought to his room, because he didn't want to encounter anyone he knew in the hotel restaurant. It wasn't that John had become a disciple of Howard Hughes. It was just that his time in town was finite, and he didn't want to waste any time in sidebar conversations.

After his talks with Andrew Gleason and Thomas Bruguiere the previous evening, John had decided to visit with Scott and Annette instead of cowardly leaving his little gifts on their doorstep. He wanted to keep open his option to skip confronting them, however, so he didn't want a chance encounter in the village to lead to a busy-body calling Annette to report a "John Sighting". He was resolutely, though guardedly, almost sure he was going to meet with Scott and Annette. He was waffling. Finally, fortified by breakfast, he decided: He was going to follow the advice of Andrea and Corky and visit his parents in person.

He shaved, showered, and dressed in his overcoat and ski hat for the walk to Annette's apartment. The town was so empty that, in the words of Scott Harrington, you could shoot a Scud missile down the main street without inflicting a single casualty. The sidewalks were covered by a foot of snow, but plows had kept the roads clear all through the night. John made his way on the deserted roadways toward Annette's apartment. When John had reached the curb across the street from Annette's apartment, he stood close by a snow-laden spruce tree and pulled out his cell phone to call Scott.

Scott answered on the second ring, "Merry Christmas," he said.

"Merry Christmas," John said.

"John!" Scott hadn't heard John's voice in over three months. "Where are you?"

"Right out front. Can I come in?"

"You're in Caledonia?" John heard Scott tell Annette to go the front window to look for him.

"Sure, right here." John waved at Annette as she looked out the apartment window at him. She returned his wave, and he could hear her scream of delight through the cell phone receiver. "Come in out of the snow!" Scott said.

John crossed the street and arrived at the front door just as Annette opened it. She was wearing a cream Norwegian sweater and navy blue corduroy pants and leather slippers with white fur trim. She held out her arms, and John gave her a hug. Scott was right behind her; he was wearing faded jeans and a mid-blue Cashmere sweater. Scott gave John his patented bear hug and closed the door behind them. Annette was bawling, so she couldn't speak. Scott took John's coat and hat and led him to a chair between the Christmas tree and the fireplace. Working through her tears, Annette brought John a cup of coffee the way he liked it.

"It's been really hard for us not knowing where you are and with no way to reach you," Annette said when she finally got her voice back. She wasn't scolding him as much as she was making sure John knew his absence had hurt them.

"I'm sorry for the way I behaved. I think I was a little crazy."

"We're all crazy," Annette said.

"What matters to us," Scott said," is that you're here now, and you're healthy."

As some of their tension released, they stopped measuring every word as if fearing offense. They began chatting spontaneously as they had in days past, back before Dan's death. John asked about the hardware store. Scott described working for Andrew Gleason's new store manager, Tilly Grosslichter. "Tilly the Hun" was how they referred to the manager behind his back. Scott said you could perform surgery on the floors they were so clean and shiny under the watchful eye of Tilly.

Annette related some top secret Brighton School intelligence, including Board Member Andrew Gleason's war against accepting as part of the reading list a book called "Roger's New Dress".

"Roger, I take it, is a boy?" John guessed. Annette nodded.

"You bet your pink *tutu*," Scott said as he rolled his eyes.

John told his parents – it was still strange to call them that — about his life since moving to Florida. He gave them a brief account of his visits with Andrea and Corky. He made Andrea into a saint for her commitment to her brother Karl. He made Corky sound like an action hero now that he had shed so many pounds. John watered down the role of Antolini, because he didn't want to be a gossip. John talked about his job in Florida. He described the daily confessions of Sid, which, if even half-true, made him the Romeo of Northern Florida.

"Every locker room has a Sid," Scott said.

"Why did you go to Florida in the first place?" Annette asked.

"It's the *un*-New England." He said it was a concept of antithesis. Acid versus alkaline. Sweet versus sour. Warm versus cold. He told them that he just started driving. He took the first exit he came to when he crossed the Florida line. It was random getting there, he told them, and he would probably leave the same way.

John gave Annette and Scott each a simple gift that he had brought from Florida. His gift to Scott was a small white starfish. Scott hung it on the Christmas tree with help from Annette. John's gift to Annette was a small wooden lighthouse also designed to decorate a tree. Annette hung the ornament and gave John a kiss on the cheek. She seized any excuse to show affection for her returned son.

"Why'd you come back?" Annette asked him.

John fiddled with his coffee cup before responding. He said he wanted to see Caledonia again. He wanted to hear the clock tower chimes. He wanted to walk over the snow crust on the Thornton lacrosse field. He admitted that, perhaps, he wanted to see if Annette and Scott were suffering, the way a little boy sneaks back to his yard after he's run away from home.

He recalled a story his Grandfather Benjamin Hardin once told him about the time Benjamin took a shotgun into the woods to commit suicide after a confrontation with his parents. Benjamin was sorting out holding the shot gun to his chin and pulling the trigger with his toe, when he started day-dreaming about his mother wailing inconsolably with grief and his father lamenting forever the loss of his son. The images of their misery were so gratifying to Benjamin that he began to smile from sheer pleasure. Soon, he was laughing. Within the next minute, Benjamin canceled his suicide, because he had sated his appetite for punishing his parents.

"I didn't plan on coming to your apartment, but something happened."

"Like what?" Scott asked.

"I went to Rambo's, and he told me about Paul Bruguiere getting killed in Afghanistan."

"I was going to tell you later," Scott said grimly.

"I went to Thomas Bruguiere's house for a little while last night. It ripped my heart out. Thomas is devastated. Without Paul, he has nothing."

Annette said, "He just wanders around from Rambo's to O'Brien's to the Inn knocking down pints of Guinness to drown his misery."

"Seeing Thomas made me realize how much I miss you," John said.

Scott, who was standing directly behind John's chair, put both of his hands on John's shoulders and squeezed.

"I miss you, John," Annette said. "I want you to be my son. I've always wanted you to be my son."

"We've talked about it a lot," Scott said. "I mean, you *are* our son. We've discussed adopting you, but we worry about Trinette butting in."

"I don't care about the papers," John said. "I don't want to drag everything that happened out in the open."

John understood that public disclosure was what his Grandmother Marie was trying to prevent all along. He didn't care if the genealogists got family trees all fouled up years from now. He wanted the legacy of the Hardins and the Lavals and the Harringtons to remain undisturbed.

Scott sat down beside John. "Being your father is the greatest honor of my life." Scott said. "But, if *you* don't care about the paperwork, *we* don't care about the paperwork."

"I worried that you'd ever come back to us," Annette said. She was crying again.

"I was a nut job when I found out about the secret," John said. "It was like the person I thought I was didn't exist anymore. I was confused and angry. I talked to Andrea about this for hours. The first thing she told me to do was to forgive myself for causing Dan's death," John said as tears flooded his eyes. He had said "Dan" instead of "Dad", because wasn't Scott his dad, now?

Annette got up from her chair and walked around the table to sit beside John on the other side of John's chair from Scott.

"It was an accident, John," she said. "You didn't cause

Dan's death."

"I'm trying to let it go," John said. "Andrea told me that I have to forgive you, too."

"Can you?" Annette asked.

"Yes." John said. He was blubbering without shame. He leaned over and kissed his mother on the cheek.

Each member of the new family unit had been forced to cope with a major loss of some kind. Annette had lost her baby. Scott had lost his eyesight. John had lost his identity. They had all lost their parents.

"John, you've got secrets, too," Scott said, "and I think you should come clean with them."

John reacted defensively. "I don't know what you mean."

"Not now," Annette pleaded with Scott.

"Yes, now," Scott said. He motioned to their bedroom. "Please, get the folder."

"Scott?" Annette wanted him to reconsider. She feared that everything they had just accomplished would be lost if she brought the folder to the table.

"We've got to address it now," Scott insisted. "No more secrets."

"What?" John asked. Scott held up the palm of his hand to arrest the conversation until Annette returned with a Manila folder.

"Find the six-page document," Scott told Annette. She pulled a document out of the folder and laid it in front of John. It was The Liberty Revocable Trust document. Scott continued, "My signature is on Page 6. Show him, Annette." She didn't have to show John; he remembered it clearly. "But I never signed that document," Scott said. "I don't think Dan ever signed it, either. I think he would have told me if he was a trustee and I was a successor trustee. I'll ask you straight out: Did you forge our signatures?"

"Yes."

"Why?"

"I was too young to open a brokerage trading account. Creating a trust was the only way I could do it."

"Why was it so important to open a trading account?"

"I knew the hardware store was in trouble. I didn't think you could get a job when you lost your eyesight. I wanted to help. I wanted to make money. I learned how to trade options, and I got good at it. My paper trading results were off the charts. I wanted to make a lot of money, real money." He appealed to them for understanding. "I wanted to be special, and I wanted you and Dan to know that I was more than a punk pretending to be Davy Crockett."

"So, you made some money?" Scott asked.

"Yes, I did."

John examined the trust agreement. It was the original. He explained how he had transferred assets from The Liberty Trust to his newly-opened personal brokerage account when he had turned eighteen. This original trust agreement was one of the few documents he had retained. He had stored the document horizontally beneath the false bottom of a banker's box which he then packed full of vertically arranged term papers, grades, and awards.

"You had to go through my personal papers to find this," John said.

"Yeah," Scott said. "I've busted my hump to execute Dan's will, and Annette has helped me all the way. We weren't trying to pry. When we had our personal effects moved out of Dan's house, your banker's box ended up with my office stuff."

John started to object, but he realized that personal records privacy wasn't the issue. The issues here, no matter how the evidence was uncovered, were John's fraudulent representations, his forgeries, and the illegality of what he had done. His obsession with numbers, his facility for trading options, and his string of successes had led eventually to avarice, pure and simple.

"We said, 'No more, secrets'," Scott said, "and that means you."

John had some explaining to do. Much of Christmas Day had passed by the time John's chronological explanation was finished. Annette had no idea of what an option was, and she couldn't follow the steps John had taken to enable him to trade options as a minor. Scott had a reasonable grasp on how options worked, but he had never actually traded an option in his life, and he was astounded by the volume of John's trades in the trust account. John answered their questions truthfully, and he didn't try to hide behind good intentions. Based on their questions, John wasn't sure which aspect was more surprising to them – his scheme's illegality or its profitability.

Scott said, "John, I doubt there's a hedge fund in America that's generated this kind of return." John felt momentarily flattered, but the look on Scott's face was more skeptical than flattering. "I don't know much about these things, but I'm willing to bet that you're taking on a lot more risk than you think you are."

"It's been working for over four years," John said. "I think I have a pretty good idea of what I'm doing."

"John, the big guys have MBAs and banks of computers and years of knowledge to rely on. If they could make this kind of return, they'd be doing it." Scott was relying on common sense. "I don't know what your current situation is, but what shoots straight up usually comes down in a crash."

"You've just said you don't have any practical experience," John said defensively.

"I'm just recommending caution," Scott said. "Suppose I get an experienced broker to talk with you and review your trades?"

"I don't want anyone else involved," John said stubbornly.

"Will you at least limit your exposure? Analyze your risk. What happens if there's a crash?"

"Sure," John said. It was Scott's first day as his father, and he was already acting like he had been on the job for fifty years. Scott's face reflected doubt. "Really, I will," John insisted.

Not many hours remained before John was to fly back to Florida the next day, so they finally abandoned the subject of John's option trading. They sat around the fireplace sipping mulled wine and relating common memories more suited for the special day. In the aftermath of wrenching emotion, the three members of this new family fell into the familiar cadence of years past when they sat on the back deck of the Dan Hardin house chatting for hours. By the time John put on his coat to leave, they were all exhausted but as content as they had been in a long time.

"Here's my cell phone number," John said. "It's not a

secret anymore."

John's boots squeaked on the dry packed snow as he walked back to the Caledonia Inn. The town clock bells tolled nine times, sharply and clearly in the frigid night air.

John invited Scott and Annette to breakfast at the Caledonia Inn the following morning. It was the Tuesday after Christmas Day, so most of the villagers were back to work. The waitress in the restaurant recognized the threesome as they entered, but she didn't start a "how-ya-been" conversation. She seated them in a booth near one of the fireplaces.

As soon as the coffee arrived, Scott said, "We talked about secrets yesterday. Here's my secret. I got this packet in the mail just before Christmas." Scott asked Annette to spread the contents of the packet on their table. She put the pamphlets in two piles and read the cover note in a low voice. Scott told John the background story on how Scott had come to know the friend who had mailed the packet.

Back in his flying days at Holloman Air Force Base in New Mexico, Scott had met some of the German *Luftwaffe* pilots who were members of two German squadrons permanently assigned to the desert base. Over their years in the United States, a few of the German pilots married American girls. In a few of those cases, the German pilots returned to the Alamogordo area with their American wives after either resigning or retiring from the *Luftwaffe*. Their resident alien status allowed them to stay in the United States as long as they wished. Some earned American citizenship.

Citizens or expatriates, the pilots took to the mountains

and the desert enthusiastically. They had the boots, the Stetsons, and the pickup trucks to qualify as authentic Westerners. One couple bought a twelve-acre apple ranch in High Rolls. Another bought a cabin in Cloudcroft, and the former fighter-pilot-turned-green-card-bearing husband became a ski instructor there. A couple of others settled in Arroyo Seco on the outskirts of Alamogordo. Hans Reichart had bought a ten-acre spread south of a little town called Tularosa. He raised llamas. The pamphlets Hans had mailed to Scott extolled the natural wonders of White Sands, Alamogordo, Ruidoso, and other towns in the Sacramento Mountains or down in the Tularosa Basin. Annette, using a conspiratorial tone of voice, read the high points of the brochures while John looked over her shoulder at the photographs.

"I'm not saying we're moving for sure," Scott said with undisguised excitement in his voice, "but we've talked about it a lot. It'd be a great new start. No baggage."

"You sound like you've already decided," John said.

"Not, yet," Scott said. "Think about it for you, too, John."

John did think about it. For the time being, he'd go back to Florida. He'd valet and he'd trade, but if Scott and Annette moved out West, he'd be there. He liked the idea of a change. He liked not knowing what the future held.

Annette insisted on driving John to the train station in Dover after breakfast. He had plenty of time to ride to Boston North Station and switch to the T for the quick ride to the airport for his afternoon flight to Jacksonville. Scott piled into the back seat for the ride. John occupied the front passenger seat, and he looked out the window as Annette drove southbound on the town's main street. As they passed by an unobstructed view of frozen Caledonia Bay, John could see the open water between the lake ice and the town docks where he had fallen through the ice — the very spot were Dan had drowned. He felt sick for a moment until he blocked the memory.

He watched church steeples pass by his window. As they drove by the Bank of Caledonia, Thomas Bruguiere, who was walking down the granite steps, recognized Annette's car. From his neck up, Thomas looked like a pirate in his ragged bush hat, eye patch, and flamboyant winter scarf. Thomas waved in a huge arcing gesture. He shouted words that couldn't be heard inside Annette's car.

"You crazy Napoleon whack-job," Thomas shouted. "I taped your check together. It's for real! Thanks, Big John!"

John waved back at Thomas.

"Bruguiere looks sober enough," Annette said. "And happy, too."

"He's one-of-a-kind," Scott said.

The trio didn't say much as Annette drove to Dover. They had pretty much done all the talking they needed to do. As Annette stopped by the curb in front of the train station, John thanked them for the Christmas Dinner.

"There's a lot more I'm thankful for than just Christmas dinner," John said. "I'll email you when I get back to Fernandina Beach."

Scott got out of the back seat at the same time John closed the front passenger door. Scott hugged John and whispered in his ear. "Thanks for the greatest gift I've ever received in my life."

"The starfish?" John smiled.

"No, Son. Thanks for what the starfish symbolizes – you. You're my star."

Annette hugged John. "I'm out of tears," she said. "I love you, John."

"I love you, Mom."

Chapter 26

PANIC

JOHN HAD MIXED feelings about the Christmas expose of his under-age trading binge. On one hand, his parents knew he had earned two million dollars while most boys his age were flipping burgers for six dollars an hour. He was more than an avoider of sidewalk cracks. He was more than a memorizer of atomic weights. He was more than a daydreamer playing the role of a diminutive French general with his hat on sideways. On the other hand, they also knew he had broken the law to get what he wanted. He was a forger and a liar. In other words, his parents knew he was a smart guy who was a bandit, not unlike his namesake – John Wesley Hardin.

Now that John was old enough to trade legally, he felt pressure to generate out-sized profits. He convinced himself that he wanted to make four million dollars to make his parents secure financially. Scott had tried to assure John that the Harrington household wanted for nothing, but John was obsessed with the idea of making them rich. He was like a puppy that can't bring its master enough tennis balls. He was a solution yearning for a problem. He didn't stop to consider that his drive to enrich his parents might be a disguise for his own greed.

John began to hedge less and to take on more one-sided positions. He began to put more of his capital at risk. It was one thing to lose money on an adverse trade when no one knew about it. If he were to lose everything now, however, under the scrutiny of his parents, it would crush him. John wanted to prove Scott's apprehensions wrong, and he wanted to blow away his parents' expectations.

Scott had warned John not to take on too much risk, but John believed Scott's opinions were "old school". In Scott's world, you saved money and bought a certificate of deposit and watched inflation erode the value of your savings. In John's world, you took a bold position: You could lose the whole investment, but you had a chance at an annualized return of a thousand per cent or more. It was hard to explain to his parents how it worked, so he would show them. His obsession to make money crowded out all other obsessions.

A few of John's bad trades leading up to Christmas had taken a bite out of his net worth to the tune of over four hundred thousand dollars. He was convinced that the market was due for a pullback, perhaps as early as the end of January 2007. His interpretation of the proprietary technical indicators he had used to make more than two million dollars now was the basis for his bearish forecast. He laid on large short positions by buying front-month puts without selling corresponding lower strike puts. Failing to vertically spread his bearish put positions required a larger outlay of capital. He doubled up on the direction of the move by selling bearish call spreads to help finance his put purchases. Unfortunately for him, the major stock indexes ground higher throughout the month of January.

He lost another $250,000 by the third week of January. The Dow Jones Industrial Average (DJIA) had climbed 500 points from 13,000 to over 13,500. John was more convinced than ever that the market was overbought, and he increased the size of his bearish positions using options with expirations in February. The DJIA hinted at a retracement, but then slogged higher to 13,900. His diary entry for February 20, 2007, read, "NAV: $967,225." He had lost over a million dollars in fewer than six months. Doubt began to gnaw at his confidence like a rat nibbling at a block of cheese. Even when he took on some long positions as a random hedge of his core bearish stance, those individual stocks betrayed him by pulling back. He felt as though he had been cursed. Logic and reason couldn't explain the dimension of his losses, so he looked to the supernatural for an explanation.

His decisions were so overwhelmingly wrong that he became paranoid. In one desperate move he actually did the opposite of what his indicators told him he should do. He lost $41,000 before closing out the position. He was routinely losing money in chunks as large as the rarest of successes he once had enjoyed. John was nervous and depressed. Diary entry for March 18, 2007: "NAV: $442,417."

The DJIA had climbed to 14,500. He had fought the market's bull move all the way, convincing himself that each new high increased the likelihood of an explosive sell-off. He was afraid to reverse his opinion and go long the market for fear of being wiped out by the overdue reversal. He had always trusted his technical analysis, and he reasoned that he had to keep trusting it now.

John had written an email to Andrea in January telling her about his reunion with his parents at Christmas. He thanked her for teaching him the importance of forgiveness. He told Andrea about the new bond with his parents. Because his brokerage balance continued to dwindle ever lower, John decided to send some of his remaining profits to Andrea while he still could. He wrote a check for twenty thousand dollars payable to Andrea and explained that it was a gift. The gift implied no obligation. No strings were attached. The money was hers to use in any way she chose — for school, for her brother, for her parents. Andrea emailed John immediately when she received the check.

"You crazy man! I will *not* cash this!"

"Cash it," John wrote in a return email. "It's yours."

In the end, Andrea accepted his gift, but the pleasure he initially felt from making the gift slowly dissipated and gave way to worries that Andrea might think he was trying to buy her affection. It complicated their relationship in a way that he hadn't anticipated. He avoided mentioning the gift again. Andrea similarly was overly sensitive to the subject. She was caught between feelings that she hadn't thanked John sufficiently and concerns that she might seem obsequious to mention it again. So, she also avoided discussing it.

John continued to lose money throughout the months of April and May. He agonized each trading day in his Fernandina Beach apartment trying to return to his profitable ways. The DJIA and other indices, however, didn't care about the quality of his analysis. The markets didn't care that

John thought they were priced irrationally. For months, John had been convinced that a retracement, possibly a severe one, was imminent, but, again, the markets didn't care.

John continued to work his valet shift, but the work was joyless. He found no pleasure in the companionship of his peers anymore because of his preoccupation with his trading misfortunes. Sid, the self-professed stallion of the valet staff sauntered over toward John and two other valet attendants who were cooling their heels in the shade.

"Hey guys," he said, "you know that blonde chick at *The Barnacle*?"

"We don't care, Sid," John interrupted him.

This slowed Sid down, but he still pressed his message. "Last night – oh, yeah." He rolled his eyes foolishly and pumped his fist as a gesture of victory.

"Sid, stop!" John barked. "Enough! Do you have any idea how stupid you are? Do you know what a liar you are? How pathetic you are? Just go away."

Sid had never been spoken to this way, so he didn't know what to do. He stood there looking puzzled for a minute before he said, "I just thought you'd want to know I got laid."

"No," John said. "We don't want to know." John's nerves were frazzled.

Sid drifted away looking hurt. Even though the other valet attendants were happy to have Sid muzzled, they drifted away from John, too.

John's nights were often sleepless. He felt groggy during the day, and he occasionally had to take a nap between the market close and the time he reported for duty at the resort. In the past, he had viewed ordinary investors as rubes muddling along with their 1.7% dividend returns and paltry 8% capital gains. Now, he was bedeviled by "what if" calculations. What if he had simply closed out all his option positions and bought equities like United Technologies and Johnson & Johnson? Just playing it safe like the mediocre masses would have maintained his net worth at well over two million dollars.

His world crashed in late May when house and exchange margin calls began cascading in on him. He spent four hours in one day simply closing positions at a loss to meet a margin call. The next day he began the serious business of forced liquidations, and, by the last trading day in May, he had been wiped out. His diary entry read, "Liquidated everything. I'm ruined. Five years of work undone. NAV: $4,332." His financial downfall had happened faster than he ever could have imagined. He had inhaled the foul odor of panic. His legs quivered involuntarily. His hands shook as though he were afflicted with palsy. He felt humiliated and exhausted and broken.

The enormity of the disaster! He couldn't discuss the panic he felt with anyone on the island. There was no one he could call to lessen the pain. The failure was his to bear alone, and the weight of his huge losses bore down on him relentlessly. His future seemed bleak. His days seemed a kind of purgatory of regrets. He had believed in his capacity to make money so completely that he had come to regard profits as inevitable, as something owed to him. He had extrapolated his historic rates of gains to forecast his net worth by the age of thirty at $63 million. His identity had become dependent on making money. Who was he now? He was a valet parking attendant lucky to have a roof over his head and no more than \$10,000 in the bank. He had just turned nineteen years old and he felt tired, jaded, and cynical.

John called Scott on the first morning in June. He told his father he was nearly broke. He felt as empty as a shell washed up on the beach. He hadn't fully understood the risks he was taking. He had made bad investment decisions over-and-over again as he fought a relentless tape. Failure was crushing him. He had no future, nothing to live for. He didn't think he could live with the shame.

At one point, John asked Scott if he could send him any money that might be due him from Dan's estate. Scott flatly refused. John felt even worse for having asked. If he couldn't talk with Scott, John felt that he could slide away into a black hole and never get out again. John's voice was chalky and his inflection was flat. Scott let John talk it out. John sighed frequently, long sighs of depression. John repeatedly berated himself and expressed how perplexed he was that his winning methods had betrayed him. Scott let John talk until the circle of his monologue turned into a vortex.

"John," Scott interrupted his son, "it doesn't matter. Even if you've lost every dime, it doesn't matter. We don't really own anything on this earth. We have the use of money and possessions for a few short years."

"But if only I hadn't blown up. I could've bought you and Annette a beautiful house!"

"We don't need a beautiful house, John. Any dwelling – any shack — that Annette shares with me is a beautiful house. Don't think you disappointed us or anyone else."

"This sense of loss, it's killing me."

"Forget your obsession for money! You know you've been obsessive your entire life. You used to turn yourself into a pretzel to keep from stepping on sidewalks cracks. That was funny; this isn't. Forget the money. Let people back into your life and start living again."

Scott gradually pulled John out of the worst of his cloud bank of doom by getting his mind off his financial woes. Scott told John that he and Annette were moving to Arroyo Seco in two weeks. Annette had given notice that she was not returning to Brighton School. Scott had given two weeks' notice to Tilly the Hun at the hardware store. They had already paid the rental agreement early-cancellation fee.

In a giant leap of faith, they had hired Raymond Delacroix to load their chattels into a rental moving truck over the coming weekend. Raymond had agreed to drive the truck to Arroyo Seco for them in exchange for the title to Annette's sedan. Watching Raymond – the reformed bully — carefully packing delicate crystal gave Annette renewed hope in mankind. Even after paying for the rental truck, fuel for the journey, and an airline ticket home, Raymond was earning a little more than the going rate for managing their move.

Hearing the details of his parents' move took John's mind off his personal crisis. He offered to go to Caledonia to help, but Scott assured him that his help was needed at the destination, not the origin. John agreed to drive Dan's old sedan to New Mexico. He wanted to live with his parents until they got settled. Scott and Annette had bought a modest new home without ever personally seeing it. Hans Reichart served as proxy for them, and he assured them that they would be comfortable in the three-bedroom home in the foothills overlooking the desert. Scott and Annette wanted to use some of their inheritances to pay cash for the house when they closed after arriving in Arroyo Seco. Hans Reichart's wife was an elementary school teacher in the Alamogordo School System and she was happy to offer to help Annette find a teaching job there.

Talking to Scott put John in a better frame of mind. He was revisited by an overwhelming sense of loss for many days, but Scott's advice gradually became operative in John's way of viewing his fiscal catastrophe. John gave notice to the resort and to his apartment landlord and packed all of his possessions into six liquor boxes for his drive to New Mexico.

Scott had reminded John that the remainder of Dan's estate was in trust to John's benefit, so John wasn't completely without funds. Despite his immense losses, John knew he was more financially secure than most people his age. The self-pity had to stop.

Chapter 27

SERENITY

JOHN'S EXIT INTERVIEW with the Human Resources Manager of the Amelia Island resort was completely different from the interview that landed John the valet job. For one thing, John wasn't wearing a suit. For another, the HR manager seemed to have learned that it was his gymnastic Adam's apple and not his humor that was getting all the laughs at interviews. He kept his side-splitting comical side in check. The manager, whom John regarded as a good soul, expressed his kindly intentions in his nasal, rural accent.

"Well", John," the HR manager said, "I guess you're not going to replace me after all."

"I guess not, sir."

"You've done a good job here, John. People here think well of you, and we're going to miss you." He checked off steps on his out-processing checklist. "I hope you have success in whatever you do."

"Thank you, sir."

"If you ever need a recommendation, you can count on me," the manager said. He passed the checklist to John for his signature.

"Thanks a lot," John said as he signed the document.

"Can I offer you a comment based on observing you over the past several weeks?"

"Yes, sir." Curiosity and common sense vetoed a negative response.

"Don't worry so much. You're a dazzling star among your peers. You're unique and you're smart. Give yourself a break, and learn to relax."

As they stood up from the desk, the HR manager shook John's hand with a vice grip that John bet came from a youth spent milking cows in South Georgia. John liked the HR manager. He was a decent guy, and John wished he could see the man's tie bob crazily on his Adam's apple — like a rodeo rider on an insane bull — one last time. Before the manager released his hold on John's hand, he lowered his voice and asked John a question.

"Why aren't you in college, Mr. Hardin?" John looked into the manager's face blankly. The manager's huge left hand capped John's right shoulder, thumb below his clavicle and fingertips over his scapula. "Great things are waiting for you, John, so don't waste time parking cars. Get into college and prepare yourself to do those great things."

John was speechless as they parted. The manager smiled benignly after him.

John drove away from that part of his life beneath a canopy of Spanish moss hanging mysteriously from branches of aged oak trees. He had come to Amelia Island burdened by a crisis of identity. He had arrived mourning the death of his father. He had earned a fortune and then lost it. And, now, he was leaving for a new life with his new parents. He was leaving the shadows of these dark mossy woodlands, their nocturnal chirping and croaking, and the incessant sound of waves crashing onto the beach for a wide, quiet land of sunbaked sand dunes, mountains, and parched earth. John was heading westward.

As the miles rolled by, John thought about the manager's advice and he wondered how he could unclutter his mind. His brain was a perpetual motion machine. If nothing was on his mind, his brain defaulted to a counting mode. He counted the seconds between telephone poles. He counted the painted yellow hash marks in the center of the highway. He still could remember the number of paces from the back deck of the Dan Hardin house to the boat dock – sixty-one. One hundred, sixty-two was the number of paces from the Post Office to Hardin's Hardware. His record for number of steps taken without stepping on a crack in the sidewalk was three hundred, thirty-seven out in front of the Thornton Prep main entrance. The only reason the record wasn't higher was that his three hundred, thirty-eighth step would have been onto a slab of concrete so fractured that it looked like a meteor had struck it. Only a pogo stick could have avoided a crack. Somehow, John had to find a way to quiet his mind.

John reviewed his life experiences with family and friends now departed, and he realized how much of his life he had kept secret from them. He had traveled a solitary path motivated by his most intense desires. His fascination with numbers and his addiction to the thrill of accumulating wealth had erected a barrier between him and the people he loved.

John saw that he needed to obsess on loving his remaining family instead of obsessing on earning their love.

John spent nights in Mobile, Alabama; Shreveport, Louisiana; Abilene, Texas, and Artesia, New Mexico on the way to Alamogordo. He found his parents' house in Arroyo Seco on the eastern side of Alamogordo. He parked his car in their driveway, walked up to the front door, and rang the doorbell. When Annette opened the door, cool air cascaded out on him from the air-conditioned living room.

"John!" Annette exclaimed as she hugged him tightly, "welcome to your new *casa*!" She pulled him by the hand into the living room. Scott entered the room from a corridor to greet him.

"Good to see you, Travelin' Man!" Scott said. "You just missed Raymond Delacroix by a day."

"There are worse things than missing Raymond Delacroix."

"Against all odds, he's turned out pretty normal," Annette said in Raymond's defense.

Annette was nothing, if not an optimist, John thought.

"Raymond had never been out of New England before, so he kept talking non-stop about his amazing adventure," Scott said. "I had to remind him that we hired him as a mover, not a story-teller."

"How was *your* trip?" Annette asked.

"Cathartic," John said. The reflection of light off the surface of the swimming pool passed through the sliding glass doors and danced on the living room ceiling.

"Get a beer from the fridge and take a swim," Scott told him. "Just swim in your boxers. They'll dry in no time, because the humidity's so low."

After his swim, John dried off in the sun and came back into the house.

"Love those anchors," Annette said in reference to the patterns of his boxer shorts.

"These were a big hit in Italy."

He, Annette, and Scott talked into the afternoon. John told them about visiting Abilene, Texas, birthplace of the World's Greatest Fighter Pilot – Scott Harrington. Scott was pleased that John had remembered. The end of the world seemed a lot further away to John than it had seemed a month earlier.

Annette told John that they were going out for dinner joined by the friends who had found the house for them. Hans Reichart and his wife Ramona were coming to the Harrington house for pre-dinner cocktails. Ramona was from nearby Tularosa; Hans was from faraway Ulm, Germany. Ramona had met Hans when he was flying German *Luftwaffe Tornados* at the air base ten miles west of Alamogordo. True to the stereotype of German punctuality, Hans and Ramona arrived one minute before six o'clock.

Hans was a stocky, mahogany-tanned character dressed in sandals, khaki shorts, a Hawaiian shirt, and an Australian bush hat which he left on his head when he entered the house. His handlebar mustache could have supported the weight of two medium-sized cockatoos. He laughed for no reason at all and his accent was a dead-ringer for Sergeant Schultz straight off the set of *Hogan's Heroes*.

"Scott told me you have been to Germany?" Hans asked.

"*Ja*," John said.

"Fluent, too?" Hans said, and he laughed boisterously.

Just looking at Hans made you laugh. He was a one-man *fiesta*. Ramona remained aloof in the manner of a patient mother tolerating the pranks of a mischievous offspring. Because Ramona was a school teacher, she acted as though she had a license to correct anyone, Hans in particular.

"You don't need another beer, Hans. We're going to dinner," she said critically.

"American beers are so small," Hans replied, "this isn't a second beer; it's just the second half of my first one." And then he laughed his rolling laughter. His laughter was infectious.

"*Aiiy, Gringo,*" Ramona said. John thought she was one of the most striking women he had ever seen. She was a terrific straight person for Hans' act. "You look just like your father," Ramona said to John as she fiddled with a wisp of his blond hair. He could almost feel the caress of her long, sensuous fingers as she twisted the strands of his hair.

"Thanks," John said.

"Shucks," Scott added. Hans howled laughing. John wondered what might befall Hans if he ever encountered some really good comedy. He'd likely suffer quadruple hernias.

They went to dinner, came back to the house for nightcaps by the pool, and the Reicharts left the house by ten o'clock. As first days in new towns go, the day had gone very well for John, indeed.

During the month of July, the heartbeat of the Harrington house fell into a welcome sinus rhythm. John got a part-time job maintaining swimming pools. Annette landed a job beginning in August teaching fourth graders in the same school where Ramona taught. Hans took John up for a flight in his glider. The Harringtons and the Reicharts went horseback riding in the mountains.

John and Scott attended a Tularosa Little League Baseball game in which Hans was serving as home plate umpire. Players, coaches, parents, and fans stood in unison and held their hats over their hearts during the playing of the *Star Spangled Banner*. Tears cascaded down Scott's cheeks as they always did when he stood in honor of the national anthem.

"Play ball!" the announcer declared.

Hans ran a tight ship at home plate. His German accent added a lot to the entertainment value of the game. *"You routdare,"* meant "strike three, you're out". He had a pretty good eye for the strike zone, however, and a fair-minded person had to conclude that he had made a successful transition from soccer to baseball. Scott couldn't actually see much of the game, but he got a kick out of Hans' antics, and the price of popcorn was right.

A thought germinated in Scott's mind as he thought about Hans' *pro bono* service to these Little League players. Hans had no children of his own. He had left the glory of flying fighters, hardly ever looking back. He spent hours every day working with his llama herd with scarcely any financial reward to show for it, and, yet, here he was giving his time to help kids have a meaningful team-building experience.

It occurred to Scott that he had been focusing too much on what he had lost instead of on what he could gain despite his present limitations. Furthermore, his emphasis had been centered on what he could do for his own benefit instead of what he could do for others. Scott had morphed from a risk-taker to a dependent. Surely, Scott thought, he wasn't destined to be irrelevant. He thought back to an image of thirty years before when he first saw a fighter pilot standing by his *Phantom* at Hanscom Field. Without saying a word to Scott, that fighter pilot had motivated Scott to embark on an exciting journey that was the highlight of his life. Scott began to believe he could be a similar catalyst to someone else, perhaps a young person. He decided to shift his attention to a new question: What could he do of benefit to someone else?

After many conversations with Annette, he took her suggestion to volunteer to mentor a high school student. Perhaps he could help a teenager overcome an obstacle, learn to study, or develop good work habits. Perhaps this was his way to be relevant again.

Two weeks of interviews boiled down to two candidates. The first was a senior at Alamogordo High School named Don "Neon" Lytz. The nickname worked because Don had an electric personality and a highly-charged ego. "Neon" was remarkably fast and elusive on a football field, and he had been observed by scouts from the University of Oklahoma, Texas Tech, the University of Wyoming, New Mexico State University, and even as far away as Northern Illinois University.

Don's father had died the previous autumn during the third quarter of the Alamogordo game against El Paso Bel Air, leaving Mrs. Lytz alone to cope with pressures of recruiters and scholarships. She needed help motivating Don to keep his academic grades up during the upcoming senior year. Mrs. Lytz appealed for a mentor in hopes of preventing a derailment of Don's hopes for using football as a pathway to college.

The second candidate was a short, stocky blind boy named Hector Ruiz. A sophomore at the New Mexico School for the Blind and Visually Handicapped, Hector had grown up in Artesia without his mother and largely without the attention of his father, Javier Ruiz, a chronically unemployed alcoholic. Hector was described as aimless and introverted, and his future was as dark as his vision.

Don Lytz' guidance counselor wanted Scott to choose Don, because Scott's Princeton credentials gilded the marketing of Don. Scott chose Hector Ruiz. The counselor asked Scott why he had passed on the potentially famous Don Lytz to choose an undistinguished blind boy.

"Because I understand what he's going through," Scott said.

Scott's duties began as bi-weekly orientation sessions with Hector at the Blind School. The campus was three miles from the Harrington house, so John drove Scott to his sessions and waited for him on an outdoor bench on the Blind School campus. While sitting on the bench during one of Scott's early sessions, John met a twelve-year old blind boy named Paco Lopez. Paco was a handsome, enormously shy boy. He was sitting on the same bench in the shade that John had selected for a resting place. John coughed slightly before speaking to avoid frightening the boy.

"What's your name?" John asked.

"Paco."

"I'm John."

"Hi."

"Are you from Alamogordo?"

"No, I just go to school in this place. I am from Carrizozo."

"That's just up the road, right?"

"It's in New Mexico," Paco said, unsure of whether it was up or down the road.

"Do you like it here in school?"

"It's okay," Paco said.

"Do your mom and dad come to see you?"

"I don't have a mother or a father," Paco said. "My *tío* takes care of me."

John thought about Paul and Thomas Bruguiere.

"Do you want a mentor?" John asked.

"I don't know what is a mentor."

"It's an older friend who listens to you and takes you for ice cream."

"I don't have anything to say, but I like ice cream," Paco said.

"Okay. We'll talk to my father. He's a mentor for another boy here in the school. They can fix us up."

In that way, John and Paco became friends. Despite, or because of, his blindness, Paco gave John insights that changed the way he viewed the world. Paco accepted the way things were. *"Es la vida,"* he often said. John swam with the little guy in the Harrington's pool, and Annette made enchiladas for them to eat in the shade on the patio. Paco rode along in Annette's pickup truck when she and John were shopping for groceries. Paco enjoyed the motion of the truck and the companionship.

"Did you see the size of that dog?" John asked Annette thoughtlessly when he spotted a Great Dane as big as an Appaloosa.

"I didn't see it," Paco said. He was innocent, and he

wasn't touchy about being blind. "It's no big deal," Paco said, "I've never been able to see anything in my whole life."

John speculated that Paco's other senses might be heightened because of his blindness. He took him for a hearing test at a nearby clinic, but Paco's hearing was distinctly unremarkable. John used an old jogging shoe, a block of blue cheese, and a mothball to conduct a smell test that showed Paco's sense of smell to be quite ordinary; in fact, he had difficulty distinguishing between the jogging shoe and the cheese. John was running out of senses. Turning a blind eye, so to speak, to the liquor laws of the State of New Mexico, he poured three different kinds of beer into small glasses to see if Paco could taste a difference among them.

"My tongue is blind, too," Paco said after he had drained the test samples and admitted he couldn't tell one from the other. "Let me try the test again."

"You're just trying to get a buzz on," John accused him.

"It's for science."

"You'll get me fired as a mentor."

John tried to figure out what Paco's strong points were – science, history, poetry, speaking, wrestling? No. He didn't appear to have *any* strong points. But he seemed so serene, so unaffected by setbacks or bad news of any kind. Surely that was a strong point. Paco's strong point was that he adapted to whatever happened in his life without complaint. He didn't retaliate when slighted. He didn't keep score of insults. He had a trusting nature. If someone kept him waiting, he didn't grow nervous or irritable. Disappointments didn't vex him. He was placid, had a decent sense of humor, and, in his own way, was more of a mentor for John than John for him. That was Paco's strong point; he was at peace. Paco was John's passport to tranquility. Once, he asked Paco if he ever found himself counting.

"I know how to count," Paco replied, "but I don't count unless I need to count."

"Well, what do you think about when you're just sitting on a bench like the time I met you?"

"I don't think about much," Paco said. "Sometimes I think about lunch."

Maybe that was John's problem. He'd never had to think about lunch, so his mind went "walk-about" in minefields of worry.

"What are you thinking about right now?" John asked.

"The wind blowing in the trees. I can hear the leaves rustling."

"Do you think about the speed of the wind?"

"I don't care about the speed of the wind. I just know there's enough wind to move the leaves so I know the trees are there."

Perhaps Paco could teach John to calm his mind, to let his mind rest. No counting. No memorization. No analysis. Just a release into tranquility.

John's diary summed up his last year: "I've been broken, saved, and redeemed."

John returned to Salzburg in September. He and Andrea had discussed his visit in a flurry of emails. They agreed that John should meet Andrea's family. He rang the Bergens' doorbell at one o'clock in the afternoon and Andrea answered the door with a hug and a long kiss. John was euphoric. He wanted to kidnap her and run from the house, but he followed her into a sitting room where her brother Karl sat in his wheel chair beside her mother and father seated on a couch. *Frau* Bergen took John's hand and smiled pleasantly. John grasped *Herr* Bergen's extended hand and gave it a healthy squeeze as Scott had advised him. *Herr* Bergen had read the same handshake manual, because he had a grip like an alligator's jaws. John went over to Andrea's brother and kneeled down in front of his chair.

"Hello, Karl."

Karl's head bobbed around and his arms moved around in front of him unpredictably. John held one of Karl's misshapen hands momentarily, and he could feel the tension in Karl's hand release. As he had before, John could feel the warmth of his own hand move into Karl's hand, and, again, John wished the heat was a healing power.

They all sat down. *Frau* Bergen offered John a plate of tarts. John took one and placed it on the serviette Andrea had given him.

"I'm very sorry about your father's death," *Herr* Bergen said.

"Thank you. Everyone in the village misses him."

"We regret that we couldn't come to visit your village," *Frau* Bergen said. She and her husband spoke English well, and that resolved one of John's fears.

"I don't live in Caledonia any longer. I've moved to the desert out West."

"A cowboy, now?" *Herr* Bergen said.

John smiled. The stereotype worked for him. He looked at Andrea.

"Do your parents know about my family?" Andrea nodded her head to say yes. "After my father died, I discover that the parents I grew up with aren't my birth parents."

"Adopted?" *Herr* Bergen said.

"It's more complicated than that. Anyway, now, I'm living temporarily with my birth parents in New Mexico."

"We have a story, too," *Herr* Bergen said. He described how he had started his business, how it had thrived, and how it had failed all in the space of twenty years. "For a time, I couldn't accept what had happened. I think you know this feeling?"

"Yes." John tasted his tart and nodded approvingly toward *Frau* Bergen.

"For a time, I felt ashamed. I had failed my employees and my family. I tried to find jobs in management positions, but I found nothing."

"But you're working now?" John asked.

"Yes," *Herr* Bergen said. "I stopped worrying about appearances. I stopped looking for management jobs and admitted I was willing to take an entry-level job if necessary."

"That had to be hard."

"Yes, it was. But, now, we have a miracle. Andrea gave me the money you sent to her, and I have used it to start a small business with another man, a younger man. We're teaching web page design classes, and our classes are full."

This was news to John.

"Yes," *Herr* Bergen continued, "we've hired additional instructors, and we're doing classes in Munich, Salzburg and Vienna. We also have small business clients who pay us for designing their web sites. Very exciting! And, soon, I'll be able to pay you back."

"Oh, no," John said. "There's no paying back. Honestly. That was a gift from me to Andrea. No paying back. It was her gift to do with as she wanted."

They drank their tea and ate another round of tarts. *Frau* Bergen talked about the work she was doing in the Salzburg school system. John told her that his mother Annette was a school teacher, and he told her about the Historic Figures Program. Their conversation became more casual. John chose his moment to tell them why he had come to Salzburg.

"I'm only nineteen years old," John began, "and I have a lot of growing up to do — a lot to learn, but I want you to know that I love your daughter very much." Andrea's eyes teared up, and *Frau* Bergen clasped her hands in front of her throat. "I'm interviewing for a job next week. And, when I get the job I'm going to work at it as hard as I can to prove myself to my new family and to the Bergen family. I want to deserve the right to ask Andrea to marry me some day. It's a long way off, because I still have to go to college, but I'll take it one step at a time, and I'll get there. I'll prove it you."

"You've already proved yourself, John," Andrea said. She moved to his side and held his hand.

Herr Bergen got up from the couch and went to the kitchen. John could hear glasses tinkling. He brought in a tray of small glasses and a refrigerated bottle of schnapps.

"This is made of a fruit called...."

"Pears," Andrea said.

"We're supposed to have a serving of fruit every day," John said.

Herr Bergen laughed and said, "As many servings as you like."

John toasted Karl with the schnapps, and Karl responded by rolling his head and making an effort to smile. After a little more light conversation, *Frau* Bergen told Andrea and John to go out alone for a dinner and to their favorite beer garden.

"Your parents know I was here before?" John asked Andrea.

"Oh, yes. And they know that you didn't try to seduce me when you could have."

"Wow, you share everything with your family, I see."

"Pretty much."

"So your parents think I'm a prude or a priest."

"They know exactly who you are, John Wesley Hardin."

A week after John returned to Arroyo Seco, Annette made dinner for Paco, Hector, John, and Scott. They swam for an hour before dinner and John taught Paco how to make real swimming strokes instead of flailing around like a frog in hot water. Paco was amazed at the speed he could generate. He smacked his head on the side of the pool when he completed his first official half lap.

"The pool isn't infinitely long, Paco," Scott said. "You've got to feel the side to know when to turn or you're going to beat yourself senseless."

"I need a helmet," Paco said.

Paco and John were sitting side-by-side on the pool steps when Paco happened to run his fingers over John's left foot. Paco's hand returned for another braille inspection.

"Man," Paco said, amazed by his discovery, "you only got three toes."

"So what?"

"That's freaky, man."

"Maybe three's normal. Maybe it's your toes that are freaky," John said, testing Paco's conventional wisdom.

"No. *Five* toes is normal." Paco said. He thought for a minute. "What happened to your toes?"

"I'll tell you all about it some other time."

After drying off, Scott, Hector, and Paco sat at the patio table while Annette and John brought dinner out from the kitchen. Paco wanted to do the three-beer test to see if he could "tell the difference". John told him he had betrayed a secret to Hector. Their conversation roamed over other equally trivial subjects through the meal and into the round of ice cream. Hector seldom spoke unless he was asked a direct question. When they had finished the meal, Scott and Hector left the table and walked into the house. When a few minutes had passed, John's curiosity steered him indoors to find Hector and his mentor. John heard Scott's voice from the study and stopped short of entering the room.

"Hector, I want you to trust me enough to talk to me. When you and I talk, we'll come up with ideas. We'll learn."

"That's cool, man," Hector said in a weak, uninspired voice.

"Hector, if I give you a dollar and you give me a dollar, we each have one dollar just like we had before. But, if you tell me an idea and I tell you an idea, we each have *two* ideas. That's the power of communicating!"

"Cool," Hector mumbled. Hector's inability to articulate

cranked Scott up.

"Hector, you have greatness inside you. I can sense it." It wasn't the first time in Scott's life that he may have stretched the truth. "Promise me you'll grow yourself mentally, physically, and spiritually to reach your full potential. Discipline! Make yourself do pushups and crunches every day. Do them until your muscles burn. The pain will keep you humble. Spend time in prayer each day to honor God. Will you do that?"

"I'm just a blind kid," Hector said. His uncertain voice made it clear that he hadn't yet recognized the greatness inside himself and he certainly hadn't bargained for such a robust agenda. This new life was shaping up to be a little more challenging than lying around his drunken father's trailer in Artesia.

"You are much, much more than that, Hector!" Scott exhorted him.

John reversed his steps quietly back toward the living room. He sensed that the revival was almost finished.

"You can be a role model for Paco," Scott continued. "You're a good wrestler. Make yourself even better. Work harder. It'll change your life!"

A few seconds later, after John had reached the kitchen and joined Annette at drying dishes with a tea towel, Scott and Hector entered the kitchen.

"Hey, Beautiful," Scott said to Annette as he wrapped his arms around her.

"Afternoon, Reverend," she said. Scott kissed her.

"What are Scott and Annette doing?" Hector asked from across the room.

"They're smooching," John said.

"That's what I thought," Hector said. "I should be over there taking lessons, because he's my mentor."

"Get your own girl," Scott said. His speech had worked. Hector was talking.

They returned to poolside where Paco sat with his feet in water halfway to his knees. John and Hector sat beside him on the rim of the pool.

"I wish I had a father," Paco said wistfully.

"You've got an uncle," Hector said.

"But I want a father like John has."

John stood up and said, "You boys bring your drinks with you and come over to the fire pit. I'll tell you a long story about a boy who had *two* fathers." The two blind boys left their perch beside the pool and stepped cautiously toward the circle of chairs by the fire pit. John helped them wrap up in towels and each settled into a chair ready to hear a yarn. Scott and Annette went inside and left the trio to share John's tale.

"Are you going to talk about your three toes?" Paco asked.

"What three toes?" Hector wanted to know.

"It's in the story," John said. He leaned forward in preparation for painting images in the minds of these two blind boys who had never seen the light of day. "Once upon a time there was this kid in New England who thought he was Napoleon Bonaparte."

On Friday afternoon, John drove Paco to Carrizozo to spend the weekend with his uncle. Carrizozo was a dusty little town situated at the northern end of the Tularosa Basin about halfway between the Rio Grande to the west and the Pecos River to the east. Paco's uncle lived in a small house surrounded by three mature trees on the west side of town. Arturo Lopez came out into the yard when he heard the sound of John's car parking in the gravel driveway. By the time Paco opened the passenger door, Arturo was there to lift him up for a welcoming hug. John walked around the front of the car to shake hands.

"Nice to meet you," Arturo said. "Come into the house out of the sun." Arturo put Paco down and held his hand as they walked ahead of John through the front portal into the house. The adobe walls and tile floors made the small home comfortably cool on a warm afternoon. "How about a beer?" Arturo asked John.

"Me, too," Paco chirped.

"No beer for you, *Desperado*," Arturo said. "You'll be lucky if I give you a Coke." He motioned toward Paco who sat on a chair at the kitchen table. "You have to watch this one closely."

"I've seen his moves," John said as he accepted the Lone Star beer.

"This one has the moves, all right." Arturo ran his hand over Paco's hair.

"John is teaching me to swim the right way," Paco said.

"It's about time you learned something," his uncle said.

They talked about the railroad history of Carrizozo and about Paco's family. Arturo showed John a picture of Paco's mother.

"Beautiful, no?" Arturo asked. John nodded agreement. "My little sister. She got all the looks in our family. I got all the calories." He patted his stomach when he said this, but he was exaggerating, because he was reasonably fit, and he had the same fine features of his sister and Paco.

"Paco told me his mother died," John said.

"When he was six years old. She was driving home down the ski mountain by Ruidoso when her car slid off the highway into the canyon." Arturo's hand patted Paco's shoulder. "This Paco loved his mother."

"I still love her," Paco said. He took a gulp of his Coke. "I can still feel her skin and her hand holding my hand."

"She called Paco the man of the house," Arturo said, laughing at the memory. "Here is this little one living in my house, drinking my Cokes, and I'm working in the sun to pave the roads, and my sister calls Paco the man of the house." He laughed again.

"I am still the man of the house," Paco said. He had his mother's smile.

"How about Paco's father?" John asked.

"Paco doesn't remember him," Arturo said, "but I do. He was all talk and no action. He was going to do this and going to do that. Anyway, whatever he's doing now, he's doing it in Chicago. He left Carrizozo a long time ago."

John thought about how spoiled he had been. How he had been nurtured by his father and his grandparents. He had never been hungry. He had always been secure. He had lived in a spacious house on a beautiful lake surrounded by neighbors who looked out for him and tolerated his eccentricities. He had gone to good schools. And he had the gift of sight. He felt ashamed for complaining about Annette's secret, for feeling hurt. He had two loving parents. Compared to Paco, John had never had a serious problem in his life.

"Paco likes you," Arturo said. "He says you are really good to him. And he likes your mother, too."

"Here's a picture of my mother and father." John pulled out his wallet and passed the pictures to Arturo, who complimented both pictures.

"Paco, you are lucky to have John as your friend," Arturo said. Paco nodded.

"I'm the lucky one," John said, as he drained his Lone Star and stood up to leave. "Paco's teaching me to relax and enjoy life."

"He's good at relaxing," Arturo said. He reached for his wallet and produced a twenty-dollar bill. "This is for your gas," he said.

John refused his offer. "Thank you, but no," John said. "I enjoyed the drive up. I've already told Paco I'll pick him up at seven o'clock Sunday evening."

Arturo shook John's hand. "Thanks for being Paco's mentor."

"It means a lot to me," John said. "I enjoy every minute with Paco." He pushed his fist against Paco's shoulder. "See you, Hoss," John said.

Paco, who had never seen anything in his life said, "See you, Stud."

In preparation for his interview on Tuesday morning, John got a haircut, trimmed his nails, pressed his suit, laid out his silk tie, shined his shoes, and starched his Brooks Brothers shirt as stiff as a coat of armor. He arranged his *curriculum vitae*, transcript, and diploma in a Manila folder. He had even washed and waxed his old sedan on the off chance that the interviewer might see him park outside the bank where he was interviewing.

John and Scott had talked several times about the proper tone and length of answers. Scott told John to remember that most interviewers would rather be in a lot of places other than an interview room. Annette had recommended that John put "quality over quantity" in his answers. Advice was plentiful. Be natural. Be truthful. Don't spike the ball, whatever that meant.

A receptionist asked John to be seated on a couch in the foyer of the bank. The prominent object in the room was an oil painting of a cowboy breaking a bronco. The two adversaries had been at it for a while, judging from the amount of dust suspended in the air. Looking at the painting made John thirsty. He wondered whether there was a subliminal message to be decoded.

After a ten-minute wait, an attractive lady named Mrs. Maria Ortega came out to greet him. Shapely in her tailored blue business suit, she made quite an impression on John. Her wide smile revealed a set of chompers to make Miss Universe jealous. John shook her hand firmly, but not the knuckle-popping kind of firmly he had used on *Herr* Bergen in Salzburg. Mrs. Ortega invited John into a small office just to the right of the bank vault. After they were seated, she scanned his resume and transcript.

"You did well in high school and in sports," she said.

"Yes, Ma'am."

He knew he had to do better than that, but she didn't look like a person overly interested in lacrosse or the 400-meter run. The light sparkled off the cuts in Mrs. Ortega's gigantic diamond ring. Perhaps, John thought, he was being interviewed by a trophy wife. He examined her face as she scribbled a note on an interview sheet. She had no pores; her skin was as smooth as alabaster and the color of caramel. Her features were delicate, and her thick black hair was shiny and perfectly cut. Her beauty was a distraction.

"What's the most important lesson you learned at Thornton Academy?" Mrs. Ortega asked as she smiled pleasantly.

"I learned that serving other people is more important than satisfying my own selfish desires." John still felt stiff. He stifled a yawn. He needed oxygen.

Was that movement of her eyebrow a mini-frown? John second-guessed his answer, an answer that struck him as simultaneously saintly and sexual. He felt he needed to be blander. His North Korean torture chamber scenario was great for throwing ice water on the impulse to laugh, but John didn't have a boilerplate daydream to promote blandness.

"What's your biggest character flaw?"

"Obsessive greed." John would have scored really well on a lie-detecting machine with that answer. Scott had warned him not to answer this question with "I'm too modest".

"How do you control greed?"

"By valuing people more than money. By believing that I'm good enough just the way I am," John said out loud for the first time in his life. "By loving other people more than myself and trusting that I'm worthy of their love." In his mind, John could see images of Paco, Andrea, Annette, and Scott.

Mrs. Ortega wrote three sentences worth of text in her notes.

"What do you know about the business of banking?" she asked.

"I think tight credit spreads may be a challenge for local and regional banks, in particular. And I think the regulatory burden is going to fall disproportionately on the smaller banks."

"Where do you get your information?" Mrs. Ortega asked as an aside.

"Cable television business programs." John could read her written notes up-side-down.

"Has a clue," she wrote.

"We have a gender-neutral compensation policy here at the bank," Mrs. Ortega said. "Do you have any thoughts on that?"

"Well," John said, his mind racing to absorb the unfamiliar phrase. "I'm open to either sex being on top."

John instantly broke into a sweat. What had he just said? What was he thinking? What did his words even mean? The temperature in the room soared, or so it seemed to John. It was almost as if his brain had shut down for a moment. Mrs. Ortega looked up at John with an expression of bemusement.

"Do you want to rephrase that?"

"Yes," John said as he shuffled in his chair. "I'm in favor of the bank's policy on gender neutrality." John blotted at his forehead. This interview was starting out horribly. At this rate, he was destined to clean swimming pools for the next forty years. Mrs. Ortega smiled knowingly and jotted some more notes.

It didn't help his concentration that Mrs. Ortega kept pulling her blue suit jacket down at the waist in a way that drew attention to her ample, possibly prize-winning bust. John designated Mrs. Ortega's bust a "no-glance zone", because he believed that not even his pathetic answers to questions could ruin his chances for employment faster than Mrs. Ortega suspecting him of being a sexual deviant. John focused exclusively on her eyes, but not in the way that Andrea had once called "bedroom eyes", because that was as risky as violating the "no-glance zone". John found interviewing hard work.

Mrs. Ortega paused thoughtfully to give the impression she had just thought of a fresh angle.

"Do you have any questions for me?" she asked sweetly.

Almost before he had formed the words, John knew he was taking a chance using information on Mrs. Ortega he had gleaned from the Internet: "I hope you don't mind me asking, but are you a former Miss New Mexico by any chance?"

She shook her head to move a wisp of hair from her left forehead, a move used by models at photo shoots.

"I was in the pageant some time ago," she said, smiling brightly at John.

"How did the other contestants accept losing?" John asked.

Mrs. Ortega laughed at that one. "I was Miss Carlsbad, but I didn't win the state pageant." She paused as if to remember the event. "I won Miss Congeniality, though," she said and she shrugged in a self-effacing way. "But, let's get back to you, because I already have a job."

John could have taken that as a rebuke, but Mrs. Ortega was still smiling, so he guessed that his bold initiative may have charmed her. If so, that was the only charming thing he had done since walking into the interview room.

"I've called two of your references," she said. That surprised John. "They both were very complimentary of your work and your character." John fidgeted in his chair again. "I asked them for a one-word description, and here's what they said. A Mr. Gleason said 'loyal' and an HR Manager in Florida said 'smart'." She smiled at John and John smiled back at her. "That's good," Mrs. Ortega said, because we're not in the market for 'disloyal' or 'stupid' employees."

John smiled again. This woman was really attractive. John focused on her cute nose and her sparkling eyes. He felt like he was being hypnotized. John had to stop thinking about Mrs. Ortega to prevent an embarrassment as profound as Raymond Delacroix's at his football physical. Imagining torture at the hands of North Korean prison guards should do the trick.

Mrs. Ortega pored over his transcript. "With these kinds of grades, you can get into college easily. Do you plan to go to college?"

"I'd like to go to college when I know for certain what my goals are."

"You don't know what you want to do?"

"Not in detail," John said. He had morphed from being a cunning word smith to being a self-confessed aimless drifter in the space of fifteen seconds.

"Where do you see yourself here in the bank in ten years?" Mrs. Ortega's face was pensive, as though she thought no one had ever conceived of this question before.

"I hope to learn enough to be worthy of replacing you when you move to a position of even higher responsibility," John said. He felt good about that one even as he admonished himself not to be smug.

Mrs. Ortega smiled again. She had heard some iteration of that answer a dozen times in the past. John rationalized that she might hire him despite his spotty answers out of compassion or just because he was reasonably good-looking and wore a nice tie. She wrote for a while on her interview sheet.

"Finally," she said with a tug on the waist of her suit jacket, "what special talent do you have that sets you apart from other candidates?"

John paused before replying. Winning and losing two million dollars was an answer, but not a viable answer.

"Well," he said as he adjusted his tie to stall for time.

"Yes?"

"I'm very good with numbers," John said.

John had no way of knowing that his Grandfather Phillip Laval had given exactly the same answer at his bank interview forty-seven years ago, and 2,505 miles away in Caledonia.